SOUL OF STARS

Also by Ashley Poston

Heart of Iron
The Princess and the Fangirl
Geekerella

SOUL OF STARS

ASHLEY POSTON

BALZER + BRAY

An Imprint of HarperCollins*Publishers*

TO ALL OF THE FRIENDS I'VE FOUND
ALONG THE WAY,
AND ALL THE ONES LEFT TO FIND.

In a shrine of ancients past
When the dark has stolen the throne,
The Goddess holds the end of times
And there she waits alone.
And when she fails its heart will beat
And consume the kingdom bright,
For no soul lives to tell the tale
Of a star to shine the light.
—*"The Goddess's Legacy,"*
The Cantos of Light

THE
IRON KINGDOM

RESONANC

LUNA

EROS

THE
IRON
PALA

NEON
CITY

JUNIPER

NEVAEH

THE STARPASS

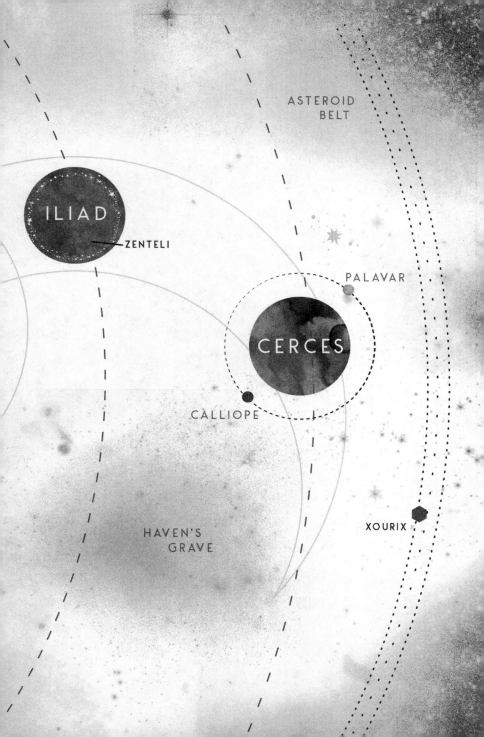

SOUL OF STARS

I

STARSHIP

MELLIFARE

The tomb could only be opened with an iron key.

Mellifare studied the intricate lock, tracing the curving metal rods and ancient cogs. From the carvings of the cycles of the moon above the door to the scriptures engraved in the lock itself, she was certain this was the entrance to not only *a* tomb, but the Goddess's tomb—the one she had been searching for.

They were deep underneath the shrine in the Iron Palace, where the nobility buried their important dead in stone coffins. She savored the musty, forgotten smell of this death-place for a quiet moment. She liked things better when they were dead. On the other side of this door was her heart, just as Father had said. He lay dead in one of the crypts in this shrine, along with the Grand Duchess, all of them freshly buried and sealed away like books in a library. The abbesses who had survived the assassination attempt on the Empress a few days ago led the mourning prayers in the shrine proper, although there was no one left to sing with them.

Her optics flickered. She swayed, suddenly, but caught herself on the side of the wall to keep herself upright. A warning flared in the back of her head. She was running low on energy.

The last few days had been especially taxing. The assassination, the fight after, letting the Empress *escape*—but what took the most of her power was—

"Sister."

Him.

The Empress had called him Di, but she had stolen that name away when she shredded his memories and installed him on the throne. He still wore his coronation cloak, as black as midnight, and his red hair was pulled back into a neat ponytail, clasped together with a golden toggle. With delicate silver stitches, he had sewn up that insufferable wound the Empress had given him on his left cheek.

Quietly, he assessed her.

"Are you well?" His voice was soft and melodic.

She hated it.

"Yes," she hissed in reply, and stood from the wall. She had HIVE'd him, but she did not have enough power to rewrite him as she could the other Metals. They were simple—but he was made differently. If he had known a little more of what he could do before she tore apart his memories, she would not have had enough power to. He could have retaliated and—well, it did not matter.

She would not be this weak for much longer.

Behind the door, in the Goddess's tomb, was her heart, and once she had it, she could tear this failing memory core out of her chest and return to her full power. And then she would—she would—

It was best not to get ahead of herself.

"The key, brother," she said, outstretching her hand. He gingerly took the Iron Crown off his head and handed it over. She pressed it into the indention in the door, and the intricate locks began to whine and rotate.

There was a sharp *crack*, and the door split open, revealing a staircase down into darkness. Anticipation tasted sharp on her tongue as she snatched the glowlight from a nearby Messier's belt and stepped down into the depths of the tomb.

As she reached the bottom, she listened for her heart to call her. The sweet sound of it beating.

There was silence.

In the center of the tomb sat an intricate stone coffin, dozens of trinkets laid around it on the floor. Vases and relics, golden standing candelabras and pouches of copper coins from long ago with a long-dead Emperor on their faces. In two strides she made it to the coffin and shoved open the lid. It clattered to the ground, revealing—

Nothing.

Not the Goddess. Not her bones. Not the heart—

Nothing.

Her face twisted in anger.

With a feral shriek, she shoved over an ancient stone statue of the Goddess and spun on her heels, her eyes crackling red with fury.

Where *was* it?

Had the Goddess stolen it already? Or was it in a different tomb? The prophecy had pointed to where the Goddess rested, and that was here, but her heart was not. She gritted her teeth, hating to be made a fool of.

The Emperor, at the top of the stairs, gave her a curious look. "Sister?—"

"Burn it to the ground—the entire shrine. I want nothing but cinders."

"But—"

She extended her hand and the invisible strings of the HIVE wrapped around his code. With a twist of her finger, she rewrote his hesitation into obedience.

"Yes, sister," he said.

From the sanctuary of the shrine came an abbess in an opulent silver robe, two abbots fresh from an Iron Shrine on Cerces a step behind her. They should have stayed on Cerces. The abbess's eyes widened as she saw the opened tomb behind them.

"Your Excellence! You aren't allowed to be back here!" she cried frantically to the Emperor. "This is the resting place of our beloved Goddess! She is—"

"She is not here," the Emperor replied.

Then, from behind the abbess, a Messier grabbed the old woman by the head and with a twist snapped her neck. The abbots shrieked and stumbled over their own feet as they fled the sanctuary. Two Messiers cut them down before they could escape.

Mellifare picked up one of the candles on a picket stand and tossed it behind the pulpit and onto the purple tapestries of the Goddess's story. It lit up in a *whoosh*. Fire crept along the curtains and reached into the rafters, crackling and popping, a sound that reminded her so pleasantly of the fire that had torched the North Tower seven years ago. There was something about fire that soothed her—the way it devoured, leaving nothing but ash in its wake.

A blank slate to start anew.

As Mellifare and the Emperor left the shrine, the flames caught on the banners of the Goddess, scorched the icons, melted a thousand candles, and burned it all away.

ANA

"I should have let you burn," a voice whispered across her ear.

Ana quickly glanced over her shoulder, but the street was empty and dark, save for a group of people warming themselves by a thermal heater. She swallowed the fear lodged in her throat.

EOS hovered beside her and beeped curiously. She shook her head.

"It's nothing," she told the small bot, and pulled her thick fur-lined cloak around her tightly. The voice was nothing even though it sounded like her best friend. It was nothing even though he had tried to kill her six months ago.

EOS didn't believe her, and she really didn't believe herself, either.

A bone-deep chill wind swept through the narrow streets, ruffling her short black hair, and she shivered. She *hated* the cold—almost as much as she hated flash-frozen fruits and corsets.

But she couldn't bring herself to hate Neon City.

It was on Eros, but it didn't *feel* like the rest of the dreamy, green landscape. Located in the southern quadrant of the planet, Neon City constantly smelled like damp cement, sewage, and fresh rain, but from a distance the city was beautiful—outlined in lights that reflected in the puddles and through the mists that drifted along the streets. Buildings jutted up into the sky like piercing daggers, slick and glittery with rain. It gave the city an eerie, haunted radiance. In the outskirts where Ana walked, darkness clung to the streets.

It had been six months since Di's ascension to the Iron Throne. Six months since he'd almost killed her when he drove a lightsword through her stomach—no, she couldn't think about that. Wouldn't. Or the scar on her stomach would throb, and she would remember the HIVE red of his eyes, and the way he whispered so softly against her ear, *"You should have burned."*

And Di—her Di—was lost to the HIVE forever.

She barely even understood what the HIVE was—part AI, part brainwashing virus. Lord Rasovant had created it to subdue difficult Metals, but the program stripped them of their thoughts, their memories . . . everything. Until they were nothing more than puppets. It wasn't until the palace that Ana realized Lord Rasovant didn't control the HIVE at all, but something else did.

The Great Dark.

She didn't know what form it took—an AI, a person, a monster—but she had seen something terrible in the red of Di's eyes as he slid the blade into her stomach.

Another gust of wind rushed through the street, picking up pieces of trash and dried leaves, and blew her hood off.

She and EOS passed an Iron Shrine, hollowed and burned out, like dozens of others in the kingdom. No one had found the arsonist yet, but the Emperor, and the Ironbloods on the Iron Council, blamed rogue Metals—just like they blamed rogue Metals for her assassination. In the wake of her *death*, the Emperor had HIVE'd so many more Metals than ever before, creating an army of thoughtless soldiers.

In response, Siege and her fleet had created sanctuaries: places where Metals, and those who supported them, could go to be safe.

Or, at least, *safer.*

The front doors of the Iron Shrine had been blown open, hanging charred on their hinges, the temple itself a gutted corpse, blackened and ash swept, and the holy tombs beneath it were desecrated. The building had stood for almost a thousand years, and even after the fire it still stood. Rogue Metals wouldn't burn a *shrine* for nothing—ransack a tomb without taking anything out of it.

It didn't make sense to Ana.

The HIVE was behind it, she was sure of it. The fires started soon after the Emperor took the throne, and every shrine was destroyed in the same way—the pattern was too exact. The HIVE was searching for something.

But what it was, she couldn't figure out.

A small group of people huddled inside, around a low-burning flame in a trash can. A lively fiddle carried across the wind, filled with voices in holy songs. It reminded her of the tunes Wick used to play and Riggs sang off-key—when she would pull Di out of whatever boring medical book he had been engrossed in and they'd dance.

Or *attempt* to.

Metals weren't very good at dancing.

Her ears perked at the familiar sound of footsteps—*Messiers.*

"Scatter!" a girl cried, and the group split in different directions, jumping out of the burned windows and between the crumbling walls.

She quickly pulled up the hood of her cloak and slipped into the shadowed stoop of a house, EOS ducking into her cloak. The patrol grew near, and she slipped her hand into her inner coat pocket, fingertips brushing against the small cubed memory core—Di's—the size of a plum and cold to the touch.

She held her breath as the Messiers passed. Pristine blue uniforms, universal blue eyes, polished boots, and polished metal faces.

When they were gone, she slumped against the door, her breath rushing out of her lips in a puff of frost.

She tapped the comm-link clasped to her cloak and traveled on down the street toward her destination. "There's a patrol in the slums tonight, but I'm almost at the coordinates."

For a moment, there was only static in her earpiece, and then her captain said, *"Of course there is. Probably there to arrest another Metal. Be cautious, darling. Robb, Jax, check in?"*

"We're standing by" came Robb's distinctly Erosian accent.

There was the soft murmur of voices in the background. Robb and Jax were gambling nearby in one of the slum's bars.

"Jax, don't let him bet too much," the captain added.

Jax gave a playful gasp through the comm-link. *"Robb? Never. He's a saint with money."*

"Yeah, with spending it," Lenda, the *Dossier*'s gunnery lead, groused.

Laughter filled Ana's earpiece, and it set her nerves steady. "I'll let you know if anything goes sideways."

The captain added, *"And be careful. If it weren't for Starbright expressly wanting to see you alone, I'd be down there myself."*

"With over a million coppers on your head?" Ana pointed out wryly. "I don't think so—no offense, Captain."

"We all have baggage," Talle, who must've been in the cockpit with Siege and Lenda, chimed in through the comm-link.

"I'll be careful—on iron and stars," she promised them, and tapped the small star-shaped comm-link on her lapel to disconnect.

The coordinates pointed to somewhere on the edge of Neon City and near the shore of Lake Leer. The buildings were rusted, and the only light came from tired neon signs and the cold glow of fluorescent bulbs. Ana came to a stop at the end of the street, surrounded by single-level buildings that looked old and feeble and weatherworn.

The appointed address was an abandoned shop across the street. The dying neon sign above flickered, spitting colors across the vacant street in short, sporadic bursts.

Her heart sank a little.

It must have been a coat shop once, but there was only one left on display. It hung tattered on a mannequin, a ghost of its former self, the red wool faded to a dull grayish pink, its lacy cuffs yellowing, brassy buttons clouded over with age. But, in better condition, it would have been the exact kind of coat she once dreamed about—red as blood, its shoulders chromed in gold, buttons polished, and cut sleek.

Behind it, standing so very still, was a shape in the window. The neon light flickered against them. Tall and humanoid.

It had to be Starbright.

She tapped her lapel, EOS hovering at her shoulder. "Robb, Jax? I found them."

After a moment, her captain said, *"Careful, darling."*

Of course she would be—she *had* to be.

But after two months cooped up in the infirmary, a month of rehabilitation, and three more of hiding and running and hiding some more, she was no closer to finding out what the HIVE wanted or how to find the AI that commanded it—commanded Di, and Mellifare, and the countless Messiers—and defeat it. She'd grown tired of running.

She couldn't anymore. There was a restlessness inside her that grew every day she sat still.

Tapping her comm-link off again, she told EOS, "Stay out here and keep a lookout," and jiggled the handle of the shop door. To her surprise, it eased open. This was either the right place, or a trap.

She hoped it wasn't the latter.

"Hello?" she called.

No one answered.

She squinted, willing her eyes to adjust to the darkness, but still she couldn't see anything. "Hello?" she called louder, and stepped through the doorway. "I'm not here to hurt you. You sent for me. I'm An—"

The front door slammed shut, and static filled her earpiece.

Startled, she recoiled deeper into the shop, reaching for her pistol, when she felt it.

At first it was a gentle tug on the metal bits of her coat— the metal buckles and zippers and cuff links and weapons on her—before an electromagnet above her grabbed them with such force that it picked her up off the ground and slammed her into the ceiling. It held tight to the daggers in her boots, the twin pistols under her arms, even the rings in her ears, leaving her suctioned against the magnetic plate on the ceiling—which hurt like *mad*.

Of course it was a trap.

"Goddess's *spark*," she cursed as she tried to pry her arms off the metal plates, but she couldn't due to the pull on her favorite heart-shaped cuff links. She couldn't even reach her comm-link to call for Robb and Jax.

"This was designed to catch Messiers," the shadow said in a monotonous voice, "but it seems you have a lot of metal on you as well."

ROBB

Robb sincerely hoped whatever Ana was walking into wasn't a trap.

He and Jax were waiting in a small bar about three streets over from the address, playing a few rounds of Wicked Luck with the locals.

The LowBar was aptly named. It was small and dark, the gray walls rusted from a leaky irrigation pipe in the building above them. Mechanics, ship workers, and hired hands alike milled about, drinking and gambling, the stench of motor oil and sea salt strong from Lake Leer. Neons on the ceiling pulsed in gentle waves—it felt like being underwater. Before, when Robb had been a Valerio, he wouldn't have even thought to step into this part of Neon City, afraid some orphan pickpocket would clean him out. But now he *dared* someone to find a copper anywhere on him.

He wasn't a Valerio—he wasn't anything. He hadn't taken Siege's name yet—her *real* name. The one she'd whispered to him in private when he had woken up in the infirmary six months ago, after the assassination attempt on Ana's life.

He . . . was rather afraid to take her name, he hated to admit.

Robb's mechanical arm twitched, and he rubbed his forearm to keep it calm. The mechanic who installed it a month ago said the glitches were normal at first—the nerves were reconfiguring themselves to the new tech—but that meant he couldn't control it well yet, and that annoyed him. It acted up at the worst times. Like when he was angry. Or sad.

Or nervous that Ana was about to walk into a trap—

"The twenty-third Emperor of the Iron Kingdom will be making his appearance in Nevaeh in just under an hour," said a reporter on a holo-screen in the top right corner of the bar. The newsfeed showed the space station of Nevaeh and hundreds of thousands of citizens crowding into the street. *"Praised as a light in the darkness . . ."*

"Nothing like putting on your holy best to order genocide," Jax muttered.

Another man grunted a laugh. He looked like one of the dockworkers, metal toggles clasping the braids in his long peppery-brown beard. "Bet that sparkly robe of his costs more than I'd make in a lifetime."

"It's easy to be rich when you don't pay your army," replied a woman at the table. She was about Siege's age, with long auburn hair and a cheek implant. "Those Messiers give me the chills, and he just keeps getting *more* of them."

An older gentleman who reminded Robb of Wick, with a mechanical leg and a bad eye, shot down the rest of his whiskey before he said, "Rumor is he's takin' criminals he catches up to the dreadnought and *changin'* them."

"Come on, Mirek, you know those rumors are bullshit," said the woman. She tapped her cards on the table.

"It'd be just punishment if it were true," added a young man with shaggy brown hair and a scruffy beard. Van—or at least he looked like a Van. Robb hadn't liked him since the beginning of the game. He hid cards under his patched-up brown leather coat, not that it had helped his losing hand. "I wonder what a *star-kisser* would look like as a Metal. Would you still sparkle?"

Star-kisser—slang for the Solani people like Jax. Robb squeezed his forearm tightly to keep his mechanical arm still. He wouldn't mind punching this son of a bitch in the face one good time.

Jax fixed his expressive mouth into a thin, hard line. "I wouldn't know. Though if he tried to come for me, I'd tell him where he could stick his punishment."

No one knew that the Emperor used to be their friend—or even that he was a *Metal,* since he looked so human—and Robb wasn't sure if Jax's threat was real, or if he was just playing the part. Maybe a little of both. Jax had known D09 as long as he'd known Ana. Robb was sure there'd been a lot of history between them, but Jax had never grieved when Di was taken— not like Ana had. Did he just not *care*? He doubted that, and Jax did seem rather angry.

"You don't like our Emperor, *star-kisser*?" taunted the man. "You know that's treason."

"And you clearly don't understand what treason is," Jax replied dryly, taking two sevens out of Robb's hand and placing them facedown in the middle of the table. "Or how to play cards."

"Two sevens," Robb added for him, and the game went on.

The bearded man named Van tossed down two fives and asked, "Why don't you like our Emperor?"

"*Goddess.*" Jax sighed, a muscle in his jaw feathering. "Can't I just not like gingers?"

"You know what I meant," the man spat.

"Maybe beat me in a card game and I'll give you an answer," Jax replied, grabbing the last two cards in Robb's hand and sliding them down onto the table. "Two queens."

"That *has* to be bullshit. I'm calling Wicked," declared the woman, her cheek implant flaring purple. She reached in anger for the cards Jax had thrown down and turned them over.

She frowned when two queens stared back at her.

"Solani can't lie, love," he told her, absently reaching for his winnings.

Van pulled out a lightblade and slammed it into the pile of coppers, barely missing Jax's fingertips. "Hold on there, *friends*. I think this is mine."

"Not this game," Robb replied, keeping his voice level. "We won."

Van grinned wide, flashing a golden front tooth. "The kingdom's got a warrant out for an exiled Ironblood and a starkisser. For *treason*. You wouldn't be them, would you?"

Robb turned to Jax and said, "Maybe he does know what treason is, *ma'alor*—"

The entrance to the LowBar buckled in with an inhuman

kick. Two Messiers stepped inside, their blue eyes scanning the crowd.

Robb took hold of Jax's arm as they scrambled to their feet—

He turned, and the mouth of a Metroid pressed against his forehead. *Goddess's spark.*

Van grinned around his golden tooth and drew back the hammer with his thumb. "You and that *star-kisser* ain't going nowhere. Maybe now I'll find if Solani Metals sparkle—"

Before Robb could so much as think of what to do, Jax grabbed the man's pistol and shoved it upward. The surprise made him squeeze the trigger, and a bullet burst the neon light above. It showered sparks onto them. He twisted the gun out of the man's grip, slamming the butt of it across his jaw, and the man slumped to the ground.

The bar erupted into chaos.

Patrons scattered for the back exit, kicking up chairs, their drinks flying.

At the front of the bar, the Messiers pulled out their weapons to fire. The ammunition glowed hot. Robb thought quick—he grabbed the table's legs and flipped it over onto its side as a hail of bullets slammed into it.

He and Jax pressed their backs against it.

A bullet bit through the table at his elbow, and he hissed in surprise more than pain, jerking his arm up. "Any escape plans?"

"Aside from not dying?"

"That would be helpful!"

Jax shook his head. "Can't really think of any, no."

"Perfect."

In the reflection of one of the overturned steel tankards, Robb watched as the Messiers slowly made their way toward them. The two androids split up, one taking the left side of the room, the other the right—odd, since they usually traveled in packs, but now they circled from opposite sides.

Prowling.

His mechanical arm twitched again.

He hoped Ana was faring better.

"Peace, citizens," said one.

"And come quietly," finished the other.

Quietly? The Messiers *did* know who they were dealing with, didn't they? He and Jax were probably wanted on at least fifteen other charges—driving in a no-fly zone, trespassing, transportation of illegal goods, gambling, hijacking a skysailer, illegal use of stolen funds. . . .

And as far as Robb could figure, that'd been only in the last six months since the assassination.

It would be easier if they could just *kill* the Messiers, but then they'd be no better than murderers. Lord Rasovant had preyed upon sick people during the Plague twenty years ago and uploaded them into Metals. For years, the kingdom praised him for creating the *perfect AI*, but as it turned out they weren't AIs at all.

It rather sickened him.

He glanced around the bar, racking his brain for some sort of plan. *Think*. What could disable Metals? What could—

His gaze caught sight of the exit door.

Who says we have to fight them?

It was a terrible plan, but he couldn't think up another one that wouldn't end in their immediate demise. He anchored himself against the table. "I got an idea. On the count of three, we push the table back into them and make a run for the door—got it?"

"*That's* your plan?" Jax hissed quietly.

"One," he mouthed.

Jax gave him an incredulous look and shook his head.

"Two."

Jax anchored himself against the table begrudgingly.

"*Three!*"

Together, they rammed the table into the Messiers, pushing them flat on their backs.

Then he grabbed Jax by the hand and yanked him toward the exit door. They stumbled into the alleyway where their skysailer waited. Jax vaulted into the driver's seat and started up the engine, Robb in the passenger seat. The engine hummed, lights igniting on the console, as golden and black wings fanned out.

Robb tapped his comm-link. "Captain—Ana? We have a problem. Some cheating piece of *spacetrash* ratted on us—"

The two Messiers exited out the back door after them, aiming their Metroids.

"—and Messiers know we're here everything's fine tell Ana to call us right now *bye!*" Jax finished, slammed the disconnect button, and, with a jerk from the controls, lifted the skysailer off the ground and into the neon lines of traffic above.

ANA

Ana glared down at the shadowy figure—*Starbright*. "As you can *clearly* see, I'm not a Messier."

"But that does not mean you are harmless, either."

She ground her teeth. She hated that she'd fallen for something this stupid—and she'd just walked straight into this trap. "Yeah, and *you're* a coward, hiding in the shadows. Why don't you come out and show yourself?"

"Very well."

Then—like twin stars igniting—moonlight-colored eyes flickered to life on a face made of metal slats, forming angular cheekbones and mouth and chin. There was a horrible, deep scrape across its temple that had been soldered closed.

A Metal.

"You . . . are Starbright?" she asked cautiously. "Then—is it true? You know how to bring a Metal back from the HIVE?"

"Correction," the Metal said. "I am the Metal who was brought back from the HIVE."

Her heart leaped into her throat, so bright and buoyant it felt like—

Like—

Hope.

She tried to pry her arms from the magnetic plate again, but they wouldn't budge. She needed to tell her captain that it was *possible*. And if it was possible for this Metal, then . . .

Then . . .

Perhaps Di wasn't lost. Not yet.

"Then we need to talk," she quickly said, unable to keep the desperation out of her voice. "I need your help. Or I need Starbright's help. And I am definitely *not* going to discuss anything while hanging from the ceiling."

"Then it looks like you'll be up there for a while," came a soft, annoyed voice.

A glowlight flickered on, and Ana turned her face just enough to find a young woman leaning against the doorway, holding the light. She was around Ana's age—eighteen, maybe—with shoulder-length silver hair that partially shadowed her sharp face, and wide violet eyes rimmed with kohl. Her lips were painted black to match the rest of her wardrobe. She was short and curvy, with wide hips and thick legs that tapered into knee-high gravity boots. She was a Solani like Jax, but her skin was darker, reminding Ana of the cold deserts on Cerces. There was a wire that looped from her right ear down into her collar and disappeared. A hearing apparatus.

"Who're you?" Ana asked.

The young woman ignored her and stepped to the edge where the magnetic plate began, studying the scars on Ana's face. Her long tassel earrings levitated, rising with the magnetism. "You *do* look like the image Koren Vey showed me. Are you the Empress?"

"Wouldn't you like to know," Ana snapped, and tugged—gently this time—on her sleeves. Her cuff links could be torn off easily enough, and she could feel that if she shifted she could slide out of her pistol holsters. Her boots were magnetized only by the daggers in them, but the magnetism was surprisingly weak through the synthetic material.

Thanks to the glowlight, Ana could make out the rest of the store now. There was a small cot rolled up in the corner, along with a few days' worth of takeout containers. It had been a hiding spot, but not a very permanent one. The magnetic trap she was currently stuck to was junk-engineered on the fly, sheets of metal taken from the roof, probably, hooked up to a ceiling outlet to make an electromagnet.

It was brilliant, and that infuriated her a little more.

The Solani girl cocked her head, and something dark flickered across her deep violet eyes—much darker than Jax's. "Leave her, Xu. I've changed my mind."

"Wait! You can't leave me up here!"

"Can't I?" the young Solani woman scoffed as she turned to leave. "If you *are* the Empress, you left your kingdom, your people, your duty. You're nothing more than a coward—"

With Starbright's back turned, Ana jerked her arms away from the magnetic plate, and with a *snap* her cuff links popped off. She swung her feet forward. As she fell, she twisted her shoulder enough to slide her arms out of her pistol harness and caught it by the straps, jumping on top of the Solani. She pinned her to the ground.

"I am no coward," Ana snapped, shoving the girl facedown

into the floor, her knees on her shoulder. She slid a dagger out of her boot and pressed it against the back of the girl's neck. "And you *will* help me."

"*Elara!*" the Metal—Xu, Ana had heard Starbright call them—cried.

In response, she pressed tighter against Starbright's neck. "One more step and I won't be nice." The Metal stepped back again, hands rising into the air. Ana turned her gaze back down to the girl pinned beneath her. "Xu—that Metal—said they escaped the HIVE. How? How did you do it?"

"Lost a lover?" Starbright—Elara—asked sarcastically. "It'll cost you. A million coppers a Metal—"

Ana tightened her grip on the handle of her dagger. "No, not just one. All of them. Every Metal in the HIVE. If we can save them, we save the kingdom."

The young woman studied her face with a furrowed brow. "Why do you care about Metals so much?"

Her grip on the hilt of her blade tightened. "Because Metals were once human."

"... *What?*"

"Like us. *Alive*," she added. "That's how Rasovant created them. He uploaded people's—their *subconsciousness* or whatever—into memory cores. The HIVE erases everything they are, and I wouldn't wish that on anyone. I want to save them. I have to."

Elara turned her head to the side, and Ana realized that the collision with the floor had broken her nose. Blood smeared her face. She and her Metal exchanged a look as if they knew something but didn't want to say what.

Ana pursed her lips. "Look, if you didn't want me here, then why did you ask me to come?"

"Well, that's a very good question—"

"Elara, they are here," said her Metal, flicking their gaze to the storefront window.

From across the street came a patrol of half a dozen Messiers. Ana heard them outside—a dozen more surrounding the store in a synchronized march. Her blood ran cold.

How had they found her?

It doesn't matter—they won't catch me, she thought, and grabbed Elara by the back of her coat and hauled her to her feet.

"Is there a rooftop exit?" she asked.

"In the back, up the ladder—"

She took her by the arm, dragging her toward the back of the store. The Metal shoved something into a dark bag before they followed. Behind them, the Messiers broke the storefront window and leaped inside.

The storage room was filled with old coat boxes and empty hangers. There was a ladder that led up to the rooftop.

"Jump to the next one!" Ana commanded, slamming the rooftop hatch down and driving her lightblade into the lock to slow down the Messiers.

"Jump?" Elara squawked. "And why in the Goddess's tits should we do *that?*"

"Just trust me, okay? You're right about me disappearing—I did. I disappeared from the kingdom, but it's not because I gave up on it. I *won't* give up on it, and I need your help to save it."

The rooftop latch rattled as a Messier pounded on it to open. The lightblade held fast. For now.

Elara visibly gulped, glancing at her Metal friend for guidance, and when the Metal nodded, so did she. "Okay—yeah, okay. Lead the way, Princess."

So Ana did, and hurtled across the gap between buildings to the next rooftop, and then the next, and Elara and Xu followed. Below them in the street, Ana counted at least a dozen—maybe two dozen—Messiers swarming the abandoned shop they had just left.

Di would've tsked and told her that there was a 92.7 percent chance of her absolutely screwing this up—but Di wasn't here, and there was no percentage of success she could bank on. She hoped she wasn't leading Elara and Xu to certain death.

After she hopped down onto a generator, and then the street, someone grabbed her by her coat and spun her around. Her vison filled with the blue eyes of a Messier.

"Identifying—" it began.

"GET DOWN!" Elara shouted a moment before something whizzed past her head. A boomerang with its blade glowing a pale yellow. It struck the Messier across the neck and lopped its head clean off.

The body stumbled back, fuses hissing from its torso.

Ana stared, befuddled, at the headless Metal. "You—you took its head off!"

"You said they were alive once, right?" Elara straightened Ana's coat, running her fingers peculiarly down her lapels. "I can't help you get them out of the HIVE if they're dead."

"But it's—it's headless!"

"But not dead," she pointed out, and stretched her left hand back toward the dead Messier, one of her bracelets glowing. The boomerang jerked out of the Messier's body and returned to Elara's hand with a *swish* through the air, and she placed it back on her belt.

Three more Messiers appeared behind them in the grimy, dark alley.

Of couse there were more.

Ana tapped the comm-link on her coat. "Robb, Jax—I could use that pickup."

She didn't wait for them to respond before she shoved Elara and Xu out of the alleyway and into the bustling crowd of a busy night market.

Vendors hawking jewelry and spare mechanical parts shouted at buyers from across the way. The sound of lutes and fiddles snaked through the din. It was disorienting—to be sur-rounded by so many people so suddenly when she was running for her life.

Jax replied, *"We'll be there—"*

The sound of a Metroid crackled through the crowd, and everyone ducked, scattering into alcoves like frightened mice.

"—Was that a gunshot?" finished Jax.

"Not the time for questions!" she replied, and looked around the market for the tallest building. The slums were low to the ground, except for an old tower that shot up into the sky like a black spike. It looked like a condemned business high-rise, lean-ing slightly to the side, its blown-out windows making it look like a skeleton with knocked-out teeth.

It would do.

"Make for that building!" she told Elara and Xu.

"That's a death trap," Elara replied, shaking her head. "I am not going—"

An electrified bullet slammed into a basket of fruit in a stall beside them, leaving a cantaloupe smoking.

"—I'm going," she quickly corrected.

Elara and her Metal set out at a run toward the abandoned building, as Jax told Ana his ETA in her ear—two minutes. That was both too much time and no time at all. The scar on her stomach seared her with pain. She pressed her hand against her healed wound, gritted her teeth, and ran faster.

The HIVE wouldn't catch her—*not today.*

Once they reached the condemned building, they ducked into the front entrance, past the forgotten security desk, and made for the stairwell and began to climb; Elara and Xu first, and Ana behind. She closed the stairwell door and blasted off the handle. Hopefully that would hold—the door buckled in— *never mind.* She turned on her heel and took the stairs up two at a time. One flight, then another. Ana could hear the Messiers' Metal gears whirring behind her. One false step, and they would catch her. Her heart pounded in her chest.

She had not been caught yesterday. Or the day before. Or the months before that. She had never been caught by a Messier or a guardsman or a patrol.

She was Ana of the *Dossier,* and she would not be caught today.

Elara threw open the door to the top level. The view stretched across the slums of Neon City, black shadows giving way to glittering windows of bright neon lights. Above them, clouds obscured the skies, thick like gray marshmallows, covering up the moving star that was the *Dossier.*

Ana's lungs burned as she tried to take a deep enough breath, but she didn't have time. "Keep running!" she cried.

Elara threw her a stupefied look. "There's a *ledge!*"

"Jump off it!"

"But—"

"TRUST ME!"

Because she trusted Jax.

To her surprise, Elara launched herself off the side of the building, ratty black cloak fluttering behind her like wings—

And landed in the backseat of a skysailer. Xu landed on the cushion beside her.

Robb whipped around in the passenger seat, throwing out his arm to reach her. "ANA!"

She could read the fright on his face—the disbelief, and then the horror—a moment before she realized what was happening. Because as she went to launch herself off the side of the building, a hand snaked up and caught her by her hood and pulled her back.

Away from the skysailer.

Away from Robb.

Away from Jax, and the *Dossier* and her captain.

I've never been caught, she thought, and then realized her mistake.

Because she had, on the dark side of Cerces all those months ago. Something she had almost forgotten because she had escaped.

Because of Di.

One moment she was launching herself off the side of the ledge, and the next she was on the floor, rolling back onto the rooftop. She heard Robb shouting her name, about to dive out of the skysailer to help her, but Elara grabbed him and held him back. Jax turned the skysailer to the sky, a rain of bullets showering them as they ascended into the night—

And were gone.

A Metal grabbed her by her arm and pulled her to her knees, slamming the butt of its Metroid into her cheek. She tilted sideways with the blow but caught herself. Her head spun, ears ringing. Her lungs burned.

She couldn't catch her breath.

Stay calm, she told herself. Her heart was racing—but not from fright. And that scared her. Because she recognized the shiver up her spine, the tingling across her skin.

It was a thrill.

Reckless, freeing.

For the first time in months—since a sword had been driven through her stomach, since the new Emperor had ascended the throne, since they had fled and hidden and waited—she felt *alive*.

Over her hammering heart, four humming Metroids clicked to ready.

All aimed at her.

She glowered up at the blue-eyed guard dogs of the kingdom. Their metal faces were impassive, their gazes unwavering. They were always unwavering. There was no thought behind them.

One said, "You are under arrest—"

"—for evading capture," the second went on.

"—and obstruction of justice," the third finished.

The fourth squatted down to her, but she didn't acknowledge the Messier as she trained her eyes on a spot on the floor. It grabbed her chin and jerked her to look into its simple metal face.

"You won't kill me," she told it—the HIVE—the monster who looked from behind those eyes.

The HIVE was looking for something. That was why it burned the shrines—she didn't know what for, but if she could trick the HIVE into thinking it needed her, she might keep her life a little while longer. And she hadn't lived with Robb for six months to *not* pick up on the delicate art of bullshitting.

"You need me," she lied. "I know what you're looking for in the shrines, and if I die? You'll never get it—I can promise you that."

"Well, that is most fortunate," the fourth Messier said in a voice that wasn't Metal, but one she knew well. A voice she had heard in her nightmares, lips pressed against her ear—*You should have burned.*

Di's voice, but no longer Di at all.

Its eyes deepened to a bloodred. *"Because I was planning to kill you slowly."*

JAX

He would never forgive himself.

"Turn around!" Robb cried, trying to grab the controls, but Jax shoved him back into his seat. The desperation on his face made Jax's stomach twist. "We're not leaving her! We have to turn back! We—"

"We *can't*," Jax snapped, and Goddess's spark he hated saying those words. He hated that his tongue did not curl with the taste of a lie. It was the truth in the worst possible way, and he hated himself more that he was the one who had to turn the skysailer away.

"We have to! Ana is back there! If he gets to her—"

"I know, *ma'alor*!"

"Then why aren't we turning back?"

"Because we'll be caught, too." He curled his fingers tighter around the controls. This was a choice that wasn't his to make.

Ana had told him back on the *Dossier* that if anything went south, save Starbright. She had pulled him behind the skysailer in the cargo bay before they'd gone down to Neon City, while

Robb had been tweaking his new mechanical arm.

Jax had hissed, "Ana, you're more important—"

"Not right now I'm not," she had said. "Starbright is more important."

"I can't promise that—"

"Please, Jax," she had pleaded, a little quieter. "If Starbright can bring a Metal out of the HIVE . . . we'll be one step closer to *stopping* the HIVE. With Starbright, we'll have a better chance at saving our kingdom."

"Not without you we can't," Jax had tried to point out, but it was no use. He knew that defiant set of her lips. He couldn't dissuade her. Besides, he had already seen how this exact excursion was going to go. He had seen it months ago when he had kissed Robb in the quiet of the medical bay, after the fight that took Robb's arm. He hadn't even been thinking when he pressed his mouth to Robb's, and the fates had swirled inside his head again. The images haunted his dreams, burned into the backs of his eyelids—

A building like a shard of black glass. A rusted cell. The Royal Captain. Di but not Di in a dimly lit control room. A skysailer too far away. A window of crackling glass. And then—

From the backseat, the girl with silver hair—Starbright? Who knew—said, "Ah, fellas, is that thing supposed to be blinking?"

A flashing red message sprang up on the windshield.

RETURN OR RESIST ARREST, it warned.

Oh, this was just becoming so much *fun.*

He swiped the warning away. "Robb, how did they ping us? We're cloaked."

"They're not supposed to be able to."

In the rearview mirror, a skysailer swirled down from the night sky to follow them. Its wings were a metallic blue. Jax tightened his grip on the helm. "Well, *now* they're following."

"They must've decoded our cloaking signal." Robb bent forward underneath the dash and slammed his hand against a door. It popped open to reveal the skysailer's onboard terminal. As he worked to input a new code into the keypad, three fingers on his mechanical hand suddenly went limp. "Goddess's *tits*," he swore.

"Less cursing, more cloaking, *ma'alor*."

"I'd like to see *you* try when your arm isn't cooperating—"

"And you're doing it *wrong* anyway. Get out of my way!" added the girl, climbing into the front seat and diving for the onboard terminal underneath the dash.

The skysailer behind them crept closer. It was sleek and silver, its fanlike wings angled back to help the ship gain speed, with a Messier at the helm. Jax hated trying to outrun androids. They didn't make nearly as many mistakes.

"Hey, Sparkles, can you buy us time?" the girl shouted at him from the floorboards.

Sparkles. There could be worse nicknames. "How long?"

"As much time as you can."

"Do I have to keep steady or—"

She extracted herself from underneath the dash long enough to give him a dead-serious look. "I could work doing a barrel roll while riding bareback on a jetcycle. I am nothing if not a professional."

Jax suddenly liked Starbright a little better. "Understood. Robb, buckle up."

His partner began to pale. "Please no barrel r—"

He reached over and pulled Robb's harness tight across his chest. "Hang on to her," he said, and Robb clamped his arms around one of the hacker's legs a moment before Jax cut the skysailer to the left. Everything in the ship—the loose change, repair tools, trash—went sliding across the floorboards.

The ship twirled, rolling over on itself, and shot toward the heart of Neon City.

"*Oy!*" Starbright squeaked. "Watch the hand!"

Mortified, Robb jerked his mechanical hand away from her rear. "A-apologies!"

Jax banked a hard left as he passed a tall glass building, curving around it, and cut between two traffic lines. Warning sirens blared as he barely missed a commercial vehicle and skimmed over the crowded streets below. People in ponchos and damp capes looked up as they swirled past.

The silver skysailer followed swiftly.

From afar, Neon City looked like a mountain of glass buildings covered in neon lights, the mist surrounding it making it glow like some otherworldly haven. It would be a fun place if it weren't for the smell of dampness and smoke and poverty that permeated the streets. Most of its residents got by illegally—selling black-market wares, or living off cheated winnings from the gambling rings beneath the city itself.

Every time he flew one way, the Messier skysailer would match him. He couldn't shake the stupid craft no matter what he did. He could keep dodging in and out of buildings all day long, but he was more afraid of the Messier ship calling for backup.

"Are you done yet?" he shouted at her.

"Gimme a *sec!*" she cried. "I'm not the Goddess here."

The skysailer began to whine as it overheated, its trail of white vapors growing increasingly gray. And still the silver Messier skysailer had no problem following.

Fine.

Fine.

If that's how the HIVE wanted to play, he'd play.

Goddess grant me a steady hand—and please ignore ma'alor*'s luck,* he added as he drove the skysailer into the sky again and cut toward a cluster of buildings that stood so closely together it looked like nothing could squeeze between them.

Robb looked up long enough to see exactly where they were heading.

"Jax," he warned.

He eased himself back and loosened his grip on the controls. The buildings came closer. They were commercial high-rises. Ironblood-owned—Malachite, it seemed. Or maybe Obsidia. Whoever it was, he hoped they had insurance.

"Jax, don't—Jax—"

Closer. Closer still.

"JAX—"

He tapped the controls, and the skysailer tilted onto its side and eased through a crack between the buildings. One moment there was sky, and the next there was steel and glass, and they were between them. The silver skysailer tried to bank up, but it was too late. It exploded into the glass tower, sending shrapnel spiraling down into the city center.

As they swirled out on the other side of the buildings, Jax glanced behind him one last time to make sure they were gone, then pumped his fist into the air. "And *boom!*"

In reply, Robb let go of the hacker's legs, his face so pale he looked like a corpse. "I'm going to puke."

The Metal, still perched in the backseat, one leg crossed over the other, applauded. "There was only a twenty-three-point-four percent chance of us surviving that. Congratulations, we are alive."

"For *now*," replied the hacker, who tapped Robb to help pull her up from the floorboards and back into her seat. She flipped back her shoulder-length hair, and Jax noticed that she was Solani as well, though she must have had hints of Erosian blood. She gave a start when she saw Jax—they'd barely glanced at each other when she first fell into the skysailer—and his skin prickled.

She hadn't recognized him, had she?

If she did, she didn't mention it. Maybe that was worse. "That signal should keep us cloaked for at least twenty minutes, but I'll say fifteen just to be safe."

"To do what?" Robb asked. "Ana's *gone.*"

In the rearview mirror, he watched as a silent conversation passed between the girl and the Metal, and then she nodded and reached into the Metal's dark bag. She pulled out a holo-pad, her fingers moving quickly across the glass. "Not quite. I slipped a tracker underneath her coat collar. No one ever looks there."

Jax turned around in the seat to give her a weary look. "Why would you do that?"

"So . . . I could find her?"

Robb blinked. "Who *are* you?"

Without even looking up from her holo-screen, she waved to her Metal friend. "This is Xu, my partner, and I'm Elara Vath'aka."

Vath'aka—a name given to Solani with no birthright. Her family had been exiled, then—either her parents, or grand-parents, or great-grandparents before that. The little knot of tension that had solidified in his chest began to unravel, because if she was born without a birthright, she had probably never visited Zenteli. Which meant she *wouldn't* have recognized him.

She didn't know he was the C'zar.

"The HIVE has her in a skysailer already. Taking her off-world and onto one of those dreadnoughts the Emperor recommissioned, if I'd hazard a guess. And that's not good. If those rumors are true . . ."

"They can't be," Jax said, pulling at his gloves nervously. "Only Rasovant knew how to make people into Metals. It's just a rumor."

"But what if someone else figured it out?" wondered Xu.

That was something Jax definitely didn't want to think about. "We should save her either way—as quickly as possible."

Robb gave him a solid look and dipped his head in to say qui-etly so only Jax could hear, "*Ma'alor,* I don't trust them. It seems so fortuitous. How did they know to contact us? That we were looking to stop the HIVE? It's too easy. We should make them promise on iron and stars to help us."

Like how Jax had made Robb's mother promise on iron and

stars to keep Robb safe, and so she stepped in front of a bullet meant for him. Jax had never mustered up the courage to tell Robb—and whether or not it had any hand in her death, he felt ashamed anyway. To hear Robb ask to make this girl and the Metal promise, it made his skin prickle. He wouldn't let Robb make the same mistake he had.

"We're not going to do that," he replied sternly.

Robb narrowed his eyes, but when Jax refused to relent, he looked away with a huff. "Well, I'm not telling Siege."

"I will tell this Siege," the Metal said.

In the rearview mirror, Jax watched Elara quirk an eyebrow at her partner. "Don't pretend like you don't know who Captain Siege is."

"She is probably quite lovely, Elara."

Jax programmed the coordinates to the dreadnought into the guidance system of the skysailer and banked up out of the atmosphere and into the star-filled sky.

EMPEROR

The orange light of morning spread across the crowd below like a slowly creeping fire. It reminded him of the way the Iron Shrine in the square below had burned, red then orange and then golden, until its insides were charred and the bone white of its steeple was the only part of it left standing. It reminded him of the way the Iron Palace had burned. The North Tower. This entire kingdom, if his sister had any say in it.

The streets of Nevaeh teemed with citizens, crowded into the avenues that crisscrossed over the city. From his perch on the edge of the floating garden of Astoria, they looked like an infestation of vermin. Messiers perched on the rooftops like prison guards, their skins glinting like flares in the morning light. Newsfeed drones orbited around him, cameras feeding his likeness onto large holo-screens so even the citizens near the slums could not escape his gaze.

The HIVE thrummed in his head like a heartbeat. It told him who he was, and who he needed to be, and what to say.

He spread his arms wide and the citizens roared his name.

"Goddess bless the Emperor!" they cried. "Goddess light his way!"

In the light spilling from the harbor above, he looked like a god, sunshine catching in his red hair, turning strands orange and gold. It reflected off the toggles and buttons on his rich black cloak, sparkling off the diamonds sewn into the fabric in galactic swirls. His cuff links burned like fire, the Valerio clasp around his neck like molten gold.

He looked like an icon—a god of the sun to rival the memory of their moon goddess.

Behind him, his Royal Guard, in their simple purple uniforms, stood in a quiet line. His sister had replaced all the human guards with Messiers after his coronation. Beside them were a few of his Iron Council—the Obsidias and Carnelians and Pyrites. Those who had pledged their unending devotion to the crown.

Also standing there was the sole Valerio who owned this floating garden. He'd never cared for the Valerio. The man looked on with a narrow sort of envy that was snakelike and wanting.

He raised his hands higher, palms out, and slowly lowered them. In return, the crowd sank into silence. There were hundreds of thousands of eyes on him, as the HIVE wanted. A beacon for them.

He savored it, only to close his eyes and see the Empress staring back at him. When his Messiers had caught her on that rooftop, he'd thought she would have been frightened, but there had only been pity in her eyes.

That irked him.

Did he *look* like someone to be pitied? He was a god. "My citizens," he began, the voice of the HIVE whispering at the back of his tongue, languid like honey, and it was so easy to stoke their fears. Humans hated things they didn't undertand, so humans hated Metals. It was that simple, and their fear made them that much easier to control while his sister searched for her heart. Once she found it, not even the rage he stoked would save them, and by then there would be no one left to stop her. As he finished his speech, he told the audience, the lie sweet on his tongue, "Follow me, and I will lead you into the light!"

The crowd roared, a hundred thousand voices amplifying the song in his head. He relished in it. Reveled—

There was a flash to his right. A sound zipped past his ear, through his red hair, a bullet missing him by a fraction of an inch.

The HIVE whispered, *Lower left, fourth building, street corner,* and his gaze lowered to a rogue Metal with a high-grade sniper rifle.

The crowd below screamed and began to heave like waves in the sea.

The Metal aimed again in the chaos, cool and composed.

In a blink, he took control of the rifle. Electricity crackled over its charger, wires whining as it overheated—

The Metal fired again a moment before the weapon exploded in its grip.

He felt someone jerk him back from the side of the floating garden and force him to the ground. His gaze refocused on the

man on top of him. Chilling blue eyes, brown—almost black—
hair shorn short with a floral design shaved into the sides. A
Valerio crest was clasped to his throat, knuckle rings glinting
as he grabbed his shoulder.

"Your Excellence," Erik Valerio said, "it'd be a pity if you'd
gotten hurt."

He shoved off the Ironblood and silently got to his feet.

The Royal Guard ushered the Ironbloods into the underbelly of the garden for safety, but he walked to the edge of the
garden again and peered down to where the Metal had been.

It now lay broken on the ground, the explosion from the rifle
having carved a hole into half of its face and chest.

They are growing bolder, said Mellifare, who had gone into
the underneath with the guards and Ironbloods.

Let them try, sister.

The streets swarmed with panic. People fled for cover, trying to find who or what had shot at the Emperor. There were
rebels in the crowd, too. Somewhere, festering like glitches in
an otherwise perfect code.

"Your Excellence, seems like the public doesn't like you
much," said the Valerio.

"They are few," he muttered.

"Maybe there are more than you think."

The Emperor gave him a sharp look, but the Valerio simply
bowed and led him into the underbelly of the garden. The other
members of the Iron Council were already gathered in one of
the hallways, and they quickly genuflected at the sight of him,
expressing gratitude that he wasn't dead.

"You were so lucky that the young Valerio saved you!" said Lord Obsidia.

Lady Pyrite nodded. "What is this kingdom coming to?"

"Heathens," added a third Ironblood. A Malachite son. "The lot of them. You're a light in the darkness, Your Excellence."

The Iron Council was to serve the Emperor or Empress in their ruling of the kingdom, but they had not helped anyone but themselves for generations. If someone assassinated him, each and every one of them had a plan in place to put themselves on the throne.

And none wanted it more than Erik Valerio, who was only twenty years old and already head of the Valerio estates after the murder of his mother.

Erik Valerio had not *saved* him because he was loyal.

He turned to Erik Valerio. "Thank you, Lord Valerio. Your mother would have been proud of you. I am proud of you. If I can repay you in any way for saving me, please do not hesitate to ask."

Erik smoothed a smile over his lips that was cold and predatory, and flicked his eyes down to the half-melted Valerio pendant at his throat. The pendant he had used to claim the throne almost six months ago.

"Seeing you alive is enough," said Erik, his eyes as cold as steel. "We Valerios need to look out for each other, yes?"

The Emperor cocked his head, imagining what it would be like to rip the Valerio's lying tongue out of his mouth, but instead simply said, "What a charming sentiment."

"Very. I expect you at my party next week—it will be *fantastic.*

Astoria is beautiful this time of year," Erik added.

"Yes, of course."

The HIVE bloomed in the back of his head, relaying that another Metal had been captured, a moment before one of the Messiers in the hallway bowed and said, "Your Excellence, we found an accomplice. We have brought it up to the garden."

"Thank you. Leave us and return to your families. I am sure they are worried." He gave a flick of his wrist to dismiss the Iron Council.

As Erik Valerio passed, he very carefully took him underneath the arm, and leaned in. The facade of the dutiful Ironblood slipped away, revealing the envy and rot underneath, and he snarled, "You can fool everyone else, but not me. We both know you're not a Valerio, and that's not your crest. Enjoy your time on your stolen throne, because it will be mine."

The Ironblood let go of his arm and left with the others to the docks.

His throne? A flash of anger spiked his processes, but he wrestled to control it and rolled his shoulders back to ease the tension. The Valerio knew how to poke at him, but he had more important matters to attend. He turned his attention to the Messiers and their captive Metal. They had detained it in another hallway that led to a kitchen, forced it to its knees. It looked up at him with glowing moonlit eyes and watched him wearily.

The Metal was dented, a bullet hole in its shoulder. It wore a leather jacket and knit trousers and shoes—although it did not need to wear anything. It was a weapon. It was not supposed to think on its own.

"Why do things like you even try?" he asked, more exhausted than anything else.

"I am not a thing," it replied. "And you are not an Emperor—"

He bent down to the android and snagged it by the chin. "*You* are nothing."

Then, with the HIVE singing in the back of his head, he pushed the code into the Metal, one line at a time.

At first the Metal twitched. Then it tried to tear out of his grip, but he held firm and fed another line of code, and then another, like humming a tune that would soon get stuck in its head. One note, and then another, and another, and it thrashed in a dance all its own, until the song sang so loud between their link it was a symphony. Its moonlit eyes faded to a soft, sweet blue, and the Messier stilled in his grip.

"Who are you?" he asked the Metal, and in reply the Messier said, through the mouth of every other Messier who stood guard in the room,

"I am the HIVE."

"See? You are nothing." He dropped the Messier's chin and, gathering his cloak, left the room. "We are nothing."

ROBB

The dreadnought was *enormous*.

It looked like a monstrous bird of prey, a ship built in an era when Ironblood rebellions were common and heirs vied for the throne. They were built as deathships by a mad emperor bent on quelling any uprising, but the destruction they caused was catastrophic—more than the Ironbloods could justify, and as soon as the Emperor died, the ships were decommissioned. There were still graveyards in space where pieces of rebel fleets drifted. Robb had studied the decommissioned dreadnoughts at the Academy, but he'd never thought he would see one in person.

The sight struck him senseless.

Over the last six months, the Emperor had recommissioned these deathships. They acted as prisons of sorts now—where Messiers took convicts and outlaws and rogue Metals. They never came out alive. Or dead. They never came out at all, really. He thought the HIVE killed them, but maybe . . . maybe the rumors were true.

Maybe the HIVE turned them into Metals.

Robb sorely hoped it was just a rumor. He hoped they weren't too late—that Ana was still alive. Elara ran a cloaking device over the skysailer to skew the dreadnought's sonar so they could get close undetected. While no one had ever escaped a dreadnought, no one had ever tried to sneak aboard, either.

The ship was shaped like a hulking boomerang. The plan was: get in, overload the solar core to shut down the power, and search for Ana—avoiding the entire HIVE in the process. They had about eighteen minutes and thirty-two seconds to cover the entire bloody ship, so he and Jax would have to split up once they got inside.

It was a *terrible* idea.

They didn't have a better one.

Jax fastened his hand on the side of the ship, his other hand holding tight to Robb, as Elara, Xu, and the skysailer fell away.

"Well, this is better than not doing anything, ma'alor," Jax said over the comm-link.

"Just barely," Robb replied, and grabbed ahold of the other handle on the opposite side of the airlock. "But why couldn't Elara or Xu do this?"

"You didn't just suggest that a Metal walk into a ship where they HIVE Metals," Jax deadpanned.

He felt his cheeks redden.

The *Dossier* was on its way, but it was on the other side of Eros, dropping off medical supplies and rations at a sanctuary. It would get here as fast as it could.

His mechanical arm twitched, and Robb quickly grabbed his

forearm to keep it still, prayed to the Goddess that he could control it.

Their space suits had been improved upon since the last time Robb went jumping onto another ship—they were the first thing Siege had bought in the wake of the assassination attempt six months ago. (The second thing Siege bought was a drink.) The space suit reminded him of old Royal Guard armor, a plated chest piece, pauldrons, arm armor, gauntlets, and a thick nylon-polymer body mail underneath. The chest piece pulsed gently with a dull light.

And, thank the Goddess, they were bulletproof.

Jax dug into the satchel and took out a small square. He pressed it against the lock. The square lit up with three red bars that slowly counted down to a green bar. Then the airlock burst open with a *snap*, spilling a puff of frozen oxygen into the air. Jax helped him inside first and followed, closing the airlock after them. The chamber gave a sigh and recompressed.

Robb pressed the button on the side of his helmet, and it folded back into the collar of his spacesuit. He sucked in a lungful of stale recycled air. "*Goddess*, I hate space."

"And tight spaces, and the word *moist*, and freeze-dried jerky with caminar pepper," Jax added, looking around the darkened maintenance hallway. "You know what I was just thinking?"

"How this is a terrible plan?"

He gave a wry laugh. "About the first time we met. Me, dashing and rogue-ish. You, bleeding all over the newly upholstered backseat of my skysailer."

"I only bled a *little* on your seat—and don't forget I helped save your life when the skysailer stalled, remember?"

"You could say I fell for you then, *ma'alor.*"

He scowled. "We're sneaking aboard a death trap and you're making jokes. What if my metal arm acts up? What if I can't defend myself and—"

"Shush," Jax interrupted, and gently cupped his face in his hands. "Worrying'll give you wrinkles. You'll be fine."

Robb hesitated as he looked into his partner's eyes. "How do you know?"

His partner gave a secretive smile, but there was a strangeness in his eyes that Robb couldn't place. He pressed a gloved thumb against Robb's lips—and kissed it. It was the only way they could kiss, with layers between them, always rotating around each other like a binary star.

Close, but never touching.

". . . Jax? Is there something wrong?" he asked hesitantly.

"Can't I kiss my partner?" Jax asked, and gently traced this thumb across Robb's bottom lip.

Maybe he's just nervous, Robb thought. "I'll see you in twenty minutes in the docking bay, then. Either I'll have Ana—or you will. We'll be fine."

For a moment longer Jax studied Robb's face, as if he was trying to ingrain it into his memory. *"Al gat ha astri ke'eto, ma'alor."*

Until the next star shines on you.

"I'll see you soon," Robb promised in reply, and watched him leave down the dark maintenance hallway and out of sight.

It's nothing, he told himself as he heaved the rucksack, heavy with the tools he needed, onto his shoulder and left down the other way to find the electrical conjunction. *Jax is just nervous, like I'm nervous.*

He easily found an open grate into the ventilation ducts, or climbed on top of a cleaning bot to lift himself inside, but he couldn't shake the feeling that something was wrong, even as everything went according to plan.

ANA

A group of six Messiers led her down a long gray hallway. Halogen lights lined the edges like trim work, the doors they passed sealed tight. There were medical wards and living quarters, vacant food halls and empty rooms, their windows dark. She didn't know where they were taking her on the dreadnought, and that made her all the more nervous.

She should be dead. She was *going* to be dead if she didn't come up with another lie—and fast. At least she knew she'd been right: the HIVE *was* looking for something in the shrines, and then burning them.

But what?

Think, Ana.

When the Messiers had loaded her into a transport shuttle, they bound her hands behind her back with magnetic cuffs and snapped a voxcollar around her neck. It hummed softly against her throat, a constant threat of ten thousand volts straight to her skin if she so much as mumbled a word. She couldn't escape it. Was this what Jax had had to deal with for a week while he served Lady Valerio in the Iron Palace? If she fought back against her captors, she'd surely make a sound.

So she had to work around that.

Somehow.

When they had brought her onto the dreadnought, the Messiers stripped her of her cloak, her weapons, her coppers, her comm-link . . .

But when the Messier had found Di's memory core, it paused.

There was a shift in its eyes, and it flicked its gaze to her—and there he was. Just like on the rooftop in Neon City, the Emperor—Di—looked out through the Messier's eyes.

He had tucked the memory core back into her coat pocket. *"For your comfort,"* he had purred, and then the Messier's eyes faded to blue, and he was gone again.

It had to be a trick of her mind—he couldn't be *anywhere,* could he?

The Messiers let her keep Di's memory core nevertheless, even as they stripped her of everything else and led her deeper into the dreadnought. She had been walking for so long, she couldn't remember how to get back to the docking bay where they'd brought her in.

Her breath came out in puffs of frost. It was so cold on the ship, she doubted the other prisoners could spend very long here without turning into human ice cubes. She shivered, darting her eyes from one Messier to the other, trying to formulate how to escape. If her hands weren't tied, she'd have a lot more options. She could try to disable one—but then the other five would take her down. Her fingers were almost numb from the cold already.

The last time she'd been this cold, she and Di had taken shore leave to one of the frozen cities of Iliad, a small town that specialized in ice sculptures and ship graveyards. The *Dossier* had been in a fight that took out two of its sails, so while Jax and the captain went to salvage replacements, Ana and Di had some shore leave and a laundry list of parts to get for repairs. It had been only a year and a half ago, but it felt like decades. With the last of her coppers, she'd splurged on a small cup of hot wine, of which Di had greatly disapproved.

"Well, fine then—if you could buy anything, what would you buy?" she had countered.

"Books," he had replied.

"Seriously? You read them once and then you put them on a shelf to take up space. Forever."

"And to reference later," he had argued, "and reread."

"You have a photographic memory, Di."

"They are also adequate weapons. They also smell nice."

"You can't smell."

He'd cocked his head, as if it confused him. "Oh. Then perhaps I *would* like their smell."

She had rolled her eyes. "Why not spend your coppers on something useful?"

"Such as?"

"Such as . . ." She had thought for a moment, sipping the hot wine as it warmed her hands. "Oh! What about that new service bot the captain's been eyeing?"

He had turned his moonlit eyes to her. "You are not serious."

"Why not? The bot'll cut your work time in half! It'll give

you more time to *reread*. And," she had added happily, "it's adorable."

He had looked away. Not angrily, but in a way that she knew meant he wanted this conversation to end. "I am ninety-seven-point-three percent sure this *can opener* will be of no help to me. I am incredibly useful without it."

Ana had frowned. ". . . I hurt your feelings, didn't I?"

"I highly doubt you could find a mere *bot* as apt as me."

"You think we'll replace you."

He had come to a stop in the middle of the market, people in thick fur-lined cloaks scurrying about them. Snow fell and crusted on her eyelashes and in her dark braided hair, and frosted over his metal skin. He gave her one of his many unreadable looks. "You would never replace me."

"Oh? That confident, are you?" she had joked.

"Yes. Because I am yours."

"That's silly." She tried to dismiss him, feeling her cheeks getting hot. She told herself it was because she was embarrassed.

"Ana—"

"You don't know what you're talking about," she had added, trying to tell herself that he didn't *mean* it that way.

Even though it sounded like a declaration.

Even though it made her heart flutter.

"Besides, I was only saying we should buy the bot so it can do all the chores that I know you don't like to—and I'm sure you could find *some* sort of use for it, and it might not be as much of a nuisance as you're thinking and— Di?" she had called when she realized that he hadn't been following.

She'd glanced behind her to see where he had wandered off to. A vendor probably caught his eye, or a window display. Instead, she found him only a few feet behind her, having paused in the middle of the market, somewhere between one step and the next.

Her heart had leaped into her throat.

". . . Di?"

On some nights after, when they visited mechanics on Iliad and listened to rumors of Rasovant's lost fleetship, she wished she had never turned around. Because Di stood frozen, shoulders stiff, legs immobile. His eyes flickered like the lightning storms on Eros, strange and all of a sudden terrifying.

It was the first time he had glitched.

And it would be far from the last.

Now she wondered how different her world would be if she had never gone in search of Rasovant's lost fleetship. If faced with the choice now, she wasn't sure what she would do to have Di back.

All the good memories in her head warred with the look in his red eyes as he sank his lightsword into her stomach. The way his face twisted, the grimace trying to be a smirk. It made the scar on her abdomen ache so deeply it went to her very soul.

She bit the inside of her cheek to keep her teeth from chattering and upsetting the voxcollar. The Messiers shoved her into a vacant room. It was a small medical ward, but it had been emptied of all equipment and stocked with spare Metal parts.

One of the Messiers grabbed her by the arm, and the door closed behind her, trapping the two of them inside. The voxcollar gave a *pop*, and the hum silenced as it deactivated.

"Where is it?" the Messier asked, its monotonous voice dipping into the brassy, familiar baritone she dreaded. It made her breath hitch. When she looked at the Messier again, its eyes were red and Di looked out of them.

She jerked out of his grip.

How could he do that—jump into other Metals? Was it a power of the HIVE?

He advanced on her. *"Tell me where the heart is."*

The . . . *heart?* The only heart she knew about was—

The *Cantos.* The Great Dark's heart.

He took a dagger from his waist. It was steel—not a lightblade. A blade made to bleed, whereas a lightblade burned. He meant what he'd said before. He would kill her slowly. She stumbled back, mind reeling—*Think, think, think!*—as he twirled the blade in his fingers and advanced upon her.

He was not her Di anymore.

He was the enemy—and it had taken six months to understand it. He wanted her dead. *He* did. Not just the HIVE. If he loved her, wouldn't he have fought? Wouldn't he *still* be fighting against the HIVE?

She eyed the dagger.

He hadn't killed her at the palace, and he wasn't going to kill her now.

ROBB

The ducts of the dreadnought's ventilation system were a lot larger than the ones on the *Tsarina*. He doubted he could wiggle his way through those now, having gotten a bit broader in the months since. Honestly, between running from Messiers and trying to find a mechanic to outfit him with an arm, he hadn't really paid much attention to his growth spurt. His trousers were a little short, and his coats didn't fit nearly as well as they had before—but it was kind of hard to find a tailor when you were a wanted war criminal.

And he definitely didn't expect to be infiltrating a prison on his seventeenth birthday.

Not that he'd told anyone. He really didn't want to—and besides, even *he* knew that mentioning it on the day Ana got arrested was in poor form.

Happy seventeenth to me, he thought. He could celebrate his birthday later. With his friends. And the boy he loved. And maybe finally tell that boy that he loved him. Yeah—he would. It'd be a fine birthday present to himself.

But first he had to find the control box, set the charges, and not die.

Not dying was imperative.

So he dropped down into the maintenance hallway at the end of the ducts and found the electrical junction, old and frightfully rusted, set the charges, and hid around a corner.

He kissed the detonator, prayed, "Goddess, let this work," and pressed the button.

ANA

As Di raised his blade, the halogen light above them gave a whining pop—and shattered. Ana winced as darkness filled the room. An emergency light flickered on in the corner, bathing the room in a bloodred glow.

She and Di, through the eyes of a Messier, watched each other for a moment.

"CODE THREE-FIVE. SOLAR MALFUNCTION," a metallic voice announced over the intercom.

It seemed to break the spell.

In that moment she shoved her fright down into her belly, where her scar burned, and launched herself at Di. She slammed her shoulder into his chest. He stumbled away from her, trying to keep his balance.

She jumped, swinging her handcuffed hands underneath her to bring her arms in front, and grabbed for the weapon on his belt—a mace. When did Messiers start carrying *maces*?

Whatever.

She slammed it into the Messier's face again, and even though it wasn't Di's face, she remembered it like points in her favorite constellation. The scuff on his forehead, the slat on the left side of his mouth that creaked, the staticky tremor of his damaged voice box. She swung the mace even as tears came to her eyes.

It's not him—

She slammed the weapon across its face again.

—It's not—

And again.

—Di.

The Messier twisted to look at her, half of its face buckled in, eyes sparking, and she gritted her teeth, raised the mace over her head, and brought it down one last time.

Die.

The Messier dropped to the ground and didn't get back up. She pushed the palm of her hand against her eyes to wipe away the tears.

A *heart*—the Great Dark was looking for a heart. She concentrated on that as she dug into the uniform of the Messier and found the key to her handcuffs and undid them, rubbing at the marks on her freed wrists.

Then she took the steel dagger from the Messier's frozen grip and slipped it into her boot.

She had to keep calm. Another Messier must have had the voxcollar key. Even though it was deactivated, she still wanted to get this bloody death necklace off her, then find a way out of here.

Suddenly, something bumped against her shoulder. She glanced up, tensing to strike—

It was a service bot, its bulbous lens narrowing to her.

No—it was *EoS*!

She recognized it from the dent in the top left corner of its cubed head where Di had "accidentally" slammed a door on it.

It beeped and extended something to her. A voxcollar remote. She took it. "EoS, thank the Goddess, you're the best fifty coppers on discount I've ever spent." She pressed it against the lock on her collar. With a click, it released and fell to the ground. She gave a sigh, rubbing her throat.

As a reply, EoS nudged her cheek.

"Did you stow away on the ship to follow me?"

It bleeped again.

"That was dangerous," she scolded. "You could've gotten killed. C'mon—I don't know what caused the blackout, but I'm not going to waste it. Do you remember the way to the docking bay?"

The bot bobbed in the air like a nod, and she told it to lead the way. It zipped out of the room and turned down the dark hallway, and she followed.

JAX

For the record, Jax *hated* this plan.

He knocked a lightsword away with his obsidian cuff and drove it down through the Messier's skull.

He didn't hate this plan because he had to play the bait in this Goddess-forsaken prison. He didn't hate it because the entire dreadnought smelled like disinfectant and old socks. He didn't hate it because his comm-links to Elara and Robb were out, or because the red lights were giving him a headache, or because the suit was making him chafe. He didn't even hate it because this was the *fourth* Messier he had disabled, and he was finally breaking a sweat—

No.

He hated the plan because he would never find Ana, and these stupid Messiers were *taunting* him.

"You cannot save her," the first Messier had said just before Jax pounded its face in with the butt of its own lightsword.

The second said, "This is senseless." He ran a blade through that one's chest.

"She is safer with the Emperor." He simply cut its head off.

"You will die here." That one he broke a sweat killing.

Muttering a string of Old Language obscenities, he wrenched his blade from the last Messier's chest and continued toward the control room. The outer wall of the hallway was a sheet of glass that looked out to space, filtering in enough starlight to give him energy to keep going. Solani didn't fare well in the dark.

He wiped his sweaty brow with his sleeve and hurried down the emergency-lit hallway. Through one of the windows he saw a large room. Once it would've been used as a mess hall or a meeting space, but now it was simply filled with lines and lines of Messiers, their eyes blue and sharp, staring straight ahead into the next Metal. There must have been a hundred—maybe two—crammed into the space. Just waiting.

There were so *many*.

And there were no outlaws or criminals. The convicts who had been brought here were nowhere to be found.

He hated to think the rumors were true.

Nervous energy itched just under his skin. His thumb-kiss with Robb lingered on his lips like a regret. He should have kissed Robb. *Really* kissed him—with tongue, just to make it worthwhile.

To leave Robb something to remember him by.

His . . .

Nervously, he pulled at the collar of his space suit.

"Jax! Jax help me!"

He whirled in the direction of the voice. "Ana?"

"*Jax!*" she screamed, so frightened her voice crumbled at the end. "*JAX!*"

He didn't even think—he just ran toward the door at the end of the hallway. It was closed, unlike most of the others. He slammed his lightsword into the door. The white-hot blade cut a molten-red line down the door. Then he leveraged the hilt against his body and began to pry it open.

With one final jerk, the door cracked open enough for him to shimmy inside. "Ana!" he called desperately. "Ana, where are y—"

He was halfway into the room when he realized where he was.

The bridge of the dreadnought.

It was dark, the consoles and panels dead. One wall of windows looked out toward space, the other down into the docking bay below.

Two Messiers stood up from their stations. Ana was nowhere in sight. His throat constricted. He remembered this bridge from Robb's stars.

"Identifying—" one Messier began, the other answering, "Jaxander Taizu." And then, like a secret, "C'zar."

"Sorry, haven't been that in a while," replied Jax, irritated. The HIVE had tricked him—the voice hadn't been Ana at all. He raised his sword to point at the two of them. "That little trick of yours has made me *very* angry, but I'm feeling generous. I'll give you a choice: Do you want to die first"—he turned the tip of his blade to the other one—"or do you?"

The Messier on the left reached for the pistol on its hip, and that was all the answer he needed. He threw the lightsword at the Messier before it could draw its weapon. The blade slammed into its chest—

As the other Messier fired a shot.

He drew up his obsidian cuff to shield his face and charged at the Messier. A second bullet glanced off his wrist with the impact of a punch, a third ricocheting off his space suit's breastplate.

Then he was on the Messier and grabbing the pistol, pushing it away so he couldn't be shot at again. He twisted his fingers under the automaton's chin slats and pulled. Wires popped out, short-circuiting its optics. The Messier stumbled sideways as Jax twisted the pistol out of its grip at last and fired two shots into its chest, shattering the memory core inside.

The Messier slumped, bits of its blue core slipping out between the bullet holes, and died.

Goddess forgive me for that, he thought, knowing that he shouldn't have aimed for its core, but he didn't want to die yet either.

Jax shoved the gun onto his belt and winced when his arm spiked with pain. He inspected it. Goddess, *seriously*? A bullet had skimmed his biceps, the only unprotected part of his arm, leaving a bleeding gash. Lucky shot, but nothing he'd die from.

Still, it'd leave a scar.

Not that he was worried about that anymore.

He couldn't change the stars this time, not like he had with Ana on her coronation day, because what he hadn't known then was that the stars took other things instead. Where Ana had been saved, someone else had not. Viera Carnelian—the Royal Guard Captain—or her brother Vermion, or Lady Valerio . . . but Jax knew, deep down, that in saving Ana he had damned Di.

Of all the things he regretted, he regretted that the most.

That he couldn't have saved them both.

He swiped his fingers across the console to wake it up out of emergency power saving, disabled the ship's defenses, and sent a hail to the *Dossier*. "This is Jax—come in, *Dossier*."

There was static across the comms for a moment, and then it crackled, and the voice of his captain came through like dawn breaking over the horizon. *"Reading you loud and clear. We are ETA three minutes and forty-three seconds. Are you safe?"*

"As safe as I can be, sir," he replied.

"Have you found Ana yet?"

"No, but trust me—Robb will find her. She'll be fine. Just be at these coordinates as quickly as possible. Robb and Ana will leave in a skysailer from the docking bay."

There was a pause, and for a moment Jax worried that he'd lost her, but then she said, *"Jax, you come back with them—"*

He exited out of the comm-link, his hands shaking. There wasn't time for regret. He pushed the Metal off the operations console and sat down. He had to open the docking bay doors or Robb and Ana weren't getting out of here alive. They would be down there in five minutes and seven seconds, so he set a timer for then, hoping he wasn't misremembering from his vision. They would be in a skysailer by the time the doors opened.

Just as he finished programming the command, the door to the bridge opened with a *snap*.

The clock began to tick down from five minutes.

4:59

4:58

4:57

He spun around in his chair.

A Metal stood in the doorway, hands on either side of the cut door. This android was different, though. It wore the same Messier uniform, but there were more bars on its shoulders. Higher in rank.

The dreadnought's XO—its Executive Officer—if he had to guess.

It turned its red eyes to him—and Jax saw the monster peering through.

Di.

Jax bit the inside of his lip so hard, he tasted the blood against his tongue, and it grounded him for a moment.

This was the beginning of the end. And he wished he had a second—just a second more—with Robb.

"Well, that's new," he told Di. "Can you patch yourself into service bots, too? Street-sweepers? Trash receptacles? I bet you're right at home there—"

"I should have known it was you," said the Emperor through the XO's mouth.

4:48

4:47

Just a little longer. He unsheathed his lightsword. "I *am* rather predictable," he replied, and launched himself at the Messier.

ANA

"Are you sure this is the right way?" she asked EOS.

All of the hallways looked the same, but she could've sworn she had already passed these doors before. She needed to get to the docking bay—hijack a skysailer and get the heck out of here. Trouble was, there weren't any bloody *signs* around this deathship. The dreadnought was more confusing than the palace—and she'd gotten lost so many times in those hallways, it bruised her ego.

EOS gave a blip and flew down the corridor. Without much choice, she followed. She passed what looked like a tech bay with darkened Metals inside, spare parts lined up on the far wall like different pieces of armor. It seemed like the HIVE had an endless supply of soldiers at its beck and call, and that worried her.

Where had they gotten so many Metals?

The more she saw of the dreadnought, the more she began to believe the rumors—that the HIVE *was* turning people into Metals, and then HIVE'ing them. But why couldn't the HIVE just create androids without memory cores—like the androids on the *Tsarina*? That would've been a whole lot easier.

It didn't make sense, unless there was something she didn't yet know.

For the length of the corridor, she and EOS clung to the red-lit shadows, until one of the corridors finally looked familiar from when she'd first arrived. The elevator to the docking bay should be close.

EOS turned left at another intersection—and suddenly recoiled backward, beeping furiously.

"What—?"

Ana barely had time to brace before someone slammed into her in the intersection, and she bit the floor hard. She gasped, trying to push whatever had attacked her off, but they straddled her and pinned her to the ground.

In the dim red light, her attacker's blond hair shone like copper, her cheekbones harsh, the arrows underneath her eyes darker than pitch. Wait—she knew that slant of eyebrows, the downward curve of her lips.

"Wait!" Ana cried as the woman wound her fist back. "*Viera*, it's me!"

The woman froze. She looked down at her for a moment as if she didn't know her. Then, slowly, she lowered her fist. ". . . Ana?"

Ana shimmied out from underneath her, not quite believing her eyes. "You—you're alive?"

Slowly, Viera's eyes widened with the same mystified look, as if they were two ghosts seeing each other in a world where ghosts did not wander. Then Viera, coming back to her senses, quickly doubled over and pressed her forehead against the ground. "Your Grace." Her voice shook. "Your Grace, please forgive me. I did not know it was you—"

Alarmed, Ana quickly pulled them both to their feet. "No—no don't. Stop."

"But Your Grace—"

"How're you alive? How'd you get here?"

Surprised, Viera looked from Ana to the bot, and then back to her. "I—I was imprisoned, but I cannot remember for how long. They were taking me somewhere. Then the lights went out and I decided to try and escape. What are *you* doing here? How did you survive?"

"It's a long story. Come on—the docking bay isn't far—at least, I think." She grabbed Viera by the wrist and pulled her down the hallway toward the elevator.

But there was someone already there.

The stranger turned around, finally hearing their footsteps, a moment before Viera launched herself at him, grabbing him by the throat, and pinned him against the closed elevator doors. In the harsh red emergency light light, Ana made out the unruly curls of brown hair, the stubble prickling against his chin. And Valerio blue eyes.

"*Mercy!*" the stranger wheezed.

Ana blinked. "*Robb?* Viera—it's Robb!"

He slapped at Viera's wrist to get her to let go of his throat, and she did. He gasped for breath. "Goddess's spark— *Vee?*"

Viera blinked at him a moment before she responded, "Robbert. You are . . . taller."

"And you're alive?"

"If you're here—Siege sent you?" Ana added, hopeful.

He shot her a wounded look. "I sent *myself,* thank you—"

"Then where's the captain?"

"She's on her way. We need to get to the docking bay and out of here—Jax is going to meet us there," he added, glancing back over his shoulder. "Assuming we make it there."

As if on cue, a patrol of Messiers came down the farthest end of the hall. Two in the front carried egg-shaped lights.

"We should probably get moving," he added, and she agreed.

Together, they pulled open the elevator doors. Starlight spilled in through the crack like a beam of light after a long nightmare. It was so bright she winced. The outward wall of the elevator shaft was made of thick glass and looked out onto space to—

. . . a fleet of schooners marked with the royal crest making their way toward the dreadnought. There were dozens of them—too many to count. And she had the worst feeling that they had come to make sure she didn't escape.

"How . . . did you say we were going to leave?" she asked absently, but Robb shook his head, because however they *were* going to leave, they definitely couldn't now. Not with all those waiting outside.

EoS bleeped slowly.

Suddenly, a streak of black and chrome cut through the formation like a knife, leaving pieces of skysailers in its wake.

The *Dossier.*

It had arrived.

Robb took Ana by the hand and squeezed it. She squeezed back. "We're getting out of here," he assured her. Then he let go of her hand and leaped across the gap to the cable. The elevator had stopped two floors up, so it was a clean ride all the way down. Viera took a running start after him and followed.

The sound of the patrol came closer. The beams of their flashlights reflected off the walls, turning the red emergency lights into a murky pink.

"EoS, you go first—EoS?" Ana glanced over at the bot.

It hovered, quiet, and then it bumped its bulbous lens against her forehead—as if to tell her not to worry, something Di had done so many times in the past—zipped down the corridor, and was gone into the shadows.

"EoS!"

"Ana!" Robb called up.

She touched her forehead where EoS had bumped against her and made up her mind. EoS knew what it was doing, and she had to trust it. She jumped for the elevator cable and followed Robb and Viera down into the murky depths of the dreadnought.

ROBB

The docking bay was a sight for sore eyes. A line of skysailers stretched out across the landing area, and through the glass windows of the gigantic bay doors, he could see a little of the firefight going on outside. The *Dossier* kept the schooners busy, but he wasn't sure how long the captain could keep it up.

Hopefully she wouldn't need to for much longer.

Where *was* Jax? He checked the holo-pad in his coat. They had less than two minutes to get out of here.

Nervously, he tapped his comm-link. *"Ma'alor?"*

There was only static.

I shouldn't worry. He'll be here, he thought, and started for the closest skysailer. "You two keep a lookout while I hot-wire this thing," he told both Ana and Viera.

"But aren't we gonna wait for Jax?" asked Ana, looking around again as if hoping he'd appear.

"We are—I'm just getting a ship ready." He hit the windshield release on the vehicle. The glass dome popped open and he hopped inside, shimmying over the passenger seat. Underneath the console was a small panel that opened up to the circuitry.

Now he was having flashbacks to Neon City.

Don't think. Just cross a few wires and—

"Is that the bridge up there?" Viera pointed toward the ceiling.

Absently Robb drew his gaze up, and wished he hadn't.

From the ceiling, a chamber jutted downward and extended out to the tip of the dreadnought, windows on all sides. The bridge. Even though it was dark, he could make out two figures inside. And he'd know that silver hair anywhere.

"Jax," he murmured with dread.

"And the XO," added Viera. They watched Jax narrowly dodge the swing of a lightsword—and barely another. "He is not going to survive."

Fuck that.

Robb had already watched two people he loved die. He would not watch another—not again. Not when he could help.

From the other side of the docking bay came a loud screech. Metal hands wormed through the crack in the door, forcing it open. There wasn't any time left. The HIVE had found them.

He twisted two wires together. There was a spark. The console blinked to life, holo-screens reading off solar core energy and oxygen levels. A counter blinked up on the screen, counting down.

00:08

00:07

00:06

Until the docking bay doors open, he realized with panic. Jax must've initiated the command from the control room. *That stupid, arrogant, insufferable—*

"Get in—NOW!" he ordered Ana and Viera, scooting over to the driver's side again, Ana taking passenger, Viera in the back seat.

The Messiers came swiftly, running across the landing pad, reaching for their swords and halberds and Metroids. He closed the skysailer windshield and locked it.

"Robb!" Ana cried, "they're coming!"

00:03

00:02

He fired the thrusters.

00:01—

The docking bay doors sprang open and, with a terrifying exhale, flung them out into space.

JAX

"Oh yikes, looks like she's getting away—again," said Jax, trying to catch his breath. The skysailer carrying Robb and Ana swirled out into space, followed by the bodies of at least a dozen Messiers. He turned his back to them and tiredly leaned against the glass window. A thin rivulet of sweat slid down his neck and under his space suit collar. He just had to keep this up long enough for Robb and Ana to get away.

That was his fate. He had seen it in the stars.

The XO glanced out at the skysailer, then back at him silently.

"Why didn't you deploy all the other Messiers? The ones in those rooms? She wouldn't have gotten away then," he added, wiping the sweat off his forehead with the back of his arm.

The XO swirled his lightsword. *"Quality is better than quantity,* nan c'zar," he replied, and there was no mistaking Di in the voice. Or what was left of him after the HIVE. He outstretched his free hand toward the skysailer Robb and Ana had escaped in. The skysailer jerked—as if Di was taking control of it.

Ak'va. He didn't know Di could do *that.*

"No!" he cried, lurching toward the XO, not sure what he could do, but he would do *something—*

A loud *thud* came from the ventilation shaft above them, and a small square bot shot out of the grate in the ceiling. It went careening toward the Metal and unfolded spindly arms from its side and weaseled them into the slats in the XO's neck, into its wiring.

EOS's lens flared a brilliant white.

"Hnng!" The Messier gave a jerk, its eyes flickering. It dropped its hand, and the skysailer was jettisoned out into space.

Jax winced, shielding his eyes, as the brightness swept across the bridge.

"Get off of me!" the Emperor in the XO cried, grabbing the bot.

The XO threw it against the window. It sank to the floor beside Jax. He pressed himself harder against the window, wishing he could sink right through it.

The XO twitched, electricity jumping across the badges and buttons of its uniform, as it raised its lightsword to Jax. *"You."*

This was the image he'd seen in Robb's stars—the moment he would die. The blade would find his heart and pin him to the glass window, and there he'd bleed out. He used to wake up gasping from this nightmare, and Robb would crawl out of his bunk bed and into his and tell him it was all right.

But it wasn't. It never would be. Because he knew he couldn't stop it.

That he *shouldn't* stop it.

He winced away, bringing his obsidian wristbands up to shield his face, waiting for the pain, the slice of hotness. Di drove the sword down—

Into EoS.

And there the sword embedded in the window and stuck fast. His heart jumped into his throat.

The stars had changed—but who had changed them?

Jax tried to push himself off the window, but the glass crackled beneath him. He froze. The lightsword spread fissures in the glass around it, feathering outward like a lightning strike in all directions. A high-pitched whistling squirreled through the cracks, oxygen swirling out.

If either of them pulled the lightsword free, the window wouldn't hold.

"Damned thing," the Emperor murmured, wincing as if in pain. The XO's eyes flickered—and its body jerked again.

Another crack inched across the glass.

"You won't catch her," he said. "She'll always be one step ahead of you. She'll stop you. She'll bring you back."

The Emperor glanced out the window, but the skysailer was long gone. *"Bring me back?"* He laughed, and the body of the XO jerked again. He crawled closer to Jax, until they were only inches apart, and Jax glared at the monster looking out from behind the Messier's glitching gaze.

The darkness that had twisted Di.

Ah vent'a nazu mah, it hummed in his head, a slight shift in the whisper he'd heard all those months before in the palace.

Where it was a promise to come then, now it was a promise come to pass. *Ah vent'a nazu morah.*

I have come from the edges, it translated. I have come from the end—

From out of the corner of his eye, he noticed a skysailer bank upward toward the bridge.

Robb.

"I will let you in on a secret, nan c'zar. There is nowhere she can hide where I will not find her," whispered the Emperor, flicking his gaze up behind Jax to the skysailer as it approached. *"She is mine."*

"Oh, metalhead"—the blue-white glow of the lightsword illuminated them, the verge of death painting them the color of a moonrise, and he looked up into the metallic face of the XO, to Di, and wished he wasn't afraid—"you were hers, too."

And then he grabbed the lightsword and prayed—

Goddess, give me light.

—and pulled the sword out.

The window gave. Space grabbed him by its icy fingers and pulled him out.

At the same moment, Di grabbed his hand—

A strange tingling sensation prickled in his belly. He knew this feeling, as the Messier's metal fingers brushed against the thin skin of his wrist, trying to hold on—

The sight took hold so viscerally, he convulsed, spiraling up into the galaxy far away. It was different from every other time he used his powers, a simple series of constellations, but these stars were—

They were *everywhere*.

In the past. The future.

Galaxies far away and then so suddenly the next sun over—entire lifetimes lacing together as though they all lived in one touch. Linked together, bright and burning and . . . and *alive*.

It was as if he wasn't seeing one star—but many. Too many.

A soul made of stars.

He felt his powers stretch and thin, the light inside him burning away in a single bright flash, so terribly quickly it stole the breath right out of him. Images raced across his eyes, swirling up through his flesh, dancing in an intricate waltz to a song that was so loud it shrieked—

He wanted to say good-bye to Robb. He wished he could have. He regretted not.

But there was no time, and not enough light inside his own soul to read a thousand others. It felt like wasting away in a dark room, light leaving every pore until he could no longer breathe, no longer think, no longer exist—so quickly it was over in a flash.

One moment he was there, and the next he was gone, and his body drifted out into the coldness of space.

II

STARLESS

EMPEROR

The Solani slipped out of his grip, his lips paled to blue, frost swirling across his skin, violet eyes wide and vacant.

Like light bulbs burned out.

He tried to reach out again, but space had pulled him too far away. The Solani—he—he *remembered* the Solani. So much younger, thirteen, sitting at a table, winning Wicked Luck rounds, grinning over his cards with a toothpick tucked into the corner of his mouth. "You wanna bet anything?" the memory asked.

"It would not be fair," a strange voice replied. Twisted, garbled like static—a damaged voice box. His? But . . . not.

"Come on, metalhead! All's fair if you use what you're given."

"I was made with these traits."

And then the Solani grinned, wider than ever. "So was I."

Now that Solani was dead.

He was dead.

He was *dead.*

Why do you care? he asked himself. *Why do you care? Why do you care he is dead? Why do you—*

A sound invaded his head. A scream—his? It tore into his programming like a white-hot dagger, and he winced away from it. Out of the XO, and into his body in the bedroom of the Iron Palace. He had just returned from Nevaeh, still clad in his diamond-embedded black robes and golden jewelry, and he was alone. The room was dark and quiet. Moonlight spilled in from between the crimson curtains, the light flaring so bright it hurt his eyes.

Whatever that *can opener* had done—whatever malware it had implanted—sizzled at the back of his teeth. He curled his hand into the cloth above his chest, his fingernails embedding into his skin there. His legs gave out from under him and he fell to his knees.

You were hers, the Solani had said.

And now he was dead.

The Solani was dead and he did not care. He did not care. He did c—

His chest burned even though he did not have lungs. He opened his mouth to try to breathe, knowing he could not, that he did not, but still it felt suffocating. His vocal box gave a staticky, gasping sound. Wheezing. As he clutched his hand to his chest and tried—to—

—Could not—

Breathe.

He knew the feeling, somehow. He knew it intimately well.

It felt like dying.

Or perhaps crying.

Both.

What had that can opener *done* to him?

Why was he calling the bot a *can opener*?

He curled his hand around the Valerio pendant clasped onto his cloak and gritted his teeth. The stitches on his cheek sizzled with electricity, crackling against his skin—and broke apart, revealing shining steel underneath, like a vein of ore through the earth—

—And realized, with a sharp crackle of fear, that for a moment he could not hear the HIVE's song.

But then the melody returned, and it washed away his anguish and pain, and the Solani was dead.

And he did not care.

ROBB

The moment both Elara's and Robb's skysailers landed in the *Dossier*'s cargo bay, the ship fired its solar thrusters and left. Robb barely gave the hull time to repressurize before he forced open the windshield. Lenda was in the gunnery beneath the stairs, fending off the schooners as the *Dossier* dipped and rolled, trying to get away from them.

Viera vaulted out of the skysailer, securing the ship with large steel cords, and went to the other skysailer to help Xu.

"Talle!" Robb shouted frantically. *"Talle!"*

Jax lay in the backseat, his eyes half open and his lips blue, and Ana had a fast and firm grip on his coat even though he wouldn't float away. Frost clung to his undone hair and iced over the buttons of his coat. He looked paler than death, his breath coming in short, staccato gasps.

"Where's Talle?" he cried.

Siege said through the intercom, her voice echoing over the booming sound of firefight and the whine of the thrusters outside, "She can't come down there."

"But—" He swallowed his words and pursed his lips together.

Okay. *Okay.* He was not going to let Jax die on his watch. Not if he could help it. He tucked his hands under Jax's arms and said to Ana, "Help me get him to the medical ward—but just don't touch his skin."

Ana gave him a baffled look. "He's *dying*, Robb—"

"Please."

"Fine." She helped lift him out of the backseat, across the cargo bay, and into the medical ward. They lifted him onto a gurney, and he pressed his thumb over the outside of Jax's coat, into the corner of his elbow. He still had a pulse, but it was faint.

He's not dead, he told himself. *He's not dead.*

The next few minutes were a blur. The ship tilted as the *Dossier* evaded the schooners, and the loose things in the cargo bay rolled and slid from one side to the other. The skysailers were tied down tight enough that they just groaned in their steel harnesses. An emergency wail let out in the solar core, and Viera quickly ducked into the engine room to fix it. The nuts and bolts in the walls rattled as a missile exploded too close to the ship, and the lights flickered.

Robb didn't understand—Jax wasn't *bleeding*, he wasn't missing any limbs. He'd been out in space for only maybe five seconds. He knew boys from the Academy who'd accidentally spaced themselves for longer and walked away laughing.

But then why was Jax—why was he—

He's not dying, he told himself. *He's not.*

The hum of the solar core reverberated through the hull as the ship tilted back and dodged another onslaught of artillery fire. Everything in the ship shifted, sliding backward with the force of gravity. Robb's metal arm shot out and quickly caught

Jax before he rolled off the gurney. Jax's head lolled to the side, his eyes almost open, gloriously plum-colored, like colliding red giants, staring past him, so far past he didn't see anything.

Fearfully, Robb held the back of his metal hand just above Jax's mouth.

But there was no breath to fog up the polished silver plating.

"I don't think he's breathing," he said aloud, but he didn't quite register his own words until Ana dove into one of the cabinets and took out an antiquated life support system—he'd seen them used before in practice, and in the Academy he'd taken a class on basic medicine, but this system was older than *either* of them. One centimeter off, and the life support would kill Jax instead of save his life.

He just stared at it, his mind blank.

"Robb," Ana snapped, and it jerked him out of his stupor. She shoved the life support disk into his hands. "Either you do it, or I will."

Either you take the gamble, or I will.

His fingers curled around the disk. "Help me open up his shirt."

With a steel dagger Ana produced from her boot, they cut Jax's coat and favorite silken shirt open, exposing his bare chest. There was an old starburst of a scar on his neck from where Robb had taken off the voxcollar at the palace, and a few other marks across his arms and torso. How did Jax get the one on his right arm? Or the slash down his left side? They belonged to stories he didn't know—stories he would *never* know if he did this wrong.

The life support system was a disk about a hand's width

long. It was dusty and the edges were rusted, and he hoped it still worked. He tried to remember what to do from his medical class, but honestly he just took it to get an easy grade. It had *not* been easy—and neither was this. Every second gone was another second Jax was lost. He sucked in a breath through his teeth, trying to calm down, placed the circular piece on Jax's sternum, hopefully above where his lungs were, and pressed the button in the center of it. A brilliant white light fed out from the center, rushing across the thin lines between the disk's plating, and it gave a sharp hiss. Needles punctured Jax's chest with a horrible snap, and his body twitched in response.

The system whirled, and suddenly Jax gasped, his back arching off the gurney, hands curling into fists, and fell back again. The life support clicked again, and he inhaled, then exhaled.

Inhaled. Exhaled.

A soft, steady beep filled the medical ward.

Jax's heartbeat.

He was alive.

Robb slowly sank to his knees beside the gurney. A bead of sweat curved down the side of his face, and he wiped it away with a shaking hand.

Ana fell back into one of the chairs. "Goddess" was all she said.

He felt about the same.

When the blood had stopped rushing to his ears, he realized everything was quiet. The firefight was done, and that could only mean the *Dossier* had escaped the schooners.

The intercom crackled and Siege's voice came through. "Report—how's Jax?"

Finding his legs, he pushed himself off the floor, stumbled around the gurney to the intercom, and pressed the button to feed him through. "Captain, we had to put him on life support. He—he stopped breathing and . . ."

And the longer he is on life support, the less likely he'll ever be off it again. And we don't even know why he stopped breathing.

But it seemed like the captain already knew what he didn't say.

"Aye. Lenda, take the helm. I'm coming down," the captain said, and ended the connection.

If it weren't for the wall, Robb wasn't very sure he would still be standing. This felt too much like his mother's death, and his father's.

He was powerless to stop any of them.

The captain appeared at the top of the stairs a moment later and surveyed the cargo bay. Elara and Xu were sitting in front of the skysailers, Viera in the doorway to the engine room. Things had been tossed around and knocked over, supplies scattered like confetti. Her hair simmered orange-red, accented by her brown skin. Talle came out of the doorway behind her, following as Siege shrugged out of her red murdercoat and hung it on the end of the stair railing.

Robb met Siege in the doorway to the medical ward. "He stopped breathing and we don't know why and Ana and I tried to—I had to—the life support was . . ." His shoulders hitched as a sob escaped his throat.

"Oh, darling." The captain sighed and brought him into a hug.

He buried his face into her shoulder and tried to keep himself together, and he felt like he was the only one unraveling. "H-he's . . . he's not . . ."

But he couldn't get the words out.

So Ana spoke for him. "We don't know why he stopped breathing—it doesn't make sense. He's perfectly fine, but . . . he just stopped breathing. I think—I think he needs a doctor."

Talle shook her head. "There isn't a hospital that'll serve us."

"Xourix?"

Siege sighed. "We just got word it was raided last night. By Messiers."

Ana gave a start. "And everyone *in* Xourix?"

"Arrested or HIVE'd."

"Oh," she said softly.

Xourix had been one of the four remaining sanctuaries Siege and her fleet had erected over the last six months. It'd been the largest and the most secure. For Messiers to go all the way to the edge of the kingdom . . .

Without Xourix, the captain was right: there *wasn't* a hospital that would serve them. They'd almost gotten arrested at a bar in the slums of a city; there was no way they would be able to waltz into a medical facility.

In the silence Jax's life support pinged again, and again.

A breath in, a breath out, keeping his heart beating, his blood flowing. There was a light sheen of sweat over his pale skin, as though it had lost its shimmer, accented only by the rush of bruises coming to the surface.

Someone coughed softly.

Everyone startled at the sound. It was Elara. Robb had forgotten she was there. She shifted her weight on her feet, Xu beside her. "I know I'm new here—but why not take him home?"

Home?

The word made his heart lurch.

It was the one place Jax never talked about, the one subject that was off-limits, that would make a cold look flicker into his eyes and bring a swift change of subject. Home was not a good place—that much Robb knew.

"This *is* his home," he said.

Elara gave him a strange look, and then her eyes widened in surprise. "Oh. You . . . don't know, do you?"

"Know what?"

The captain began to answer when the monotonous voice of Xu intervened. "If there is a place that can help the C'zar, it is his home. Zenteli."

C'zar.

He—he knew that word.

It was always said in passing. How many times had he heard it whispered at the Academy, or tossed around in Wicked Luck rings? The missing C'zar, who ran off and died at the hands of mercenaries. The last of the Solani royalty, chosen by a council of elders to lead their people.

A C'zar.

A prince.

Jax.

ANA

Siege didn't waste any time hailing Zenteli. It was as if she'd known this would happen eventually. She had a private line to the city's port authority, which was odd because usually when the *Dossier* came calling, officers were sent to arrest them, not welcome them.

The communication line crackled, and a voice patched itself through. *"Aven'ta za mar Dossier."*

It was the Old Language.

Siege responded in kind. Ana didn't realize Siege knew the Old Language—at least, Ana had never heard her speak it before. She thought only Ironbloods and Solani knew it.

"We will have personnel on scene to take nan c'zar from you," the man replied in the common tongue. *"Be advised."*

"Da'thoren," Siege said, and Ana at least knew that to be *thank you.*

Zenteli was on Iliad, which felt like a billion light-years away from where they were in Eros's orbit, but was only about half a day's flight by the calculation on the starshield. Siege brought

a timer up in the corner of the shield, and it blinked in count-
down to their destination. Ana quietly watched the counter from
the communications console, her fingers digging into the plush
armrest stuffing.

So much *time*.

Siege instructed Elara, who was sitting in one of the emergency foldout seats on the back wall of the cockpit, to erect
another of the cloaking bugs she'd used to throw off the HIVE
in Neon City, and again at the dreadnought. The codes were
more complicated than any of the ones the *Dossier* used, and the
less they got pinged by searching spacecrafts, the quicker they
would arrive at Zenteli. Every second counted.

But what if the life support . . .

She swallowed thickly, her nails still digging into the armrests of the communications chair. *Don't think about it*, she
coached herself. *It'll be fine. He'll be . . .*

Why couldn't she convince herself?

There was a soft knock on the cockpit doorway, and Xu
poked their head in to say that Talle had made a stew, and the
captain dismissed Elara to go grab some food.

When they were gone, the captain asked, "Aren't you going
to eat, darling?"

"I'm not very hungry."

Her captain turned in the pilot's chair to face her and, as if
reading her thoughts, said, "What happened to Jax wasn't your
fault."

Oh—*oh*, that made it so much worse. She just wanted her
captain to scold her and tell her to do better next time, because

at least then Ana would know that there *would* be. That Jax would . . . that this wasn't . . .

The captain just didn't understand.

"How can I stop the Great Dark, save the Metals from the HIVE—save *Di*, if I can't even save my friends?" she asked. "It's impossible—"

"Don't say that." Siege leaned forward, across the console that separated the two chairs, and brushed her thumb across Ana's scarred cheek to wipe away the tears. "I didn't teach you to give up when things got hard, did I?"

"Y-you didn't see what was in that dreadnought, either. It was horrifying. I was trapped with the HIVE, and if it wasn't for Robb and Jax cutting the power, I know they would've tortured me—he *said* he'd torture me." He—Di, but not Di. Not her Di. "I was *helpless*. I don't—I don't know what to do. I don't know *how* we can defeat that thing. We've been trying for six months and . . . shouldn't the Goddess be able to save the people she loves?" Her eyes stung with tears. "If I'm the Goddess, shouldn't I be able to . . ."

She tried not to cry, really she did. But the last twenty-four hours finally caught up with her. The running, the capture, the dreadnought—and she couldn't get the moment Jax was sucked into space out of her head, the way the glass glittered around him, the lightsword shining bright, the way that terrible XO had reached out to him as if it wanted to keep him. She couldn't stop thinking about how cold he felt when she pulled him into the skysailer. How his lips were blue. How he had stopped breathing.

Her shoulders gave a shake, and tears fell down her cheeks,

and she didn't want Jax to die. It would be another life scratched into her soul, added to the number of people who had already died for her.

Barger. Wick. Riggs. Di. Jax.

She wasn't worth their lives. Even if she was the Goddess.

No one was worth the life of someone else.

Siege took her hands tightly. There were small pale scars across her captain's fingers. She leaned forward and pressed her lips against Ana's forehead in a soft kiss. "Go and get some rest, darling," she said gently.

Though Ana knew she probably wouldn't get any sleep at all, she nodded anyway, unfurling her fingers from her captain's, and left the cockpit. When she got into the crew's quarters, she sank down into one of the chairs on the back wall.

It was quiet there, at least.

She dried her eyes, and waited. That was all there was to do.

·) ● (·

Ana had dozed off in the chair when Lenda knocked on the door. She jerked awake, scrambling to pull herself up in the chair. For a moment she was disoriented—was she still on the dreadnought? Had a Messier come to kill her? Turn her into a Metal?—until she recognized Lenda, dirty blond hair tucked back behind her ears, her blue eyes rimmed with exhaustion. She motioned behind her, toward the galley. "Food's getting cold. Want some?"

Ana shook her head. "Oh—no." She still wasn't hungry. "Go ahead."

"*Good*. I eat when I get worried and that entire pot of stew is calling my name," she said, and began to leave—but then she hesitated in the doorway and turned back to Ana. "You know we're with you, right? That all of us on this ship are with you. In defeating the HIVE and saving the kingdom. None of us blame you for Jax. He wouldn't want you to blame you, either."

Ana looked away. "I appreciate that."

"I mean it."

"I know."

Lenda frowned, knowing that Ana didn't believe her, but then she just shook her head and left for the galley again.

Ana checked the time. It had been only three hours since she'd dozed off. Nine more to go. Slowly, she stood, her muscles screaming, and peeled off her coat. She took out Di's memory core before she put the coat in the dirty clothes basket in the corner of the room. She tried not to linger on Jax's empty bunk, or on one of his favorite coats hung on the hook over his bed. She touched the soft velvet of the sleeve.

"We'll fix you," she promised softly, not to the coat, but to Jax. "And then I'll let you punch the Great Dark first when we find it—"

"Ana?"

She whirled around as Viera ducked into the crew's quarters. She had taken a shower, her platinum hair pushed back against her head, the dirt and grime of the dreadnought scrubbed clean. There was a blanket and pillow tucked underneath her arm. "Talle said I could take one of the bunks, but I'm not sure . . ."

"That one." Ana pointed to Wick's old bunk on the bottom, opposite hers. "There's more room inside the pod than it looks."

The ex–guard captain put down her blanket and pillow on the mattress and leaned inside. "Oh, there are charging ports and everything."

"There isn't much privacy on this ship, but we should be to Zenteli soon. Then you can find a ship to . . ." She hesitated, frowning. "Where'll you go?"

To that, Viera shrugged. She sat down gingerly on the edge of the bunk. "I am not quite sure. The kingdom thinks I am dead, yes?" When Ana nodded, she frowned. "Then my family does, too."

"Are you okay?"

The woman blinked. The arrowhead-shaped markings under her gray eyes made her gaze sharp and narrow. She remembered that Wick had markings as well—splotches under his eyes. "Yes."

"I mean, after . . ." *After the HIVE got you.*

"I am fine, Ana."

She didn't think Viera was fine at all, but she didn't want to push her. "You know, if you ever want to talk . . ."

To that, Viera ran her fingers through her wet white-blond hair. "I thought you were dead these last six months, Ananke. I thought I had failed. I had never failed before."

Does she think her imprisonment was punishment? The thought horrified her, and she quickly leaned forward and said, "It wasn't your fault. You didn't know."

"Yes, well. Now I do."

"And I'm alive."

To that, Viera smiled, but the expression never quite reached her eyes. "That you are."

EMPEROR

He was just about to sit down in the Moon Garden, the charred remains of the Iron Shrine in the distance, to read a book he had found in the library, when the Iron Council called an emergency meeting. Glancing up at the sky so he would not be tempted to roll his eyes, he put his book down on the side table and stood from the white wrought-iron chair.

"I did not know you read," Mellifare commented from her perch on a nearby bench. She had been in the head of another Messier a few moments before, her body rigid and still. She flicked her dark eyes to him.

"It passes the time," he replied, but he honestly did not remember why he wanted to read it. The book sounded interesting. It helped him forget about that Solani boy—but something about the C'zar still bugged him. He paused before he left the garden, judging that the steward was still out of earshot, and turned back to Mellifare. "We could have turned him into a Metal."

"Who?"

"The Solani prince."

She blinked, pulling herself fully back into her body, and gave him an annoyed, pointed look. "And why would we need him?"

"It seemed like a waste, is all," he replied. "We could have used his talents to locate your heart. The girl now knows you are searching for something in the shrines. It would be . . . beneficial if we found your heart before she did."

She sighed and came over to him, placing a hand on his cheek. "Oh, brother dearest, do not worry."

He began to argue, but the moment he found the words, the song in his head stole them away. He blinked, frowning.

What had he been worried about, again?

Her gaze drifted behind him to the impatient steward. "I believe you are expected."

"Yes, sister," he mumbled, and left her in the garden.

The herald hurried after him, carrying a navy suede evening coat with sapphire cuff links, which he shrugged on over his starched white shirt. Then he tied his hair back with a black ribbon, and made his way to the council's chambers.

"Your—Your Excellence!" the steward added, raising up the Iron Crown.

Oh, he had almost forgotten it. His mind felt strange and cloudy, but he tried to shake it away as he put on the crown.

As he entered the council's chambers, the holograms of Ironbloods rose to their feet and murmured greetings. He quickly moved around to the head of the obsidian table. Their images wavered a little, their projections grainy against the one Ironblood who had actually decided to show up.

It had to be Wynn Wysteria. He was quite certain that she was the reason this council was called to begin with.

For the last few weeks, Wynn Wysteria had requested multiple meetings with the Emperor at the palace—in person, no less, so her being here again did not surprise him. It only annoyed him. Every evening she would return to her ship docked in the moonbay, and her personal guards would keep watch until morning. She did not trust the palace.

Perhaps she knew more than she let on.

He sat down at the head of the table, and the holographic images of the other Ironbloods in the meeting followed. "To what honor do I owe this occasion, Lady Wysteria?"

Wynn curtsied to him. "I am glad to see you well. I heard of the assassination attempt on Astoria. It would seem we were lucky to have Lord Valerio there."

Her voice grated on his nerves. "Indeed."

She nodded. The young woman was dressed in black, her long strawberry-blond hair pulled back in intricate braids. Perhaps if she were a bit more demure, her late father could have sold her off with the right dowry to breed instead of infuriating him—

A shard of pain sliced through his head, knocking him dizzy—as if something inside his own code scolded him. *The glitch?* He rolled his shoulders back to disguise the discomfort.

"So why did you call us?" he asked her.

"I have troubling news. A number of citizens had reported seeing the late Empress in Neon City—alive."

He set his mouth into a thin line. "A rumor and nothing more."

"It's our sworn duty to these citizens to hear their voices," said Wynn. "What if this *rumor* is true, and she's alive? The citizens have not been kind to us lately. Your taxations on trade and travel to fund your pledge to gather these *rogue* Metals have taken a toll on each of our worlds' economies. The poor are dying and the rich are doing nothing, and our Iron Shrines are burning. Who are we if not in service to our people—and our late Empress?" she challenged him. "If she is indeed alive, we should find her."

He drummed his fingers on the obsidian table. He could just kill Wynn Wysteria. It was tempting. Her *and* Erik Valerio, but the HIVE pulsed gently in the back of his head, Mellifare telling him to play their game.

He leaned forward and steepled his fingers. "You have a fair point, Lady Wysteria. I'm sure we could *entertain* your parlor gossip, if you so wish."

Her eyes widened. "It is *not* parlor gossi—"

"But to expend such resources, I would need council approval."

The other dozen members looked at each other, murmuring in soft tones. One chair was empty, he noticed, the one belonging to Erik Valerio. He wondered where that unreliable snake was. Plotting behind his back, no doubt.

Trouble—all these flesh sacks were *trouble*.

"Well," he said after a moment, waiting for another Iron-blood to rush to Lady Wysteria's defense, but no one did. "It seems as though the rest of us will not entertain your rumor—"

"There is footage," Wynn interrupted hurriedly, "of the Empress, or someone who looks like her."

The murmurs grew louder across the table.

His lips drew into a hard line.

She lifted a panel on the obsidian table in front of her and pressed a button. A holo-screen popped up in the middle of the table. The video had been captured from one of the taverns in the Theo District—the slums, most of Neon City called it. It showed a girl racing down the street, pursued by—

He tapped his first finger on the table again and made the holo-screen glitch. The video froze, pixelated, the only thing discernible Neon City's skyline.

"All I see is a corrupted file," he said.

Wynn paled and tried to upload the video again. "It was just there!"

The other council members began to mutter, shaking their heads at her. He hid a smirk behind his hand and lounged back in his chair. "Lady Wysteria, your efforts to discredit me are astounding. I applaud your creativity, but perhaps you should be a little more subtle."

Her mouth dropped open. "I—I wasn't . . ."

He stood from his chair. "Now, if you will excuse me, I am sure we all have most pressing matters to attend to today. Thank you for your *diligence*, Lady Wysteria," he added, trying not to sound too snide as he left the room.

The lady had been correct about one thing: he *did* need to find the Empress. She was becoming a thorn in his side.

When he returned to his chair in the Moon Garden, Mellifare was gone. To the palace, she was still a chambermaid, and her body was off cleaning one of the rooms, no doubt, but *she* was hosted in a myriad of Messiers on Cerces, tearing down the door to another tomb. Empty, like all the others—and he heard her scream through the HIVE, light fire to the shrine, and kill the abbesses who begged for their lives.

He opened his book—*The Swords of Veten Ruel*—to where he'd left off, licked his finger—although he had no saliva—to turn the page, and tried to ignore Mellifare.

ROBB

Zenteli was a city unlike anywhere he'd ever been before. It shone alabaster white in the sun, almost indistinguishable from the clouds surrounding it. The city was one of the last safe havens away from the HIVE and Messiers, because of an age-old treaty with the kingdom that barred kingdom influence in the Solani city. Located on the peak of a mountain range near the northern pole of Iliad, it should have been cold, but the sunlight kept the city warm and comfortable. Beneath the mountain was a valley where the original Solani ark had crashed over a thousand years ago. As the *Dossier* broke through the clouds, the sight of the ruined ship was monstrously large—more like the carcass of a living creature than a ship at all.

A small fleet of Solani ships sat in the dock when the *Dossier* came in to land, shining slivers of silver that looked as sharp as arrows. A team of doctors took Jax away on a hover-stretcher, and two guards—*Solgard*, Elara had called them—in obsidian armor escorted the rest of them through the city to the Shining Spire.

The moment the *Solgard* saw Xu and Elara, they reached for

the swords on their belts, and Captain Siege reached for hers.

"They're with us," said Siege.

The *Solgard* spat something in the Old Language—Robb could make out *exile* and *ark* and *Metal*, but the other words were too fast—that made Siege purse her lips.

"Then they'll stay here, won't you?" the captain added to Elara and Xu for confirmation, and both of them nodded. He wasn't as surprised as the rest of them to learn that Siege knew the Old Language.

He knew her last name, after all.

"Lenda will make sure they don't go anywhere," she said, motioning to the muscular blonde to her right.

"I don't do well in cities," Lenda agreed, eyeing Elara and Xu. "Besides, I've got repairs to do on the ship. You two can help."

The *Solgard* sneered but agreed. It must have been because Xu was a Metal. The Emperor's lies even reached as far as Zenteli, it seemed. The rest of them followed the *Solgard* through the streets to the Spire. People paused in the street and leaned out of windows to get a look at them as they passed.

"That's them—the ones who brought the C'zar back," he heard a fabric vendor say to a customer.

Another said, "Those are the kidnappers."

"Wait until the Elder Court gets to them."

The whispers unnerved Robb. It seemed like everyone had known who Jax was except Jax's closest friends. He felt like a fool.

While the outer walls of the city were made of sandstone, most of the buildings built into the top of the mountain were made of marble. The city was clean and well kept, far older than most cities on Eros. It also had one of the only Iron Shrines that still stood untouched, a shard of white blending in with the rest of the buildings.

Robb caught Viera looking out toward the shrine in the distance. "Reminds me of the Academy a little," he said to her as they were escorted through the city.

She was quiet.

"Do you remember that time—"

"*Yes*, Robb, I remember," she interjected, annoyed, and excused herself from the procession. "I would like to go pray," she said as she disappeared into the crowd, a *Solgard* following as escort.

He frowned. He and Viera had never been close, but something was strange about her. Perhaps six months in a dreadnought did that—but then why had the HIVE kept her alive? Not that he wasn't glad she *was* alive. It was just . . . odd.

The guard led them through a large archway into the Spire. It was just as bright on the inside, the scratched walls so thin the soft midday light bled through them. But on closer inspection, the scratches were names—of millions of Solani. On every wall, in every hallway. The guard led them up a few flights of wide stairs and into a bright garden filled with plants he recognized but couldn't name, long-petaled flowers and swirly-stemmed bushes. Where the Valerio garden was cluttered with so many beautiful flowers they all seemed to blend together, the ones in this garden were chosen carefully and planted around a dais in the center, with stone pathways spreading from it like rays of light. The ancient dais turned slowly with the fall of the sun, telling time in the ancient way.

Ana went ahead and explored the garden. He hung back, feeling into his pocket for the old iron ore his father had given him, and began to spin it between his fingers. Rust coated his fingertips, but he felt safe doing it. He knew what would happen when he touched iron. He was certain of that, while it felt like the rest of the world was spinning out of control. From the garden, he could see the bones of the Solani ark well, lying at the base of the valley like the carcass of an ancient creature.

A little way away, on a bench, he heard Siege and Talle whispering between each other. He had half a mind to walk away before he heard too much until—

"Is this my punishment?"

Talle drew Siege into a tight embrace and kissed her cheek. "Shhh."

"I heard him, starlight. When he . . ."

He tore himself away from their conversation. What had Siege heard? Robb had been with Jax the whole time in the medical ward. Had he contacted the *Dossier* while on the dreadnought?

It didn't matter.

He finally sat down on a bench and stared out at the green valley, and everything was quiet and beautiful and still. Here, for a moment, he could pretend the kingdom was not at war with itself, and that his clothes didn't still smell like gunpowder, and his arm didn't ache with phantom pains.

And he would trade it all for a firefight if only Jax was with him.

·☽ ● ☾·

It felt like hours passed before someone came to get them.

"You must be the crew of the *Dossier*," said the woman. Her dress looked as if it doubled as armor, with wide epaulets that curved up like horns, a breastplate decorated with images of constellations he didn't recognize, tapering to a long skirt that trailed behind her in a train. Her skin was pale like Jax's, and glittered in the noonday sun with the radiance of Cerces's diamond mines, her short hair cropped in jagged edges, making her square jaw all the more striking.

He knew this Solani before she even introduced herself.

Jax's mother.

Siege stood, her fingers intertwined with Talle's tightly. *"Ma c'zar,"* the captain greeted her.

"Siege, is it?" The *ma c'zar*'s voice was as warm as the recesses of space. Before Siege could confirm or deny it, the Solani woman raised her hand and struck it across Siege's face.

Robb stood, dumbfounded, until Ana went to lunge for her, and then he took her by the arm to hold her back.

"What was *that* for?" Ana snarled. "We brought him back so you can help him!"

"Ana," the captain said softly.

The woman turned her cold violet-eyed gaze to Ana. "Empress," she greeted her.

"She didn't deserve that," Ana said. "If anyone does, it's me. Jax risked his life to save me, and now he's here. Why don't you stop slapping people and just help him?"

The *ma c'zar* looked away, and Robb felt the ball of panic in his chest tighten. "Child, there is no cure for the dark fever."

The *dark fever.*

Jax had talked about it a few times, but only in passing, like when he was trapped in a dark room for too long, or when he felt sick or cranky. It was a passing thing, like a head cold, and the moment starlight touched his skin again he was fine.

He was always fine.

Ana blinked at her as if she didn't understand. ". . . What?"

"There isn't a cure," Jax's mother reiterated. "It comes to all of us in time, usually when the light inside of us finally goes out. It is also this light that grants C'zars the power to read the stars, but at the cost of their own life span. Most C'zars aren't fortunate enough to live past their second decade. That was the future my son ran from, and yet he will die early all the same."

Robb heard a sob hitch in Talle's throat, and she turned away. He felt numb. He couldn't comprehend. Jax was—he was out of light?

"Is there any way to refill him?" he asked, and the *ma c'zar* gave a soft chuckle.

As if it was a joke, and he was a child.

"Your life support only gave him borrowed time, and for that I must be grateful. Will you please follow me, Captain? You and your wife are the ones who raised him. I would expect that you would want to see him before . . ."

"I think Robb should see him," Siege said absently, and motioned to him. Her hair had lost its glow somewhere between the woman slapping her and learning of the dark fever. He realized, quite suddenly, how gray her hair had become over the last few months.

The woman looked surprised. "The *Ironblood*?"

"Robb," the captain corrected. "Your son calls him Robb."

No, Jax called him *ma'alor*.

And he never would again.

The woman didn't seem to understand, but she agreed to it all the same. She led Robb, numb and aching, to the very top of the Spire. Cloudy crystalline walls separated one room from another, the doors clear as glass. It was so bright, his eyes watered. The medical ward looked more like the inside of a star. Robb followed the *ma c'zar* to the end of the hallway, to the last room, where two *Solgard* stood guard.

He was afraid to go inside—afraid of what death looked like in these brightly lit rooms. He was afraid that the last image of Jax he would ever remember was one where he was dying. He didn't want to remember Jax like that. He wanted to remember Jax . . .

He wanted . . .

He didn't want to have to remember him at all. He wanted to be able to wake up every morning and see his face on the pillow next to his, trace the lines of his sharp cheekbones, and know he would be there again tomorrow.

That was what he wanted.

His mechanical arm jumped, twisting, and he quickly grabbed it by the biceps to hold it still.

The hospital room was small and bright, without furniture. Medical apparatus and holo-screens reading off Jax's vitals hung on the headboard wall. In the middle of the room rested a familiar boy in a bed, the antiquated *Dossier*'s life support device still suctioned to his chest. It pulsed faintly.

He stepped into the room, one foot at a time, slowly releasing his mechanical arm, and reached for Jax's hand. It didn't matter now, whether he could see the stars or not, because there was no light left to see them with.

And it felt like there was no light left inside Robb, either.

He felt like the carcass of those burned Iron Shrines, once filled with grandeur but now nothing but ash. He sank to his knees at Jax's bedside, and kissed his knuckles, and whispered with the intent of all of the words he had never gotten the chance to say, *"Ma'alor."*

JAX

This was not a dream. But he wasn't awake, either.

Last he remembered, Di, in the XO's body, had him cornered and there was no way to escape. But then . . . then what happened? It was all a blur. He was scared to die, even though he knew this was where he did—but . . . something had happened. The scene hadn't gone the way it had in the vision. Something had changed.

He remembered pulling the sword out of the window. It fractured—one moment a sound and then nothing at all as space swept in. He knew he'd only be out in space for a few moments, so he hadn't been worried. He'd been spaced before.

But then Di had reached out to him, touched him, and then—

So many stars. So many souls. Thousands of them. They invaded his head and showed him so many fates. Paths not taken and paths that were. Lives twisting, braiding, in an intricate web of *should haves*. That single touch drained his light, like a candle snuffed out—

Oh.

Every time he read a fate, a little more of his light vanished, a little more of his life drained away, and in the span of a moment he had read *thousands*.

He was dead, that was simply it. He had to be.

But . . . if he *was* dead, he expected darkness—a void, perhaps? The Moon Goddess welcoming him home, a land of bountiful fruits and gold and . . . he didn't know. The Solani didn't believe in an afterlife. When they died, they became stardust again, and the cycle continued.

He didn't expect . . . to be *here*.

Wherever this dimly lit hangar was. It stretched endlessly on both sides, the halogens above casting sickly white light across the makeshift medical stalls. The sounds of people moaning, sick and diseased, clogged the cold air, making it hard to breathe. He'd heard about these Plague hospitals—they still sat on Eros, falling into ruin where no one dared to go, fearing that the Plague might still cling to a gurney or hospital robe or food tray. But he never expected to see one, and he never expected it to feel so . . . so *wrong*.

Because these Plague hospitals were twenty years gone, but it seemed like time had no meaning here, and even the noises felt like they were trapped, rebounding back against each other, quieter and quieter, until they were nothing but whispers.

He pushed back the white cloth to the first medical stall.

There was a young man not much older than himself sitting on the edge of a hospital gurney. He wore a white hospital shift, his left wrist tagged with a plastic band that read his patient number and allergies. His hands were blackened, and Jax could feel how much they hurt—twisting, excruciating pain, as if he was being devoured alive.

He was reading a book. There were dozens of them piled up on the makeshift half shelf behind him. They looked dirty and old, having been read a hundred times. Jax tilted his head to the side a little to read the title. *The Swords of Veten Ruel.* An old classic about as enjoyable as watching paint dry.

The young man seemed to be enjoying it, though.

His hair was shorn short, the color of blood to match his thick eyebrows. It was startling, how much he looked like the Metal he and Robb had found on the *Tsarina*, though his eyes were a gradient of browns and reds. Rust colored.

Still, he looked like . . .

"Di?"

The young man glanced up—and through—him.

No, he wasn't D09. He couldn't be. What were the odds that the person D09 had been actually looked like the body Robb had uploaded him into? This was the boy—the original one— who looked like Di's body. This was the real version of that mold. Human—

And very much dying.

There were footsteps behind him. He turned to watch a girl come down the aisle toward them. She looked around sixteen, in a ratty gray shawl and a hood that covered half her face. The tail of a straw-colored braid curved down her shoulder, and she played with it around her finger. He recognized this girl from Robb and Ana's stories of her. What was her name— *Mellifare?*

Quickly, before she could see, the young man hid his book underneath his pillow.

"Hello, Dmitri Rasovant," she greeted him in a feathery voice.

Dmitri Rasovant—this was Lord Rasovant's late son?

So this was the past, then.

Quickly, Jax glanced around the hangar again. Now he could see the threads of light between one gurney stall and the next, the places where one fate ended and another began, stitched together to create this illusion of the past. He had never seen the past in the stars before, but it wasn't unheard-of. Time flowed like a river, and the past was just a bit upstream.

But why am I here?

The redheaded young man, Dmitri, shifted uncomfortably at her knowing his name. "And who're you? You're not supposed to be here—and I'd appreciate if you didn't get closer. Or you'll get the Plague, too."

She cast an amused glance at the other Plague victims. "I cannot contract it."

"You're immune?" he asked doubtfully.

"Something like that."

"Did Mari—Marigold—send you? I told her not to. I told her to forget about me and—"

"No," Mellifare said softly, warmly, a pleasant hum in her voice, "I am here of my own accord. To see you. To offer a proposition."

Simply being near her made Jax's skin crawl. Ripples of something terrible slushed off her, so heavy it made his mouth taste like ash.

It seemed like the young man felt the same, and he shook his head. "I think you've mistaken me for someone else. I can't do anything—"

"But you can." She tilted her head, her eyes drifting down to the young man's blackened hands. "Are you afraid of dying, Dmitri Rasovant?"

The question seemed to surprise him. ". . . Y-yes?"

"Would you do anything, if I said I could save you? If your own *father* could save you?"

Dmitri's eyebrows furrowed. "Save me? How?"

She smiled. "Your father is a brilliant man, and I wish to give him all the knowledge I possess to save the kingdom—and to save you. You see, I am not from this kingdom. I am from far, far away and I have lived a very long time, and I need his help."

"You are delusional," Dmitri replied, and his heart monitor began to beep sporadically. "Leave before I call a ward—"

As he reached for a buzzer to summon a nurse, she grabbed him by his blackened hand and jerked it toward her. Her eyes widened, pupils to irises flooding with a brilliant red light. He stifled a gasp and stopped struggling against her. "Now do you believe me, Dmitri Rasovant? I can save you. I can save you all."

"Don't," Jax murmured under his breath, because even though he was in the past, he saw the future unfurling like a tapestry of fire and darkness.

Ana had said that Metals were once human, but he didn't believe it until just then. How could Rasovant have uploaded people into machines? But Jax knew now, without a shadow of a doubt, that with the knowledge Mellifare had given him, Rasovant had done just that. Taken their souls and made them ghosts inside metal shells.

And this was where it all began.

Was *this* what the stars wanted him to see?

Dmitri Rasovant studied Mellifare as though it was too good to be true—and it was—but there was desperation written into the way he bit his bottom lip.

From the top of the row of sickbeds, a doctor stumbled down, dragging his left foot behind him. Jax thought it pretty strange that a doctor would be in a Plague hospital—until he realized the doctor was infected, too. Could all of these souls be the Metals who'd been HIVE'd? That was a terrifying thought.

The girl quickly looked at the doctor and then back at Dmitri Rasovant. "I need your answer. Do you not want to see your friends again? Do you not want to go *home*? What would you give if I granted you that?"

"Don't," Jax pleaded. "Please, don't."

But the boy glanced down at his terrible rotting hands, and then back to her. "Anything," he replied. "I'd give anything."

"A heart will do." She grinned, and suddenly everything slowed to a stop. Noises echoed until they sank into whispers—

And then silence.

Jax glanced around at the rest of the hospital, but everything was so still it looked like a photo. He turned back to Dmitri and was susprised to see that Dmitri saw him, too.

"Why did you *do* that?" he hissed, wanting to punch him.

The young man scrambled to the back of his gurney, frightened.

"Was it worth it? Did you give her your heart? You probably ended up dead! Forgotten in the body of some HIVE'd M—" His words caught in his throat, and his tongue tasted ash.

I'm lying?

This boy hadn't been forgotten. But how did he know him—from *where*? He studied him for a moment longer, shorn red hair and brownish eyes, and the realization dawned. What were the odds of it?

A thousand to one—a million.

But as he said his name, his tongue tasted sweet. It was truth.

". . . Di."

"How do you know my name?" the boy—Di, *Dmitri*—asked, and then his eyebrows furrowed. "Don't I know you?"

Di. Dmitri *Rasovant.* Lord Rasovant's son.

Oh, of *all the people* Ana could have fallen in love with. Of all the thousands of Metals, hundreds of thousands of Solani, millions of Erosians and Cercians—she had to fall in love with the son of the man who tried to *kill her*?

The boy who let the Great Dark into the kingdom?

He took a step back.

"I know you," Dmitri went on. "I feel like I must."

"Why did you do that?" Jax snapped. "Why did you sell us off to the Great Dark? You—"

"I was afraid!" he replied. "I didn't want to die."

The anger in Jax cooled into a dull, aching throb. Because if Dmitri had never sold out the kingdom, he would never have become a Metal. Never met Ana. Never met him. In two strides he came up to Di and took him by the shoulders. He was so thin and gaunt and sick. Jax hated to see him like this. "Look, metal-head, I don't know if this is a dream or a memory or what—but you *have* to remember her."

The young man looked confused. "Who?"

There was a sharp sound, and one of the fate threads above them unwound, tearing the rooftop open like fabric, to a deep, unending darkness. Seams began to unravel down the walls, across the floor, picking apart the scene thread by thread, swallowed by a darkness so loud it rattled his bones.

He turned his gaze back to Di as black tendrils swooped down and ate the privacy sheets, the hospital bed, the floor, and began to pick at the edges of Di. "You'll know her—you'll always know her, I promise."

Piece by piece, the darkness took him. He tried to grab ahold, to keep him a little longer—

Because this was Di, *their* Di, and Goddess he wanted him to remember the rounds of Wicked Luck he lost—and he wanted him to remember Ana and Robb, and Siege, and Talle, and Wick, and Riggs, and even that bastard, Barger—to remember *him*. To remember all of them.

But most importantly, he wanted Di to do the impossible—

He wanted him to come back from the HIVE.

Because he was family. Jax's family.

And Jax had never thought he'd have something like that.

One moment, he had his fingers curled around Dmitri's arms, and the next Dmitri had unraveled into a string of light, and snaked away, up and up, like a streamer caught in the wind—and vanished.

Jax fell into the darkness.

And fell.

And fell.

So far, and so fast, he soon forgot he was falling at all. The warmth in his chest where his light once resided was gone, replaced by a deep and hollow emptiness. Bit by bit, the darkness began to take him, too. First a speck, then another, until he was disintegrating like a statue of sand. His hands gone, his arms, his legs . . . fading into a nothingness.

And he was so tired.

In the distance, he heard a voice. It was familiar, but he was so tired, and the nothingness in his brain felt so comforting.

"Ma'alor."

He held on to the sound of Robb's voice like a light across a vast and dark sea.

EMPEROR

Wynn Wysteria was going to be a problem—especially if she began comparing notes with Erik Valerio.

He drummed his fingers on the desk of his vanity, staring at the broken silver stitches across his cheek. Erik Valerio liked to run his mouth, and Wynn Wysteria poked around in places she should not. He could not just dispose of them; the families they came from were too prominent. He would have to get rid of them some other way.

Absently, he plucked the suture pen from its stand and began to restitch his cheek—

"Careful—do not sew them too close together. Do you want me to do it?" a voice, grating and metal in his head, asked.

With a jerk, something snared him by his coding with so much force he bent forward, dropping the suture pen. He gripped the edge of the vanity.

It felt as though his chest was on fire—the stifling, terrible need to breathe—

It was an image—a memory. In that old and rusted medical ward.

A young woman—fifteen, with unruly black hair braided atop her head—glared at him. Golden eyes. It was the Empress. "I said no. I can do it."

"On your own leg? Just allow me."

"C'mon, let me try it for once."

"Why?"

She looked him defiantly in the eye. "Because someday you might not be around to stitch me up."

"I doubt that."

—And then he was sitting on the stool of his vanity again. The reflection in the mirror looked back at him, eyes the color of moonlight, and said, *"You were wrong."*

He screamed and lurched off the bench, stumbling away from the mirror, and fell flat on his back. But as soon as he looked back at the mirror, it was vacant.

It had been an illusion.

A virus that bot had injected into him.

A—a *glitch.*

He curled his hands into fists of rage and slammed them against the floor. And again, this time with a scream. Again, and again, until the skin on his knuckles cracked, revealing the silver veins of his metal skeleton underneath.

That damned can opener did something to him, and he could not zero out the virus quickly enough. It was leafing between his programs, as soft and subtle as water between his fingers. Some sort of malware—but every time he tried to isolate it, the program disappeared. Then reappeared elsewhere. He felt constantly distracted. Constantly unmoored, dredging up memories that were his but not.

And it had something to do with that *girl*—

"Your Excellence?"

The voice startled him, and he glanced behind him at the herald standing in the doorway. He quickly got to his feet, brushing off his pants, and cleared his throat. "Forgive me—is there something you need?"

The steward went on as if he had not just seen the Emperor banging his fists on the ground for theoretically no reason at all. He was very good at pretending. "Your Grace, Erik Valerio is scheduled to see you today. He is very adamant."

"Of course. Tell him—tell him to meet me in the library. I have a book to return."

"Very good, Your Excellence," said the steward, and then he added, "It is very nice to see the library visited. It is one of the best in the kingdom, I must say so myself. It even has copies of my great-grandfather's research on the *Cantos* for the mad Emperor."

That gave him an idea. "There is a section on the *Cantos*?"

"Oh! Yes, Your Excellence. The palace's library has the most extensive collection of scholarly essays, as well as the original text. I must say it is quite a resource."

"Thank you. I think I will go explore it."

"Oh—you're—you're welcome," the steward replied in surprise, and bowed as he left.

Was *thank you* really that odd of a phrase for him? He rubbed at his mouth and went over to his wardrobe, picking out a pair of black gloves and fitting them over his ruined knuckles. Now there was another thing he had to hide. He put a flesh-colored bandage over his cheek, grabbed the book he had finished in the garden, *The Swords of Veten Ruel*, and left to meet with Erik Valerio, knowing that if he had to kill him, there were enough corners in the library to hide the body.

ANA

Ana stood in the garden, looking up at the Spire.

It had been an hour since Robb had disappeared into it, and Siege and Talle had retreated to the other side of the garden. Ana had survived the HIVE—and she had learned what it was looking for, some sort of *heart,* but all she could think about was Jax, and all she wanted was her captain to come over and comfort her, and tell her that he would be okay—that he would get better. To give her permission to get back in the fight—to save her kingdom.

Siege always knew what to say. Ana needed that now more than ever.

But Siege never came over, and so Ana stood alone on the other side of the garden, torn between her love for Jax and the end of times. When Di had been crowned six months ago, she hadn't thought he would be in power for so long. The Emperor blamed rogue Metals for the world's ills, and the citizens listened. It seemed like fear was a motivation that, stoked like fire, could burn down an entire kingdom.

And oh Goddess, was the kingdom burning.

Ana was pacing back and forth between lavender flowers and a patch of moonlilies when a Solani swept out of the garden gates to Siege and Talle and told them they could see Jax now.

Ana bristled as she quickly came over. "And me?"

"The *ma c'zar* said the child should wait out here," the guard said.

"She does know I was put in charge of a *kingdom*, right?" asked Ana, but the captain made a motion for her to calm down.

"She'll wait," Siege said, and then she told her quietly, "Don't—just don't do anything while I'm gone. And when I return, I . . . I need to tell you something."

"Like what?" she asked. "That you're harboring *another* prince or princess on the *Dossier*? That Lenda's secretly the heir to some grand fortune? *Aragon* maybe?" Because the last of the Aragons had died with the late Grand Duchess, her daughter killed by an assassin some twenty years ago. Siege flinched as Ana continued, "No, I'm fine not knowing, thanks."

"Ana—"

But she'd already turned away from her captain. Siege sighed and left with Talle. Ana stormed off toward one corner of the garden, resisting the urge to kick a flower in her anger. The flowers didn't deserve it.

The comm-link on her lapel flashed, the silver band on her ear that also served as an earpiece crackled, and Elara's voice hushed through. *"You seem irate, Princess."*

Ana jumped, startled. She whirled around the garden, but

she was alone, save for the *Solgard*, looking bored and unhappy, guarding the entrance to the garden. "Elara?" she whispered. "Where are you?"

"*The* Dossier, *where I'm supposed to be. The* ma c'zar *is certainly as cold as ever.*"

"You were listening this whole time?"

"*Just a bit.*"

Hackers, Ana thought, and realized that there was nothing she could do about her anger, so she just let out a long breath. After a moment she said, "Did you know? That Jax had the dark fever?"

"*I . . . had hoped that he didn't.*"

"And you recognized him as the C'zar when you first met him?"

"*Yes,*" she replied carefully.

Ana kicked a pebble, and it skittered across the cobblestones and into the bushes. "You seem to know a lot about us, and we know almost nothing about you." When Elara didn't respond, she added, "Does it have to do with that person you mentioned back in Neon City? Koren Vey?"

"*Yes. She helped me rescue you.*"

"How?"

"*Can you take out your holo-pad, Princess? It's easier to show you. And find somewhere . . . quiet.*"

That meant find somewhere discreet where the *Solgard* couldn't see her. There were plenty of bushes and trees and flowers in the garden, so she simply slipped between two budding rosebushes, thorns catching her coat, and settled down behind them, on the lip of the garden. It was a sheer drop into a cluster of official buildings a hundred feet below, where more trees and flowers and grasses bloomed in the shade. Zenteli was a strange place, a mixture of white marble and green spaces.

She took out her holo-pad. A screen appeared, prompting a code, and it filled in itself and opened a strange program Ana didn't recognize. "I assume you hacked it?"

"So, don't get mad, but I've been . . . looking at you for a while."

Ana made a disgusted noise. *"Spying?"*

"Not in the traditional sense. Here." Elara prompted the program on Ana's holo-pad, and three screens expanded to fill the glass. They looked like windows into the *Dossier*'s galley, hull, and cockpit. Lenda was stocking the galley with supplies she'd bought in the market. There wasn't any sound, but by the way her head bobbed she was singing something. Probably that snappy tune Wick played for her all the time.

Ana looked closer at the screens. "How did you do that? The *Dossier* doesn't have cameras. Did you install them when we weren't looking or—"

"Nope. About a month ago, I patched myself through the Dossier's *holo-screens and rewrote the projection to not only export images but input them as well. It's part of a code I stripped from Xu while they were HIVE'd. It's how the HIVE can be anywhere and take control of anything. The code literally creates a back door, wipes the slate clean, and rebuilds it to its own specifications. That's how it controls Metals."*

Ana frowned, looking through the hazy images on the screen. So that was how the HIVE could control Di. It erased him, then built him back to serve it. His memories were still there, but *he* wasn't.

"How did you get Xu back if it wipes the slate clean?"

"*Honestly? I didn't think I could, but Koren Vey said that while the HIVE can erase data, it can't erase* them. *I locked them in a lead-lined room to dampen the HIVE's signal and started rebuilding them piece by piece, memory by memory.*" The three screens minimized, and Elara's face appeared. She looked like she was hunkered down in the *Dossier's* cockpit, sitting in one of the emergency foldout chairs. Her hearing apparatuses glowed purple in the dimness. "*I could do it because I knew Xu—everything about them. I'd have stayed in that room as long as it took—years, decades. But then, partway through my rewriting their first memory, Xu's memory core started . . . well, it started to rebuild itself. Right in front of my eyes. And in a matter of seconds, Xu was back.*"

Ana's heart fluttered at the thought. Di's memory core in her pocket felt heavy and important—so much more so than it had been before. "So if we destroy the HIVE, we can bring all the Metals back at once?"

"*No,*" Elara replied, sounding troubled. "*It's not that simple. From what Koren Vey and I found out in the coding I stripped from Xu, all the Messiers are linked to one AI.*"

Ana sat a little straighter. "Who?"

"*The* D'thverek."

The Great Dark.

She had been right all along. She had looked into Di's red eyes, and she had seen it, had almost been *killed* by it. A chill prickled her skin.

"*Metals are a part of it now*," Elara went on. "*They're all tied together in this weird symbiotic relationship that we know as the HIVE. The* D'thverek *feeds off of them somehow. If it dies, so do all the Metals it's connected to.*"

"But there are thousands—tens of thousands—of Metals in the HIVE by now! It'd be impossible to detatch them from the HIVE one by one. We can't possibly—"

"*Maybe we can. That's why Koren Vey sent me to find you.*"

"How does this Koren Vey know so much?"

"*It's complicated—*"

Robb crashed through the bushes, effectively cutting her short. He picked a leaf out of his hair, absolutely oblivious to the conversation. "Ana, there you are! Siege said you'd be in the garden, but I didn't think I'd have to fight *nature* to find you."

"Robb!" She gave a start and scrambled to her feet. "How's Jax? Is he really . . ."

His mouth wobbled, and he shook his head. "He's not good."

She didn't think she'd heard correctly. They were here so he could get better. Not because . . . not because . . .

Because Siege brought him here to die, that terrible voice confirmed in her head.

He went on, struggling to find the words. "Like the *ma c'zar* said, his light is—it's gone. There's no way to get it back—"

"There has to be a way," she replied numbly.

"There isn't, Ana."

"Can't they just hook him up to some sort of light-feeding machine and—"

"He's not a Metal!" Robb snapped. "We can't just *magically* transfer him into a new body, or replace his parts, or charge his battery!" He ran his fingers through his hair, turned away from her, and sighed. "I'm sorry. I didn't mean to . . . I'm sorry."

"Oh, Robb." She gathered him into her arms and pressed her face into his shoulder, and he rested his cheek against the side of her head, and they hugged each other for a long time. She didn't think she could cry any more than she already had. There were tears in her eyes, but her insides felt numb, like a ligament that had lost circulation.

After a while, he said softly, "If we don't stop the Great Dark, his death'll be for nothing."

"But we don't know what to do, or where to look—"

"Koren Vey can help."

Robb jumped, glancing around the garden. "Elara?" he called, rubbing his tears off his cheeks.

Both of their comm-links lit up with the signal. *"Koren Vey can help,"* she repeated. *"They're waiting in the ark."*

"The one down in the valley?" Ana asked.

Robb added, "Why would they be in a thousand-year-old shipwreck?"

"You're just going to have to trust me, Smolder," Elara replied evenly. *"Meet me at the north gate of Zenteli—and swing by the* Dossier *for provisions. Lenda'll ask if I take them."*

"Provisions? Why would we—"

"We're going on a hike."

Then both of their comm-links went dead. They glanced at each other.

Robb muttered, "I don't know if I trust her."

She took him by his mechanical hand and gave a tug so he knew she was holding it. "What do we have to lose?"

Goddess bright, she prayed, even though everyone thought she was the Goddess, and it felt a little weird praying to herself, *help save Jax, so we can save the kingdom.*

She pulled Robb with her toward the garden gate, where the *Solgard* let them into the Spire and down the front steps. They passed the Solani chiseling Jax's name into the wall, and she tried to ignore it, but the *tck, tck, tck* of the chisel got under her skin.

Another name carved into her soul. Another person lost.

And she wished, like a thousand times before, it had been her name instead.

·) ● (·

They stopped by the *Dossier* as Elara asked. She had apparently slipped away when Lenda, after a brief shopping trip, had inserted herself into a fight ring and won a few hundred coppers. Now there were at least twice as many people working on the *Dossier* as before—all of whom had lost to Lenda in the ring.

Apparently, it was very boring down by the docks.

Lenda was taping up her bruised knuckles, sitting on a fold-out chair in the mouth of the hull. "What? It's not my fault they lost." A guy passing them carrying new coils for the solar engine high-fived her. "Besides, work's been pretty sparse with all the shit going down in the kingdom. And I'm still payin' them."

Ana quirked an eyebrow. "With what money?"

"The money I won off 'em in the fighting ring, obviously. Oy!" Lenda called around them, pointing to a squirrelly man folding up some of the *Dossier*'s laundry on the docks. "Fold the towels *left* side first! Goddess's spark, gimme a minute." Slamming her hands on the armrests, she pushed herself up and strode down to the dock.

Xu had pulled out a box and was sitting on it at the edge of the ramp, their legs crossed beneath them, letting a beautiful monarch butterfly rest in the middle of their face where, if human, their nose would be. The butterfly flitted its wings, fanning them out like a skysailer in full glide. Ana couldn't imagine this Metal, with the patience of a saint, ever donning the Messier uniform.

But then again, she'd never thought Di would, either.

Ana and Robb grabbed a rucksack with a few provisions from the galley—a few fruit preserves, a flash-dried nutrient bar—and as they were about to leave, Lenda asked, "Has the guard captain found you yet?"

Ana frowned. "No, I thought she might've come back here. Maybe she's still praying?"

"She isn't one to just disappear on us, though," Robb added, slinging the sack over his shoulder.

"What would you do if you were tortured for six months?"

To that, he pursed his lips.

"Perhaps she needs time," said Xu, startling the butterfly off their face. They watched it flutter away before adding, "I am sure she still has . . . things she must sort out on her own."

Ana agreed. "And we'll be here when she wants to talk. Lenda, if we're not back by sundown . . ."

"Tell the captain, yeah," Lenda replied, looking up from her taped knuckles. "You know, Xu says the ark is off-limits. To everyone."

Ana rolled her eyes. "What are they gonna do, arrest a dead Empress?"

"They could arrest a live one," Xu replied.

She sighed at that. "Do *you* know about this Koren Vey?"

The Metal shook their head. "I cannot say. I made a promise."

The more she thought about Elara's timing in contacting her as Starbright, the more suspicious all of this became.

Lenda ran her fingers through her hair. "Just be careful. I don't want the captain having my head."

"She'll have mine," Ana replied. She and Robb hurried down the ramp of the *Dossier* to the docks, and onward to the far gate at the edge of the city.

·) ● (·

Elara squatted outside the wall, almost invisible to the naked eye. When she saw them, she got to her feet and gave a wave. "Did you get the provisions?"

Ana offered out a rucksack.

Elara grabbed it and rifled through it for a can of peaches and popped it open. She turned down the dirt road and began to eat. "Oh man, I was *starving*. Thanks, Princess."

"You do know I'm not—"

"A princess, yeah. No one followed you, did they?" She glanced behind them to make sure. Ana and Robb shook their heads, no. "Good, good. Come on—it's a long trip down into the valley, but at least it's not raining right now. *That* would suck."

"But who exactly are we going to meet?" Robb asked as Elara paused and turned back away from them. "I mean, you didn't tell us anything, and we're not just going to follow you to *follow you.*"

Elara ate another slice of peach and started down the path again, and almost helplessly they had to follow. "Long story short, my parents were archeologists. They wanted to study the ark down in the valley." She pointed down the mountainside, toward the enormous bone-like carcass reaching out of the tree line. "So they did, even though it was forbidden, and the elders in the city didn't much like that. They exiled my parents—and me—from Zenteli, and stripped away our last names."

"Why can't we take a skysailer down into the valley, though? Why do we have to—" In classic Robb fashion, he tripped over a tree root to exemplify his point. He caught himself and jerked upright again, coolly smoothing down his shirt. "Why do we have to *walk?*"

Elara pointed a half-eaten slice of peach up to the top of the wall. "Because you see those guard towers? It's someone's duty to watch over the ark and make sure no one gets close, and with all the Messiers swarming and shrines burning, they're *definitely* on high alert. The ark's basically holy remains, after all. The last of our history." She rolled her eyes and tossed the rest of the peach into her mouth. "It's just *rotting* down there in the valley. Our entire people's history is sitting in that ark, and instead of trying to learn about it, we just watch as time eats it away."

Ana tugged at the collar of her coat and glanced at the canopy of the trees above her. She really didn't much like nature. All the dirt, and bugs, and humidity. "Why did your parents get in trouble for studying it?"

"The ship's been unstable since we crashed here a thousand-odd years ago. The elderberries up in that cushy Spire are scared that if we mess with it too much, it'll go boom and take with it the history stored in its databases. But if we don't even try to access that history—learn it—isn't it already, you know, *kaboom?*"

"And so this person, Koren Vey, is hiding in the ark?" Robb asked skeptically, and shot Ana a regretful look.

I know, she wanted to tell him. *I'm feeling pretty regretful right now, too.*

Elara said, to their surprise, "It's not like she can leave, Smolder."

"And here's where we just have to believe you, I suppose," he deadpanned.

"Yep."

Well, at least it was better than waiting in that stupid garden.

She didn't want to admit that maybe she was just running from the inevitable—because as long as she was moving, pushing forward, doing something, time wouldn't catch up with her.

Time that Jax no longer had.

Because of her. Because she was reckless.

Elara dug into the can, realized it was empty, and tossed it out into the forest. By now, Elara had eaten all the provisions, and both Ana and Robb realized that the provisions had been because Elara was hungry—not because the trek was long. The path they followed was almost not a path at all, overgrown with roots and vines. There were buzzy . . . *things* . . . everywhere, and she kept swatting them away.

Ana was raised on a starship.

She wasn't meant for *nature*.

It had taken only an hour or so to get down the side of the mountain, with the help of a few pulleys and antiquated zip lines hidden in the foliage. The last bit of the trail was a hilly descent into the valley, and the ark already looked impossibly big.

It had once housed hundreds of thousands of Solani—but Ana hadn't realized how big it was until she was halfway down the mountain and the bones of the ship stretched from one side of the valley to the other, like the skeleton of some great beast of lore. It wasn't a natural valley, but a crater made from its impact.

Elara stopped them at the edge of the forest and looked back up to the city on the peak. "This is the tricky part. The lookout will definitely spot us here."

"Then we can't go any farther?" Robb asked, irately batting away a fly that had started pestering him about half a mile back.

"Nonsense, Smolder. We just have to go faster!" Elara spun back to them and dug into her own bag. She produced two fist-size plates. Ana recognized them from the *Solgard*'s belts. "I managed to slip away with a few of these. They're shields. You just push the middle button here and"—she pressed the button in the center and a sheet of silver whirled out on all sides to form a fairly decent shield that covered most of her body—"magic!"

Ana and Robb each took one.

"And why do we need shields?" Robb asked dryly.

"Watch and learn, Smolder." Elara dug out a third shield for herself, extended it, and took a running leap over the hill. She tucked the shield underneath her feet a moment before she landed on the grass, and went surfing down toward the ark at a remarkable speed.

Robb's eye twitched. "We couldn't have used hoverboards for this?"

Ana popped out her own shield and patted his shoulder. "Well, if I die, it was nice knowing you, *Smolder.*"

She heard Robb squawk in protest at the nickname as she made a running start for the edge of the hill, launching herself off it. She tucked the shield underneath her feet and landed hard on the grass, then surfed off after Elara.

The grass was smooth under the shield, and a laugh bubbled up out of her throat despite herself. She threw her arms out to keep her balance. As the wind whistled past her ears, the towering bones of the ship rose into the crystalline sky, curving inward like a rib cage. It was longer than any ship she had ever seen before—as big as the dreadnought, but not nearly as frightening. Slowly the shield came to a stop at the base of the ruins. She glanced back to see how Robb was faring, and he . . . had sat on his shield and was bobsledding down, a little slower than the rest of them but with a triumphant look on his face.

Well, Jax had never claimed Robb was *cool*.

She found Elara standing in the mouth of the ruins and retracted her shield, snapping it to her belt. "How will this Koren Vey help us defeat the HIVE when we can't kill it because of the Metals inside—"

Elara huffed. "You are *relentless*. You love him that much, huh."

She paused, surprised. "Who?"

"That Metal of yours. The reason you're doing all this."

"I'm—I'm doing this for the good of the kingdom," she quickly replied.

The silver-haired young woman gave her a knowing look. "Princess."

She winced and gave up the pretense. "It . . . was my fault he was HIVE'd, so I have to save him."

"I actually know the feeling. About a year ago, Xu and I ran into some trouble. This was back when the kingdom, under the late Grand Duchess, just HIVE'd rogue Metals and not all of them. We got into a bad lot, and our employer, the bastard, ratted on us. Xu protected me. They let me escape and . . ." Elara trailed off, then put her shield back on her belt. "What if you can't save him? What'll you do then?"

"I'll try anyway."

"And if you have to choose? Between him or the kingdom?"

"I don't believe in *choosing*," she argued, but when the Solani girl rolled her eyes, she grabbed her by the arm tightly to stop her and said in a sharp voice, "Enough people have died *for* me, and it stops with Jax."

"And if *you* die?"

"Then I'll have tried—"

"*Bullshit*, Princess. You know that if you die, it's over, right?" Elara asked angrily "The kingdom will follow you if you just tell them you're alive. That's why everyone's protecting you and you can't even see that—the C'zar, that Ironblood, the nefarious *Captain Siege*."

"They want to do the right thing."

"Because they believe in *you*," she snapped, and threw her arms into the air. "Argh, whatever! It's no sense arguing with you." She shoved open the green curtain of vines and disappeared into the ruins.

Why do they have to follow me to do the right thing? She bit her tongue so hard, she tasted blood. *Why am I their conscience?*

Robb came to an inching stop in the shadows of the ruins and stood, brushing the dirt off his trousers. "Well, that was exhilarating—where's Elara?"

She jabbed her finger into the ruins.

He minimized his shield and put it on his belt. "Did . . . something happen?"

"No," she said quietly, wanting to ask Robb if it was true—if he would die for her, too, like Jax had, but she thought better of it. She'd rather not know, because she might just strangle him if he said yes. Together, they pushed back the vines that hung in the mouth of the entrance.

Her anger quickly evaporated.

"Oh, *Goddess*," Robb whispered.

They stared up at the ark in awe. It was hard to be angry in the midst of something this overwhelming.

The ancient ark stood in all its ghostly glory. It was so much *larger* than Ana could have anticipated, its crystalline structure reminding her more of fossils found in the earth than a ship at all. Great vine-covered pillars curved inward, reaching five hundred feet in the air to make a sort of rib cage for a great beast. The ark spread out in both directions, so long it faded into the trees on either side. It was like nothing in the Iron Kingdom because it wasn't made of iron or copper or gold. It was ivory and ancient.

Elara walked up to one of the enormous ivory pillars and tenderly placed a hand on it, as if it was dear to her.

Home, Ana realized. An ageless part of it.

"The *allahlav*," Elara began. "The ark. It brought us here a thousand years ago. My grandmother used to tell stories her grandparents told her, and theirs before them, of how our galaxy used to be. Stories of cosmic beasts who protected our worlds and kept us safe. The *allahlav* were our ships. Living organisms with wings and teeth and circuitry as their blood. But then the Great Dark came, the stories say, and we couldn't stop it. This was the last *allahlav*. It helped us flee, and then it died here."

"So it was an animal?"

Elara shrugged. "A tech-creature? A bio-automaton? I don't know. They're fairy tales, Princess." She patted the pillar and added, "We just have the bones now. Come on—Koren Vey is through here." She nudged her head into a darker part of the ruins and traveled on.

For a moment, Ana let the image sink into her memory, the sun-drenched bones of a gaping rib cage, eaten by time and trees and ground. There was so much of it, she felt small. A dust speck in the great expanse of the universe.

Beside her, Robb stared up at the ship with his mouth agape. "I wish . . . I wish Jax could see this."

"Me too," she replied as they followed Elara into the depths of the Solani ark, so overwhelmed she didn't notice the plume of inky smoke rising across Zenteli from the Iron Shrine.

ROBB

The ship was dark from the vegetation and old trees that had sprouted between the remains of the ship to form a canopy above them. It smelled of moist earth. Elara took out an egg-shaped flashlight and shook it to illuminate the ruins around them. Ropes of creepers, ivy, and moss hung draped across tree branches and the ruined structure of the ship. There were remnants of doors and furniture and staircases and long-petrified wires, and some of the collapsed walls had a strange glittering, scaly texture to them. The longer he walked, and the crunch of leaves and roots and ancient ship dust echoed under his feet, the more he felt the distinct sensation that he was somewhere he shouldn't be.

He hadn't actually *believed* Elara when she said the Solani came here in *creatures*—it sounded like a fantastical story, something out of a fairy tale—but the longer he followed her into the bowels of the ark, the more he began to doubt his own judgment. The Solani weren't from this galaxy. Their skin glittered as though they'd had been sprinkled with diamond dust. Jax could *read the future*.

Just a year ago, he'd thought the most fantastical thing that existed was an iron ore that rusted between his fingers, but as Elara raised her light to illuminate the heart of the ark, he began to realize just how little he knew.

Perhaps Ana was the Goddess.

And perhaps there was magic in the galaxy, after all.

In the center of the ark sat a platform with a gigantic crystal at its center, as tall as a person and the color of clouds. It made him uneasy as they approached. The crystal sat in the middle of a great spherical astrolabe. Or maybe it was an armillary sphere? Robb didn't really know much about ancient navigational contraptions. Once, the spherical framework of rings would have turned around the giant crystal in the center, twisting as they rotated to map the coordinates of the stars, but centuries and vegetation had frozen them in place. There were words—letters—in the Old Language written on each circular band, but they were too faded for Robb to make out.

Elara slipped between the rings of the astrolabe and made her way toward one band that had come to a stop at her height. The bands dipped into troughs in the floor so they could rotate around the crystal at its center.

"What now?" Ana asked, her voice echoing in the cavern as she caught up with them.

Elara reached up to the ring and gripped it tightly. "Now," she said with great bravado, "we wake her up."

"*Her?*" he asked.

Ignoring him, Elara pulled down on the band with all her

might. The ancient structure gave a groan, but with all the vines and vegetation woven through the rings and into the joints, it barely moved.

Elara gave them an annoyed look. *"Well?* Smolder, help a girl out!"

He shook his head, the hairs on his arm standing straight. The crystal in the middle made him uneasy. "I'm not sure—"

"Come on—the sooner we help her, the sooner we can leave." Ana went over to the same ring as Elara and reached up to help her pull it down.

The contraption gave another loud groan, vines popping apart, leaves sighing off, and with a hitch, the ring broke free and glided down into a trough in the floor, the other side of the ring rising like a seesaw. The first ring knocked against the second and began to spin it, and the third, until all seven of the spherical bands moved around the crystal in a rotation that rattled Robb's chest.

He took another step back.

Ana jumped out of the way before a swirling ring caught her behind the legs.

The rings began to move faster and faster, trapping Robb and Ana and Elara inside.

A gnarled, terrible knot of panic began to fester in his stomach.

"Are you sure this is a good idea?" he shouted over the noise of the contraption. "Didn't you say it could explode?"

But if Elara heard him, she didn't reply.

In the center of astrolabe, the crystal, buried under a

thousand years of vegetation and dirt and dust, began to glow a beautiful starlit white. The light fed across the rings, igniting the words on the bands, and traveled across the floor under their feet, awakening designs that, to Robb, looked like constellations. Beside him, Ana stared up at the machine in wide-eyed wonder. Didn't she *sense* something was wrong? It couldn't be just him. He rubbed his arm, smoothing down the raised hairs, trying to calm himself down.

You're just spooked. It's nothing. It's not going to explode—

The crystal shot out a series of lights into the words on the rings, and through the other side the words projected stars and planets and entire constellations. The air became thick with a map, clouds of holographic galactic storms and sweeps of astral gases. Nothing looked familiar, but he recognized it from the tapestries in the Spire.

It was a map of the Solani home kingdom.

"Ak ven'na nat Elara."

Robb jumped at the voice.

It came from everywhere at once, rebounding through the ancient hull. He reached for the *Solgard* shield he stashed in his waistband and froze.

The blue image of a Solani swirled to life in the midst of the projection, glitching in and out like a weak video signal. Although the tech was ancient, the image was much crisper than the hologram used for the Iron Council. The Solani was tall and thin, with long hair and obsidian armor that reminded him a little of the *Solgard* in the Spire, carved with swirling filigree. When she spoke, her tone was soft and sweet.

"W-what is she saying?" he asked, concentrating on the ancient Solani's lips, but he couldn't quite make out the words. "And who is she?"

"The C'zar," Elara said in a little more than a whisper. "Koren Vey. The one who led the arks here. Her light is trapped here. Koren Vey is the one who led me to you, Princess." Then she told the hologram of the Solani something in the Old Language.

The image glitched and replied quietly. Elara's eyebrows furrowed. She listened more intently.

"What's she saying?" Ana asked, and then turned to the projection. "Do you know how to defeat the Great Dark? Or at least how to find it and—"

"*Yes*," the hologram replied.

Robb blinked. The words felt fuzzy and strange, like when his foot went to sleep and left it tingly. "Do you hear that? I understood her."

The hologram turned to him with an unwavering violet gaze that reminded him so achingly of Jax. "*Your C'zar had his light stolen.*"

Robb felt gooseflesh ripple across his skin. "How . . . how do you know that?"

"*I have foreseen it a thousand years ago. I have been waiting for you—and you, daughter of the moon*," she added to Ana. "*We do not have much time.*"

Koren Vey raised her arms. "*You want to save your kingdom, but to understand how to, you must understand how we have come to this moment. The entity you wish to destroy has no beginning, and no end, but the story of the* D'thverek *is the same in every galaxy."*

The *D'thverek*—it was the Solani word for the Great Dark.

"It is a creature that feeds on light—life. In each galaxy, the Goddess is born to stop it, but in each galaxy she fails, and the D'thverek *drains their light, destroying all living things, and moves to the next. It cannot survive without light, for it has none of its own. When it came for us, our C'zars had foreseen that we could not defeat it, so we fled. This ark was the only one to escape. And here it rests, where you stand in its bones."*

The holographic galaxy morphed into a set of constellations Robb knew well—the Iron Kingdom. It looked so different, though, from all the maps he'd studied over the course of his life. It was the Iron Kingdom from the C'zar's perspective. Eros was not the shining planet that the maps depicted, and Iliad was not dark and damp, and Cerces was larger than both of them combined, all wrapped together, surrounded by the asteroid belt that kept whatever lurked outside from coming in. The kingdom looked so small and delicate. How could it defeat something that had lived lifetimes by feasting on the lives—even worlds—of others?

Looking at the map of his home, he realized just how terrified he was. The Great Dark had always been a myth—a bedtime story to tell naughty children—but now that he knew it had taken his *ma'alor*, that it was coming for the rest of them, it suddenly felt viscerally real.

It wasn't a myth anymore, but a nightmare he could put a face to.

"We took our final stand here, where the Goddess was reborn,

and she joined us in the fight. She was barely older than you are now. In our scrying, we could not find a path to a future where we survive the D'thverek—*save for one."* Koren Vey stood straighter, raising her chin. *"Instead of trying to defeat the* D'thverek, *we stole the mechanism that allowed it to feed off the light of others. The* D'thverek *called it its heart. We couldn't destroy it—we didn't know how to. So the Goddess buried it with her in an unmarked tomb, and we would be safe, but only for a thousand years."*

The planets in the map swirled, again and again, one year to the next, faster and faster until the planets and their orbits were a blur—and then everything stopped, and the map was the galaxy Robb knew—the Iron Kingdom just after the Holy Conjunction six months ago.

Koren Vey put her hands calmly behind her back.

"We gave you a story—a prophecy—to warn of its return."

"The *Cantos*," Robb realized.

"So now the Great Dark's looking for its heart," Ana said quietly, shooting a cautious glance at him. "It's burning shrines and HIVE'ing Metals to amass an army—"

"No. It is simply staying alive. It has found a way feast off people's light by transfering their souls into machines. It needs Metals to survive, but the more it gathers in the HIVE, the more energy it takes to control them. The D'thverek *is dying still. It* must *die,"* said Koren Vey. *"You must not let it find its heart."*

Ana hesitantly exchanged a look with Elara. "But . . . if the Great Dark dies, then it'll take all the Metals in the HIVE with it."

The horror of what Koren Vey was asking them to do slid

across his skin like icy fingers.

To save the kingdom, they had to let tens of thousands of Metals perish.

"You are asking us to kill them?" Ana's voice shook.

"*Do not let the darkness find its heart,*" Koren Vey replied. "*I fear that if you try to save the Metals, you will fail.*"

He watched as Ana's hands slowly bunched into fists. She didn't say anything for a long moment.

"She might be right, Ana," Elara said, crossing her arms over her chest uncomfortably. "I've done countless computations on the code used on Xu. I've tried everything. We don't have the resources to get them all out of the HIVE, and we're running out of time."

Ana didn't say anything.

"Where *is* this heart?" Robb asked.

"*The heart is hidden in a tomb in an ancient ruin on Eros.*"

"There are hundreds of those. That certainly narrows it down—"

Koren Vey raised her hands again, and up from the ground came hills and valleys that reminded Robb of the backs of those scaly lizards Erik used to put in his bed as a child to scare him, but then he recognized the strange-shaped pool of water in the valley. "Hold on. That's Lake Myriad. And that pass in the mountains is the Rigid Bone. I know these landmarks. It's in the Bavania Range"—Robb motioned to the mountains—"because that's the valley near . . ." He went very quiet.

"The valley near . . . ?" Ana prodded.

"Near the Academy." His gaze lingered on the dot where the tomb was located, pulsing at the base of the mountains. He . . .

he *knew* those coordinates, the town nearby, Resonance. The memory scratched at the back of his head, but he couldn't quite place it. "There're ruins there where students used to run off to before the Plague came."

Before he could try to remember any more about Resonance, the image rippled again and burst into bits of stardust, startling him out of his thoughts. "*You must keep it safe. The Goddess will help you—*"

Ana jerked ramrod straight. "I *am* the Goddess reborn. I'm the first girl born to the Armorov line in a thousand years—"

The C'zar looked at her sadly. "*You are not the Goddess.*"

"But the prophecy—*your* prophecy—said I would be!" she argued. "If not me, then who? Who *is*?"

"*I am sorry. I do not know that answer, but—*" She cut herself off with a gasp. The crystal in the center of the giant astrolabe gave a flicker. Fear crossed the woman's cool, sharp features. "*Elara, I fear we have spoken too long.*"

Elara gave a start. "What? Why?"

Koren Vey flickered, pain creasing between her brows. "*Get out,*" she commanded, and then more frantic. "*Leave!*"

"What? No—I can't—" Elara began, reaching for the woman even though she was only a hologram, when the crystal gave a pulse, and the rings began to spin faster. A terrible, high song echoed through the cavern of the ark, so loud it rattled Robb's heart in his chest.

He cursed. Of all the times for a thousand-year-old piece of technology to decide to blow up, it had to be *now*. Koren Vey had told them to leave, and he didn't need to be told twice. "Elara! We have to go!"

"I won't! We must do something," she replied, turning back to the ancient C'zar. "Can't we do something?"

Koren Vey tried to take Elara by the shoulders, but her hands passed through her, and her eyebrows furrowed all the more. How many times had Elara visited this ark while her parents studied it? How many conversations had they had? Elara must have been the first person Koren Vey had seen in a very long time. *"Please, you must leave before—"*

There was a loud *crack*, and a fissure opened down the middle of the crystal like a bolt of lightning. He spun around, trying to see if there was an exit or some way to jam the rings—*some way* to get out of this death trap. His metal arm twitched, gears whirring as dread began to pour into his blood.

"Shit," Ana hissed between her teeth, and whirled back to Koren Vey. "Can't you stop it? Can't you do something?"

The ancient C'zar shook her head. *"I'm sorry. I'm only a part of it—I can't control it."* And then she said something quieter to Elara in the Old Langauge, pieces that Robb picked out between the high song of the rings whistling through the air.

It sounded like *Sorry* and *failed you.*

Elara stepped back, shaking her head. "No—no, there's a way out of this. I'm not going to let you die!" Determined, she walked through Koren Vey to the control board beside the crystal, brushing off centuries of rubble and dirt and leaves to reveal the strange console underneath.

The crystal began to whine, emitting a strange energy that prickled at Robb's skin.

"No, Elara, don't touch—!"

The moment Elara touched the controls, the crystal sent out a sizzling shock wave that threw her back. She skidded like a rag doll across the floor, again through Koren Vey, who tried to catch her, and came to rest an arm's length away from the spinning rings. She didn't move.

"Elara!" the ancient C'zar cried, and her body flickered again. The core was failing.

Goddess, he prayed as the loud, high roar filled his ears, and he clung to Ana, death so close he could taste the bitter fear of it on the back of his tongue, *I wish I could see Jax again.*

JAX

"Darling, I need you to wake up."

He knew that voice. He had heard it a hundred times before. In a small starship sailing across space—*he piloted starships?* That felt . . . impossible. He was a C'zar. He was a weapon for his people against the darkness. Trapped in a role he couldn't escape. He couldn't have been a starship pilot.

But that voice . . . it was so familiar.

It reminded him of a woman whose hair changed colors with her mood, in a red murdercoat with polished buttons and too many secret pockets. The first time he met her, he had just tried to pick one of those *secret pockets* in the Market District of Nevaeh. He'd snagged a piece of jewelry—a strange crest that wouldn't fetch much, all dented and rusty. A bird with outstretched wings, catching the tail of a star. He now knew it to be an Ironblood crest—a rare one.

He took it and ran.

The woman, who had been walking beside another woman with long black hair, had noticed a few moments later and shouted after him, "Oy! You little—"

But he was too fast, and he knew all the hiding holes in this space station since he'd stolen his way aboard a few months ago. He hadn't had a good meal in ages. This would at *least* get him—

As he rounded the corner where a shopkeeper sold watches, he slammed into someone else. He backpedaled, about to apologize, when the tall woman with long black hair took him by the wrist and twisted it just far enough to make him let go. She had a grim set to her face.

A moment later, the woman with burning orange hair caught up with them. Jax struggled against his captor, but her grip was like iron. She tossed the crest back to the woman he'd stolen it from. "You seem to keep losing that, Sunshine."

"The little bugger nabbed it right out of my pocket. The Duchess would've been *furious*."

"The Duchess thinks you're dead." Then, "I could always cut off his hands."

Jax had felt a cold chill down his spine—and briefly wondered if, without hands, his curse would go away—before he realized how utterly *stupid* that was. He tried to twist out of her grip again. "Don't *touch* me! Let go!"

So the tall woman did.

He stumbled back. He could try to escape, but he had the feeling they wouldn't let him go. The optic-haired lady tucked the crest into a different, more-inner pocket and appraised him. She touched the goggles around his neck, much too big for him, and noticed the ring of hacking keys on his belt loop. He'd won them off some idiot in a Wicked Luck game the first night in Nevaeh. They underestimated a ten-year-old boy. Everyone did.

"These are mighty fine for a street rat like you, darling. Orphan or runaway?"

"No one," he had replied tightly.

"No one? What a pity." Then she turned away with her partner, and they began down the market street, and for some reason his skin tingled as they left—as if something was passing him by that he would regret. They were talking about the mechanics of a ship, their ship, and it sounded like the same conversation from earlier when he pickpocketed her.

Before he could stop himself, he piped up, "A decompressor switch won't work."

The two women paused and turned back to him. He kept his eyes trained on the ground. *What are you doing?*

"Oh?" the tall woman asked.

He shook his head. "That'll only limit the output to the main thrusters and make your ship slower. Cercian class, right? Maybe a level eight?"

"Seven," the other woman said, her hair shifting from orange to red. "You know a lot about ships, darling."

"My mother worked on the docks of . . ." He stopped himself. He couldn't say Zenteli. If the Elder Court had put out a missing-person request on the newsfeeds, then it would surely clue them in. He had his silver hair tucked up into a black beanie and too-large gloves tied up to his elbows, so there would be *no* accidents, but he didn't want to risk his truth-telling mouth to rat him out. So he said instead, "I was raised around ships."

"Huh." She looked at her partner and back at him again. "Say, would you want to come and look at my ship?"

"He's a *child*, Sunshine," the tall woman said.

"All the more extraordinary." Then she looked back at him, yellows and blues bleeding deeper into her hair. "And if—only *if*—you can figure out what's wrong with the old girl, I'll take you on."

"Take me . . . on?" He didn't understand.

"I'll teach you how to fly with the best of them. Better, in fact. I'll teach you to be the best pilot in the kingdom. And you'll have somewhere to sleep and food in your belly. It'll be hard work, and it won't be safe, but I don't think you're looking for safe."

He wasn't sure *what* he was looking for. Food sounded good, and somewhere to sleep without risk of being pickpocketed or kidnapped or killed. The maintenance tunnels underneath Nevaeh, where the orphans and runaways lived, smelled, and it was hard to sleep when you were constantly surrounded by people who wanted to steal from you and sell you to a diamond mine. But why would some lady captain and her partner want to take *him* on? "Is . . . there a catch?"

"No catch. I just thought you looked miserable enough for me to offer," the captain admitted, and added after a thought, "Perhaps you could change your stars."

His eyes widened. Change his stars—even though he had already seen his fate. He hadn't thought of trying to change them. "Who *are* you?"

The captain smirked and outstretched her hand. "Siege, and this is my wife, Talle."

Jax hesitated for a moment and then took her hand. "Jax," he replied, "and I'll be the best pilot you've ever seen."

Captain Siege was the only person he had ever confided in—the only person who really knew him, down to the bone, and never said a word. She pushed him to be better. To be different.

To change his stars.

But that was a dream. It had to be. He didn't fly *starships*. In no past, in no present, in no future. All fates flowed in a river of time, and it was impossible to swim against that kind of current.

He was so tired from trying.

He was so, so *tired*.

"Darling," the voice said, and he felt lips press against his cheek. There was a sigh, and a warmth spread into him like dye in water. "I know it hurts, and I know you don't want to be here—but we need you a little while longer. The Iron Shrine in Zenteli is burning, and the Great Dark is getting closer and we need you." Then, quieter, "Robb needs you."

Robb.

Dark curly hair and kind blue eyes and a smile that cut to the bone. A boy who always looked sad when he thought no one was looking, and liked to lace their hands together, one finger at a time, with so much care Jax could cry. Robb, who had found out about his curse and didn't care. Robb, who never once mentioned how they could never kiss lips to lips, or touch skin to skin, and loved him nonetheless. Robb, who accepted him while not knowing he was the C'zar and all the baggage that came with it.

He wanted to hear his voice again—just once more. He wanted to tell him what *ma'alor* meant. He needed to.

"He's in trouble, darling," Siege said, because Jax knew it was Siege, from her rough cadence and her soft words. He knew her voice as well as he did his own mother's. "And you need to wake up."

The warmth spread through his body, numbing the hunger in his bones. It was light, but a different kind. A light as hot and bright as the sun. It drew him back to the surface, to the edges of his skin, and gave him the strength to open his eyes.

Siege's hair glowed as brilliant as a supernova, and she smiled.

ANA

Goddess *damn* it all, she'd survived *too many things* to be blown up by a weird ancient space contraption.

"I can try to delete myself from the allahlav's *mainframe,"* said Koren Vey. She was crouched down beside Elara, who was breathing but unconscious. There was a terrible wound on the back of her head where she had struck the floor. *"My light powers the core."*

"You would kill yourself?" Ana asked, surprised. "No—there has to be another way."

Koren Vey gave her a sad look. *"Daughter of the Moon, I have been dead for centuries."*

"If you're here, you're not dead" was Ana's reply.

The crystal was only a few feet away, but as soon as she stepped toward it, her head swarmed dizzily. Around them, the vines seemed to shiver and grow with the strange energy pouring out of the crystal, buds flowering into wide pink and purple and blue flowers. Her chest felt tight, her skin buzzing like it did when she got too close to a live wire; she stepped again and stumbled.

Robb grabbed her underneath the arms and pulled her back to a safe distance.

He helped her back to her feet. "Are you okay?"

"I—I think?" she replied as the floor slowly stopped spinning. "I can get near it."

Robb set his jaw. "Maybe I can."

"No, don't—"

Of course he didn't listen to her. He stood and marched toward the console, but as he reached his metal arm out toward it, the wires in his arm sparked. He gave a cry and backpedaled. His metal fingers jerked and swiveled every which way. He cursed between his gritted teeth. "This is *not good.*"

"I *told* you!"

"I had to try!"

She snapped back, "If I told you, 'Hey, that's a live wire,' would you still touch it just to make sure?"

His jaw worked angrily. Finally, he settled on "Maybe."

She gave him a pointed look. "Jax was right—you *are* insufferable."

"You cannot get close to it," Koren Vey said, standing. She watched them apprehensively. *"Your body cannot withstand the energy. Only certain Solani can. Now do you understand?"*

Ana was shaking her head. "I told you, we'll find a way—stop!" she added as Koren Vey disappeared, then reappeared next to the console and reached up her hand to the crystal. "Please, stop! *Listen!*"

To her surprise, Koren Vey did. Her eyebrows furrowed at the sound. Above the whine of the astrolable, the hum of a skysailer drew near, until it crested over the treetops beyond the bony ruins. It flew into the cavern of the ark, and a silvery-white-haired young man stepped out of the ship.

The ancient C'zar stared in wonder.

"*Nan c'zar,*" she whispered in disbelief.

ROBB

Violet eyes, sharp cheekbones, a star-shaped burn scar on his neck from where he had pried off a voxcollar half a year ago. The life support on his chest pulsed in quick, staccato waves, and it looked as though it took him all the energy he had to walk.

"Jax?" he asked.

The young man turned his deep violet eyes to Robb, and they looked like home.

He *was* here.

He began to walk toward them. The gigantic rings swooped around so fast, Robb knew he couldn't make it through them. He tried to shout—to warn him to leave because this place was about to explode, to go to Eros, to get the heart and run as fast as he could out of the kingdom—when Jax stepped into the circle of rings. He raised his hand as one swooped down toward him—

And stopped.

The ring just—just *stopped*. Hovering an inch above Jax's raised hand, it quivered, shaking off the ivy that had somehow still clung to it.

Koren Vey appeared beside Robb, her hand outstretched toward the rings. It shook as she tried to keep the rings from moving. Her face pinched with concentration. *"You should not be here."*

"I can't be anywhere else, *nan c'zar*," Jax replied, and turned his gaze to Robb. "Come on, *ma'alor*. Out you go. Ana," he added, and she hurriedly retrieved Elara, pulling an arm over her shoulder. Elara gave a pathetic groan as she dragged her out of the astrolabe and toward the skysailer.

"I thought we were dead," Ana said in relief. "I thought *you* were dead."

"Dead?" Jax gave her a smile, although it didn't reach his eyes. "You know I'm too pretty to die."

The astrolabe gave another groan, and the crystal flashed. A wave of energy swept across the ground, bringing up dust and dirt in a wave. Robb staggered as it passed him, his heart fluttering in his chest.

The life support on Jax's chest sparked, and he winced.

Koren Vey shook her head. *"I cannot hold it much longer. All of you, go as far away as you can."*

Ana ducked underneath the rings with Elara, hurrying toward Siege and Talle and the skysailer, but Robb stayed rooted to the ground. Something felt off, like that moment on the dreadnought when Jax kissed him.

His partner inclined his head. "You don't have much time, *ma'alor*." The rings groaned; Koren Vey's hand shook. "Please."

"Not without you," he replied, and his voice broke. "I can't without you."

Jax sighed. "Of course you won't, *ma'alor.*"

Then the Solani prince leaned forward and kissed him on the mouth.

There were no flashes of the future. The stars did not reach down and show Jax Robb's fate—not of the Great Dark or the heart or the shrine. Robb knew this because he felt Jax in the kiss for the first time, no magic or stardust or curses. It was simply a kiss between two people who loved each other very much, and thought they had all the time in the world to say it, and now knew they never would, and it broke his heart.

"Al gat ha astri ke'eto, ma'alor," Jax whispered, and then he grabbed Robb by the jacket, pulled him out of the rings, and stepped inside.

Robb caught his footing and spun back just as the rings snapped back into motion with a thunderclap, whirling faster and faster. They trapped Jax inside. The bright, ravenous light of the crystal lit the entire cavern like an inferno. The power it gave off made it hard for him to breathe. His metal arm twisted and jerked, but he didn't care—he didn't want to leave Jax. He *couldn't* leave Jax—

He screamed his name over and over again, but Jax never turned around. He never looked back.

The Solani prince walked up to the crystal, a shadow against the blinding light, Koren Vey barely an outline beside him. The wind created by the swooping rings fluttered at his hospital gown and undid his loosely clasped hair, fluttering around him like silver streamers. The strange energy from the crystal didn't seem to affect him, or if it did he pushed through it and swiped his fingers against the console at its base.

"Robb!" Siege shouted above the sound of the astrolabe, vaulting out of the skysailer to get him and drag him into it.

But he couldn't take his eyes off Jax. He was talking to Koren Vey, and there was a surprise on his face that Robb couldn't quite understand. He wanted to hear what they were saying. Was Koren Vey telling him that it was hopeless? That he was sacrificing his life for nothing?

Tears burned in his eyes, and he was helpless. The wind picked at his clothes and hair and stung at his eyes so badly they teared up. He didn't want to face the Great Dark. Not without him.

It all felt so meaningless without someone to fight with.

Without Jax.

No, he thought, *no no no*—

Siege grabbed him by the shoulder to take him to the skysailer, but he wrenched away from her.

Koren Vey lifted up her hand, palm out, to Jax, and he did the same.

Suddenly, the astrolabe gave a terrible cry, and a radiant light swept through the cavern, swelling like an expanding sun—

One moment, he was watching the light fill the ark until only the shadow of Jax remained, and the next he was lying on his back a few feet from where he'd been standing, Siege covering him with her body. The skysailer Ana, Talle, and Elara were in had been pushed back against one of the bone-white pillars, and there it sat smoking. His ears rang, his head spinning.

"C-Captain?" he whispered.

She slowly unfurled herself from over him, bits of ivy and

ancient ark sloughing off her back. She sat beside him, bleeding from her hairline. Her hair simmered a soft, hesitant blue. "Are you okay?"

He nodded.

And realized, quite suddenly, that the roar of the astrolabe's rings was gone. The air was thick with silence.

The ark was still there, standing, despite whatever happened.

That could only mean—

"*Jax,*" he gasped, coughing as he inhaled the dust lingering in the air and scurried to his feet.

The shock wave had knocked the vines off the ribs of the ark, and the evening light poured in like fire. Whatever was left of the interior had crumbled, and the last of the creature's skin, hanging on to the bones, fluttered down like pebble-size metallic snowflakes. One landed on his shoulder, but he brushed the scale off. The rings of the astrolabe had come off their rotation and sat on their sides on the floor, encircling the crystal, which was now clear all the way through—like glass.

"Jax?" he called, coughing against the ancient dust, as he climbed over the rings and onto the center dais. Dirt and dust stuck to the tears on his cheeks. He wasn't sure if he was sobbing or calling his name. "Jax?—"

As the dust settled, he saw him.

The Solani prince was standing, staring down at the palm of his hand, surprise and confusion lacing across his silver eyebrows. His hair cascaded down his shoulders to his lower back, glimmering like spun steel in the sunlight. There was a new color in his cheeks, and the bruises across his arms and under his eyes seemed to dull by the moment.

He was alive, and Koren Vey was gone.

His hands went to the life support on his chest. Robb tried to stop him—but Jax shut it off before he could say a word. The disk went dark, needles coming undone from his chest, and it clattered onto the ground.

Jax took a deep breath.

Then another.

There was an odd light in the ancient ark that didn't come from the sunlight streaming in overhead, and it seemed to get brighter with each breath Jax took. At first, Robb thought it was a trick of his eyes, but as he came closer, the light didn't fade. It was the same soft shimmer from the crystal, but now—now it was coming from . . .

"You're . . . glowing," Robb whispered, quite unable to say anything else. And he *was*. Robb blinked the tears out of his eyes just to make sure, because it looked like a million stars shimmered, dim, just underneath Jax's skin.

Startled, the C'zar turned to face him, his violet eyes impossibly wide. *"Ma'alor?"*

"Y-yes?" He came up to him, pressing his metal hand against Jax's cheek. He *was* alive. He was okay, and Robb had yet to stop crying.

"I think you should catch me."

"What—why? Goddess—*Jax!*"

The Solani's eyes rolled into the back of his head, and he dropped like a sack of lead, but Robb caught him before he hit the floor.

EMPEROR

He scoured the rare book selection in the palace's library, combing through the contents of numerous dissertations and nonfiction accounts of the Goddess's reign. He even flipped through one of the first translations of *The Cantos of Light* from the Old Language, but there was nothing he didn't already know.

He licked his thumb, his tongue dry, and it surprised him for a moment before he remembered that *of course* it was. He did not have saliva. His tongue was merely . . . *there*. Which, if he thought too hard on that, was a little odd—and he flipped through an older tome, the leather dry and brittle in his hand. It was a novel detailing accounts of the Great Dark's descent into the Iron Kingdom. It came in the form of a Solani, because it adapted to whatever galaxy it absorbed, like how it looked human now. The Great Dark—Mellifare—came to absorb the light in the kingdom, but the wording was strange.

There were some words in the Old Language—the language the Solani brought with them—that really had no common tongue equivalent. The translation read *light*, but that word . . .

He tapped his finger on the ink-smeared page.

That word—*andor*—was not light in the old tongue.

Andor.

Souls.

The glitch festering in the back of his head sparked with a *pop*, and he winced. His sight pixelated, and suddenly he was no longer in the library but in a cold laboratory with a screen spread across the wall, reading off vitals and data usage and RAM. A strange contraption sat on his chest, heavy and cold, pulsing a strange white light.

"Father, what are you doing?" a voice—his?—asked, and pulled at the straps that tied him to the operating table, but he was too weak, and his bones hurt—everything hurt. From the inside out, like he was rotting to the core. An inky blackness crawled up his skin like vines, eating away at him. The Plague.

"It will be pleasant, Dmitri," his father had said, shushing him. "You'll barely feel a thing. I can save you. I *will* save you."

"I don't— Father, this isn't—" *This isn't right, this isn't what I wanted*, he wanted to say, but he was breathless just from speaking. His heart gave a terrible lurch in his chest.

The light on the contraption flickered, and then he noticed it—the small cube placed in the center, where the light came from. He took another shuddering breath. Black dots ate at the edges of his vision. He felt strange and distant, like his body was there but he was slowly, slowly not.

"I want to save you," his father said, and his voice broke with it, and stroked his hair like he had when he was little. But there was a strange sort of desperation in his marbled eyes. "I've lost everything—I can't lose you, too. She said I wouldn't lose you."

Who?

But he remembered then—the girl with flaxen hair who had come up to him in the Plague hospital, asking what he would do for a cure, for life. *Anything*, he had said, and all she wanted was a heart.

Her heart.

The heavy piece of tech on his chest flashed again, and he tried to suck in a painful, burning breath, but he—he—he couldn't—

The book in his hands clattered to the ground, and it jolted him from the memory. He was . . . he had been . . .

"Your Excellence," the steward said, startling him. He whirled around to the short and paunchy man, fisting his hands so the man would not see them shaking.

"What—oh, it is you."

"Yes, Your Excellence. I thought you would like to know that the shrine in Zenteli was set ablaze by Metals, but the guards there caught it early, and it suffered only minor damages, thankfully."

"Was anyone injured?" he asked.

The steward looked at him in surprise. He had never asked anything like that. He was still shaken from that glitch—that was what it was. "Um—not that we know of, Your Excellence," said the man. "It seemed there were a few citizens praying who managed to get the fire under control, but there is again no trace of the arsonist." And then he fidgeted, shifting from foot to foot. "Forgive me if this is out of place, but do you really believe rogue Metals are behind it—"

"Are you questioning me?"

"No! No, sir, no, Your Excellence. I would never."

You just did, he wanted to point out, but instead he picked up the book he had dropped and returned it to its spot on the shelf. "Send a correspondence to Zenteli, that if they need any assistance—"

"Have I come at the wrong time?" the oily voice of Erik Valerio interrupted as he approached them, his hands behind his back. He leered down at the steward, who shrank into his collar, bowed, and took his leave. After the servant had gone, he lazily turned his gaze back to him. "I hope you haven't waited long."

Twenty-three minutes, forty-two seconds, and fifteen— He fixed his face into an impassive look. "Not at all."

Erik Valerio inclined his head. He was dressed to be impressive—in a sleek black evening coat with geometrical designs across the cuffs, and a bloodred ascot at his throat. His hair was slicked back, but it curled around his ears, like his younger brother's did, though Erik's was darker and his eyes were a sharper shade of blue. He had tried to mimic them for months, but while his looked glassy and cold, Erik's were soulless. It was harder to mimic being an outright bastard than he thought.

"What pleasure do you bring to me today?" he asked Erik. "Should I genuflect to the man who saved my life?"

"Oh no." Erik dismissed the notion with a wave of his hand.

His smile turned wolfish. "Although I do come bearing good news! I've—"

"You have canceled that party of yours?" he interjected.

Annoyance crossed his face. "No, of course not. I live for parties, and Astoria is beautiful. I've found the Empress. She's hiding in Zenteli—where a shrine just burned, if I heard your steward correctly."

"It was saved," he amended. His anger was irrational, and now even his favorite room was soiled with the stench of Erik Valerio. He turned out of the aisle and left the library.

As he shouldered open the door, he called to Erik, "And as you probably *also* heard, Zenteli is not in our jurisdiction. We would have to obtain permission from the C'zar to visit."

Erik scoffed, following him out the door and into the long and marbled hallway. "From the rumors I'm hearing? The C'zar's dead—"

"Then take it up with their Elder Court."

The Ironblood quickly stepped in front of him and stopped, blocking him from leaving. "*Or* we can take care of this ourselves. Kill her."

He raised a single eyebrow.

"If the Empress returns, I doubt you will keep your throne, and *she* deserves it even less than you."

"Bold, Sir Erik."

"She was raised by outlaws," Erik added.

"And you think you deserve the throne?" he snapped back, even as the Great Dark sang in his head to *play along*. He could not stomach playing with Erik Valerio any longer. "You can take up finding her on Zenteli with their Elder Court—"

As he tried to leave, Erik grabbed him firmly by the arm. His voice was low and livid. "If she comes back, then you won't be in control anymore. You know as well as I do that this kingdom will rally around her—they follow you only because they think she's dead. But when the kingdom finds out that you lied to them, Your Excellence? That your Messiers tried to have her *killed*?"

He held back a retort—the Messiers were not his—they had not been since that bot had uploaded the strange virus into him. He could barely command a simple *door lock* at the moment. It was like there was this cold shard inside him every time he tried, this errant line of code that kept pulling him back, yelling—*screaming*.

It was a problem he did not like.

Erik leaned in close, the blue of his eyes almost glowing against the shadow of his brow. He was meticulously put together, with pruned eyebrows and a clean-shaven face. The vines buzzed into the sides of his head were particularly sharp today, his hair atop expertly styled.

"You understand the great risk she poses if she *is* still alive," said Erik in a soft growl, leaning back as a Messier made its rounds down the hall.

He would have thought it was Mellifare spying, but he knew she had taken over a Messier on Cerces, ransacking another ruin. She rarely used the crown anymore, and simply tore through the iron-locked doors with vicious strength.

He tried to reach out—take control of the Messier down the

hall—but the cold spike of code drove into his head again, and he winced, snapping him back into his body.

The Messier moved on without so much as a pause.

When it was gone, Erik curled his fingers tighter into his arm, pinching his skin. "You have full authority in this Goddess-*damned* kingdom, Your Excellence. Why don't you use it?"

He jerked his arm out of the Ironblood's grip and walked around him. "That is true. But I would rather plot murder with a pile of dirt."

With a snarl, Erik spun around and shouted, "You're the Emperor! Do something!"

Ignore him, he told himself, his fingernails biting into his palms. *Ignore the bastard.*

"Or are you scared? Scared that I'm *right*? That if she comes back, you won't be in control. Or maybe you don't care because—"

Goddess, it would just feel so *good* to rip that Ironblood's head from his neck.

"—someone controls *you*!"

The words made him stop. Because the Great Dark was scratching, hissing at the back of his head. A feeling he had only just recently come to hate. How it sang and sang over every thought he made.

And oh that *damned* voice underneath, where the glitch festered and someone shouted—screaming, raging—

He could not get the dead C'zar's face out of his head, or the girl's golden eyes, or the memories whispering, prodding— memories that were not, *could* not, be his—

He turned back to the elder Valerio, trying to control the resentment in his words. "Tell me, *sir*, who do you think controls me?"

Erik took one look at him and retreated a step. "I—I didn't mean—"

"*Who* controls me?" he repeated, his voice rising, but he did not let Lord Valerio reply before he went on, "You are an Ironblood by birthright and so you are bred and taught to fill a role. Like the HIVE, you are given orders, and you are told to behave with a certain decorum. You are—what is a good word—brainwashed? *Conditioned?* Why do you bow to me if you think I am not deserving of this crown? Because you are told you should. Why do you ask my permission? Because that is how you are instructed." He took another step toward the man, and his words were like venom. "It is because *I* control *you.*"

Lord Valerio's blue eyes turned sharp. He could see the fire in them, as deep and raging as an inferno. Good. He liked hatred. It was something he could quantify. "I don't take orders like some mindless *Metal scum.*"

Metal scum.

He had never wanted to kill someone more in his life. Electricity crackled across his knuckles.

Above them, the lanterns swirled around like the eye of a hurricane, their orange lights flaring so brightly their bulbs began to whine, fissures cracking across the glass.

"What the . . ." Erik whispered, and slowly sank his gaze back to him. "What *are* you?"

Not *who*.

Because he was not a person. He was a tool. A component. A part.

He took a step toward the human, so close he could smell the sweat and fear on his skin, and before he could stop himself, the carefully crafted Valerio blue of his eyes flickered a monstrous red. He whispered, to answer his question, "I am your Emperor."

Erik took another step back, then another—and then he turned on his heels and fled out of sight. The swirling lanterns above him burst. Shards of glass rained down, plinking against the marble floor. Well, it looked like he had just uninvited himself to Erik's *party*.

He began to fix his cuffs when heard a gasp, short and fearful, and turned to the young woman who hid in a doorway. But when he looked her way, she left in a flash of mourning dress and strawberry-blond hair.

Wynn Wysteria.

He had been careless.

He closed his eyes, trying to wrestle them back to blue. He should not have scared Erik Valerio. *Mindless Metal scum*, that festering flesh sack had called him.

It made him vibrate with anger, fresh against that terrible memory from the library, rubbing him raw and hollow. Another Messier came down the hallway with that familiar vacant look in its blue eyes. Mindless.

He quickly turned toward the nearest room, reaching out for the keylock, and with a flick of his wrist opened the door, locking it behind him so no one else could come inside.

And in the silence his head throbbed, and the voice in the glitch screamed and screamed, and the Great Dark sang its song, and the noise was so loud he could hear nothing else.

The curtains across the room shifted in the evening breeze from the open window.

There was a girl standing there, her gown the color of opals and her skin an earthy bronze. She turned to him, her golden eyes catching the afternoon light—

Honeysuckles spilling through vines, her eyes wide and hopeful, leaning toward him, pressing her soft lips on his metal mouth . . .

I will always come back for you, I promise on iron and—

He blinked, and she was gone, and the wind whispered through the curtains.

III

STARLIT

ANA

The *Solgard* descended from the watchtowers. Their silvery skysailers reflected the evening light off their hulls and made them look like comets streaking toward them. The dust had barely settled, and they hadn't caught their breaths.

"Take Elara and *hide!*" Siege ordered, her hair as orange as the undersides of the *Solgard*'s ships.

Ana didn't really understand. "But what about you and Talle and Robb and—"

"The girl's an exile. If she's caught, they'll never let her leave."

"But—"

"Siege is right," Robb agreed. Jax was slumped against him, unconscious. "We'll be fine. You'll think of something."

"We could all hide. Scatter and—"

"*Ana.*" There was an unspoken warning in Siege's voice.

Ana cursed under her breath, looping Elara's arm over her shoulder. The girl was still unconscious, her head lolling to one side, silver hair draped into her slack face. Ana barely had enough time to haul her underneath a waterfall of ivy hung from one of the ark's tall rib-like bones before the fleet of *Solgard* ships crested over the ark and landed in the green clearing. The guards pried Jax, unconscious, away from Robb, and arrested them. Within moments, her family was gone, taken back up to Zenteli.

A small group of *Solgard* lingered behind, poking through the weeds and undergrowth in the ark, looking for her and Elara, who began to wake up against her. She groaned, and Ana shoved her hand over her mouth to quiet her—but not quick enough.

One of the guards came near, jabbing his spear into the underbrush. Her heart thundered as he poked a spot just over her shoulder, and another by Elara's knee—

And then walked on.

She quietly lowered her hand from Elara's mouth. The girl was fully awake now, and they stayed as still and quiet as they could as the *Solgard* inspected the area, the ancient rings, the glass-clear crystal, until they were satisfied. They seemed a little jumpy, spooked by being in a place like this—a relic of their ancestors—so they didn't stay long, thank the Goddess, and hurried out without so much as a glance back.

When they were gone, Ana and Elara slipped out of the ivy.

"What happened? Where did everyone go?" Elara asked, rubbing the back of her head. Her hair was matted with blood, and she hissed as her fingers touched her wound. Ana had gotten enough stitches to know Elara needed them.

Ana told her what had happened as they moved through the

ark to where the bones met the grasslands and looked up to the watchtowers.

"We have to get them out of prison then," Elara said, pulling back a handful of vines to judge the distance between them and the edge of the forest. The sun had already begun to set, but for some reason the visibility wasn't getting any dimmer. The bones themselves were *glowing*. Like giant sunsticks. And the little flecks of scales that littered the ground reflected the light in a beautiful oily sheen. Elara kicked one, and it skittered out into one of the shadows cast by the glowing bones. "We should be able to stick to the shade if we hurry before the sun sets."

"Do you think you can make it up the mountain?" Ana asked, motioning to the hacker's head injury, but she just waved it off like it was nothing.

"I'll be fine. Let's go."

They hid in the shadows cast by the incredible *allahlav*, keeping to the contour of the hills, until they reached the forest. The way back up the mountain was marked by small marker lights to show the path. Neither of them spoke much as they ascended to Zenteli, until finally Ana said, "I'm sorry. About Koren Vey."

To that, Elara shrugged. "You said they touched hands, right? And Jax was glowing afterward?"

"Yeah."

"Then I don't think she's really dead. I think she might've given her light to Sparkles. Quite genius, really. She redirected her light into Jax from the crystal, depowering the engine."

"Solani can do that?"

She nodded. "I think she could only because Jax didn't have

much light of his own left. So I don't think she's dead—she's just . . . different now. Something else. Energy or light or stardust. Whatever we become after. She had the best stories, though, about who we were. About our old kingdom before the *D'thverek* came."

"Can you tell them to me?" Ana asked, and Elara smiled. As they climbed, she told her the stories Koren Vey had told her, about cities built in the clouds and creatures that swam in the air. Of great ships like the one in the valley that shimmered all sorts of colors as it floated among the skies, and brilliant parties in lavish crystalline palaces, and the more Elara talked about it in her out-of-breath, wistful voice, the more Ana began to dread what the Great Dark would do to her kingdom.

If it could destroy a place so beautiful and powerful as the Solani kingdom, then how could the Iron Kingdom stand a chance?

She needed to find the heart. She wanted to see Jax first, to make sure he was okay—but there wasn't time. The higher the twin moons of Iliad rose into the night sky, the more the voice in the back of her head itched that she needed to go. To make sure, no matter what, that the Great Dark never found its heart.

By the time the city gates came into view, the moons were high in the sky, coating everything in a bright silver that reminded Ana of Jax's hair. A *Solgard* stood guard out front, apparently stationed there to look out for them if they decided to come back to the city. He spotted Ana before she could duck into the bushes with Elara, and she quickly held up her hands.

"I'm not armed," she told him as he pointed his sharp spear at her. The end glowed a hot white—a lightblade.

"You're that girl—the Empress we're looking for."

"If I said no, would you believe me?" When the guard narrowed his eyes, she sighed. "Could you just let me into the city? I won't make any trouble."

"The Elder Court said to arrest you on sight." He reached for his comm-link on the collar of his uniform. If he called to the rest of the guard, she doubted she'd be able to get into the city at all.

"Wait—"

A glowing boomerang arced into the air, narrowly missing his face. He stumbled back, eyes wide, and spun around to try to find the weapon. It arced into the air behind him and came back around with a fierce twist, slamming into the side of his head.

He fell to the ground like a rock.

Elara climbed out of the bushes behind Ana and took up her boomerang again, placing it on her waist, and then she rummaged through his pockets for some spare coppers and the keys to the gate.

"Don't *steal*," Ana hissed.

"That's ironic coming from an outlaw," replied the hacker, sliding the coppers into her pocket. The guard groaned. He'd have a good bruise on his head when he woke up with empty pockets. She tossed the gate key up into the air and caught it. "Okay, so if the heart's in those ruins, then we have to get your captain out of prison and go find it—c'mon, help me pull him into the bushes."

They each took an arm and dragged him a few feet into a shrub.

"*I* have to go find it," Ana corrected, wiping her sweaty forehead with the back of her hand. "Alone."

Elara gave a start. "*What*? Princess, that's suicide."

"We're the only ones who know where the heart is—you, me, and Robb. I need to go *now* and get it before the Great Dark finds out the location. There can't be many other shrines left before it gets to those ruins. And we don't know how long it's going to take to get the captain and everyone out of prison, or whether Jax even *wants* to leave."

Elara hesitated.

"Trust me," she added to try to win her over, but when she realized that Elara wasn't going to come around she added, "You can't stop me."

"*Ak'va*," Elara groaned, rubbing her face with her hands. "Okay, but—help me get this uniform off him."

"Are you going to steal that, too? I don't think you'll be able to sell that without—"

"I'm going to put it *on*," Elara explained. "I can't exactly sneak into the Spire looking like I am."

"Oh. But if you get caught . . ."

"I know," replied the Solani girl, and cast her eyes down to the unconscious guard, already unlacing his pauldrons. "But I've never really had a crew before—or anything to be a part of, really. It felt nice on the *Dossier*. You kind of welcomed me in despite—well, *everything*. I hadn't had that before. So you get a head start, and I'll go free your friends, and they'll go running after you. I might not be able to stop you, but *they* can."

Ana didn't point out that the crew had tried to stop her a hundred times before, but she'd always run off on her own anyway. It had been how this entire mess started, in an Iron Shrine going to meet Mokuba about a lost Ironblood ship. She didn't *want* to go alone this time, but every second counted—and every second the Great Dark looked for the heart, it was a second closer to finding it. Ana helped Elara undo the rest of the guard's uniform and put it on her. The breastplate was surprisingly light, as were the greaves, and every time she touched the curious metal, it rippled like water. When Elara was dressed, she stepped out of the forest, pulling her bob into a ponytail behind her head, and together they slipped into the city.

The streets were sparse and dark, the only sound coming from the taverns, casting golden light and the smell of sweet mead out onto the streets. They bade each other good-bye and began to go their separate ways, when regret tugged on Ana's heart, because the last time she had gone alone, it hadn't ended well.

"Hey, Elara?"

The girl turned. "What?"

"They're your friends, too. Not just mine."

To that, the hacker smiled. "Thanks, Princess."

"And can you tell Jax that I'm sorry? For everything."

"The dreadnought wasn't your fault," Elara had tried to say, but Ana was already heading for the docks where the *Dossier* sat, because it *was* her fault. That much Ana knew.

Ana kept to the shadows and back alleys on her way to the

docks, and when the sight of the *Dossier*, black and chrome, rose up in the distance, she felt a pang of relief. Hired workers were still, patching the hull and stringing up brilliant new chrome lightsails.

The *Solgard* had brought back their skysailer from the ruins, and it sat wilting on one side of the hold. It was banged up, and she hated to think of how Jax would react when he saw it. That skysailer was his baby.

Inside the ship, she didn't see anyone, so she quickly climbed the stairs, took out her old rucksack from her chest in the crew's quarters, and piled it full of provisions. Di's sage coat hung on a hook where he had left it six months ago. It still smelled like rust and gunpowder as she shrugged it on and pressed her nose against the collar, inhaling deeply. It smelled like him. The coat was loose in the shoulders and too tight in the chest, but if she didn't zip it up, it fit perfectly. She slipped Di's memory core into one of the inner pockets and hurried to leave again before anyone found her.

"I bought a new comm-link for you" came a voice as she crossed the hull.

Oh, busted. Again.

Ana spun around to find Lenda ducking out of the engine room with a grease towel tossed over her shoulder, followed by Xu. "We've got to stop meeting like this."

"Where's Elara? Robb?"

"We . . . ran into some trouble."

"How come I always miss the good stuff?" Lenda grabbed one of Talle's flash grenades from one of the weapon workbench in the cargo bay and held out to her. Ana gave her a curious look, and the gunner rolled her eyes. "Rucksack, Di's coat, sneaking around? You're going somewhere, so instead of trying to stop you, I'm arming you. Be careful with this thing, yeah? I think Talle tweaked it to pack more of a punch."

"Thank you," Ana replied gratefully, slipping the grenade into her coat pocket. She would be lying if she said that she wasn't a little nervous. Her anxiety wound like a tightening rubber band, ready to snap.

She glanced around the hull one last time, frowning. "Where's Viera?"

"She still has not returned," replied Xu. "I believe she is helping at the shrine. She is a little . . . *odd.*"

"She's just—she'll be fine," Ana replied. "I just have a feeling the Great Dark did something terrible to her while they had her."

"Yeah, about that . . ." Lenda rubbed the back of her neck, leaning against the side of the skysailer. "Why didn't they turn her into a Metal?"

To that Xu said, "Perhaps she knows a secret they want. Metals do not have the function to retain their human memories. Or at least my memory core did not. Perhaps Lord Rasovant created others that could."

Like Di's new body, perhaps? Had he remembered who he was? She wished she'd asked when he found her in the palace, before the HIVE took it all away from him.

"Well, whatever secret that is, it must be important," replied Lenda, and fished for something in her pocket. It was a star-shaped comm-link. "Here." But when Ana reached for it, she jerked it away. "You don't have to go and do this stuff alone, you know. I don't know everything that's happening, but I do know you think you have to do everything solo—"

"I know," she interrupted, unable to meet Lenda's gaze. "It's just safer this way."

Or at least, that was what she told herself.

The burly woman gave a frown, seeing right through her where Elara hadn't. "Riggs and Wick and Di weren't your fault, so stop carrying them around."

Ana thought of Di's memory core sitting deep in the pocket of her coat and shook her head. "I'm the Empress. They were my responsibility."

"And you were their family, so you were theirs . . . just like you're ours. So don't die on us, okay?" Lenda finally outstretched the comm-link again. Ana took it and pinned it to the collar of Di's sage coat, syncing her earring to it.

"Okay," Ana promised, pulling the strings to seal her sack, and looped the strap over her shoulder. The gunner pulled her into a strong hug. Lenda was just a few years older than Ana, but sometimes she felt decades older. She never talked about her past or where she'd come from, but Ana always got the feeling that she hadn't come from a place of love. Ana was glad she was here now.

"I won't die," Ana promised. "Stars keep you steady."

"Iron keep you safe."

Ana didn't look back as she left down the ramp and wove through the nighttime crowd toward the transportation vessel on the other side of the docks. It was the last one to Eros for the night, and she quickened her pace to catch it, rummaging through her rucksack one last time to make sure she had her fake ID—when she collided headfirst with someone.

She stumbled back. "Oh, I'm sorry—*Viera!*"

The ex–guard captain gave her a careful look, her gaze lingering on the rucksack over her shoulder. "You are leaving."

"Yeah—but the *Dossier*'ll be leaving soon, too. If . . . if you want to come with us. What's that on your face?" she asked, pointing to a soot spot on Viera's cheek.

Viera slid her finger against the mark and smeared it. "I was praying in the Iron Shrine when Metals set it on fire earlier. I helped put it out, but I could not follow them."

"Are you okay? Did the smoke get to you or—"

"I may not be a guard captain anymore, but I can take care of myself," she snapped, and Ana took a step back.

"I'm—I'm sorry."

Viera rubbed the bridge of her nose and gave a long sigh. "No, I am sorry. It has been a long few months. Where are you going?"

"Oh, um. Eros. I gotta do something," she told her. "I'm going to make sure that whatever the HIVE did to you they'll never do to anyone else again. I promise. And I'm sorry I wasn't there to stop it—but we'll stop it now."

"How are you so sure?"

"Because I'm going to find its heart," she replied cryptically. Viera opened her mouth to ask what the heart was, but the freighter had powered on its thrusters, and she cursed. "I'm

sorry—Elara'll explain everything. I'll see you in a bit, okay?"
Then she drew Viera into a quick hug and tore off through the
crowd toward the freighter ship, and she didn't looked back.

But as Ana found a seat in the galley of the freighter, curling
her fingers around a warm cup of coffee, her eyes darting to
all of the people around her who could be human or Metal or
HIVE'd, she wondered if maybe she should've brought someone
with her—Lenda or Viera or even Xu. But that would've been
asking them to risk their lives for her again.

It's fine, she told herself, pulling her hood lower over her
brow. *No one knows where I'm going.*

But still, she couldn't shake the feeling that she was being
watched.

EMPEROR

The golden-eyed girl left the freighter on a waystation near Eros and boarded an S-class transportation vessel bound for a small town in the Aragonian District called Calavan. An agricultural town—hardly worth the trip, except for its proximity to the Ironblood's esteemed Academy. Most people going to Calavan were merchants and travelers and rough-looking mercenaries searching for business. The girl didn't fit in, though she tried. She held herself too tall—like that captain of hers.

He struggled to keep himself planted in the Messier as he watched her buy a ratty cloak from a vendor on the ship and throw it over her sage jacket. As if that would disguise her.

Was she just *bad* at hiding, or could he simply recognize her out of a crowd of thousands?

She could make it a little more difficult—

The glitch tore through his thoughts again, screeching like a stereo with a receiver too close, and forced him back into the redheaded Metal body. He despised this glitch with every number in his AI programming.

He blinked and refocused his gaze on the entrance to the North Tower. It had burned to cinders almost eight years ago. No one was allowed in. He touched the bulbous lock on the door. He did not know what had led him here. A feeling, perhaps?

It annoyed him. He was having a great many of those—*feelings*—when just a few days ago all he knew was hatred—for moonlilies, for people, and especially for girls with golden eyes. Whatever this glitch had done to him, he had to fix it before Mellifare found out.

He was afraid that if she knew, she would think him no longer useful.

He was not sure what she would do with him then.

The two Messiers who stood guard by the door watched him with careful gazes. He recognized Mellifare in them. She was spying on him. He quickly turned away from the North Tower, setting a course to return to his room.

He passed a closed door at the end of the hallway and paused, that strange feeling again, like electricity at the back of his molars. He turned back to it. The red light on the panel indicated the door was locked. Familiarity scratched at the back of his head like a dog at a door. He reached into the keylock and clicked the access to green.

The room opened.

It was a study.

Dust-covered books lined the left wall, beside bone-white skulls and golden astrolabes. There was a desk on the right side of the room with a computer embedded into the wood, but it was long-since dead, blackened marks stretching out across the oak as if the computer had fried itself.

He ran his fingers along a globe of Eros and spun it. The axis creaked, but he already knew it would.

"And how do you think *you* can help?" a voice in his head snarled, and he jumped in surprise. It was old and gravelly, and familiar.

"I don't know, but I have to try, Father," he replied, but it was not him.

In his head he saw the scene: a Royal Guard who looked like him, agitatedly twirling Eros, while a man with a braided beard and chains around his neck—the Iron Adviser—sat at the desk. The man from the memory of his lab.

"I can't let innocent people die," he said, and he felt the anger in his words. "If the Plague is a pathogen, or some sort of nano-tech, I want to help. What if it's the Great Dark?"

The man scoffed. "The Great Dark—it doesn't *exist*. It's an old fool's tale. If you leave, I can't protect you. No, you're staying here and that's final."

He stopped the spinning planet, shaking his head. "You can't protect me from everything. I'm sorry, Father."

And left.

Blinking out of the memory, he stopped the globe. His hands shook. The smell of moonlilies and rosemary filled his nose, the feel of that old man's neck under his grip, how easily it snapped. He clutched at his chest, fingers curling into the satin of his blouse, that burning, aching feeling returning.

But he recognized the source now—

His memory core.

The room spun, and he leaned against the desk to brace himself.

"This room belonged to Lord Rasovant," Mellifare said. Startled, he looked to the doorway where she stood, braiding her hair down her shoulder, with all the airs of a cat waiting outside a mouse hole, her face expressionless except for the slight tug of her lips into a smile. *"Father,* I guess he was."

"Why . . . did you call him Father?" he asked. *Why did I?*

She cocked her head. "Because, in a way, he made me. He made me strong, and he made me many." As she said that, her voice echoed in the hallway outside, from the Messiers standing guard. Then he felt his own lips move, too, and her voice come out of them—*"He made me unstoppable."*

He quickly pressed his hands over his mouth.

She smiled in delight at his discomfort, and he felt her control leave him again. "Now, I know you were spying on our Empress. Do you know where she is going?"

". . . Calavan," he said slowly, not trusting his voice, but thankfully it was his.

"And pray tell, *why* would she go there?"

"I . . . do not know."

It was not a lie, but he did not tell her he thought she was going to find the Goddess's tomb, either. It was only a hunch, and he was only 83.76 percent sure. He did not want Mellifare going on a wild-goose chase, or so he convinced himself.

The Great Dark, humming its soft song in his head, did not seem to notice his lie—

Until Mellifare flicked her black-eyed gaze to him. "But I *did* notice, brother."

And then her voice rang in his ears, *I am in your head.*

Between his code, pulsing with a red anger, was the song— *"I am the Great Dark,"* a memory purred in his ear. He was in a room tied to a chair, and Mellifare had whispered into his ear. He had been different then. He had been—he had . . .

He had forgotten.

His body went rigid.

She came to stand so close to him they almost touched, and she looked up into his eyes. "She has gone to find the tomb with my heart, and she knows exactly where it is."

"Y-yes, sister," he whispered.

Suddenly, the song changed. It grew heavy and dark and erratic. He did not have to listen to the commands to know what it said.

He hesitated. "Sister?"

"And why did you not tell me?"

"I felt that—"

"I am tired of your *feelings* and *ideas,*" she said, and flicked her hand at him. The HIVE clawed into his head. An explosion of pain rocked through his wires, like molten lava under his skin, and he dropped to his knees. He swayed, unsteady. She came up to him and pressed two fingers against his forehead before he could stop her. "Remember that you are *nothing.*"

The red code pierced through his pain and betrayal like an arrow—between the memories of the study, of her whispers, of the Great Dark—and left him hollow yet again, filled with only the song.

She took him by the chin and made him look into her red eyes. "Now, I think it is high time we met Ananke Armorov again and let you make good on your promise, Dmitri—and *give me my heart.*"

JAX

When he finally came to, he was in the Spire's medical ward again—alone. He plucked the IV out of his arm and sat up in bed, trying to parse together what happened between the ark and returning to the Spire. He still had the C'zar's voice in his head.

Van ma'alor, she had said when she raised her hand, prompting him to do the same. Take my light.

And he had. He stared down at his bare fingers for a long moment, watching it shift underneath his skin like a living thing. He had never felt something so . . . *visceral* before. It was like his entire body thrummed with light.

He rubbed at the place where they'd stuck the IV, but he couldn't find the mark anymore. The wound was gone. Was this how powerful his ancestors' light was—even watered down after a thousand years? It was almost frightening.

He concentrated for a moment on the strange power—and then outward, sensing the two guards standing outside his medical ward, their own light bright like bonfires. Then the hundreds of people in the Spire below him, his captain, and Talle, in the prisons underneath. He could feel all their lights, too.

But Robb's was different. It didn't burn like a bonfire but swirled and danced and beckoned, almost like—

He jerked his gaze toward the doors to the ward just as a boomerang clipped one guard in the head and slammed into the next one. They both slumped to the ground. Their assailer, another *Solgard*, picked up the boomerang, put it back on their waistband, and opened the door.

Jax blinked at his visitor. "... *Elara?*"

She stopped in the doorway, not even trying to disguise her surprise. "Goddess, are you *glowing?*"

He quickly crossed his arms over his chest, hiding his hands, although he couldn't hide the rest of his skin, which did ... *glow.* It let off a soft yellow-white light.

"Never mind, we don't have time. You glow, that's fine." She shook her head and bent down to the longer *Solgard*, grabbing him by the arm to drag him into the ward. "Help me get this armor off him."

"What? Why?"

"Because—"

"Ana's gone," he interrupted, the light inside him flickering, whispering her words to him a moment before she said them, like he could see brief shadows of the future a moment before it happened. His throat tightened in panic. "She's gone to the ruins."

"Um ... yes. She has. You can't read minds or anything, can you?"

"No. I just knew what you were going to say—and she *is* gone? She left?"

"Yeah, Sparkles. She's gone to the ruins."

"Ak'va!" he cursed, and snapped at her in the Old Language, "Why did you let her go?"

"Let her? She said she'd go either way! Don't blame this on me."

"Oh, I'm blaming you," he replied, and helped Elara quickly undress the guard. The guard's armor was a little tight on him as he laced up the breastplate and fit on the pauldrons and greaves. He finally stood and began looking through the drawers for a pair of gloves. He couldn't go anywhere without them—what would happen if he touched someone?

Last time, he almost died.

He didn't want to die again. At least not in the same way.

"Sparkles, hurry up," Elara urged. "Someone could come by any minute."

"I can't go anywhere without gloves," he singsonged, and noticed that the more anxious he grew, the brighter the light under his skin seemed to flicker.

"You would make a good flashlight."

"Shut *up.*"

"Is that what our light used to look like? In the old kingdom?" she asked seriously, and he thought as he shuffled through the final drawer and pushed it in.

"I . . . don't know."

"It is indeed beautiful."

That was not Elara's voice, and his heart stilled at the sound.

Slowly, he glanced over his shoulder. It was his mother, her hands clasped together in front of her, silver hair short and eyes like raw amethyst.

Ten years had barely changed her. She looked almost exactly the way she had the night he left—her chin high, her eyebrows arched, her lips pursed into a thin and often-disapproving line. His memories didn't do her justice. He had forgotten how she stood like an unbent tree, and how her hair was whiter than silver and shimmered like spun glass. How she commanded the attention of every eye in the taverns down by the docks, and now he was sure she caught the eye of every person in the Elder Court. While the years flying with Siege had been kind to him, the years in the Spire had whittled her down to a point. She was nothing but edges now.

"Mother . . . ," he whispered.

Her steely gaze lingered on him. *"Nan c'zar."*

His heart clenched. *Nan c'zar.* Not son. Because first and foremost, even to his own mother, he was a weapon. He stuffed those feelings down into that deep, frigid part of him that had decided not to tell Robb he was the C'zar, the part of him that was glad he found out only after he had almost died, and said, *"Ma c'zar . . . ."*

"It seems I found you just in time," she said, indicating his *Solgard* wardrobe.

He glanced down at it and swallowed. "I can explain—"

She held up her hand, and his words lodged in his throat. "The Elder Court has asked me to . . . propose an agreement with you. Stay and take your oaths as the C'zar and lead our people, and if you do, the Elder Court will drop all charges against your friends and, under the promise that they never return to Zenteli, release them."

Then Siege would be able to go after Ana.

He didn't like the sound of the bargain. It was too clean. For an Elder Court that couldn't read the stars, they had made a very precise bargain. Unless . . . "They were never going to let me leave, were they? If I tried, they would've arrested the captain and everyone else for—for Goddess *knows* what."

His mother nodded. "Your captain has a very prolific record."

Then . . . he was trapped. He could either walk himself and leave his crew—his *family*—in prison, or he could take an oath to become the C'zar and let the captain go without him. If he had more *time*, he could orchestrate some sort of escape, but the light itched nervously under his skin, telling him that time wasn't something that he had.

And he was inclined to believe it.

Elara hesitated. "Sparkles, you're not *actually* considering it, are you?"

"What other choice do I have? I don't want to be the C'zar, but if my power can help save people, then I can't be afraid of it anymore. Ana's in danger. I can feel it."

"But Sparkles . . ." Elara wilted, because it was predictable which option he would choose—the only one he could. While he loved his life as a pilot—he loved the *Dossier* and his captain and his family, and oh how he would miss the terribly cramped crew's quarters, and the smell of exhaust in the engine room, mingled with Siege's cigar smoke—he couldn't bring himself to sacrifice that for his own freedom.

No, he refused to.

"'Tell the Elder Court I will be down in a moment," he said, beginning to undo the clasps of the uniform, when his mother put a hand on his arm to still it.

"There is one other choice," she said, and finally opened her fist. In it sat a small electronic key—a master key. "This will open any of the cells down in the prison. The guard shift is about to change, and you can leave through the service door in the rear of the prison. It will lead you out to the market square. From there, the *Dossier* has clearance to leave. You are my C'zar whether you sit on a throne of crystal or a filthy leather seat on a decrepit ship."

He hesitantly took the key out of her hand. He twirled it between his fingers. "You planned all this? To let me leave?"

The smallest of a smile graced her lips. "*Let* you? *Nan jour*"—*my son*—"I wasn't ever planning for the possibility that you would stay. The Elder Court does not deserve you," she added, motioning below her, down floors and floors, to where the Elder Court held their session, in crystalline chairs. "Ever since your father died, I have been biding my time to show them exactly how I feel. They only care about preserving their own future, and that will not stand. Especially if they plan to destroy my own son in the process. Now go, you're wasting time."

He pursed his lips and quickly drew her into a hug, and she was so much smaller than he remembered—or he was that much taller, but she still smelled the same. Like starlight and lavender, where all his childhood memories rested. "I've missed you."

"I missed you, too." She returned the hug, and then pulled

back and looked into his eyes. "You've grown up. I couldn't have wanted better. Siege did so well."

"I'll—I'll send you a message once we're clear of the harbor and figured out our next moves against the *D'thverek*."

"Please do, and if you need me—or our ships, our stars— don't hesitate to ask. *Al gat ha astri ke'eto, nan jour.*"

"*Al gat ha astri ke'eto,*" he echoed, and he found himself turning away from her, toward Elara, toward the elevators, and left.

His mother was right—the guards were changing, and they thought he and Elara were the next to take their posts. They didn't notice his glowing skin, but then again the guards left so fast they didn't even trade names. Jax rotated the master key around his first finger nervously as he hurried down the cell blocks holding his friends, and with a swift twist of the key the door popped open.

Siege glanced up from her perch on the bench; Talle's head resting in her lap. Robb jerked to his feet.

"Ana went to the ruins to find the heart by herself," he told them, "and we need to go after her."

Robb's eyebrows furrowed. "How did you . . ."

He pulled off his *Solgard* helmet, his silver hair spilling over his shoulder, the glow of his skin so much more apparent now. "Trust me, *ma'alor.*"

Elara added, "Yes, he's glowing. Yes, I let Ana go. And yes, we should probably get out of here," as the elevator at the front of the prison dinged, and the *real* guards for the shift change arrived. "Like, three seconds ago."

Everyone hurried out of the cell, slipping through the

shadows that clung to the dark walls, and out of the door his mother had told him about. It was a passageway that led out to one of the twelve gardens in the Spire, and they slipped quietly through the streets of Zenteli. By the time the *Solgard* noticed them missing, they were already at the docks.

"Are you sure you want to leave, darling?" Siege asked as Elara and Talle went ahead of them and up the ramp into the *Dossier*, where Xu and Lenda were putting the last fixes on the sails. "Once you do . . ."

"My home's here," Jax replied, and his gaze drifted to Robb, who lingered on the docks, his gaze set on another ship—a freighter destined for Eros. "*Ma'alor*?"

Robb hesitated, rubbing his mechanical arm. "I—I think I need to do something."

"Then I'll come with you—"

"No!" he said quickly, and then said again, softer, "No. I think I need to do this alone. Koren Vey said something, and I want to . . ." He frowned, unable to express the words, but the light in Jax whispered anyway.

"Resonance," he filled in for him.

The Ironblood seemed surprised for a moment and then nodded. "And it's almost guaranteed that the HIVE will track the *Dossier*. It'll be better if I split off and go to Eros alone. I won't be in any danger, but we all know Ana attracts it."

"Doesn't she," he agreed.

"Then I'll go with you," Elara said from the top of the ramp, and cast a nervous glance back at Xu. "Xu can run the cloaking while I'm gone."

Why not me? he thought, but in truth Robb hadn't met his gaze once since he'd woken again, and a lump settled in his stomach. Because things were different now. He was the C'zar, and Robb *knew* he was the C'zar, and Robb knew he had lied to him for so long.

"Be careful," Xu said, and Elara kissed her cheek.

"Never." She hurried down the ramp to Robb, and Jax didn't leave the ramp until they had disappeared into the crowd. He still felt their lights, pulsating, flickering, anxious and afraid, and so was he.

Siege called from the hull doors. "Jaxander?"

He tore his eyes away from the crowd and hurried into the *Dossier.*

ANA

Only she could go after the heart. It couldn't be anyone else.

She kept telling herself that as she drove from the outskirts of Calavan into the wilds of Eros, toward the coordinates on her holo-pad. In the distance, the Bavania Range rose up like spiked ridges on a monstrous backbone, white-capped with snow. The shrine was nestled at the foot of one of those mountains. So close, and yet so far.

She would find the heart and destroy it before the Great Dark could get it. Somehow. The skysailer hummed quietly as she skimmed across the grassy road overgrown with weeds and brambles.

She tried a few times to contact the *Dossier*—Lenda, at least—but every time she tried, her comm-link just gave a crackle—jammed. Or broken.

When the trees began to swallow up the road, she banked the skysailer up and skimmed the tree line. The wind had a chill to it, but the sun was high and the air smelled fresh and clean, and her hands were clammy with sweat. The chill in the air—the smell of winter—reminded her of the time the *Dossier* escorted an ex-con from the city-state of Tavenktcha on Iliad to the northern quadrant to Neon City on Eros.

He had been an imposing man, as thick as two men. He had a braided red beard that reached halfway down the front of his barrel chest, and it glowed with optics the way Siege's did, although Ana much preferred the way they looped into her curls. Di had not trusted him from the start.

"*Shh*," she had shushed, hoping Redbeard hadn't heard. "The captain trusts him, so we should, too. Stop being a worrier. You'll get wrinkles."

Di blinked at her. "I am more likely to rust—I believe my components are freezing, it is so cold out here."

She laughed. "You can't even feel the cold. It doesn't matter whether you're a Metal Popsicle."

"No, but what will happen when all of this frost thaws?" he had asked. "The condensation will get into my hardware and I will short circuit and rust and you will need a new partner."

Grinning, with her hands shoved into her pockets for warmth, she bumped her shoulder against his. "Nah, I'd just fix you."

He had been wearing his favorite coat—sage-colored leather with fasteners up the side, his hood pulled over his head to help disguise that he was a Metal. She liked to remember him best like this. Moonlit eyes and a dent on his forehead from where she ran him over in a skysailer and a set to his mouth that was never argumentative—but also never approval. She liked to remember that moment on the frozen docks of the city-state

Tavenktcha, if only to remember the way the evening light shone across the slats of his face and reflected off his frosted cheeks.

"Are you sure you wouldn't want a new partner?" he had asked. "Someone else you could run over with a skysailer?"

She gave a mock gasp. "You're *still* on that? It was an accident! I thought it was in park!"

"I believe that."

"That sounds like sarcasm."

"I am unable to convey sarcasm."

"That *also* sounds like sarcasm," she had deadpanned.

Redbeard, who had been walking a few paces in front of them, had belted out a laugh and glanced over his shoulder to both of them. His eyes were like black pinpricks, but he had the kind of face that wasn't nearly as scary as it should have been, with the scar raking across his eyebrow. "Ye know, when Siege said she had a rogue Metal on her ship, I was a little worried. But ye ain't too bad."

"I shall take that as a compliment," Di had replied nobly.

"Good. Maybe ye won't be HIVE'd."

"*Maybe*? He won't be," she had argued.

"And if he is?"

"Then I'll get him out."

"With love and sarcastic quips, eh?" the ex-con had asked, and unlike Di, she could hear the mockery that dripped across his words.

It pissed her off enough to say, "Yes. With love—and *especially* sarcastic quips." Then she looked away, pursing her lips, as the ex-con howled with laughter again, making her cheeks burn with fury.

The next morning, Redbeard had tried to steal Siege's lockbox and jettison off to the next city as soon as they landed in Neon City. Siege found him, of course, and returned with three of his golden teeth and a bloodied nose as payment.

"We're never doin' that again," she had groused, but now Redbeard captained one of Siege's fleetships stationed out near Cerces, the *Illumine*. Last she'd heard, he had been trying to board and take down a dreadnought of his own—like Robb and Jax had done to save her.

If Ana saw Redbeard again after all this was over, she wanted to tell him that he had been right—Metals could not be saved with love and sarcastic quips. Ana wasn't even sure they could be saved at all, although she held on to that hope like a ship clinging to its mooring.

She would get the heart. She would defeat the Great Dark. And she would bring Di back.

She would.

She had to.

As the skysailer buzzed over the fir trees, she kept squinting down into the thicket for any sort of ruins. The console relayed a holographic map, but all she could see were trees and mountains and blue sky—

And then the firs gave way to alabaster stone and felled pillars, and the ruins of what looked like a temple.

An Iron Shrine. One she had never seen before. It was ancient, the way it fit into the foot of the mountains as if it'd been carved there. Through the hole in the roof, there was the barest glimpse of a white stone face both foreign and familiar.

The Goddess.

Ana set the skysailer down at the edge of the ruins. Everything was quiet.

Good—she hoped it would stay that way.

She grabbed her rucksack, looped it over her shoulder, and checked the ammo in her Metroid before holstering it under her arm and climbing the alabaster stairs toward the ruins.

This Iron Shrine must be over a thousand years old, having fallen to time and memory, built when the Goddess still existed in flesh and bone. The downed pillars held sconces in the shape of the Goddess, her hands hooked to hold the flames. The Old Language was chiseled at the base of the fallen doors leading into the temple. The forest had slowly encroached for centuries, vines and roots upending the floor and crawling up the walls. Small white flowers bloomed between the flagstones like weeds, but she'd seen their star-shaped petals before, and she knew their sweet scent like a lullaby.

They were moonlilies.

Cautiously, she stepped into the shrine, tugging up the hood on the tattered cloak she'd bought on the freighter from Iliad. The afternoon light fell in strokes between the fallen slats of roof, painting golden bars across the autumn-leaf- and vine-covered ground. It was peaceful, and quiet—too quiet. There were no birds, no nature, no buzzing of insects. There was just air and sunlight and ancient marble, and slowly she drew her hand to her pistol.

She didn't trust this kind of silence, and she quickened her pace.

Halfway into the shrine, she noticed writing on one of the walls. At first it looked like nothing—errant age marks—until she came closer. The drawings were faded and written in inky black charcoal. It was graffiti.

MARI + SEL, one said.

NICHOLII THE GREAT (although *NICH* was changed to *DICK*, which Ana thought was *really* classy).

There were drawings—stick figures and tic-tac-toe games. A little farther down, there were scenes from landscapes she could see from the shrine—the forest in the distance, the valley beyond, and one of the broken Goddess statues just a few feet away. They were signed by *M.V.*

Robb had said that students at the Academy a few miles away used to come here before the Plague. These drawings must have been the work of those students.

She ran her hands along the words.

If they were Ironbloods who went to the Academy twenty-something years ago, the last names had to have been families she knew.

M.V. Mercer *Valerio*?

And Nicholii—her father, the late Emperor Nicholii?

DI'S A SPOILSPORT, another message read, although that had been crossed out three different times to *DEVILISH ROGUE, SARCASTIC SMARTASS, HANDSOME BACHE-LOR*. She grinned at that one.

"These sound like jokes Jax and I'd make to you, Di," she

murmured to the memory core in her pocket, and closed her eyes to recite a prayer that Siege had used just a few months ago when they sent Riggs to rest.

"To those who set sail into the night," she whispered, and a part of it felt like she was saying it to her own Di, too. The one lost to the HIVE, and the fragment in her pocket, and the memories that still haunted her head. "May the stars keep you steady, and the iron keep you s—"

A rock skittered across the uneven flagstones.

Ana jerked to her feet and whirled around toward the entrance of the shrine, reaching for her pistol—

And froze.

A long shadow stretched into the shrine from the open doorway, lengthening in the waning afternoon light. Her throat began to tighten, each footfall making it harder to breathe, until she couldn't at all, and the scar on her stomach burned with pain like it never had before. She quickly pressed her hand against it, feeling the knot of skin. She tried to breathe. To think. To run—Goddess, she had to *run*—

Goddess help me, she prayed, even though she was certain the Moon Goddess no longer listened.

And he stepped into the shrine.

"You are trespassing."

It was a voice she knew, a voice that haunted her when she closed her eyes. He was in every good memory in her head, and he was in every nightmare.

She couldn't run.

She could barely even move.

The heart was here, and so was he, and whether she had unknowingly led him here or he had been lying in wait . . . it didn't change the shape of his shadow. And a part of her was *happy* he was here—alive—

At least she knew.

He prowled down the aisle toward her, over crinkled fall leaves turned golden in the chill, and roots slowly upturning the flagstones, lined with broken benches. His steps were slow and methodical.

She swallowed the knot in her throat.

Don't turn around, she told herself. *Whatever you do, don't turn around.*

Because this was not her dear friend. This was a monster, truly, the thing Di had been so afraid of becoming. And that gave her a little more courage, because he was not her Di. She had to repeat that.

He was not hers, he was not hers—although it sounded wrong in her head. Hadn't he said he was hers so very long ago?

"Turn around," he ordered.

She slowly reached into her ratty cloak and pressed her hand against the solid square in her coat pocket—Di's memory core. She'd managed to hold on to it despite the dreadnought and the ark and the universe trying to pull him away from her. She took a deep breath and remembered that he was with her. And she wasn't afraid.

She *wouldn't* be afraid.

He clucked his tongue to the roof of his mouth. "I prefer looking into the faces of the people I kill—"

"Did you always like to hear yourself talk?" she interrupted, quite unable to stop herself. "Or is it a new *glitch*?"

She turned around—and wished she hadn't.

Her heart faltered.

He looked just as she remembered, bloodred hair and fake Valerio-blue eyes. The wound she had given him still looked fresh on his cheek, stitched together with steely thread. He wore the Iron Crown atop his head and a black cloak that rippled as he came closer, a black jacket emblazoned with golden buttons and sunbursts stitched into the shoulders and sleeves, and black trousers. There was a great deal more gold and jewelry on him now, decorative cuffs on his ears and a thick choker rising up his long neck, a jeweled clasp keeping his cloak shut—he looked *overwhelming.* As though he didn't even try to hide his power.

No, that was not her Di at all.

Even though he had the same sharp chin, and the same lips that curved perpetually downward, and the same thick red eyebrows, his eyelashes the color of oil. High cheekbones, and a narrow nose. The curve of his neck was the gentle slope she remembered pressing her lips against, once upon a time.

But this—this was the monster who had tried to murder her.

And yet . . .

"Di," she whispered, unable to stop herself.

He recognized her and came to an abrupt halt. His eyebrows furrowed. *"You."*

Not that she thought he would call her by her name, but she missed it all the same.

His face darkened. "You will not escape me this time."

Then he outstretched his hand.

It happened so fast, she couldn't even draw her weapon. A crackle of lightning surged from the comm-link on her cloak collar. She cried out, trying to wrench it away—and dropped her guard.

He rushed toward her, so fast he was a blur.

But just as he grabbed for her, he winced as if he'd been stabbed in the eye. He stumbled to the side and shoved the palms of his hands against his eyes. *"Damn it,"* he swore. "No—not again."

Run, she told herself.

Run, Ana.

So she did.

Over an overturned pillar and around the broken head of the tallest Goddess statue, toward the back of the shrine where the tomb usually was. She ran through fractured glass on the ground and colored light from what remained of the stained-glass windows above her. Past the base of the fallen Goddess statue, around to the doorway to the inner shrine, where only the abbesses and priests of the Goddess were allowed to enter.

The heart was here somewhere—in the Goddess's tomb. *Find the tomb,* she told herself, trying to keep control of her panic. *Find it and get the heart and—and run.*

The room was small and circular, with a pedestal in the center that used to hold a rusted water bowl that now sat knocked over beside it. Her skin crawled with the feeling that she wasn't supposed to be here. The murals on the walls were once bright, but now the tiles were faded from years of sunlight through the missing side of the roof and the vegetation that had crept in. She could still make out most of the images, though—telling of the defeat of the Great Dark. There was the Solani's ark, a living ship that had carried them across light-years to the Iron Kingdom, but the panels that told of the heart and what happened to it were cracked and broken, as if someone had purposefully destroyed them.

She stumbled on a piece of loose tile, glancing back to see how close he was—not close at all. Was he even following? On the other side of the circular room was a strange and intricate lock that seemed to twist in on itself, so detailed it was impossible to open without a key. Something circular? With prongs?

She glanced around—but there was nothing else here.

This was the door to the tomb. She was sure of it.

And with no way to open it, this was a dead end. She could use Talle's grenade to blow it open—but then she would lead him inside, too.

Her fingers curled into fists.

She had unwittingly led the Great Dark directly to the Goddess's tomb where its heart resided. Had this been its plan the entire time? Behind her, she heard footsteps come into the room. She reached for the Metroid in her underarm holster as she spun to face him.

Count your bullets. Remember where they—

Standing where Di should have been were two Messiers.

"Do not struggle," said one.

The other followed, "For you will not esc—"

Ana didn't give it the chance. She raised her pistol, took aim, and fired. She didn't think.

She only counted the bullets.

One. In the head.

Then she aimed to take out the other one, but just as she did, a hand punched through it, grabbing its memory core, and ripped it out. The Messier gave a jerk, its eyes flickering, and slumped to the ground, revealing the Emperor behind it, the gentle pulse of a blue square memory core in his hand.

"I am the only one who is allowed to kill you," he purred, glaring up at her from beneath his thick eyelashes, and crushed the core. "No one else—*gnnh!*"

He winced, and his blue eyes flickered red—as hot and bright as a flame—and his face slackened, lips untwisting from their snarl. His body unwound, and he righted himself and stood as still as a statue. His glassy gaze no longer stared at her but through her—

As if she was suddenly not there at all.

"Forgive my little pet," said a honey-sweet voice that Ana recognized—the same voice that belonged to the girl who had helped her dress for a week, who laughed at her terrible jokes, who told her she would make a great Empress. "Sometimes I fear it would have been better if I had deleted his functioning facilities—but we both know he is more entertaining when he thinks."

Ana lifted her aim to Mellifare.

The flaxen-haired young woman came into the circular room. She no longer wore a lady-in-waiting uniform, as she had at the palace, but trousers and a pristine white blouse with a ruby broach clasped to the high-neck collar. She was a Metal like Di—and Ana wondered when the Great Dark had assimilated her, and how long she had been stationed in the palace, lying in wait. Mellifare stepped over the ruined Metals and curled her arm around Di. Emotionlessly—like a puppet—he kissed her forehead, and Ana's stomach twisted.

"Don't move," Ana warned, "or I'll kill you."

"And I'll kill him," She motioned to Di.

Ana forced a laugh. "What'll you do? Does the Great Dark really want *you* killing its Emperor?"

Mellifare tilted her head. "Dear me, what do you think *is* the Great Dark?"

"Some—something that stays hidden, controlling you and Di and the HIVE and—"

Mellifare snapped her fingers.

Ana winced—but nothing happened.

Until Di gave a bloodcurdling scream and fell to his knees. The crown on his head clattered to the ground and rolled to a stop in front of her feet. She stood her ground, fighting the urge both to comfort him and run. He clutched his head, his fingers curling into his hair, pulling at it. "It hurts," he sobbed. "It hurts."

Mellifare looked on with a growing smile.

"Stop it!" Ana said. "What are you doing?!"

"Simply tricking his pain receptors to feel like his entire body is on fire. I am sure you know that sort of pain. I gave *you* that sort of pain once."

Oh, she had been a fool.

"*You're* the Great Dark," she whispered. "You set the fire. You killed my parents—my brothers."

"I did," replied the young woman. "Too bad I didn't kill you."

Ana stared in horror. She remembered that sort of burning pain, bubbling up like a fresh nightmare, the way it seared and boiled. How it seemed so deep in her bones that it felt like her soul was burning up, shriveling to ash and cinders. It was a feeling of a thousand knives raking across her skin, flaying it, drenching her thoughts in a single, unending scream.

The pain traveled with her everywhere she went, the memory like ash in her mouth.

"Now take the crown and open the door," said Mellifare, and flourished her hand toward the tomb's entrance. "You should do the honors. You did find it, after all."

A key hidden in plain sight, so heavily guarded that only one bloodline could even touch it. A circular disk with prongs.

A *crown*.

She gritted her teeth. "I'd rather *die* than open that door."

Mellifare tilted her head. "Very well."

Di screamed louder, pulling at his hair. He thrashed, his body rigid and trembling. The sound made her heart shudder. Her fingernails bit into the palms of her hands. She wouldn't— she couldn't. If that crown opened that door, then she would unleash the Great Dark into the world. Mellifare would get what she needed to kill this kingdom.

Ana could not do that.

But then Di looked up at her, his red eyes wide and filled with agony. "Please—please help."

It's not him, the rational part of her head whispered, and she *knew* it wasn't really him . . . but he was really hurting.

That wasn't a ruse.

"You are making him hurt," said Mellifare, and the edges of her words were sharp with impatience. "He is screaming in pain and it is your fault—"

"Okay, fine!" She gave in, her words like lead on her tongue. Her mind raced—even if she didn't put the crown into the door, Mellifare would.

But if Ana unlocked the door first, she would be the first in. The first to the heart. The first to—to—

Talle's grenade sat in the pocket opposite the one with Di's memory core. Lenda had given it to her. Said it packed more of a punch. It wasn't much, but these ruins were ancient and crumbling, and if she couldn't destroy the heart—she could bury it.

"Then take the crown and put it into the door, and perhaps I will stop." The monster's eyes flashed red as her smile widened, and she offered the crown to her. "After all, the Goddess should open up her own tomb."

She thinks I'm the Goddess, Ana realized as she took the crown from the ground at her feet, curling her fingers around the prongs. But the real Goddess was out there, somewhere. Maybe she was coming to save Ana. Maybe she had given up a thousand years ago.

Maybe she knew there was no stopping Mellifare, so she didn't even try, and left Ana to fill shoes that were impossibly big.

And Ana had failed.

She stepped up to the tomb's door, her grip so tight on the crown, the prongs left indentations in her palms.

Di screamed on the ground, curling into himself.

The crown fit perfectly into the groove, and she twisted it to the right. There was a *thunk*, and the dozens of turning tumblers began to shift and click, rotating into place like cogs in some of the ancient clock towers on Eros. As it revolved, she began to recognize the sharp lines and circles, the connecting dots and the strange angles.

It was a map of the Iron Kingdom, and the crown was the sun.

What have I just done?

When the last tumbler fell into place, the door popped open with a sigh.

And Di stopped screaming. He untangled his fingers from his hair, his hands shaking, and glanced up to her. And for the first time since he had been HIVE'd, Ana thought she saw something familiar in his face, only for a moment, before it disappeared and he rose to his feet.

Mellifare was smiling so wide, her eyes shone. "Now that was not hard, was it?"

"Why are you toying with me?" Ana asked, her voice shaking. "Why don't you just kill me?"

"Oh, because I will enjoy turning you into a Metal all the more. You saw inside my dreadnoughts, did you not? It is so poetic—to trap the Goddess in an android. I could kill you twice then, and bring you back, and kill you again, and again, and again. It will be *exquisite*."

She fisted her trembling hands. *But I'm not the Goddess—I don't have another life to try to stop you.*

Talle's grenade was growing heavy in her coat.

"I think the *worst* part of all this," Mellifare went on, hands placed neatly behind her back as she came up beside her and looked down into the darkness of the tomb, "is that you still think you have a chance to win. Under all that skin and bone, somewhere in that fleshy heart of yours, you think you can still stop me." Her voice lowered. "You could not even stop me from taking the Metal you loved."

But a part of Di was still with her, tucked deep in her pocket, small and square. Love didn't have to be a big thing. It just had to be present, and she carried him wherever she went, and it gave her all the hope she needed.

There is a 97.3 percent chance that you are about to make a terrible decision, she heard his voice in her head. Yeah, he would say something like that. Terrible decision or not, it was the only plan she had.

And she had to try.

So she shoved the ancient doors wide and ran down the steps, into darkness.

EMPEROR

"After her," Mellifare ordered.

Obeying, he followed the Empress into the tomb and descended the steps. The tomb was much deeper than he'd thought. Mellifare followed, humming happily under her breath. He felt her, a soft and subtle pulse of song. His functions still felt jittery from the pain. Mellifare had summoned it without warning, and it left a strange, ringing sound in his ears. He could remember little else.

Mellifare took out a flashlight and shook it. The warm yellow light illuminated the steps that led down to a small and cramped room. There were no decorations of great battles, unlike the grander tombs they'd destroyed—as though whoever was buried here was meant to be forgotten. Ancient dust and cobwebs hung from the corners, draping across the walls like curtains. There was no coffin. It was empty of everything.

He had the fleeting thought that he had been here before, led by a brown-skinned girl with fiery wires in her hair, hoping they would find the—

He blinked, and the thought vanished.

"Oh, Anaaaa," Mellifare called, "have you found the bottom yet?"

Mellifare's light crept across the walls and found her at the far end of the tomb.

"Memory cores," the golden-eyed girl began, her voice strangely calm. "They're designed after your heart, aren't they?"

"I taught Lord Rasovant how to build them," replied Mellifare, "to trap souls in them, so that I could harvest their light without my heart."

"And the people inside the cores? Those souls?" Ana asked.

"They are easy enough to overwrite, as you well know."

He winced as she said that, a spark of pain in the back of his head—and a memory of the Iron Palace, grabbing a small worker bot out of the air and pushing a command into it—a little of himself—the voice now lodged in the back of his head. That same can opener that had attacked him on the dreadnought.

The one that had made him glitch.

Mellifare raised the glowlight to illuminate the girl. Eagerness thrummed in her song, infectious and loud.

The girl stood facing the wall, staring down at a hunched-over skeletal figure, knees once drawn to its chest. The white bone and cloth had decomposed so thoroughly it was almost dust. The person had died pressing something against their chest.

The heart—

But it was gone.

All that was left was the faintest outline—a square the size of a plum—in the decomposing leather of the corpse's skin.

When Mellifare realized, the song twisted like an errant wind into a harsh, discordant cry. He winced against it.

"Where is it?" Mellifare hissed, rushing up to the skeleton, shoving the girl aside. She picked at the bones, defiling them, as the skeleton crumbled, skin turning to dust. The rest of the bones lost their shape and fell into a pile with an exhausted tremble. She whirled around to the girl. "WHERE IS IT?"

The girl stood her ground. In the glow of Mellifare's light, her eyes looked liquid. "It isn't here," she said calmly.

"WHERE IS IT?" Mellifare roared, and took her by the front of her coat.

"I don't know," the girl replied. "But it's not here. It seems the Goddess beat you to it."

"The *Goddess?*" Mellifare's voice crackled and quaked.

He winced again against the song. It was screeching now, angry and desperate.

"Oh, I didn't tell you? I'm not the *Goddess*, Mellifare. As you said, I couldn't even save the Metal I love."

I promise, a memory whispered in a small, dark lab, a ruined Metal on the ground beside him, pleading with this girl with golden eyes. *I will leave if you let me save you*—

He jerked his head to the side and zeroed out the errant glitch.

"The Goddess must've already come," said the girl, "and you're too late—"

Mellifare snarled, and he felt the death threat in the song, wanting to snap the girl's neck. To leave her body here to rot in this forgotten ruin—

Do not, he thought. *Do not kill her*—

But why did it *matter*?

The voice in his head was screaming, scratching against his skull.

And the next thing he knew, he had lunged toward Mellifare and caught her wrist to stop her. And they both froze. What— what had he just done? In horror, he wanted to let go. He *needed* to let go, but his hand would not cooperate.

The voice—it wailed in his head, so much louder than the song now.

Mellifare gave him a dangerous look. "Let go of me, brother."

"I—I—I cannot," he replied, and his hand holding Mellifare's shook in terror.

Her eyes narrowed.

Suddenly, a spike of pain drove through his skull like a javelin, hurling through his programs, grabbing his ligaments like puppet strings, and his hand dropped hers. He could not stop himself. He could only watch as his body shoved the Empress against the far wall and pressed his lower arm against her throat, pinning her with his weight.

Mellifare patiently began to back up the stairs as the song tore through his head, telling him to crush her windpipe. The bones of the Goddess rattled on the ground, crumbling under his heel.

The girl gasped for breath, her eyes wide.

There is a grenade in her coat, Mellifare told him, and his hand did as she commanded and reached into her sage coat pocket. He found the grenade and brought it out, and he was helpless as his thumb brushed the pin.

Mellifare turned back for a moment from the middle of the stairs. "Brother, if you want to be *hers*, why not die with her?"

Die—

The word rang in his ears.

Die.

The girl gave him a frightened look. His hand shook, his thumb prying off the pin.

He was—

That was his—

"She's wrong," she whispered, and she stopped trying to claw away his arm and put a hand on his cheek. Her touch was soft and warm and—and she—she smiled. At him. Even though she was frightened. "You were mine, and I was yours. I was always yours, Di."

Di.

Mellifare made his thumb pluck the grenade pin out. And the glitch in his head screamed—

I AM, it roared. *I AM.*

A voice that sounded—it sounded like—

Like *him.*

Electricity curled across his body, lashing up from the floor like vines. His hair levitated with static, the buttons on his intricate midnight cloak sparking. The song crackled, digging its claws deeper. It hurt—everything hurt so much. The song wailed, and the voice inside his head screamed, and between every red thread of code and angry integer, suddenly—there she was, this girl with golden eyes and a scar of constellations and a voice that was soft and sure—

There she was like the dawn.

With a cry, he grabbed ahold of himself, rebelling against the song, and tossed the grenade behind him.

Toward the stairs.

Toward Mellifare.

Then he pulled the girl against his body as the grenade exploded in a sharp hiss of white light.

The shock wave filled the tomb. Stone and shrapnel bit into his back. He clamped down on his tongue to keep himself from screaming as a sharp piece of rock jabbed into his shoulder. A loud crack split the ceiling above them. In surprise, he glanced up. The sandstone heaved—and dropped.

Suddenly, he felt hands on his chest, and the girl pushed him out of the way. A rush of stone and sand came tumbling down, and then there was silence.

And nothing more.

ANA

She came to with a gasp.

Everything was dark, and her tongue tasted like sandpaper. For a moment, she didn't know where she was or what had happened—until her blurry vision slowly sharpened and she stared down at the body of Di beneath her. She had pushed him out of the way and must've fallen on top of him when the ceiling collapsed. Slowly, as if expecting to find something broken, she sat up; pebbles and debris sloughed off her back. She blinked wearily, rubbing the grit out of her eyes as she coughed. She tasted blood in the back of her mouth, and everything hurt—but especially her ribs. She sucked in another breath, and her side spiked with pain.

Yeah, definitely her ribs.

But that also meant she was alive—for the moment.

The tomb had caved in on itself, but most of the ceiling had somehow missed them. When she looked up, she saw the stained-glass windows of the shrine and tree branches breaking through the holes in the roof. Orange evening light streaked through the settling dust. Her gaze drifted down to Di beneath her. He wasn't moving.

She touched his cheek. "Di?"

His eyes finally looked robotic, the optics in his pupils reminding her of antique camera lenses. He had saved her from the blast, and she didn't know why.

"Di, wake up," she pleaded, shaking his shoulders, but his gaze stared beyond her, and his face didn't move, but in the still of the settling ruins she heard the whir of electricity through his wires.

He was offline, but not dead.

And she hated that she was afraid he'd wake up. That she'd have to fight him again.

Mellifare was nowhere to be found. Had she escaped? Or was she still somewhere in the rubble? Ana hoped the latter, but she doubted the Great Dark could be killed so easily.

A rumble startled her, and the far wall shifted precariously. She needed to leave before the rest of the tomb caved in, or she'd be trapped here like the Goddess had been.

Fighting to keep herself together when all she wanted to do was unravel like a ball of yarn, she grabbed his arm and looped it over her shoulder, and with a sob she pulled him to his feet.

As the dust settled across the ruins of the tomb, she climbed the stairs—until she saw that the door was blockaded. She was trapped. There was no way out.

And no one knew she was trapped.

Another rumble shook the tomb, and she tensed, waiting

for the ceiling to cave in. Di hung limply at her side, and she held on to him all the more tightly. "I wish you were with me," she whispered to him, who was not Di, who would never be Di again. "I was always so much braver with you."

What she really meant—what she wanted to say—was that she did not want to die, and she was afraid to.

The blockade at the top of the stairs shifted, and she pressed her face into his hair, waiting for the tomb to cave—when a spear of light broke through the dark stones barricading the exit. The door crumbled open.

In the light stood a shadow, her hair blazing the color of the sun, burning so bright it drove the shadows in the tomb away.

"Darling," the light said, "let's get you out of there."

Hope welled in her chest like birds singing at dawn, and with renewed strength she pulled Di higher on her shoulder and climbed toward her captain.

The moment she stumbled through the door, Siege took Di's other arm and helped her drag him out of the ruins and down the shallow embankment to a meadow where the *Dossier* sat, thrusters humming, ready to fly. The cargo door lowered and Lenda rushed out. "Captain, Jax's got two Messier ships incoming—" She paused at the sight of Di. "Is he . . ."

"Offline," Ana said.

"But is he . . ."

HIVE'd.

"I don't know," she admitted.

Lenda hestiated, but then she shook her head. "Doesn't matter.

What's that sound?" She cocked her head and spun toward it.

In the distant dusky sky, two silver streaks broke through the atmosphere, trailing white smoke behind them. They swirled down through the clouds, leaving pinholes for a moment before the clouds rippled.

The captain turned toward the ships, too. She pursed her lips. "They're here. Lenda, take Di," she ordered, and Lenda did, letting the captain rush into the ship and hurry up the stairs.

"*Shit*, he's heavy," Lenda muttered. "Are you okay?"

"Yeah. When you landed, was there anyone else here?" Ana asked as they hauled Di up the ramp and into the ship.

Lenda shook her head. "No one."

Then where was Mellifare? Ana hadn't seen her in the tomb, and even though Di had thrown the grenade back toward her— it couldn't have been that easy.

Once inside, the hull doors closed and the *Dossier*'s thrusters hummed as it picked up off the ground, the solar core in the engine room burning so brightly, the light leaked out from underneath the door. Lenda helped her lay Di down in the medical ward. The ship gave a shudder as it banked around—a little too sharply—and took off into the stormy sky.

"Is she all right?" called a voice from the top of the stairs, and Viera took them down two at a time. "Lenda, did you get her?" The guard captain paused in the doorway to the medical ward, her eyes settling on Di. Her lips thinned. "Are you sure this is wise?"

"I wasn't going to leave him," Ana replied, curling her fingers tightly around the midnight black of Di's cloak. "I won't leave anyone else behind—"

The ship veered again.

"But he is HIVE'd," Viera argued, "and there is no way out of it."

Ana replied. "There *is*, though."

"Love will not save him," she went on, and the words felt like a poker twisting her insides. "Love will not save anyone. It did not save me."

"I didn't know you were alive, Viera. If I had—"

"If you had, then *what*? I guess I should have been in love with you, then, to have have been noticed," Viera snarled.

The *Dossier* gave a shudder as an explosion rattled the screws in the old ship.

Ana caught herself on the side of the gurney as the lights crashed to black and the red emergency neons dimmed on. Through the intercom, Jax cried, "*Stations!*"

For a moment longer, Ana and Viera glared at each other, until Lenda put herself between them and said, "We can discuss the metalhead later—the Messiers are after us, and they won't stop until we're dead."

"We are as good as dead anyway," Viera ground out between her teeth. "How many people are going to die before you finally give up on him, Ana?"

The words were like a slap. *How many people?* echoed that bitter part of her brain, because so many had already died. Riggs and Wick and Barger and Lady Valerio and the Grand Duchess and—and so many others during her coronation. Jax had almost died, and Robb, and *herself*, multiple times.

And Di . . .

Ana bit the inside of her cheek and looked away, because she didn't have an answer for Viera.

JAX

"Get us out of here!" the captain roared.

He was *trying*. He gripped the controls tighter, and he could feel his gloves growing moist from the sweat of his hands. Which was, above all else, the second-worst part of this entire fiasco.

The first being that *they were being chased by the Great Dark itself*.

Three more warnings flared up on his screen, the computer charting the missiles' trajectories, and he dipped to the left to avoid them—barely missing the explosions. He brought up the windows for the ship's solar core, the speed of the solar winds, the tautness of the riggings to the sails. Goddess, it would've been nice if he'd had a chance to give the *Dossier* a tune-up before getting into another firefight.

Think—you have to lose them. You're the best pilot in the kingdom, aren't you? But his mind was a mess.

The light inside him fretted and pulsed, and he could barely control it—never mind *ignore* it. He used to be able to sense the stars gently orbiting around him, but now everything felt weirdly visceral, and the more he tried not to think about it, the worse it got.

"*Ak'va*, think, you stupid *star-kisser*," he muttered to himself as two schooners fell in line behind him. Artem-1S, both of them.

Talle said from the communications console, "Thrusters are maxed!"

"Tell me something I don't know!" He took one hand off the controls to check the ship's inventory. There had to be something he could use. Three solar-flare rockets and about a thousand rounds for the gunnery . . . .

Ana, quickly followed by Viera, stumbled into the cockpit and pulled down two emergency seats in the back, securing themselves in.

He pulled the ship up through the thunderheads and into clear sky. The clouds flickered behind him, and he wasn't sure if it was lightning or another missile. "*Goddess*, love, what did you *do* to make them this mad?"

"Well," replied Ana, "the heart wasn't in the tomb, and I kinda blew it up, so Mellifare definitely *isn't* happy with me right now."

"That's an understatement, darling," Siege muttered, positioning herself behind Jax's chair.

Jax flipped a switch to bring the wings in as they crested past twelve kilometers. "Captain, you should buckle in, too."

She didn't move from her station behind his chair. "What're you doing?"

"There are two schooners after us, and they're so heavy I'm *hoping* they can't flip-turn on a dime like our girl, so that's exactly what we're going to do, and hopefully they'll be eating our pretty little exhaust as we jet into the stratosphere." Then he flicked on the intercom again and said, "Xu, you're in the engine room, right?"

"Yes," they replied immediately.

"I need you to reroute all the solar power to the thrusters— to *nothing* else. Can you do that?"

"I hope there is nothing in the refrigerator that needs saving," they commented.

From the comms console, Talle said, "Just some salmon I was hoping to cook . . ."

"I'll buy you more, starlight," the captain promised, and grabbed one of the leather holds in the ceiling of the cockpit. She wound her hand around it twice and planted herself where she stood. "Okay, we're clear."

"Oh!" Ana gasped, jolting up, "but Di's on the gurney—"

"Stop worrying about that murderer!" Viera snapped, and Ana scowled at her.

"He's not a murderer."

Goddess's *spark*, he did not have the patience for this. "Xu, on my mark." With a flick of the propulsion, he eased out of their ascent. The *Dossier* swirled, passing through the raging gray thunderheads, toward the ground again—

At an alarming angle.

The schooners followed.

Lighting spiraled through the clouds around them, so bright it was blinding.

"Now, Xu!"

He waited for the thrusters to read the power flux. One second, two.

Come on, *come* on—

The ship lights went dark, energy rerouted to the solar core. The red emergency lights blinked on. Praying to the Goddess this worked, Jax slammed one control back, the other forward, and the thrusters shuddered. The entire ship vibrated—

And flipped backward on its head.

There was ground, and suddenly there were the glorious, angry thunderclouds. The thrusters shuddered as they tried to catch the *Dossier* out of its descent, propelling it upward again. This had to work.

The two schooners came down at them fast.

Someone screamed as he tilted the *Dossier* just enough to squeeze between the two ships, rocketing upward. Something clattered far back in the ship, plates and cups upended in the galley, a cacophony of noise rushing up from the back of the ship. He didn't want to even think about his poor skysailer.

Orange heat licked at the sides of the starshield as they climbed against gravity, breaking through the thunderclouds again, up into clear, wide sky.

Twenty kilometers, thirty, forty—

The schooners behind them couldn't reverse-flip and had to swing around the old way. It cost them seconds the *Dossier* gained as it sped up through the atmosphere. The distance from the surface of Eros increased as the seconds passed.

Ninety kilometers, the holo-screen read.

Clouds dissipated, and the skies darkened to a bluish black. The thrusters shuddered, the power reserves dwindling. Just a few more kilos and he could deploy the sails. Just a few more—

One hundred.

Gravity released the *Dossier* like a sigh, and the ship went swirling up into space.

"You're a lifesaver, Xu."

"I have been told that many times," the Metal replied. "Rerouting power back to other functions now."

"Thank you," he replied, relieved, and a moment later the lights blinked back on across the ship. He threw his hands in the air. "Yes! Who's good? I'm g—"

Siege put a hand on his shoulder. "Don't celebrate quite yet, darling."

His words lodged in his throat, and he quickly grappled for the controls, reversing the thrusters. The *Dossier* slammed to a halt.

Ana leaned forward, her eyes wide. "Is that . . ."

It was.

In front of them, a ship as large as it was wide seemed to take up the entire starshield. A dreadnought. The same one he had died on, it seemed, from the shoddily patched bridge window, and the scrapes along its wings from where the *Dossier* had knocked off a few of its short-range cannons.

Ana whispered, "Oh."

The dreadnought aimed its two large cannons in their direction, and the *Dossier* was so close he could see the detonations pulsating inside the barrels. It was both a beautiful and terrible sight.

And there was no escaping it.

EMPEROR

He was in a Plague hospital on Eros. And then on a rusted old Cercian-7 ship. Then in the Iron Palace. A derelict space cruiser. A Cercian diamond mine. Nevaeh. The Academy. Then an ancient shrine. Friends writing his name with charcoal on the side of the wall. "Is this considered desecrating a holy place, Mari?" he had asked a brown-skinned girl who never smiled. Then he was in a study, his father pinning a badge to his uniform. Dark eyes and a kind smile.

Then the same man again, snarling down at him tied in a chair. In a small, suffocating room. A girl with soulless eyes bending toward him, taking him by the hair, invading his thoughts.

Thoughts that bled red—like human blood—there one moment and then plucked away. People. Memories. Words. Nouns. Names.

Dossier.

Dossier. Siege—

He stumbled out of one scene and into another, and then

another, and another. In a firefight on Iliad. Then pressing his forehead against that golden-eyed girl's. Playing Wicked Luck with blurred faces.

A palace burning.

—*Dossier. Siege. Robb*—

He was on a ship with the crest of a nine-tentacled octopus, outnumbered by Messiers, with a man who looked so familiar—so terribly familiar, with dark hair and a thick beard and sky-blue eyes—shoving a girl into his arms, pushing them into an escape pod. His side was painted with blood.

"You will take her, won't you? You'll take her and take care of her—please," he gasped. "Di, save her."

Who was—?

A boy on a hospital gurney, his hands blackened. That flaxen-haired girl again, bending down to him, whispering secrets. Promising that he would live if only he—if he—

A hand grabbed him by the shoulder, and he spun around to another memory.

—*Dossier. Siege. Robb. Jax*—

A silver-haired Solani punching him in the shoulder. A boy with blue eyes falling from a skysailer. That same boy in a palace hallway, startled to look at him, saying a name he didn't know.

But did.

He did know that name. It was . . .

—*Dossier. Siege. Robb. Jax. Tsarina*—

The door to an escape pod opening. A woman with blazing orange fiber-optic hair, so wild it reached toward the sun, peering inside. He had seen her before, when she never smiled. She should have looked fearful, but her snarl quickly turned to concern for the girl in his arms.

She belonged to a ship of black and chrome. To a crew of kind, misfit faces.

He reached out for them. To the dark-skinned Cercian, to the older man with a braided gray beard and a mechanical leg, somehow knowing that they were—

—Dossier. Siege, Robb. Jax. Tsarina. Nevaeh—

Gone, and he stumbled forward into a garden stairwell. A doorway full of honeysuckle vines. "Di," the golden-eyed girl whispered. Then a kiss—

Goddess, a *kiss*. Deep and passionate, the orange light from the garden fading into a dark bedroom. The Iron Palace. The smell of moonlilies lingering on her skin.

—Dossier. Siege, Robb. Jax. Tsarina. Nevaeh. Cerces. D-D-D—

He winced as the redness twisted in his head, pulling like fishhooks in his brain, threading through it like a monster with claws and teeth. Shredding, ripping.

IF YOU ARE NOT MINE, it roared, louder and louder. *IF YOU ARE NOT MINE, YOU ARE NOT AT ALL.*

IF YOU ARE NOT MINE, YOU ARE NOT AT ALL.

IF YOU ARE NOT MINE.

IF YOU ARE NOT.

IF YOU ARE—

YOU ARE—

"—My best friend," said a sweet voice. Hands cupped his face. He opened his eyes to her. The girl with bronze skin and golden eyes and a scar of constellations. They stood in a palace hallway, she in her coronation gown, the HIVE in his head.

And he remembered that if he'd had a heart, it would have broken.

It did break.

It was breaking as he watched the moment, lips pressed against her ear, relishing her smell. Of honeysuckle vines and dusky sunlight falling across her cheeks. His hand shook with the sword pressed to her stomach.

—DOSSIER. SIEGE. ROBB. JAX. TSARINA. NEVAEH. CERCES. D-DI. A-A-A-AN—

"I should have let you burn." His voice. His body. His hand pushing the sword into her. He heard her gasp, felt her wilt, his heart breaking, breaking.

And she looked at him with molten golden eyes—a color he had seen so often, in so many different shades of light, at dusk and dawn and midday and midnight, stitching him together again.

And he remembered.

—ANA.

IV

STARCROSSED

DI

Somewhere in the distance, emergency sirens wailed.

The floor was cold and hard against his cheek. His head throbbed as he slowly came to, programs flaring back to life one by one. His optics focused, and he blinked and pushed himself to sit up. Deep red lights bathed the room—a medical ward? It looked familiar, but his head was so jumbled he could not think of it. Absently, he dragged his finger along the stitches on his cheek, one, two, the rest broken, and tried to think—at all, really.

His head was so quiet.

"Lenda, steady on that dreadnought!" shouted a voice as strong and striking as a bell. "Hold course!"

He knew that voice.

And—and he knew this *room*. The medical ward. Pieces came back to him slowly, like figures through a fog. He pushed himself to his feet, scrambling to the door. This was—this ship was—

The ship tilted so fast, he lost his balance and slammed

face-first into the doorlock. It bleeped and slid open to a hull he knew well. To a skysailer he had driven before. To a rusted and antique Cercian-7 transport vessel.

This ship was the *Dossier*.

Was—was this a nightmare? The HIVE playing a trick on him?

He took a step out as the ship shook again, and he gripped the doorway tightly.

Those are explosions, he realized. They were in space—that he could feel—somewhere deep in the kingdom. There was a beacon pinging the *Dossier* over and over again. It was the call of a Messier ship, as loud as a foghorn.

COME BACK TO ME. YOU ARE MINE.

The code was familiar, the song so sweet it curled his teeth.

The HIVE—no, the Great Dark.

Mellifare.

Someone was on the gunnery in the back—Lenda, he guessed? And a Metal was in the engine room—although he did not recognize them. A woman with platinum hair climbed the stairs. The royal captain from the palace, but every time he thought about her his mind went fuzzy—like a radio signal gone out of tune.

This *was* the *Dossier*.

Somehow.

He shoved off from the doorway and stumbled up the stairs to the first floor, but the woman was gone. He skimmed his hand across the rusted wall to keep himself steady as he made his way to the cockpit, the pain in his head intensifying until he

could barely see straight. There were all of these memories—
moments he half remembered and could not possibly. Flashes of
playing Wicked Luck in the galley, but then a memory of dying
in his father's lab and the Plague eating up his skin, and then
the feeling of the cold Iron Crown as he placed it on his head.

It—it was too much. He could not *think*—

And suddenly he found himself in the doorway to the cockpit. Out of the starshield, looming like a great black shadow,
was a dreadnought. One of four in the kingdom. He knew—
he *remembered*—reinstating them to the Messier force some
months ago.

Two bright flares lit from either side of the gargantuan ship.
By their speed, trajectory—they were missiles. Solar-grade,
high-impact. They would not render this ship prone; they
would obliterate it.

Through the haze of his jumbled, warring memories, he
knew he had to do something. Whether this was a dream or
a nightmare or the HIVE playing with his head, he could not
let . . . he refused to . . .

His thoughts warped and stretched. What was the *Dossier*
again? What was he doing here? Where was—

Home, whispered a voice between his memories, scratchy and
garbled from a damaged voice box.

This was—

Electricity jumped between his fingertips.

He moved into the cockpit and reached out his hands toward
the incoming missiles. One moment he was standing, the next
his thoughts were rushing toward the missiles at the speed of

standing still, just as he had on the *Dossier* all those months ago, when he took control of the ship. He had done it a thousand times since then, with the Great Dark singing in his head.

But this was different. He had control, and he knew this body now—he knew its capabilities and its limits.

He felt himself snag onto the missiles' guidance systems, threading apart their code number by number. The left missile wavered and went careening off course, up and up, until it exploded like a silent, distant flash of white. The other was a little harder.

FIVE SECONDS, the warnings on the starshield read.

FOUR.

THREE.

TWO—

He pushed his right hand to the side with a noise of protest. The missile wobbled—and went screaming past them, scraping the wing of the *Dossier*, and exploded in a flash. The *Dossier* rattled with the quake of it.

He reached farther toward the dreadnought and felt the commands from the bridge to the gunnery to send off another round of fire, and sank into the colossal ship's onboard computer. He zipped down the multitude of hallways, past the vacant crew's quarters and galleys.

YOU BELONG TO ME, the Great Dark sang, Mellifare's voice laced with sudden bitterness. He winced as he burrowed into the ship's mainframe, clawing between the red code as though it was sticky mud. *YOU ARE MINE—*

No, he was not.

He rerouted his own power away from tertiary necessities, prying energy from his skin and his aches and his senses. He had to stop the dreadnought. He had to stop *her.*

The engine room was easy enough to find, its console like an open door—

His vision flickered. He was overheating.

YOU ARE NOTHING WITHOUT ME, the Great Dark roared. *YOU ARE NOTHING.*

He knew that. He was less than nothing. He was a boy who had died long ago. He was a ghost of himself. He was not even human. He was nothing—but if he overheated, at least he could take the dreadnought with him—

He felt a hand on his arm. Barely.

"Di," someone whispered, and the voice pulled him back.

His outstretched hands wavered, electricity receding back into his fingertips, pulling his scattered AI back into himself. Out of the bridge, the halls, the locks, the escape pods. Pried it from the core of the dreadnought like plucking splinters out of a flesh wound. As he left, he rewrote a single code. That was all it took to take down the gargantuan ship. Not an elaborate program, but a single set of numbers.

100101010101—

It was the deny code to power its solar core. One the Great Dark had to find before it could fix. It was like searching for a single star in a sky of billions. One by one, the lights flickered out, stranding the ship where it floated.

YOU ARE NOTHING.

YOU ARE NO T HI N G.

YOU . . .

The Great Dark's voice faded as the ship went dark.

As he pieced himself back together inside his body, easing power back into his other functions, he began to realize just how little power he had left.

His eyesight began to dim.

Voices sounded far away—

"*Ak'va*—what in the Goddess's *spark* did he just do?"

"I'm reading a system-wide shutdown . . . Sunshine, I think he turned off the lights."

"He can *do* that?"

"Jax, do you have an escape route?"

"Ready and waiting."

"Take it."

—The voices were so familiar. He glanced around at the blur of faces. His chest was still hot, overheated, burning as it tried to cool itself down. He could no longer feel his extremities. He waited for the pull of the Great Dark to tear into his head again—

But there was nothing. Only his thoughts.

Only him.

Di, and not Di, and Dmitri, and D09, and he remembered everything. The Plague and Mercer and Marigold and Nicholii, and Mellifare visiting him as he died, and waking up a Metal, and not remembering himself, and the years spent in the service of Nicholii, who found out, and Mercer, older and bearded, who shoved a little girl into his Metal arms, and Marigold finding their escape pod, and the light-years spent in love without knowing what it felt like, what it meant, that he was not broken or glitching, but that he was *mortal* and—

The hand on his arm tightened. "Di?"

He looked over.

A heart-shaped face and bronze skin, and golden eyes. His gaze fell across her scars, as intricate as a night sky. As he turned to her, his vision narrowed into a pinprick, and he fell into darkness with her name on his lips.

ANA

Ana frowned, crossing her arms over her chest tightly, as she looked in through the window to the medical ward. Inside, Di sat restrained in a chair in the middle of the room, well away from anything he could use to murder anyone. His eyes were half open but unseeing, as they had been since he'd fainted in the cockpit, and the longer the minutes dragged on, the more worried she became.

He'd saved them from the dreadnought. That wouldn't be something the HIVE would do, would it?

She wouldn't know know either way standing on the opposite side of the door, but she remembered the terror she'd felt in the tomb, the way he'd pinned her against the wall, red eyes searing, ready to kill her—

But then he hadn't. He had saved her life.

It could've been a trick.

The HIVE's done that before, she reminded herself, absently brushing her fingers against the scar on her abdomen, but then she paused and began to wonder. *Hadn't it?*

She had seen the lengths Mellifare would go to to kill her because she thought Ana was the Goddess. It seemed odd— almost fantastical—that Di hadn't killed her the first time.

Or in the tomb.

It couldn't have been a coincidence.

Gathering up her courage, she unlocked the door to the medical ward and it eased open with a sigh. She kept a hand on her pistol as she crept toward him. "Di?"

His blank stare didn't waver.

She brushed a lock of bloodred hair out of his face and pinned it behind his ear—

He jerked awake with a start. For a moment he looked afraid, as if he'd just awoken from a nightmare. He struggled against his bindings.

She took a step back and without thinking drew the dagger from her boot.

His eyes snapped to hers, and they weren't dark like in the palace, but a brilliant white like they had been in his old body, pitch-black pupils ringed with the color of the moon.

"Ana," he whispered, and his voice broke at her name. It broke like she was a ghost who had come back to haunt him, and suddenly, she was angrier at Mellifare than ever before. Mellifare took and destroyed, and even the things that came back weren't the same. They were twisted and hurting, like Viera—like Di.

Like herself.

His gaze lowered to the silver dagger she pointed at him, and he flinched away. He couldn't meet her gaze. "Let me speak to the captain."

She stared at him, uncomprehending. "Di . . ."

"Please."

His eyes were trained on the floor, and they didn't waver. A muscle, or a gear, or *something* in his jaw throbbed. The longer she waited, the stranger the silence grew between them.

She lowered the dagger.

"You are not safe in here. What if I am still HIVE'd?" His voice was cold and detached, so different from his old and damaged voice, that she wondered if he was the same at all. "I could break these handcuffs and kill you now. Is that not what the HIVE would do?"

In susprise, she blinked. "The HIVE wouldn't have asked."

His shoulders stiffened. She now recognized the motion of his jaw working—the grit and throb of it—because it looked like the movement of someone trying not to cry. Metals couldn't cry, but she wondered what the feeling of *needing* to felt like. He said, "You cannot be so sure."

"You're right," she replied, putting the dagger back in her boot and leaving the medical ward.

As the door slid shut, a hot tear fell down her cheek, but she quickly wiped it away. Why was she *crying*? She was angry— angry that she was relieved to be out of that room, angry that he wouldn't talk to her, angry that she left.

Angry that . . .

Angry that she couldn't tell if he was her Di, or another trick of the HIVE. Angry that, if he was hers, he wasn't the Di she remembered. Something terrible had settled between them, prowling the ten feet that separated them, teeth bared. Her fingers pressed against the ropy scar on her stomach, not sure if it warded off the monster or kept it tethered there.

She had dreamed of wrenching her Di out of the HIVE so many times. She had envisioned exactly how it'd go, because she always thought it would feel like coming home.

But maybe her Di was only in her head.

Maybe she didn't love him at all—did she? Love was stubborn, and love was impatient, and thoughtless and self-centered and vainglorious. It hid in the crevices of your soul when you thought it had run away, and it never left—like a scar: deep and ugly and enduring.

She wiped another hot tear from her cheek when she heard Jax come down the stairs.

"We'll be arriving in Haven's Grave in a few hours. Is the metalhead awake yet? I really don't want to go in to dock with him still unconscious." He didn't realize she was crying until he came to stand beside her. He gave a start, the light under his skin flickering. "Oh, love! Is everything all right?"

"Fine." She quickly wiped her eyes with the back of her hand again. "I'm fine. He's awake."

"Oh." He glanced in through the window. As if he heard them, Di lifted his moonlit eyes to the window. "So he is."

"He won't talk to me."

"At all?"

She shook her head and wrapped her arms around herself tightly. "He asked for the captain."

"Huh." He clicked his tongue to the roof of his mouth. "Do you think he's still HIVE'd?"

She hesitated. "It's reckless to say no, isn't it? I know he could still be tricking me, but . . ."

Jax didn't say anything for a long moment. The light under his skin shifted quicker than before, as if under duress, and his frown deepened. "Without Elara here, there's no way to prove to him that he isn't still HIVE'd—" His words caught in his throat. "Actually, I've an idea. Don't get the captain yet."

"What are you going to do?"

"I'm not sure yet, but if you hear me scream, please come running—with a gun," he added, and unlocked the medical ward door.

JAX

The light beneath his skin whispered softly, warning him. Not of Di. Not in the way he expected. But of what would come after. He had an idea, but he was hard-pressed to actually believe that it would *work*.

He took the chair from the corner of the room and came right up to him, spinning it around to sit backward on it. They were but a few feet away from each other, and if the HIVE *was* still banging around in Di's head, well, then it would make quick work of him. Jax should have been afraid of that, but he was afraid of plenty more things much larger and scarier than this boy lost in time.

When he sat down, Di glanced up at him and then straightened in his chair. "Jax, I need to speak with— You are glowing," he interrupted himself in surprise. "How did . . ."

Jax waved him off. "It's a long story, but yes, I'm a glowlight. It makes reading in the dark *riveting*."

In reply, Di's lips twitched, as if trying to form a smile, but it quickly fell away again. He shifted in his chair. "Jax, I need you to smash me."

That was not what he was expecting.

"My memory core is in the center of my chest," the Metal went on. "I can help you aim for the correct location and—"

"Are you asking me to *kill* you?"

He winced. "I am not alive, so no. You would not *kill* me. It is the only way to ensure I am not HIVE'd. I do not trust myself. What if I hurt Ana again? Or *you* again?"

Oh, no, all of this was beginning to make a lot of sense now.

"And that's why you asked Ana to go get the captain, right? So you could ask her to do it?" he asked angrily.

"No, I would have provoked her into doing it."

He pinched the bridge of his nose. "Di, there are other ways to—"

"Are there?" Di snapped. "There is no way to tell if I am still under the influence of the HIVE. The program it uses, is so perfectly tuned that it is difficult to pick the HIVE from my own thoughts and actions. I was not under the control of it. I *was* it. Its thoughts were mine. I would try to rebel and then it would—it would *correct* me, as simply as if turning a knob. Metals have never left the HIVE—"

"Yes, they have."

"Liar."

"You know very well I can't lie. We have a Metal on board— Xu—who escaped the HIVE," he informed him, nudging his head toward the door. Xu was up in the galley helping Talle prepare a snack for the crew.

Di bit his bottom lip and looked away.

Above them, the halogen light flickered, as if in reaction to the Metal's mood. It seemed like Jax wasn't the only one with strange powers. He folded his arms over the back of the chair and rested his chin upon them. "So, the question remains, how did *you* escape?"

The Metal rolled his shoulders, clearly uncomfortable, but he didn't really need to say anything.

The light whispered under Jax's skin, the image of Di at the palace, grasping ahold of—

"EoS," Jax murmured, and Di gave him a surprised look. He went on as the past whispered to him through his skin, "You implanted data into the bot, and when it found you again in the XO, it uploaded the data back into you. Well, that explains why EoS had shocked the ever-loving spark out of that Metal."

The halogen light above them flickered again, this time more distraught, reflecting the confused look on Di's face. "How did you know that?"

"You aren't the only one with new powers—could you stop that?" he added, pointing up to the light.

Suddenly, it blinked back to life and stayed on.

"Sorry," Di added sheepishly. "I cannot control it sometimes." "Mmh."

Di went on, "With the data EoS gave back to me, I began to remember who I am, but the point is moot because I do not know if I am still under the HIVE's influence or not. Ana is right not to trust me."

He feigned shock. "She said that?"

Di gave him a deadpan look. "Jax, the window is glass—it is not soundproof."

He grinned. "I know. I just wanted you to admit that you were eavesdropping."

"I was *not* eavesdropping—"

"Were too."

"You really are insufferable."

"I won't kill you," he said suddenly.

Di ground his teeth. "Then bring me the captain, who *will*."

"I don't think she will, metalhead. I don't think any of us will. Well, except Viera, but we aren't letting her within ten feet of you," he added as an afterthought, remembering the way the ex–guard captain had looked at Di just after he had saved them from the dreadnought: like she wanted to murder him.

With a frustrated growl, Di tugged at his bindings, and the metal cords groaned with his strength. "I almost killed everyone!" he snapped. "I almost killed Ana and I *enjoyed* it!"

"That was the HIVE—"

"Was it?" Di snarled. "Or was that who I really am?"

"No, it wasn't, *Dmitri*."

The sound of his name caught him off guard. Jax knew from the light flickering under his skin that it was the first time Di had been called that name in twenty years, and the sound was strange and wrong, like a crown that had once fit but now felt too small. And then Di began to tremble. "I am a *monster*, Jax. I kill everything I love, so I should just—"

Like a wind bending the trees, the light inside him took hold of his body and leaned him forward, and he cupped Di's face in his hands. The light thrummed, pulsing out of his skin, through his clothes and his gloves, surrounding them in a celestial golden-white light. Di's eyes widened as the light sank into his synthetic skin, and across his wires, and found the soft core of his soul.

And suddenly, it was no longer a Metal sitting there but the shorn-haired young man from the Plague hospital, tears fresh in his brown eyes.

"You are good," Jax said.

Dmitri heaved a sob. "But it's all my fault."

"You are good," he repeated. The light faded, and as it did, Jax found himself looking into the moonlit eyes of the red-haired Metal again. He wiped a tear from Di's cheek, a tear that shouldn't have been there.

Di blinked. "How did you . . . ?"

"If you were a monster, you wouldn't have a soul," he said, and thumped his knuckles against Di's chest. "Remember when you tried to save me on the dreadnought? You reached out to me and grabbed my hand, and before all hundred-thousand-something souls sucked the life out of me, I saw you—and I saw every other soul in the HIVE. But just then? There was only you."

Jax wasn't a fool; he knew that Di understood what that meant. That the HIVE no longer infested his code. That it was him, and wholly him. And slowly, his old friend gave in to the truth, and his shoulders drooped as if in a sigh.

"We need your help, Di," he said carefully. "We must stop the *D'thverek*, but if she finds her heart, then we're all dead, and you're the only one who has been in her head who can help us."

"And the only one I trust," added the captain in the doorway, her hair swirled up into a topknot, pulsing orange then red then orange again. As she stepped into the medical ward, Jax quickly got to his feet. She motioned to Di. "Release him, and then I need you to make some calls."

He gave a start. "To whom?"

"Everyone. I've a feeling we don't have a lot of time left."

"Yes, Captain." He quickly undid Di's bindings. The steel cords clanked heavily against the ground. Di massaged the side of his neck, rotating his shoulders, and nodded a silent thank-you to Jax. He smiled in reply and left the ward. It wasn't until he was halfway up the stairs that he glanced over the railing and through the window, as Di stood and faced his captain.

And he wondered why Di looked so afraid.

ROBB

The Valerio manor was an empty shell of itself.

It was winter in Ablos on the planet Eros, and the skies were a cotton gray that stretched to the edge of the horizon, just a shade darker than the thick layer of white snow that clung to the wrought-iron fence at the entrance and covered the barren grounds.

He hoped that his memory hadn't failed him. While he'd sat in the prison in the Spire, he had finally remembered why Resonance had been so familiar. Once, when he was fourteen, he had slipped into his mother's study to try to find some clues about his missing father. He had scoured her desk, her computer files, her cabinets and books, and when he'd found a decrepit holo-pad, he had powered it up. On it were files labeled *Resonance*.

He hadn't gotten a chance to look at them before he'd heard his mother, stashed it back in the drawer where he found it, and leaped out of the window and into the hydrangea bushes.

Frost bit at his arm where metal met skin, and he rubbed his shoulder, hoping he didn't get frostbite. Even his thick fur-lined coat couldn't keep the chill out. He rarely visited the estate in the winter. His mother would have spirited him off to the Academy in the fall, and he wouldn't return until the lilies were blooming again in the spring.

"I'll wait right here with the skysailer, Smolder," said Elara, curling her Cercian fur-lined cloak around her. "You go do your thing. Yell if anyone kills you."

He rolled his eyes. "Thanks. You're a big help."

"I try— *Wait*." She grabbed him by the shoulder and nodded up toward the mansion. The hearing apparatuses flickered bright purple in her ears. "I hear something."

"Right, I'm sure," he sighed, and she squeezed his shoulder tighter.

"I'm not joking."

Oh. That wasn't good. "Messiers?"

She hesitated. "I'm . . . not sure. Be careful. I don't like this."

"I never liked this place." He pulled his lightsword cross-body over his shoulder and started up the long path to the Valerio estate. Snow crunched underfoot. The grounds looked to be empty as he wandered up the driveway to the main house, but he didn't trust the silence.

It was too quiet.

The estate had been a castle in ancient times, but over the years it was outfitted and refortified until only the front wall was the ancient, crumbling sandstone of old. He made his way up the steps to the front door, his breath coming out in puffs of steam. It didn't *look* like anyone was here. He tried the front door, expecting it to be locked—but it eased open at his touch. There were scrapes against the doorway. Someone had forced their way inside.

Fear curled in his gut like a poisonous snake, tail rattling. He didn't like this at all. Was he too late?

Quietly, he stepped into the foyer and hung his coat on the hook by the door, resituating his lightsword on his back and closed the door behind him.

"Hello?" he called.

But there was no answer.

His mechanical arm twitched, and he pulled it tight against his chest to keep it from moving. The stairs whined loudly as he ascended to the second floor, toward his mother's study. Upstairs, his old room had been completely renovated, his things sold, but his mother's room had gone untouched. A thin layer of dust covered the armoire, the dressing table she'd loved so much, where he had the most vivid memories of her sitting, brushing her long peppery-black hair with a fine-toothed comb. Nothing was out of order or misplaced. Her dresses were in her wardrobe, her bed made, her books neatly displayed on a wall of shelves.

But she was gone.

In the blink of an eye.

And while he'd loved her, he hadn't always *liked* her—and he was sure she'd never liked him. Which was why he never understood why she had shielded him with her body so that he, the son she clearly despised, could live. The son who, just a few hours before, had disavowed his Valerio name.

He just didn't understand why she couldn't love him that much while she was alive.

Closing the door to her room, he crept down to the end of the hallway lined with portraits of past Valerios, all dark curls and sky-blue eyes, each as dour and dapper as the last. At the very end were his mother and father, holding each other's hands, staring out of the portrait as if judging his ratty winter coat and glitching arm.

While his father smiled, one side of his mouth slightly higher than the other, his mother's lips were pressed into a thin, disapproving line, as if to say, *Look how far you've fallen.*

He tried to ignore the portrait as he came into her study. The first thing that hit him was the smell of leather—leather-bound books and leather-covered chairs—and then the muskiness of old wood. The same thin layer of dust coated every inch of the mahogany desk and the towering bookshelves and the regal busts of Emperors of old. He crept into the study, the Calavanian rug beneath his snow-stuck shoes soft.

His metal arm twitched again, and he hugged it tighter against his chest. *Not now.* His arm had done so well—*so well*—the last few hours. He was beginning to realize when it acted out—when he wanted to be impulsive but made himself measured and cool. It rebelled against everything his mother had taught him.

Funny, he thought as he fisted his gloved metal hand, *my mother always said I wore my heart on my sleeve.*

He remembered that the file had been in the bottommost desk drawer, so he went there first—and paused. Fingerprints had broken the dust on the desk. Someone had been in here recently.

"Shit," he cursed and opened the bottom drawer.

There was nothing there.

"It's amazing what you can find with a little digging," said a voice.

Robb glanced up. His brother stood blocking the doorway in a deep brown leather jacket with mink fur at the collar and dark trousers. His boots were well polished and decorated with the Valerio insignia—a snake eating its own tail. He filled the doorway just like he had in Robb's nightmares, his hair short, the sides shaved with celestial designs, and he narrowed his eyes like their mother always did—disapproving, but not surprised, as if nothing Robb would ever do would be worthy of approval. In his gloved hand was a derelict holo-pad, and he wagged it playfully. "It would seem as though our mother funded all of Lord Rasovant's early research. It's all quite startling, really. Ancient tech found in the ruins of a shrine. Apparently, Lord Rasovant looked for it for twenty years, and my mother had hidden it right under his nose."

"Erik," he said carefully, reaching out a hand. "I need those files."

A wolfish smile curled across his lips. "Do you now? And what would you give me for them?"

"I'm not here to play a game."

"The crown?" Erik asked. "Your life?"

"Erik . . ."

He tucked the holo-pad into an inside pocket of his coat and reached for the lightsword at his waist. He pulled out the long sword, blade glittering across the mirrors and gold-foiled titles of the books on the shelves. "I think I'll take the latter anyway."

"We're family—Father said family doesn't fight each oth—"

"You are no Valerio I know!" he snarled, and charged.

Robb sprang away, reaching for his own lightsword on his back—and couldn't. His mechanical fingers refused to unfist to grab the hilt. This was exactly what he had been afraid of these last six months, a moment when he would need to fight back and realize he couldn't. Not to the same caliber as before, at least. He was useless without his sword arm.

He dodged under Erik's first attack and drew his sword with his nondominant hand. A moment later he raised the blade to block—

Sparks flew between their lightswords, as bright as evening stars. He parried one way, then another, backing out of his mother's study and down the hallway again, until his back was pressed against the railing of the stairway balcony. He wasn't nearly as fast as his brother, and the sword in his nondominant hand felt sluggish in comparison. Erik lunged. Robb sidestepped and vaulted over the stairs, landing so hard it knocked the wind out of him. As his brother raced down the stairs, he managed to scramble back to his feet, a sharp pain slicing through his chest. Oh, he must've cracked a rib. That wasn't good.

Above them, a large crystalline chandelier hung, sending rays of sunlight spiraling down onto the hardwood floor, and they sparred between them, one second blinded, the next in shadows.

"Erik, can't we talk?" he wheezed, trying not to plead, but really he didn't want to fight.

"I was supposed to be Emperor! The Iron Kingdom was to be *mine!*" Erik shoved him back and slashed again—and again.

Robb blocked and sliced—he didn't want to *kill* Erik. And maybe that was the difference between them. That made him a second too slow, a fraction too late.

Because Erik most certainly wanted to kill *him*.

"I was supposed to be Mother's crowning achievement! I was supposed to bring our family greatness! And you *ruined it*!"

Seeing an opening, Erik slammed a foot into Robb's middle, and if Robb hadn't had a cracked rib before, he *definitely* did now. He stumbled back, gasping for air, trying with all his might to keep hold of his lightsword and bring it back up before—

His heel met the first step, and he went toppling backward onto the stairs. Erik knocked his lightsword out of his hand. It went skittering across the deep crimson carpet, burning holes into it as it toppled and then fell dormant.

Erik pointed the sword at his neck, so close he could feel the heat from the white blade. "You ruined *everything*, and what's more, you killed Mother. She'd still be alive if it weren't for you."

I know that.

Robb had blamed himself for so long, he didn't know what it was like to think, just for a moment, that it *hadn't* been his fault. He knew he should have died when Mellifare pulled the trigger, but it was as if his mother had been there waiting the entire time. She could have left. She could have run.

But she hadn't.

Because Valerios did not run away.

"And where were *you*?" Robb snarled. "Fleeing like the good little Ironblood you are?"

The lightsword pressed to his throat shook with Erik's rage.

He ground his teeth, unable to find an answer worthy of a Valerio, and Robb knew it the moment he saw the crease in his brows. He'd run—and no one had caught him until now.

"Toriean el agh Lothorne," Erik said, his voice barely controlled rage. "Glory in the Pursuit." Then, with a cry, he raised his blade for one last strike.

Robb was helpless. He was pinned to the stairs without any way to block, his sword too far to reach—

His brother's blade came down.

He felt his mechanical arm move, and he caught the blade in his hand. It heated his fingers and burned his glove away to reveal his metal fingers. His arm—his hand—saved him.

Something clicked then where it hadn't the last six months. He might have lost his sword arm at the palace, but he had survived.

And he was stronger now because of it.

Erik stared, wide-eyed. "You have a metal arm?"

"Unlike you, I didn't come out of the coronation unscathed," Robb replied as the gears in his arm whined, louder and louder, until his grip broke the blade in two.

He . . . hadn't realized his arm was *that* strong. Then again, he'd never thought his arm was anything more than a nuisance. He hadn't let himself accept it, but it was a part of him nonetheless, wires and all.

With Erik stunned, he slammed his foot into Erik's stomach and kicked him back. Then he pushed himself off the stairs and grabbed Erik by the collar, forcing him up against the wall. An antique Baseren painting rattled with the force. His metal arm smoked, fingers slowly dulling from a vibrant orange, leaving burn marks across Erik's collar. "Can we *stop* fighting? We're brothers, for Goddess's sake, and there're bigger things to fight about than whether you have your damn *crown*. We're all going to die, Erik, if you don't give me that file."

His brother gritted his teeth as if just the thought repulsed him. They were almost the same height now, which was strange to Robb. He had always been shorter—but now that he was at eye level with his brother, he began to wonder why he had been so afraid of him all these years. He looked like any other insufferable asshole in the world, who took and took and never thought about giving back, and Robb pitied him.

But only a little.

"Fine," he hissed between clenched teeth. "Take your stupid file."

Robb extracted the holo-pad, putting it into his own pocket, and then let go of his brother's coat with a shove. He went to retrieve his lightsword and sheathed it onto his back. "Elara," he said into his comm-link, "I'm leaving."

"You can't beat it," said Erik as he left. "Whatever that thing is—whatever the *Emperor* is. I had to watch that monster sit on *my* throne, and command *my* kingdom, and tell everyone to praise *him*—and he isn't even human!"

No, Di wasn't human.

Then Erik said, "He's a monster."

Robb slowed to a stop with his hand on the front doorknob. "He isn't."

"You've never even met him—"

"He isn't a monster," he insisted, and in the stained glass of the front door, he watched his brother come up behind him and take something out of his pocket—silver and glinting. His knuckle rings. "I fear you are."

Then he spun around and slammed his metal fist into Erik's pretty face so hard he was out before he even hit the floor. Erik was right about one thing—Robb *wasn't* a Valerio. He was someone else altogether, and it was high time he started acting like it.

"Sorry, swung too hard," he told his unconscious brother, before he tied Erik's hands and dragged him out of the house by his feet. A skysailer came up the front drive to meet him halfway.

Elara lifted her goggles. "Robb!"

He dropped his brother in the snow. "What's wrong?"

"I just got an emergency call from the *Dossier*. Siege is calling in her debts. All of them. I think something happened at the shrine."

That did not sound good.

"They want us to meet at a waystation in the ass end of nowhere— Is that your brother?" she added, giving Erik, groaning on the ground, a pointed look.

"Sadly," he replied. He knew Siege well enough to know that if she was calling in debts from her career, then things were dire indeed—and the sooner she got the information on the holo-pad, the sooner they would know what they were fighting. "Help me get this sack of shit into the skysailer. We can take my family's ship out."

She helped him heave Erik into the back of the sailer. "The *Caterina*? You sure they'll let us on?"

"One way to find out."

Erik didn't wake up until Robb and Elara *almost* had him on the *Caterina*, and then he flew into a raging spittle-infested fit about why the militia needed to listen to him. "He's a traitor!" Erik screamed. "I am the one true Valerio!"

But by a strange connection of coincidences, the same guard who Robb had paid time and again to keep his mouth shut about Robb's . . . *escapades* (the last being on Nevaeh) was now the captain of the militia, and he didn't much care for Erik.

None of them did.

"So where to, Sir Robb?" the old guard asked.

"Just Robb, please, and Elara can tell you the coordinates," he replied as two militiamen carried a struggling Erik onto the ship, and they followed the guard captain inside.

DI

Memories warred in his head.

Of Siege, the nefarious captain of the *Dossier*, and Marigold, the daughter of Duchessa Aragon. A woman with hellfire hair and a girl with a smile for trouble. He hesitated as he faced her, unsure of what to do—of what to say. The last time he saw her, he was D09 in this new, strange body, and now he was Dmitri in the same body, but with the knowledge that it had been made for him. He longed for a moment without emotions—without the bubbling fizz of anxiety and the heavy weight of guilt—and all he could do was twist his fingers and look away.

Until she took him by the face and made him look at her.

Marigold and Siege, childhood friend and starship captain.

"Captain," he greeted her carefully.

"Metalhead," she replied, and let go of his chin. Her hair simmered like a slow-burning bonfire, crackling like the question in her eyes. He rubbed the back of his neck, trying to find the right words—but how do you explain to someone who thought you've been dead for twenty years that you were alive? And had been right under her nose? The words didn't seem to want to come.

Because while she was twenty years wiser, he was still that lost teenage boy who had sold his soul to the Great Dark.

But then the captain drew her arms around him and pulled him tightly into a hug. She burrowed her face into his hair and murmured, "Welcome home."

Home.

After so long, after all those months with that cold, red song in his head. The word *home* felt too large, and he too small and too undeserving. He curled his fingers into the back of Siege's coat as the dam he had built up cracked, and all the emotions came pouring out. A sob escaped his lips, even though he could not cry. He was home, and yet he had betrayed it.

He had almost killed Ana.

But he never would again—that he would make sure of.

ANA

The *Dossier* reached Haven's Grave a few hours later. It was a graveyard of sorts, halfway between Cerces and Iliad, where derelict ships congregated through some strange cosmic magnitism, and in the center of the graveyard was a waystation only a few knew about. It was where the captain had asked for her fleetships to meet, because she had called in all of her favors. She had never so much as called in *one* before.

Not many merchants traveled through Haven's Grave, not many mercenaries camped there, and not many outlaws lived there. It simply existed as a respite, like Xourix at the edge of the asteroid belt. There were already three ships there by the time the *Dossier* docked. Two of them Ana didn't recognize, but the third she knew well—it was an Ironblood ship, the crest of the Wysteria family.

Wynn.

She hadn't seen Wynn since the coronation. She hadn't realized that the Wysterias owed Siege a debt. Then again, Ana didn't know about half of the debts Siege called to collect.

"I hope Elara is safe," said Xu as they both looked out of the starshield to the nearing waystation. They were dressed in a simple frock coat and breeches, and had shined themselves so nicely, Ana could clearly see her reflection in their face.

Jax, from the pilot's chair, eased the ship in to dock. "I haven't heard anything from her or Robb since they landed on Eros."

Xu nodded decisively. "Then there is a high percentage that she is in trouble."

"I hope not."

"Robb *is* very good at getting into trouble," Ana added, earning a glare form Jax.

"You're one to talk—"

"The three of you better stop chatting and get back to work. Darlin', are you really going to wear *that* to the meeting?" Siege added as she stepped into the cockpit, giving Ana's wardrobe a pointed look. "You haven't seen Redbeard or Cullen in years. Don't you want to look your best?"

Ana could care less about her dirty, sweat-stained clothes. "Is Di okay?"

"He's fine. He just needs a little time. I have him recalibrating the thrusters for something to do," she added, "since we no longer have EoS to do it. And I meant what I said about wondering if you're wearing *that* to the meeting."

"I . . . didn't think I'd be part of it?"

"You're the Empress of the Iron Kingdom; of course you'll be."

The Empress of the Iron Kingdom. She didn't feel much like one, and even if she freshened up she doubted she would suddenly become the hero the kingdom needed.

Jax spun around in his chair. "And the rest of us, Captain?"

"Only you two," the captain replied, nodding to Xu and Jax. "It's a small room."

If Ana remembered correctly, the room in question was *not* small. It was a meeting hall, able to hold well over fifty people. It was also one of the most secure rooms in the kingdom anywhere outside of the palace. The waystation itself operated on a self-sufficient program and didn't communicate with the rest of the kingdom. The only way to get a signal out was to do it manually, but Ana still worried that the HIVE could be listening.

She had a feeling that her captain had the same fear.

"Who else are we meeting?" she began to ask. "Any other Ironbloods? How do we know that we can trust them if—"

Her captain slid her a knowing look.

"I'm the Empress of the Iron Kingdom," Ana argued, using Siege's own words against her. "Shouldn't I know who we're going to be dealing with?"

"Aye, so you want to rule a kingdom now?" her captain asked.

Ana glanced away, the tips of her ears burning. "I didn't say that."

Siege belted a laugh. "Go change, and meet us in the waystation, darling."

Realizing she had lost that argument, she ducked out of the cockpit and took a quick shower, gently scrubbing the dust and grime from the tomb off her skin; but washing the dirt away wouldn't rid her of the memories of Mellifare raging about her lost heart. She had been terrifying. The sound of the tomb caving in still rang in her ears, and no matter how much she scrubbed or how loud she hummed a song, she couldn't seem to escape it.

Even though her captain had joked, how could Ana *think* of ruling a kingdom when she'd failed so often, and so terribly?

In the crew's quarters, she slipped into her undergarments, pulled on the only nice pair of trousers she had, and rummaged through her trunk for something at least *somewhat* formal to wear. She picked through her clothes, old shirts and worn cotton smocks, until she found a gold blouse and pulled it out and held it at arm's length.

Was it *too* wrinkled?

She heard something clatter to the ground and gave a shriek, spinning around with her blouse clutched tight to her chest.

In the doorway stood a wide-eyed Di, having dropped his holo-pad. "Sorry—I am sorry. I did not realize—you were in the middle of—your shirt is off," he finished awkwardly.

They stood stalemate for a moment.

His gaze dropped to the scar on her belly where his lightsword had pierced her through. Then he promptly grabbed his holo-pad from the ground, turned on his heel, and—

"Wait," she called.

He froze in the doorway, his back still turned to her. "You are undressed. I will *not* wait—"

"You've seen me practically naked," she deadpanned, "and I'm wearing underclothes."

His shoulders stiffened. He didn't have an answer for that.

"Di . . ."

"Your wound healed nicely," he said, and closed the door as he left.

Her fingers came to rest on the rippled scar tissue just beside her navel. Then she fisted her hand and darted across the quarters and slammed open the door. "Because of you!"

He was almost to the stairs when he turned around and quickly winced, closing his eyes. "Clothes, *please.*"

She marched up to him. He was a little taller than she remembered, a little more angular. For six months she had seen him on the newsfeeds, a golden god of the kingdom. He had seemed so much larger than life—and it struck her suddenly how very small he really was, someone she knew she would tear apart a galaxy to save. When she didn't move, he slowly peeked open one eye, then the other. The black lenses of his pupils, ringed in moonlight white, slowly dilated, refocusing on her, and then her nose, and then her lips—and something in her chest kicked.

Something massive, and monumental, and terrifying, in the way gas giants and twin suns were terrifying. Awe-striking.

Then he turned abruptly on his heel and marched down the stairs.

With a growl she shoved her head into her golden blouse and followed. "Why do you keep running away?"

At the bottom of the steps, he paused. "I almost killed you. Is that not a good enough reason?"

She scoffed. "Almost only counts in horseshoes and hand grenades."

"You're so childish!" he said bitingly in reply, and left for the other end of the hull.

She gritted her teeth, anger vibrating through her, and grabbed for the nearest thing she could—the carcass of EoS on the workbench—and threw it at him as hard as she could. It clipped the side of his head, and he whirled around. EoS clattered to the floor. He looked down to it, then to her. "Did you just throw the can opener at me?"

"Childish enough for you," she snarked.

A dangerous glint sparked in his coal eyes. "Do not test me, Ana."

"You're so *infuriating*!" She grabbed a wrench and hurled it at him. He dodged. She picked up an omnitool and chucked that, too, and now he was walking back to her with that same patience he had used in the tomb. But she was not scared this time.

She was *furious.*

"Stop throwing things!" he cried.

"Do you honestly think"—she threw a screwdriver; he dodged—"that I'd blame you? When it was *my fault*?"

She had almost run out of things to throw, but there was a soldering iron on the hood of the skysailer, and she turned to grab for that. But when she went to throw it, Di was closer than she'd realized. He caught her wrist.

"It is not your fault," he replied, his hands tightening around her wrist. "It was mine. From the very beginning."

"That doesn't make any sense."

"My name is Dmitri *Rasovant*."

Her rebuttal caught in her throat.

The son of the man who'd murdered her family and tried to kill her. His grip on her wrist loosened.

"But my friends called me Di," he added quietly.

Di—like the graffiti on the wall of the ruins.

The name she called him, too.

She studied his face, searching for any sign that this was a joke—a lie. Something that told her that she could laugh this off, because he couldn't be . . .

But his lips were pressed into a thin, wobbling line. "When I was dying of the Plague, Mellifare came to me promising that she would make me well again. I just had to introduce her to my father. So you see, Ana, I sold the fate of this kingdom to her for my useless life—"

"It's not useless."

His shoulders slumped, and he looked away again. His mouth worked, trying to find the right words to tell her that yes, he was useless, that she should have left him, that he was dead and unworthy, but in truth he was just stubborn and noble, and she hated that so much about him. She hated it because that was what she loved the most, no matter who he was.

Dmitri, D09—

Di.

"So you see," he said quietly, stepping away from her, "all of this is because of me. If it were not for me, you would still have your family. The kingdom would not be on the verge of ruin. The Great Dark would be nothing."

She caught the front of his shirt before he could walk away. "Your father could have said no—my father could have stopped him. And who's to say Mellifare wouldn't have tricked someone else? Someone I met said this was the only future, where we defeated the Great Dark. So I'm glad you're here, Dmitri."

He leaned forward and pressed a kiss to her forehead. His lips were cold, but soft.

"Thank you," he whispered, and departed the ship for the waystation.

·) ● (·

Once she dried her eyes and straightened her blouse, she set off into the waystation. It was cold, and the air tasted stale—like it had on the *Tsarina*. Not many people traversed this area of the kingdom. It was in no-man's-land. She wondered who kept up the place. It definitely didn't look *homey*, and she doubted they received many provisions in the ass end of space. The station was well kept, though, with barely a drift of dust. Where there would be a market for trading, the stalls sat empty, curtains closed over most of the cubicles. There was a bar with a neon light flickering at the entrance, and a few crew members from Siege's fleetships sat around drinking something that smelled stronger than bourbon. Just like the *Dossier*, Siege's other ships collected the lost and the forgotten—Cercians, Solani, Erosians, and once-Ironbloods and a few Metals. The last time the fleetships had all come together, it had been to mourn the passing of the *Prospero*'s late captain. She wished there was a more joyous occasion to call everyone together, but it seemed like even the end of the world wasn't stopping them from drinking.

"Lookin' for something, lass?" a gruff, ginger-bearded man called. He had kind eyes and a wide smile, and Ana recognized him instantly—the captain of the *Illumine*. And the ex-con pickpocket who'd tried to steal from Siege.

"Redbeard!" Ana cried, and ran to the burly man.

With a laugh he scooped her up in his thick arms and swung her around. "It's so good to see you, lass! Heard you've been getting into trouble." He set her down again. He smelled like motor oil and leather, and he looked like he hadn't aged a day.

"None at all," she replied with a smile. "I heard you'd been tussling with the dreadnought out near Cerces."

"Ha! Tryin' to. It's almost impenetrable!"

"Almost," she reminded him, tapping the side of her nose, and his compatriots howled with laughter.

Redbeard leaned to one of his crewmembers, a fresh-faced young woman with dark blue hair, and said, "This's Captain Siege's daughter. Finest troublemaker in the kingdom."

"I expect nothing less from her," added a familiar voice near the back of the bar. Ana spun around to the owner of the voice, a tall androgynous person with long black hair that reached well below their waist, and warm brown skin, decked in gold jewelry and a coat the color of a nebula. They grinned at her, and the neon implants in their cheeks glowed a brilliant teal.

"Cullen!" she greeted. "Your hair's longer!"

"So is yours," they replied. "What's Siege's girl doing in a bar like this?"

Siege's girl.

Even though Ana remembered her parents now, and the rest of her family, the thought of being Siege's daughter still swelled her heart. It was a moniker she had always wanted to be worthy of.

She still sometimes felt like she wasn't.

"Looking for the meeting room, actually. I'm a little lost," she admitted.

Redbeard pointed out of the bar and gave her the directions. "I'll be along in a jiff and leave this crew to drink without me, aye?"

"Aye!" his crew agreed.

Ana laughed. "Don't have too much fun, now. I remember what happened last time you were all together—don't burn the bar the down this time," she added, waving good-bye, and followed the directions he gave her. Down the hallway to the fork at the end, and then left—

And found Viera instead.

She gave a start. "*Oh!* You scared me!" She put her hand over her heart and gave a wry laugh. "You lost, too?"

Viera gave her a brief look and nodded. She had combed her hair back against her head, but even in the dim waystation light it shone like plantium. She had borrowed some of Lenda's clothes—a dark shirt that was a little too big for her and trousers cinched in at the waist. She had a gunsling strapped to her hip, and she tapped her finger on the grip of her pistol apprehensively.

"This place reminds me of the dreadnought," she said after a moment. "I do not like it. We could be ambushed from anywhere. Why am I not invited to this meeting?"

"It's just for Siege's trusted—"

"Am I not trustworthy?"

"No, you are! It's just . . ."

Viera studied her for a moment before she said, "Siege is wary, because the heart was not in the tomb, and we have a traitor in our midst."

Ana pursed her lips. "Di's not a traitor—"

"I do not mean him," the ex–guard captain replied, and gave Ana a meaningful look. "Someone must have told the HIVE where you were, or else how would the Emperor have known?"

She opened her mouth to reply and then closed it again as the realization slowly curled down the back of her spine. There was no way the Emperor or Mellifare would have known where she had gone, unless they had intercepted her somewhere between Zenteli and Calavan, but she had gone under forged travel papers and never slipped her hood. "Maybe . . . I hadn't been careful enough, and a Messier saw me at a port and they followed me."

"Or," Viera replied, and leaned in close to Ana, so close her skin prickled, "perhaps you do not know your crew as well as you should."

Then she retreated back down the hall, toward the *Dossier*. Ana stood there for a long moment, reeling in the possibility Viera had presented. No, Ana *knew* the crew. They wouldn't rat on her—not even Elara or Xu. They were good people. Everyone on the *Dossier* was. But she couldn't deny the thought that someone had sold her out.

Redbeard and Cullen passed her on their way to the meeting, and Redbeard tipped his invisible hat to her. She nodded absently, trying to compose herself.

Who could have told Mellifare?

There was another clip of boots.

"Oh, no, I know that look," said Jax.

She glanced over her shoulder. He had freshened up as well, dressed in an embroidered lavender coat. His hair was braided down his shoulder, secured with golden toggles that glimmered in the flickering halogens. His kohl eyeliner was fresh, and his smile set her nerves at ease. "You look handsome, as always."

"I do enjoy cleaning up for a good party," he replied, and offered his arm. "Shall we, Your Grace?"

She took it. "Aye, *nan c'zar.* This is giving me flashbacks to the Iron Council all over again. What if I say something wrong? What if I mess up? I wasn't good at this the first time around."

"Except this time, you aren't alone."

Relieved, she squeezed his arm. "No, I'm not."

Together, the Empress of the Iron Kingdom and the C'zar of the Solani stepped into the meeting room.

A long oval table sat in the center of the room. Ana and Jax took one head of it, while Siege and Talle sat at the other. There were maybe half a dozen people gathered at the table, and her heart sank by the moment. Had so few answered Siege's call? Wynn sat beside Mokuba and Redbeard and Xu. There was the captain of the *Prospero,* Cullen, and the mercenary leader of the Red Dawn.

The only person she did not see was Di.

Pitchers of ale were passed around, and when everyone's cups were filled Siege threw a document into the holographic window in the middle of the table. "All right, Lenda, thank you," she said, and Lenda closed the doors behind her.

She's standing guard outside, Ana realized with a bolt of surprise.

Viera was right—and Siege knew it. There was a spy on the *Dossier.* But why hadn't Siege mentioned it? And why wasn't Di here?

"What I am about to say can't—and *will not*—leave this room," Siege began. "Are we clear?"

The sparse room murmured.

"And everyone else, are you on a secure line?" she asked, raising her head.

Everyone else?

She glanced around to make sure she hadn't missed anyone—and then, to her surpise, faces burst up on the walls. The mercenary bandit Cavorn; Machivalle—who she honestly thought was dead; Jax's mother, along with the rest of the Elder Council; and countless other faces she half remembered from the years spent with Siege, and some she didn't know at all. They were mercenaries and smugglers and info brokers, starship captains and shopkeepers and waystation officers and Ironbloods from myriad points in the kingdom, and for a dumbstruck moment she wondered how Siege had gathered them all.

Siege's girl, Redbeard's crew called her. She had lived with her captain for seven years, but she'd never really understood what that meant until now. There were dozens of the most powerful people in the kingdom.

When all the people videoing in nodded in agreement, Siege leaned forward on the table, her hair shifting from a prickly orange to yellow, and she told them everything—about how the HIVE was the Great Dark, like in the prophecy, and how it was now looking for its heart. She told them what had transpired with Ana in the palace, and what they had learned in the Solani ark, about how Rasovant had created Metals, and how the Great Dark stole the light from Metals to fuel itself, and how it was growing stronger.

"If we don't stop it soon, then it will be too powerful to stop, and once it has its heart, it will kill us all," she finished. "We need to get the heart first, and we need to stop the Great Dark."

For a tense moment, no one said anything, until Mokuba shifted in his chair and finally leaned forward. "So you're saying, Siege, that we need to defeat what amounts to a god."

"Sounds like a job for the Goddess," someone said through the video feed—one of the Ironbloods.

Ana fisted her hands under the table, because she wasn't the Goddess. Under the table, Jax put his hand over hers comfortingly.

"The fate of the kingdom should not fall on one person," said another voice from the doorway, "but on all of us."

Oh.

Everyone in the room turned toward the Metal Emperor as he stepped into the room.

DI

They did not want him here.

Wynn Wysteria saw him first, and jumped to her feet as though she had seen a ghost—or perhaps worse. Probably worse. They had been in the palace together just a few days ago. He had seen her down a hallway, mourning dress and curls of hair retreating, having eavesdropped during his argument with Erik Valerio.

She had seen his eyes turn red, the lanterns above his head swirl.

"You," she hissed, and jabbed a finger at him. "What is *he* doing here?"

Her voice was so sharp, he winced.

Her shock rippled across the table as the other guests lurched away from him, as if he himself was the Plague.

The captain made a calming motion with her hands. Her hair was the color of agitated coals. "Let him speak—"

"Speak?" the captain of the *Prospero*, Cullen, snarled. "What would the Iron Kingdom's heartless *Emperor* know?"

"He ordered the assimilation of Metals," Mokuba added. "He

ordered my friends who protected them to be killed—butchered like animals!"

He did.

He remembered every word of those orders, because his memory was as perfect as his deeds were dark. There was nothing he could say to change them. He wanted to explain and tell them the truth. That he had been HIVE'd. That he could not control what he said or did. It had still been he who did those terrible things.

He made himself stand there, and he listened, trying to hold on to the words Jax had given him in the medical ward. That he was good.

He wished he was good.

He wondered, quietly, if he ever would be again.

"He ordered his Messiers to open fire on my ships!" one of the video callers added.

He had.

"He dragged my crew away to the dreadnought! I haven't seen them since."

No, because they were Metals now.

Mokuba added, "I spent the better half of six months in a constant state of panic trying to hide our sanctuaries!"

And oh, he'd been so close to finding them and HIVE'ing all those Metals.

"So why," said Wynn coldly, "is this *monster* here?"

Monster.

He stiffened his shoulders against the word, clenched his fists to bear it.

And still he stayed silent.

"And what of—"

"QUIET!" Ana slammed her fists down on the table, spilling her drink. The room plunged into silence. The ale slowly spread across the table. She glared at the people at the table. "The HIVE did that—*Mellifare* did that. Not Di."

Then she turned her golden gaze to him. He had forgotten what that was like, the trust in her eyes.

"He's here to help us," she went on, "and Goddess knows we need it. *I* need it." Then she sat down. The table was quiet, even if the people in the videos murmured to themselves. It was quite clear that no one agreed with Ana.

Why should they?

He had done so many terrible things—

Mokuba's eyebrows furrowed. ". . . Did you just call him *Di*?"

The name of Ana's Metal. Everyone in the room knew D09. They thought they knew what he looked like—Metal, like Xu. He had memories of almost everyone at this table. Redbeard, who gave him oil one year to grease his joints. Cullen, who gave him the sage coat he loved so much. Mokuba, who he knew from the incident at the Iron Shrine, and the leader of the Red Dawn, and almost every face across the walls. He knew them, their names, their debts to Siege, and the ones who simply came to help.

They did not know him—but they should.

"Yes," he replied for Ana, and turned to Mokuba. He felt the color of his eyes change, like shrugging off a coat, to something much lighter. Coal dark to moonlight white. "I am."

The guests who were not standing jerked to their feet in

shock. Murmurs of "D09" passed across the video feeds, and across the lips of the people at the table, wondering how he looked so human. A few wondered whether he was a monster.

He was.

That was not up for debate.

"Di . . . ," Wynn murmured, and then her eyes widened. "Oh! Ana—*that* Di? The one you . . ." Her voice trailed off, and Ana nodded sheepishly.

Di was not sure whether he wanted Wynn to finish that sentence. The one Ana what? Whatever it meant, Wynn's demeanor toward him softened instantly, and she pressed a white-gloved hand against her mouth in surprise.

He bowed low to all of them. "I am sorry that I hurt you."

"Siege had said you were HIVE'd." It was Redbeard who spoke. He had not taken his eyes off Di. "But I hadn't thought that meant you were . . . I'm sorry."

Surprised, Di looked back up to him. "For what?"

"For what happened," filled in Xu, and turned their white gaze to him. "For what we went through."

He had avoided the Metal, partly because he was afraid he would miss being like them—unable to feel shame or guilt—but when he finally looked at Xu, he found that the same memories he had while in the HIVE reflected on their face. They were more alike than not, both having done terrible things, and unable ever to rectify them. They had to live with it—no, not live.

Exist.

That was a better word for it.

He was neither Metal nor human anymore. He existed some-where in between.

"So we're just going to believe him?" one of the Elder Court scoffed.

Siege pressed something on a small control panel on her end of the table and cut their video feed. "Di, let's get to it."

"Yes, Captain." He threw his hand out toward the center of the table, hijacking the holo-screen. He summoned up a grid of the HIVE as he last remembered it, its tethers spread across the kingdom like kite strings. The map was almost entirely red. It reminded him of the synapses of a human brain, the way it lit up and traveled information.

"This is the HIVE. As of last count, there were twenty-seven thousand, five hundred and two Metals inside. The Great Dark created it to harness people's life force. That is how it survives. It is fueled by the light in people, and with it the Great Dark will be able to take life directly. No need for Metals or the HIVE, and everyone inside will die. Conversely"—he dropped the hologram and looked out to the table—"if we kill the Great Dark—Mellifare—then we will also murder all twenty-seven thousand, five hundred and two people who have been assimi-lated into the HIVE."

"Then we can do nothing." It was the first time Jax's mother, Avena Taizu, had spoken, her face relaying nothing but cold emotion on her video screen. *"If the* D'thverek *wins, we lose the Metals in the HIVE, but if we win, we still lose the Metals."*

"Then let's find some way to save the Metals *and* defeat the Great Dark," said Cullen as they reclined back in their chair, propping their polished boots up on the table. "I mean, if Rasovant found a way to put a soul in a robot, then there's gotta be a way for us to get a dark goddess out of a supercomputer."

Mokuba barked a laugh. "Yeah, like we got *that* technology." But then he tilted his head. "But I can put my ear to the ground to see if any of my contacts know anything about the heart."

"And in the meantime, Zenteli can harbor the rogue Metals left—the sanctuaries can't be safe for much longer," Avena Taizu added, and the Elder Court grumbled in agreement. *"We aren't under any kingdom jurisdiction, so any attacks the Messiers might make will be in direct violation of our treaties."*

Jax gave his mother a wary look. "Are you sure?"

"Solani do not cower" was his mother's reply, to which Jax held his hands up in surrender.

Cullen and Redbeard, their heads bent together, nodded in agreement before Redbeard said, "We'll keep flying interferrence for those eyesore dreadnoughts. Give you some time to find the heart."

"I can outfit weapons for anyone who needs them," a shop owner added.

"I can lend a few ships."

"Some men," the Red Dawn leader added, nodding seriously toward Talle.

Not a single one of them again brought up Di or any grudges against him. Voices chimed in from across the video feeds, offering food and shelter and warm beds and help. They were the voices of a resistance. He glanced to the head of the table, where Siege sat quietly, a hand propping her head up, her fingers masking the edges of a grin curling across her lips. Her hair flickered blue at the scalp, trailing to bright golden ends. As if she had expected no less. Her eyes lifted to his, and then to the door at the far end of the meeting space.

The doors kicked open.

"These are all very fine ideas—*or*," drawled a distinctly Erosian voice above the idle chatter, "we could just go get the heart."

Di knew that voice, but Jax was the first to turn to their uninvited guest.

ROBB

The hardest part of walking into this meeting wasn't kidnapping his brother and hauling him to the ass end of nowhere, or seeing all the debts Siege had called in and realizing that this was either the beginning of the end or the beginning of something new. No, the hardest part was was facing Jax. Well, that and getting past Lenda, who stood quite helpless in the doorway behind him.

"I tried," Lenda told Siege, who waved her hand, and Lenda closed the doors behind him again.

He didn't know whether he could—*should*—look at Jax. He didn't know the correct protocol. Should he bow? Curtsy? All he seemed to be doing was standing there after his bravado had faded, at a loss for what to say.

If anything *was* right enough to say.

Jax looked so achingly elegant, while he had flounced in here in a dirty travel cloak that still smelled like sweat and snow, his hair in wild curls. He opened his mouth to say something—*anything*—

"Hello, friends," his brother greeted them instead in his smooth, oily drawl. He tried to shift away from Robb, but he held firm to the cords. "I see you started the party without us."

Jax pushed himself to his feet, his violet-eyed gaze looking from Robb to his brother and back again. Erik really did look the worse for wear. The black eye Robb had given him was purple and swollen, and his black evening coat was crumpled and disheveled, ascot untied.

But instead of asking about the state of Erik Valerio, Jax asked, "How do you know where the heart is?"

No *Nice to see you.* No *I'm glad you're okay.*

Not that Robb had really expected that, but there was a small part of him that was still disappointed. Did Jax even look like he missed him? Robb couldn't tell.

He took the antique holo-pad from an inner pocket of his coat and slid it down the table to the other end. Siege caught it and turned it on. "Because," he said, "my mother found it almost seven years ago. The night of the fire, when the royal family and my father found out the origins of the Metals, they must have also found out about the heart. Mellifare killed them for it. But my father must have sent her a communication after he stole away on the *Tsarina*. She found the heart, and she hid it—from everyone. Including Lord Rasovant and Mellifare."

"Well, well, Cynthia," Siege murmured, her hair dimming to a burnt coal. She skimmed through the files and handed them off to Talle. "Surprising us even now."

Talle's eyes widened at the coordinates of the heart. "Sunshine, this is . . ."

"Astoria," Robb filled in for her. "My family's floating estate in Nevaeh."

A murmur swept across the table.

"Well, great, we can just steal the heart and launch it into the sun and *boom,* we're done here," said Cullen, pushing back their chair to leave. "I expect you have it from here—"

"No can do, Snarky. The HIVE will know where we're going, and I'm sure the old clunker'll figure it out." A screen popped up in the middle of the table, and Elara's face materialized. She looked like she was sitting, very comfortably, in Jax's pilot chair. His eyebrow twitched. *"Sorry, I didn't really want to make a grand entrance into your little meeting, and I really* had *to take off my pants. I can cloak us into Nevaeh, but I can't disable all the security cams on the garden and the space station."*

Mumbling darkly, Cullen sat back down.

Mokuba asked, "Then how'll we get in?"

"Well," Robb began, but Erik beat him to it, which rather irritated him.

"I've got a party tomorrow night in the garden, as luck would have it. Every Ironblood is invited to commemorate the occasion. The Emperor is supposed to be there. Though I didn't expect him to be *here,* too," he added. "Pleasant seeing you, Your Excellence."

The room turned to Di expectantly, and he shrugged helplessly. "Do not look at me—I hated him HIVE'd, too."

"Yeah, and good luck getting into my party. My guards are no fools and—"

"And if you don't help us," Siege interrupted, her voice level and bored, "then I'll personally break every bone in your right hand, and then your left. And then if you still won't, I will personally break all one hundred and fifty-one—"

"Fifty-two," Talle politely corrected.

"—Fifty-*two* bones in your body," she finished.

"It will be a pleasure to have you at the party," Erik replied nervously.

Robb resisted the urge to smirk. It wasn't every day he got to watch his brother sweat. "So. I've got a plan. We sneak in during the party, get the heart where my mother hid it, and leave before Mellifare ever finds out. It's a long shot, but luckily we excel at those."

The room was quiet for a moment, and he hoped it was because he had wowed everyone there, but the longer the silence stretched, the more he began to think he simply wasn't welcome with this harebrained idea and—

Di rubbed his bottom lip in thought and then conceded, "There is a seventy-four-point-seven-eight percent chance that might actually work."

"That's a bit low," Wynn remarked.

"It's pretty high considering," said Ana.

The captain was nodding, too. "It might just work—do we have the resources?"

"Over two hundred Valerio militiamen," Robb volunteered, "and if Wynn pledges her guards, there will be close to three hundred."

"Not to mention the fleetships," said Talle, "and the others who've pledged themselves—I think it's a start."

Siege nodded. "Then a start's all we need."

They would still need to solidify the plan, and place people on the ground in Nevaeh in case things went south, and fortify the sanctuary there, and a myriad of other things, but for the moment it felt like this could actually work. That perhaps they could win where no one had before.

Goddess bright, Robb prayed, *I hope we get out of this alive.*

From across the table, the captain turned her warm gaze to him, and she looked proud in every way his mother never had. She raised her glass to him and mouthed, "You did good."

And for the first time in what felt like years, he smiled.

ANA

After the meeting adjourned and the room emptied, Ana stared down at her spilled ale and her reflection in it, the murky amber distorting her face in ripples. She didn't look much like a hero—or the Goddess.

She didn't look much like an Empress, either.

Robb had asked her, the captain, Talle, Di, and Jax to stay. Xu left to start building codes with Elara to disable Nevaeh's securities to get the *Dossier* into the harbor unnoticed. Not only because of the HIVE, but also the *Dossier* had quite a few docking tickets unpaid, and Siege really didn't want to deal with that. Robb showed them the Resonance files and the map to where his mother had hidden the heart. It wasn't on Astoria, and that confused her for a moment.

"Didn't you say it was—" she began to ask, but her captain put a finger to her own lips, and suddenly she understood. Even in a safe meeting room like this one, Siege didn't trust the Great Dark not to be listening in.

After they made a few quiet plans, they quickly dispersed so as not to draw attention. Ana put down her drink and began to leave when the captain drew her out of her thoughts. "Darling, can I speak with you?" Siege leaned against the table beside her. They were the last two in the meeting room, and the doors were closed. The captain spoke quietly. "When you left for the Goddess's tomb, who did you tell?"

Ana shook her head. "I didn't tell anyone! No, wait, that's not true," she added, frustrated. "Robb and Elara knew, and maybe Jax? I told Viera and Lenda I was going to Eros, but not *where*. So the crew knew, mostly, but no one else."

"And no one saw you on the trip? No one recognzied you?"

"I mean, someone could have. But they wouldn't have known where I was going."

The captain gave a long sigh. "That's what I feared."

"Is that why you didn't allow the rest of the crew into the meeting? Because we have a spy?"

"It is," the captain admitted. "I wish you'd never gone to the ruins."

"I thought I could destroy the heart before the Great Dark ever got to it." Ana looked away and chewed on the inside of her cheek. The ruins still haunted her. She had been helpless. If Robb's mother hadn't stolen the heart before she'd gotten there, the Great Dark would have it now, and if Siege hadn't come to rescue her when she had, Ana was sure she'd be dead in a caved-in tomb. "I was stupid to think I could do it alone—or at all. I mean, I'm not the Goddess. I can't defeat the Great Dark."

Her captain cast a bemused smile. "Oh?"

"Koren Vey said I wasn't, when we went to the ark. She said,

'*You are not the Goddess*'—just like that, straight faced, soul crushing." She sighed and sank down in her chair. "I'm no one, Captain. I'm just an orphan."

The sunny yellow tips of Siege's hair bled up the rest until it was completely golden, shining like the sun. "You are Ana of the *Dossier*. You are my daughter," she replied, kissing Ana's forehead, "and wherever you go, you carry me with you—you carry all of us with you. Always."

But what happens if you die? she wanted to argue, through she didn't want to imagine that kind of universe.

She couldn't.

"Try to get some rest before tomorrow," her captain said. "It's going to be . . ."

"I know," Ana replied quietly.

A wrinkle crinkled between Siege's brows, as if she wanted to say something more. Something comforting, perhaps, something to soothe the rising fear in Ana's bones, but that had never been the captain's way, really. Her comm-link flickered, a private message only she heard, and she sighed. "Get some rest," she repeated, pushing herself off the table, and left.

Ana sat there for a moment longer, her hands curled into fists in her lap.

Ana of the Dossier. The captain's daughter. Siege's girl.

It was a mantle she felt too cowardly to be worthy of. Siege was brave and steadfast, and here she was afraid that tomorrow would be her last, and she didn't want to die. She didn't want anyone to—

Stop it.

A cleaning bot opened the door and gave a timid bleep.

"All right, all right, I'm leaving," she told it.

She needed some quiet, but the only quiet place she could think of was the medical ward. She always felt most at home there. It might've been from when she was young and recovering in the ward—it was safe and familiar. Or it might've been because whenever she was in there, she could remember Di the best. The hum of his circuits and the sweet sound of his motion.

But when she arrived down in the ward, Di was sitting on the gurney. He looked up as she entered and hopped to his feet in surprise. "Ana."

"Sorry, I'll leave you—"

"I think this is yours." He offered out something he had been turning around in his fingers. The Valerio crest—the one she once wore around her neck and had given to him so long ago. Hesitantly, she took it, running her finger along the melted circle like she used to. He started to leave, and the room began to feel cold and lonely and too immaculate and quiet—

"Wait."

He paused, a hand on the doorway. A finger tapped on the frame, as if deciding whether to stay, but then he turned around. She hopped up onto the gurney and patted the indent from where he had been sitting before. He returned and scooted up beside her. The gurney was high enough so their feet dangled off the ground, and she swung hers, because she couldn't sit still. It was strange—she could still feel heat coming off him as if he was alive, and it made goose bumps shiver over her skin. She rubbed her forearms to get the chill out. It was all she could do not to lean against him, probably closer than he would like. He seemed to keep her at a strange distance, afraid to touch her, to look at her too long, and she was suddenly reminded how different he was from the D09 she knew.

She wanted to ask what parts were *Dmitri* and what parts were *Di*. She wanted to know if he was split in two, or in threes, or if, with his memories returned, he was just a jumble of forgotten moments stitched together.

Had he ever loved her—had those kisses in the palace been Dmitri, or Di, or D09?

And how did he feel now?

She didn't know why it felt so monumental. There was the looming threat of the Great Dark, encompassing every corner of the future, and yet here she was, fixated on the inches between her hand and his, trying to figure out what rested in the distance between.

"You know," she began, "I realize that I never apologized."

He bristled. "Ana, please do not blame yourself. It was not your fault. It was mine and—"

"For running you over with a skysailer," she interjected.

His words caught in his throat, and he put a hand over his face to mask the embarrassment. But there was a grin spreading across his lips, and Goddess, a smile looked so much better on him than the dour frown he wore. "No," he chuckled, "you never did."

"Then let me make this my formal apology," she said with great bravado, and crossed herself for the Moon Goddess. "You were, of course, right. I can't drive. I humbly apologize for running you over."

"No, no—you ran over and then *backed over* me, if I recall correctly."

She found herself smiling, too. "Yeah, I just apologize for the running, not the backing."

He pressed a hand over his heart, feigning shock. "You wound me!"

"Now *that's* a leap. I only dented you."

They laughed, and for a moment the space between them wasn't so far. She had never laughed with him before. It was only ever her laughing, and telling him it was funny. And then when she had met him in this body, with emotions, it was in a time when neither of them could afford to laugh. And that felt strange, because for the first time she realized that however much of a stranger he now was, *Goddess*, did she love this new Di's laugh.

But then their laughter died, and that strange silence sank between them again, taking up space for being neither friends nor—nor anything more.

She shifted, spinning the crest between her fingers. "I'm kind of afraid of this plan."

"Me too. There are too many variables. There is at least a ninety-three-point-four-eight percent chance this will end badly for at least one of us."

Perhaps it will be me, she thought, because she had escaped death too many times.

"What's the percentage we'll all make it out alive?" she asked, and he pursed his lips.

"I would rather not—"

"Di."

"Two-point-three-seven."

"Oh." She blinked in surprise. "That is much higher than I thought it'd be!"

"Really? It is much lower than I would like."

She knocked her shoulder against his playfully. "It always was."

They sat in silence for a moment, and in their closeness she could hear the hum of his parts, and they sounded as soft as a sigh.

"Is it weird?" she finally asked.

"Is what weird?"

"Being able to compute things in your head knowing—and I guess remembering now, right?—that you used to not be able to?"

He gave a shrug. "I cannot say one way or the other. What *is* strange to me, though, is not being able to use contractions. *That* is weird."

"Really? Can't you overload a code or something?"

"Overload a co— Ana, please never try to program. Literally *anything*."

"Ha! Fine, fine. Fixing you didn't really work out the first time, anyway. We were shot at, lied to, left on a derelict ship with puppet Metals. . . ."

Di folded his arms over his chest. He had taken off his coat, and it hung on a hook beside the door. His silken shirt was dirty, still smelling of the ancient tomb, and he'd rolled his sleeves up to his elbows. His arms were muscular and well defined, rather like Robb's, and he'd undone the top button of his shirt, his tattered ascot lying under his collar, to reveal a sliver of pale chest. He caught her staring and glanced down at himself. "Is something the matter?"

"This might sound weird," she started, and poked him in the arm, and it *felt* solid, "but do you have muscles?"

He pursed his lips together hard, as if trying not to—

"Don't laugh! It was a genuine question!" she cried.

"I am sure it was." He hopped down from the gurney. "I believe I am going to take a shower and find some clothes."

"How about a belly button?" she called after him. "Or—I don't know—nipples? Do you have—"

"I am leaving, Ana," he called over his shoulder.

"Wait!"

He paused in the doorway again, his arms folded over his chest, and turned back around to her. The edges of his lips twitched up, as if he was fighting off a smile. "Yes?"

She let out a long breath, trying to memorize the way he looked in the doorway, his hair catching the fluorescent light in oranges and reds, and said, "I've missed you."

She didn't care if he felt the same, because in the end it didn't matter. He had his entire life ahead of him, and she had hers, and for the moment they were in the same room together.

"I have missed you, too," he replied, and left the medical ward.

And her heart leaped and thrummed in something akin to happiness.

ROBB

As he made his way down the hallway of the *Dossier* to the way-station again, and then back to the *Caterina*, he rubbed at his mechancial arm. It twitched sporadically. It hadn't been still since the meeting, and he *knew* it was his nerves, and he hated that. He thought he had left a can of oil in the crew's quarters, but either Xu must have used it or someone else had; really, though, he was looking for Jax, and he was nowhere on the *Dossier*. He needed to get back to his brother, because Goddess knows what he was cooking up while unsupervised. Perhaps a coup to overthrow Ana once this was all over. Perhaps a way to murder him in his sleep—there was no telling.

Ducking out of the crew's quarters, he started for the hull again. Maybe there was a can of oil at the weapons module, or in one of the junk boxes in the engine room—

"Robb?"

He turned at the call of his name. Coming out of the bathroom was Di, his hair freshly washed, in dark trousers and a towel hung around his neck. And here he'd thought he would have the priviledge of never seeing Di half naked ever again. The first time on the *Tsarina* was enough, honestly.

"Di," he greeted him, clearing his throat. A sore, uncomfortable feeling crept into his mechanical arm, but he rubbed at the ropy tissue where his skin met metal. His fourth finger began to twitch, and he couldn't stop it.

Di motioned to Robb's arm. "May I see it?"

He hesitated. *You did this to me*, he wanted to say, and just *looking* at Di made his phantom wrist burn in pain—he remembered how unbearable it had been, the sharp white-lightning agony that whispered up his arm until—

"I do not want you going to Nevaeh with it malfunctioning," Di added. "Besides, I know a thing or two about mechanical arms." For emphasis, he held up his hands and wiggled his fingers, showing that he had metal fingers and metal arms and . . . well, metal *everything*.

". . . Okay," he conceded.

Di took ahold of Robb's arm gently with both hands, one at the wrist and the other his elbow. He rotated his wrist and moved his elbow up and down slowly to assess the arm. "For what it is worth," Di said slowly, "I am sorry. For what I did to you."

Somehow, that felt like the wrong thing for Di to say. Robb thought it was what he wanted to hear, but when Di said it . . .

"It wasn't your— *Fuuuuck!*" As Di's fingers lit up with electrical sparks, his knees almost gave out from the pain. He felt Di sink into the circuits of his arm, command his hand, telling his fingers to flex and clench. The pressure building in his arm died with a *pop* of relief, and Di extracted himself again.

"It should not act up anymore. There was a malalignment in the central nerve connecting to your . . . Oh, never mind. Is it better?"

Hesitantly, Robb flexed his fingers and rotated his wrist. His eyebrows furrowed.

Di read his expression. "Is it . . . *not* better?"

"It feels like my hand," he replied, surprising himself. Like, *just* like his hand. No more glitching, no more weird twitches, no more half-second lag.

"You will still have to check your strength, but—"

Robb reared back and slammed his fist into Di's face. The Metal stumbled back a few paces and hit the ground. "There. *Now* I feel better."

The android lay still on the ground. "I am . . . glad," he replied, not sounding all that convinced.

Robb rotated his shoulder back, flexed his fingers again, and then offered his metal hand. Di hesitated for a moment, but then he took it and let himself be pulled up into a hug. "It wasn't your fault, Di. I'm glad you have my back."

"And you mine," Di replied, and grabbed his towel from the floor. Then he said, "I believe Jax is staying on the waystation tonight. He wanted a room apart."

"Oh—oh, thank you."

The Metal gave a one-shoulder shrug. "I just thought you would want to know, if you need him." Then he squeezed around Robb and into the crew's quarters.

JAX

The waystation was very much deserted, and thank the Goddess for that. Siege's fleetships were already en route to Nevaeh to begin the plan, and his mother's ship was readying to leave as well. While the Solani could not infiltrate Nevaeh without raising suspicions, they were to wait a few klicks away with as many aid ships as possible in case things went south. In case Mellifare appeared. In case she got to her heart.

His mother's ships were the contingency plan—if there ever was one.

One of the waystation's robotic attendants led him to a hostel room that had been vacant for Goddess knows how long, but it was quiet and clean, and honestly that was all he cared about. He shrugged out of his evening coat, tossing it onto the modest single bed, and he sat on the edge, closed his eyes, and could finally hear himself *think*.

The light whispered underneath his skin, giving him glimpses of moments just past, and he couldn't tune it out.

And Robb had returned.

He pulled his fingers through his braid to unravel it when there was a knock on the door.

"Come in," he called, not thinking.

The door slid open, but he didn't hear any footsteps come inside. A cold chill crept down his spine. He was unprotected in a waystation. Open, vulnerable. The reality of it came crashing down. He glanced over his shoulder—

The light whispered, *Ma'alor*.

Robb.

Jax quickly stood. "Um—aah—Robb. Hi."

Hi? He had been a kiss away from professing his love on the dreadnought, and all he could say now was *Hi?*

Goddess, I used to be suave.

"Do you need something?" Jax asked, and mentally kicked himself again. Robb wouldn't *be* here if he didn't need something—

"I don't care that you are the C'zar," blurted Robb.

He blinked. "Um . . . all right . . ."

Robb added hurriedly, "I mean I *do*, but not in a bad way. I think it's amazing that you are the C'zar, and I understand why you didn't tell me. It's hard to let someone see who you really are, because you're afraid they won't still love you." He rubbed the back of his neck, standing in the doorway with his shirt buttoned low and the silver rings on his fingers glinting softly in the waystation halogens, and his hair wild from travel, and a red blush coming across his cheeks. And Jax wanted to take that memory and paint it in the stars. "But that . . . that's not who I am. And if tomorrow's our last day, I just want you to know—I want to be with you *because* you are you, not in spite of it. Um—*A-A've nan amar*," he added quietly.

Jax's eyes widened.

I love you.

In the Old Language.

He opened his mouth. Closed it again. Opened. His mind was as blank as this room was quiet, and he couldn't for the life of him think up an answer in *any* language.

"Did—did I say it wrong? *A've nan amar*—"

In two steps, Jax reached out and took Robb by the face and crushed their lips together just to *taste* the Old Language on this insufferable boy's tongue. And *Goddess*, did it taste sweet, like starshine and midnight winds and breathless climbs. The light whispered beneath his skin, bright and bouyant and—

And he didn't see Robb's stars.

The pull was there, just out of his reach, just far enough that if he wanted, he could take the tether and follow it up to his constellations, and watch Robb's fate unravel in the stars, but he didn't *have* to.

The light under his skin sighed and swayed, and he wanted to sob.

This was the gift Koren Vey had given him: the ability to control his curse.

Robb made a surprised noise, but then he melted into Jax, threading his fingers through his long silken hair.

Jax broke with Robb's lips long enough to say, "Is that a good enough answer?"

"But—my stars—you can't—how can you—"

"Stop thinking, *ma'alor.*"

In reply, the Ironblood grinned—no, he *smiled,* which was very disconcerting because an Ironblood smiling never used to be a good omen—kissed him again, and pushed him back into the room. They stumbled all the way back to the bed, where Jax fell flat on his back, and the Ironblood bent over on top of him, pressing their lips together again.

Robb smelled like mechanical oil from his new arm and fresh linens because he *always* smelled fresh. There was never a moment when he didn't. He was like a blouse fresh out of the wash, the rosemary scent lingering on his stubble, and *Goddess,* he wanted nothing else than to sink into Robb's embrace and live there.

His fingers moved toward the buckle on Robb's waist and began to undo it, when Robb grunted and stilled his hand.

"Wait, wait." He paused, detached himself from Jax, took off a shoe, and threw it at the key lock. The door closed with a *clink.* "Now, where were we?"

"You were kissing me with both shoes on," Jax reminded him.

"Ah, will one do?"

"One shoe? *Ma'alor,* you rogue."

Robb grinned and kissed his neck, lips so light and feathery it made gooseflesh ripple across his skin. "I think I know what that means now."

"Rogue?"

"No, *ma'alor.* It means 'my heart,' doesn't it?"

Jax laughed. "Almost." And then he smiled, so wide he couldn't help himself. "It is closer to 'my soul'—my other half.

As though the stardust inside me, and the stardust inside you, were once one and the same."

"Ma'alor," Robb said, and Jax loved the way it sounded on his lips, slow and languid like a song.

"Can you say it again?"

"Ma'alor," Robb purred into his neck, planting a kiss every time he said the words. *Ma'alor,* on the pulse on his throat. *Ma'alor,* the point of his jaw. *Ma'alor,* the crest of his cheekbone. The bridge of his nose. The center of his forehead—

Then his lips.

Tears burned in the corners of his eyes. "I never thought I'd have this," he whispered.

"Have what?"

"You and me. I thought I'd . . . I always thought I'd . . ." And he couldn't help that he was crying now. "I thought you'd never come back."

Robb pushed a lock of his silver hair out of his face and kissed the tears off his cheeks. *"A've nan amar, ma'alor."*

V

STARDUST

ANA

Nevaeh stood against the darkness of space like a rosebud about to open. It hadn't changed since she last saw it, a prison of folded metal, streets teeming with malcontents beside estates as large and grand as they were empty. It still smelled like a beggar who had put on too much rose cologne—heady and sweet at first, with an undeniable scent of rot underneath. From a distance, the city inside looked as though it was chiseled from silver itself, gleaming in the sunlight reflected down from the harbor above them. The last time she had visited Nevaeh, the *Dossier* had docked there, but now it orbited on the other side of Eros—empty and hidden.

"We're not going to draw attention to ourselves—the longer Mellifare's kept in the dark, the better," Robb had said earlier as they sat around the galley's table. Talle had cooked everyone a breakfast of sausage and eggs and ham—she said she was nervous, but Ana got the feeling that she was cooking everything perishable. "Wynn will arrive with Viera—do you know where you're meeting?"

Viera nodded. "Yes."

"Good. Lenda, you'll stay with the captain and Talle."

Lenda nodded. "Right."

"Jax, you'll be our getaway driver"—to that his partner gave a half bow—"Ana, you'll make your grand entrance like we proposed, and Di, you'll watch her from the shadows."

"I can't go into the garden?" Di argued. He'd borrowed one of Jax's ties to pull half of his hair back in a desperate attempt to get it out of his face.

"You might not be HIVE'd now, but it might take you again," the captain said in Robb's stead. She tapped her finger against the table. "We can't let you."

For a moment, Di looked like he was about to fight her, but then his fingers curled around the fork loosened. "Very well. I understand."

"Good," the captain agreed, spearing an egg.

"Meanwhile, Elara and Xu, you two keep a lookout for any sign of the HIVE. We know Mellifare's bound to make her appearance, and if things don't turn out the way we want, we need someone who can throw some communication to Siege's debtors waiting in Nevaeh."

To that, Elara saluted. "Xu and I'll be happy to camp out far away from the masses. Although I hate that I'm going to miss the party, Smolder."

"We can throw our own party," Xu resolved.

"Party for two, please!" Elara threw up two fingers, as if ordering from a waiter, and grinned. "I don't mind. And what'll you do, Smolder?"

"*I* will take those Resonance files and find that heart," Robb concluded.

Siege ate a piece of egg and reached for the hot sauce. "To be fair, Robb, you probably shouldn't be going at all."

The Ironblood choked on his coffee. "*What?*"

"You were disowned, then dead—you'll be the talk of the party."

Viera said dryly, "Oh, Goddess forbid *that*."

Jax agreed, "He does like attention," at which Robb turned a bright red.

"I do *not!*"

Everyone laughed—even Di. Ana tried to, but it felt like her stomach was full of live worms. She anxiously picked at her sausage and eggs, knowing she had to eat, but she wasn't hungry. At least she wasn't the only one not eating—Viera wasn't, either, and she seemed oddly stoic. They still hadn't found the spy, and that made her almost sick with worry. *What if we fail? What if* I *fail?* she thought. *What if—*

Di noticed her frown and asked in a quiet voice, only to her, "Is everything okay?"

"Yes—yeah, fine," she replied automatically, but when he gave her a long blink, she wilted. "What if we can't find the heart? What if we don't get to it first? Or what if we do, and it doesn't matter? What if . . ."

The table had gone quiet, even the clank of utensils on metal plates, and Ana quickly realized that she had been too loud. She stared down at her untouched plate self-consciously.

"I mean, it's probably going to be fine," she amended.

"Of course it'll be fine," replied Lenda, setting down her fork. She was already dressed for Nevaeh in a rough-spun shirt and trousers, her dishwater-blond hair slicked back, to blend in with the crowds. The faintest hint of a mercenary brand peeked out from beneath her collar. She looked around the table. "You know, I've never been one for sentimental stuff, but I trust everyone here with my life. And I know they trust me with theirs. I never thought I fit in anywhere until I came here. To this crew—you're like a family to me. The only one I've got. And if some Great Dark wants to try to destroy that, I'll fight with everything I've got."

"I'll toast to that," Jax added, and raised his glass of juice. "To family."

The rest of the crew raised their cups in toast to her. "To family," they echoed, as if it would protect them against bullets and blades, but Ana knew deep down that it wouldn't. It hadn't protected Wick or Riggs or the Grand Duchess or Lady Valerio. It hadn't protected Di, even though he'd come back. Death had more often than not been a specter that came when you least expected it and stole you away before you could say no.

She didn't want anyone else to die, because as with Lenda, this was the only place she belonged, and she had fought so hard to get here. She wanted them to stay like this forever, gathered around in the galley, enjoying Talle's good cooking and each other's company, everyone happy and alive and here.

But nothing stayed forever.

She had raised her cup and echoed, "To family."

Now as Jax eased the skysailer up toward the Valerios' float-ing estate, she wished she had spent more time playing Wicked Luck in the galley, and she wished she had enjoyed Talle's food more often, and spent more time listening to Di read his books aloud and Lenda recount her tales of being a mercenary and Wick's and Riggs's songs that still sometimes echoed through the ship like ghostly melodies.

They were about to try to defeat a monster who had every advantage, who had an ear in on their every plan. No one had stopped the Great Dark yet—in this galaxy or any other. Why were they foolish enough to believe that they could?

That's why we mislead it, the captain had said in the safety of the meeting yesterday, after everyone else had gone, when it had just been the captain and Talle and Di and Jax and herself.

But what if Mellifare had heard that too?

Ana sat in the back of the skysailer, beside Erik in his finest gray coat and frivolous ascot, his legs spread wide across the seat, taking up most of her space. She couldn't *stand* him. Jax and Robb sat up front, disguised as Valerio militiamen. The crimson of their uniforms reminded her of the coat she had once seen in a shop window. For some odd reason the memory of it tugged on her like an errant kite string. Perhaps because the coat was long gone by now, or perhaps because it represented a future she'd never have.

Or maybe she just really, *really* hated being in Valerio mili-tia colors. The jacket was too tight, the pants too long, and it itched *everywhere.* She had been more comfortable in some of the dresses she was shoved into at the Iron Palace—and Ana never thought she'd ever feel that way.

"Receiving the docking codes," Jax said, swiping up two notifications on his dash before he eased up through the lines of traffic toward the Valerios' floating estate. "They definitely stepped up security since we last popped in. Sir Erik, would you like to be dropped off at the front or on the side?"

Erik Valerio glowered at him. He wasn't detained any-more—he'd agreed to help them, after some cajoling—but they were definitely *not* seeing eye to eye. Erik wanted to kill Di— blaming him for Lady Valerio's murder. That was one of the reasons Di had opted to go with Wynn and Viera instead, so that he could stay as far away from Erik as possible. It'd been easy enough to keep them separated on the *Dossier*, but here it would be a little more difficult.

Jax tapped his fingers on the helm and glanced over his shoulder. "Well, Ironblood?"

Erik Valerio pulled himself to sit as tall as he could and said, "The side is for paupers and Ironbloods too stingy to hire their own drivers."

"The side it is," Jax replied, much to Erik's disgust, and eased into the docking canal in the marina underneath the garden.

"It took *months* to renovate this place after you heathens trashed it," Erik was saying as Jax parked in one of the docking stations. Mechanical arms came out and hooked onto the bottom of the ship to steady it. "Do you know how many good ships were destroyed?"

"Hopefully plenty," replied Jax. "Now out."

Gathering her Metroid and lightsword—which, *ha*, Ana

used about as much as a comb at this point—she hopped out of the skysailer and reached a hand back for Erik. He took it, leering at her, and stepped down off the skysailer, followed by Robb.

"Hey, Jax?" Ana turned back to him as the docking latches unhooked from the skysailer.

"Yes, my love?"

"Be careful."

He smirked and gave her a salute, and the skysailer dropped from the marina and disappeared into the steady stream of traffic below.

"I really should have killed him when I had the chance," Erik mumbled, earning a look from Robb that could have melted the sun.

She took a deep, calm breath. She just had to keep Robb from kicking Erik off the garden for a little while longer.

"You know, this party is going to go so *different* from what I imagined," Erik Valerio went on, and started down the docks. The last time they'd been in the belly of the Valerios' floating estate, she'd been a much different person, chasing wide-eyed after a rumor.

She wasn't chasing things anymore but coming to meet them.

And oh, the image of that red coat burned in her brain.

It *was* the path not taken. The life not lived. When Di had pushed that lightsword through her stomach, she could have faded away. She had died in the kingdom's eyes. All her threads had been severed, her obligations cut. She could have been whoever she wanted. She could have been a girl of the stars—a nameless ghost on a ship of black and chrome. There could have been stories about her, or no stories at all.

But the thought had never crossed her mind. Not once.

Was that a testament to her character or her stubbornness? The more she thought about it, the less she was sure of anything. Other people would surely have stepped up to defeat the Great Dark. Other people might have succeeded far quicker and lost far less. Perhaps she never gave up because of Di, because she loved Di more than her heart could hold, but . . .

But there was another reason, needling in the back of her thoughts—

Because she did not know how *not* to try. She could have flown away, she could have turned her back, but every particle of stardust inside her would have rebelled until she had come back.

And that made her feel a little better.

Ana followed Robb and his brother up the stairs to the underbelly of the garden, where irrigation pipes hummed in the ceiling, rattling with the rush of water to all the different areas of the garden. It all looked the same, from the darkened hallways to the kitchen teeming with waiters and waitresses.

Robb took out his holo-pad and pulled up the Resonance files again. "It should be in the garden," he said, tugging at the collar of his too-tight uniform. "I don't see any Messiers. . . ."

"So Mellifare doesn't know yet," Ana finished.

"Are you coming up with me or staying down here?" called Erik ahead of them. He tugged at his cuff links, looking bored and unhappy. "I hardly need a *bodyguard* for—what are you doing?"

Robb unbuttoned his jacket and pulled it off to reveal a smock coat underneath, the color of crushed marigolds, and tossed the uniform jacket to Ana. He retied his white ascot and tucked it in again. "What, did you really think you'd go up there alone?"

"You are *disowned*—"

"I'm not going as a Valerio," he corrected.

"Then *what* are you?"

"Who, actually." Robb tapped the crest on his lapel. Ana had seen the crest a few times before, in passing at the palace. Her eyebrows knit together. It was the late Grand Duchess's crest.

Erik's face pinched. "Aragon. There aren't any family left. The old dame was murdered and her daughter went missing. How do you have that crest?"

"Wouldn't you like to know."

"Fine—it doesn't matter, you'll always be filth."

"And you're still as pleasant as ever," Robb replied, but Ana couldn't pry her eyes from the raven crest pinned to his coat. Because she remembered it from somewhere else entirely—in her captain's study. "Well, we shouldn't keep the public waiting," he added, and hugged her tightly. "Good luck, cousin," he whispered, so low Erik couldn't hear, and then departed with his brother up the steps, through the honeysuckle vines, and into the waiting crowd.

She pushed the thought of the Raven Crest to the back of her mind. She couldn't get distracted now.

Ana stood at the bottom of the stairs, wringing her fingers.

Misdirection is key, the captain had said. Make a show of one hand while the other takes the winning card from a pocket. Always suspect that someone is watching you. A few waiters passed her with delicate food on silver trays, and for an instant it felt like déjà vu, because she had been here before, dressed in an ill-fitting uniform at an Ironblood party. She felt like a different person now, even though she had been here just six short months ago.

It might as well have been an eternity.

Quietly, she crept up the steps and peered through the honeysuckle vines.

The garden was filled with extravagantly clad men and women in their finest dressing robes. The colors for the season had changed from frothy pastels to nebulas—pinks and purples, greens and blues, melding together like star-stuff. Of *course* colors she liked better would be in season *after* the kingdom thought her dead.

Just her luck.

The Ironbloods ambled around drinking rose champagne and the best brandy on this side of the kingdom, laughing and flirting in the way only Ironbloods knew how. She watched as Robb and his brother sank deeper into the crowd, Robb in his marigold yellow, Erik in bloodred. Her palms grew sweaty the longer she watched.

The orchestra began to play the royal march.

She rubbed her sweaty hands on her jacket and took a deep breath—

At the bottom of the stairwell, she heard the sound of

footsteps and quickly turned, reaching for her Metroid, *knowing* that the HIVE would show up at some point—

The boy was not a Messier, though. In the faint golden light through the honeysuckle vines, strands of his red hair flickered orange—like a blazing fire. He wore his midnight cloak from the shrine and a freshly pressed evening coat borrowed from Jax, so he cut a stark and tall figure even in the shadows. On his head was the Iron Crown. He looked every bit an Emperor as he had before, except when he looked up at her, his eyes were moonlit; he didn't dampen or darken them anymore, a deafening tell that he wasn't human, but he wasn't *other* either.

He was both.

He looked as though he wanted to say something, but then a strange pink tinge rose on his cheeks, and he quickly looked away. *Goddess*, it felt like centuries ago when they'd last stood here, looking out at the garden. What she wouldn't have given to be that girl again.

She quickly took her hand off her pistol. "Anything?"

He shook his head and climbed the dozen steps to stand beside her, peering out of the vines into the garden. The way the dusky sunlight fell through the curtain of honeysuckle upon his face reminded her of a far-off fairy tale. "Viera is posing as Wynn's personal guard. There are no Messiers on the north side, or the east. I cannot sense any on the garden at all."

"That's not good, is it?"

"No, it is not."

A cold chill raced up her spine. "You think it's a trap." He nodded slowly, and the orchestra quieted its royal march. Ana brushed back the vines. "It's almost your cue."

"I know," he replied. "You should go."

"I feel like I should be the one going out there—to show the kingdom that I'm fighting for them. That I'm still here."

He touched her arm gently, comfortingly. "You will. When this is all over, you will be the Empress they need."

"And what about you?"

He gave a one-shoulder shrug. "It will not be that hard to kill me off."

"*Di!*"

"I am joking." He laughed, and then added, "Mostly—*ow!*" She punched him in the arm, and he hissed in pain. "That hurt."

"Did not— It's Mellifare!" she gasped, spying her through the crowd of Ironbloods. She stood near one of the extravagant topiaries, dressed in a beautiful sage-colored gown, her flaxen hair pulled back into a refined bun. She had a glass of rose champagne in her hands, speaking with—

With Erik Valerio.

"There really is a spy," she added morosely. "Mellifare's here because she thinks the heart is here in the garden."

"Well, at least we know we tricked her."

She hesitated, wishing that Mellifare wasn't here at all. "Do you . . . do you think you can face her? After what she did to you?"

"I do not know, Ana." There was a thoughtful, distant look in his eyes. "But I am not afraid."

"Aren't you?"

He shook his head and then turned his moonlit eyes to her.

There was a sadness there that sank down to her toes. "If I die, at least I got the chance to see you again."

"But . . . that's not good enough."

His eyebrows furrowed.

"It's not good enough because—" And she took a deep breath, pushing away the cowardly part of her that told her *Later, you can tell him later,* when there might never be a later. "—I don't think I could love anyone the way I love you, and I don't want you to die, Dmitri Rasovant, because I am the moon and you are the sun and I shine so much brighter with you beside me."

"But I am . . . but I . . ."

She reached up on her toes and pressed her forehead against his. "You are mine and I am yours, until the end of time."

Then, with all the strength she had, she turned away from the honeysuckle vines and left down the stairs again. She didn't look back. She was afraid that if she did, it would be the last time she'd ever see him, and she refused to think about that.

She took the stairs down to the bottom of the gardens two at a time, nodding to Ironblood servants as she passed them, hoping they didn't recognize her. Most of them were too flustered, attending to their duties, to pay attention, and when someone finally recognized her, she was already at the docks again and heading for a skysailer.

Nevaeh looked so small from up here, a tiny city filled with tiny ants, and once she had thought that was how the Goddess saw them. But now she was sure the Goddess wouldn't have looked down, but up from the ground.

You are not the Goddess, Koren Vey had said.

No, but she *was* Captain Siege and Talle Fior's daughter, and somehow that felt all the more powerful.

She pulled out Lady Valerio's decrepit holo-pad and powered it on. The screen glitched, warming to a neon green. When she had first seen the files, she could hardly believe her eyes. Lady Valerio had depicted the Great Dark's heart in painstaking detail, rendering it in blueprints and meticulous descriptions, analyzing what it was made from and what could destroy it, but the most startling thing of all was that it looked just like any other Metal heart.

She knew from the Goddess's tomb it was small and square, but she wasn't prepared for it to look like the memory core she kept in her pocket, made from an unknown metal that could be destroyed only if enough heat was applied.

Lady Valerio could never do that. *The possibilities are endless with this technology,* she had noted. She had kept it as a leveraging tool.

Ana now understood what sort of power she held over Rasovant. She had been a terrifying woman indeed.

At the zenith of Astoria, look north across the city. I hid it in the hands of the Goddess, protected by years, she had written in the files, the only clue to the heart's whereabouts.

Astoria was at its zenith, in the center of the skyscape above Nevaeh, at the highest point in the sky. Four other floating gardens gently twirled around it, a hundred feet below, patches of flowering moonlilies and deep lavenders. She faced north and looked across the city, but all she could see were towering buildings that shone gold in the sunlight that poured from the lip of the harbor above, and lines of traffic, and—

And the burned remains of a cathedral—the Iron Shrine—protruding up out of the city like a shard of obsidian.

I hid it in the hands of the Goddess, Lady Valerio wrote.

There was a statue of the Goddess in the shrine.

That was it.

She put the holo-pad away and quickly ran to the edge of the docks, calling for Jax and his skysailer. A moment later, a ship eased up from the traffic lines, though it wasn't Jax at the helm. It was Siege.

"Where's Jax?" she asked, climbing into the craft.

"Staying. Where to?"

Ana nudged her head toward the Iron Shrine. "There."

The edges of her captain's hair darkened with foreboding. "Aye, I was afraid of that."

DI

Out in the garden, Erik Valerio climbed up onto the dais in the center of the garden.

"It seems our Emperor will not make it today," he started, and in the crowd Mellifare looked pleased, just as Di had hoped. There had been a spy on the *Dossier*, but it was not anyone in that private meeting Robb had called. "Though we do have another guest with us. I have told you that she is alive—and with Lady Wysteria's help we found her. We have been lied to, friends, about everything. About our late Empress, about her death. You see, she is not dead at all, and I have brought her here to show you. Your Grace, if you would," he called, turning everyone's attention to the honeysuckle vines.

Di steeled himself, willing his eyes to be Valerio blue one last time, and stepped out into the garden.

Erik stared at him, mouth unhinged, one moment in surprise—and then he realized what was happening: he had been tricked.

Of course he had. He had not *actually* expected Ana would

show herself here, had he? She had more important matters to attend.

"I am afraid Empress Ananke will not be coming," Di began, earning the attention of the entire garden, and with him came murmurs, rumors rushing behind him like a tide. As he moved past the Ironbloods in their pretty frock coats and dresses swirled with galaxies, he caught their attention like a ripple in a placid pond. The crowd parted into a wide clearing, where Mellifare stood—as if she was waiting. Perhaps she was. And perhaps this was a trap. But like Robb said, they were quick on their feet, and they courted the impossible as surely as the worlds waltzed around the sun.

Mellifare stared at him as if she had seen a ghost. He did not hear the song, but he knew it was there. *"You."*

"Me, sadly," Di replied.

He came to a stop in front of her, and oh how he remembered all those long nights sitting beside her in his bedchamber because neither of them needed sleep. He remembered how she braided his hair so tenderly and told him what she would do to this kingdom once she had found her heart. The promises of death and revenge and darkness. He could not even remember why she was so bent on destruction, and a part of him knew she did not remember, either.

The Great Dark existed just to ruin. It had forgotten any other purpose.

Di hoped to make sure it would never ruin anything again.

He noticed Robb stepping back into the crowd, away from his brother, and disappearing around a bush and into the garden.

On the other side of the crowd, Viera stepped back too—and followed, even though she was supposed to stay with Wynn. He curled his hands into fists.

"I am sorry I am a little late—I am glad you started the party without me," he said, taking a flute of champagne from one of the waiters' trays.

The chorus of murmurs grew louder, and Di turned to the Ironbloods, who got more confused and frightened by the moment.

"I fear I have not been very truthful to you all these last six months. You see, I do not rust for the crown, but it is not because I am worthy." He took off the Iron Crown with his free hand, and like before, he eased the darkness out of his eyes, like color draining from a tapestry, to pale moonlight. "It is because Metals do not rust."

As he'd expected, the closest Ironbloods recoiled, the gasps of *monster* and *murderer* falling from their lips.

He pointed the crown at Mellifare. "And she is the Great Dark."

ROBB

He slipped behind a line of shrubbery, following the neatly trimmed bushes down the length of the garden. He ran his hand along the wall of leaves, feeling twigs catch against his fingers. The orchestra had gone silent. That could not be a good sign.

Don't think about it, he told himself, traveling deeper into the garden. Out of the corner of his eye, he spied a flash of platinum hair, the pale blue of a Wysteria uniform, and he traveled deeper. He used to play in Astoria's garden when he was little, getting lost in the hedge maze as his father pursued, playing hide-and-seek. He had been wicked good at finding Robb, but then again Robb never really made it a sport to hide all that well. It was one of the few blissfully untouched memories he had of his father.

"Night star bright, where is your light?" his father used to call in his warm baritone, and Robb had to answer:

"Out of sight!"

Even now he felt his father in the garden. He could hear his laughter, almost picture him standing at the edge of the hedge maze in his royal best, crimson coat pressed and dark beard trimmed, waiting for Robb to come out.

But he wasn't playing a game anymore, and it wasn't his father following.

He stopped under a willow tree, the sound of Ironblood chatter dim voices now, and ran his hand along the names carved on the wood. Viera stopped a few feet away, and he turned to look at her—*really* look. He should have known. It had been too easy to find her on the dreadnought—alive, anyway, especially when Mellifare took and took. At first he had wondered why the Great Dark had spared Viera, afraid to think anything else.

But now that he looked back at her, it all seemed so clear. The fire in the shrine on Zenteli, the ruins where the heart was kept, how the dreadnought had caught them so easily in Eros's orbit.

How Mellifare knew they would be here today.

"Is the heart here?" Viera asked, putting her right hand on the holster of her Metroid.

He studied her. They had been schoolmates once. He'd dueled her on the rooftop, lost to her in strip poker. He should have realized earlier. He should have recognized.

"Since when have you been ambidextrous?"

Her gaze narrowed. "You are worried about that now?"

"You're left-handed," he pointed out.

"This is not the time for casual chatter. Where is the heart?"

He reached for his lightsword at his hip, his mechanical hand curling around the hilt. "It's not here . . . and you are not Viera."

The woman's gaze darkened. "You tricked me."

"And you fell for it."

Her eyes flashed red—the color of the HIVE, the Great Dark, the heart of a burning coal—and before Robb could even take out his lightsword, she raised her hand and a bolt of lightning shot out of her fingers. He felt a flash of pain, his blood boiling, his muscles tensing—and then nothing at all.

DI

Mellifare's eyes flickered red. He heard the whisper of the song—the HIVE—and he knew in that instant that she had caught on to their ploy. She bared her teeth. "You *tricked* me!"

Di took a cautious step back.

The Great Dark outstretched her arms and curled her fingers, as if gripping strings in midair, and pulled them taut. The garden suddenly shifted. Di felt it tilt just enough for a champagne glass to slide off a dessert table and go rolling into the bushes. A couple stumbled. A mumble rushed across the crowd.

"What's happening?" someone shouted. "Why's the garden—"

Mellifare raised her hands just a fraction, and the entire garden lurched. "I must say," she said with a smile, "he is not incorrect. I am the Great Dark. Too bad no one ever lives to tell."

Like a tug of kite strings, he felt the HIVE.

Its commands spiraled out like a spiderweb.

He felt them like a thousand red needles through him, so painful it made him stumble and catch himself on a tree, the song no longer sweet and melodic but a cacophony of out-of-tune notes screeching—*screeching*—so loud he could barely think. He winced, pressing his palm against his temple.

Foolish Dmitri—Mellifare came into his head, her words like needles—*you will give me my heart.*

No—*no*—

Not again—

Not—

But you are not my tool this time, and the song left as quickly as it began, left his head ringing—but whole. He blinked, realigning himself, until a wave of command swept down like tethered strings, grabbing ahold of the garden itself. He tightened his hold on the trunk of the tree and began to tremble.

Where was Robb?

Below him, the HIVE tore down the programs to align the magnets, erasing the guidance system that kept the estate in stationary orbit around the station, dismantling every bit of code that kept it running. He felt the garden bleeding out as sure as he felt the song itself.

It was going to fall.

He lurched toward the middle of the garden the moment Astoria dropped from the sky. It would only take moments to reach the ground. Faster than a breath, a blink—and they would be dead, crushed from the weight of the fall—

He reached out, like he had on the dreadnought, and took hold of the garden. Spread his reach across it, rearranging the scattered code in its simple computer core, warming the magnetics, realigning them with—with—

Something.

The city itself. The city was metal. Not as strong. Not as charged. But made of metal. And if he rewired the magnets underneath Astoria, he could put out enough friction to slow down the garden's descent—not by much—but slower than it was and—

He did not have the luxury to guess.

He had to act.

Sparks burst across his body as he reached the middle of the garden and caught the tethers that kept it floating. The magnets groaned, catching themselves again, still dropping but not as fast. Electricity sizzled over him like scattering cobwebs, his hair levitating from the power of it.

Overheating, a warning blazed in the back of his head.

He boxed it away.

"You cannot choose both, Dmitri," Mellifare said, and from the hedge Viera dragged a prone Robb by the collar of his coat. Her eyes blazed a terrifying red. She tossed Robb onto the grass in front of her, and he groaned, slowly regaining consciousness. There were blackened marks across his coat like lightning blooms.

Viera . . . was a *Metal?*

How had he not sensed her before?

Now, where is it, brother? He winced as the Great Dark tore through his thoughts, picking through his memories, his programs. He tried to stop her, but with his functions split between trying to fend her off and keeping the garden afloat, he was not strong enough.

She found the node of information and picked it from his head.

So, the shrine.

No, no, no no no—

From Viera's mouth came Mellifare's voice: *"Do you save the Ironbloods, or do you save her?"*

Then they both turned away. He tried to stop them, but if he moved and let go of the garden, it would crash. He did not know how many casualties, but was he prepared for that? His grip on the garden began to falter, lean to one side, imaginary tethers snapping off and disintegrating into nothing.

Mellifare and Viera were ten feet from the edge, then five.

Then Mellifare pulled up her hand, as if commanding a puppet, and a skysailer swirled up from below and settled down level with the floating garden. Mellifare boarded, Viera behind her—

And they left.

Straight toward the heart. The shrine. Ana.

Di watched the skysailer become a pinprick in the Nevaeh sky, too far away to do anything, and he gritted his teeth. He sank his anger down into the garden and pulled as hard as he could to stop its descent. He could feel the ground close, but not close enough.

His arms began to shake.

Ironbloods were clutching the ground around him, crying, curling into each other waiting for the impact. For death. It reminded him so terribly of the Plague hospital, of the rows and rows of people just waiting for the inevitable, hope growing thinner and thinner until it snapped.

He had had enough of hopelessness.

OVERHEATING, the warning in the back of his head said again, and he could feel his insides this time beginning to burn. It hurt somewhere in his chest cavity.

With a cry, he pulled all the energy in the garden into the magnets. From the lampposts, the electric doors, the sky-sailer docking clamps, the levers for the irrigations systems— *everything.* And with an enormous groan, the garden slowed its descent foot by foot, until its bottom clanked against one of the market streets of the city of Nevaeh and began to tilt over like a top that'd stopped spinning, and settled on its side.

Di waited a moment for the garden to move again, but when it did not, he slowly drew himself out of the control systems and relinked electrical currents. The fountains began spurting water, and the lampposts flickered on with a *pop.*

He sank to his knees, trying to stand but unable.

His vision narrowed.

Around him, Ironbloods uncurled themselves, looking at him in horror. But he could not make out what they said, nor did he care. Mellifare had the coordinates to her heart. They had tried to mislead her, buy Ana some time, but—not enough. It was never going to be enough time.

His fingers curled around the grass beneath him, blades springing between his fingers. He had been a part of Mellifare for *months.* How could he have let his emotions get in the way? The thought that they *could* defeat her? Outsmart her? It was never to be that simple.

He had been a *monster*. He should have thought like a *mon*—

"He saved us," one of the Ironbloods said, helping her partner up. "The Emperor."

Another said, "What did he just do?"

". . . And he stopped the garden from falling! What is he? A Metal?—"

"—A *monster*—"

"He saved us."

Slowly, he got to his feet again. He had to go after Mellifare.

"Jax." He reached out a comm-link to the skysailer in question. "Mellifare is heading your—"

Suddenly, a lightsword slid between two of his metal ribs and came out the front, and a voice hissed in his ear, "This is for my mother."

ROBB

"NO!" Robb cried, his head spinning as he scrambled to his feet, but it was too late.

Erik wrenched his lightsword out of Di's back, and the redhead sank to the ground. He twitched, sparks hissing from the wound, and then lay still. Erik sneered, flipping his sword the other way to thrust the tip into Di's head—

When Robb slammed his shoulder into Erik's side, tackling him to the ground. The lightsword went skittering to the edge of the garden and then tipped over it.

"What are you *doing*?" Erik hissed, shoving him away.

"You killed him!"

"I took *revenge*—more than what you could do!"

"He didn't kill her! *Mellifare* did!"

"He stole my crown," Erik snarled, his voice shuddering. "My throne—he stole everything!" Then he lunged at Robb, fist pulled back in a punch.

There was a split second between dodging and watching Erik stumble past when he did the wrong thing. He should have dodged the other way. He should have grabbed his brother by the coattail, he should've pinned him to the ground. But it was a split second in which Robb dodged, and his brother stumbled past and slammed into the railing. And by then it was too late. Erik lost his balance and went tumbling over the garden rail, but he managed to catch himself.

"Erik!" Robb cried, racing to the railing, and outstretched his hand. "Grab on!"

His brother, dangling from the edge, glared up. "I don't need you."

"Don't be stupid—"

But then Erik reached up and knocked Robb's hand away. "I said I don't need—"

Erik's fingers slipped off the rail.

Robb dove for his brother, snagging his gloved hand, and tipped over the railing, catching himself on the edge. His mechanical arm whined with the strain. No—he could hold on. He could definitely. It was a *metal arm*, for Goddess's sake. It couldn't—

His hand began to slip.

Oh, just *curse* his luck.

Below him, Erik snarled, "Let go—I said, let go of me!"

He gritted his teeth, willing his mechanical arm to stay together. "Not on your life."

If Robb had been looking down at his older brother, he would've seen a strange look pass over his face. Not quite surprise, and not anger.

Something akin to pity.

Because Erik felt his hand slipping out of the glove Robb held. He felt gravity and death grip him all at once, and oh, oh Goddess, was he *terrified*. Not that it mattered. Nothing he could have done mattered just then.

Gravity pulled, and his fingers slipped out of his glove. One moment he was grasping onto Robb's hand, and the next air, and he was falling, and falling, and falling, leaving Robb dangling from the railing of the garden, holding his black glove.

Robb screamed, but he couldn't let go—all he could do was watch, but by the time he turned his eyes down, his brother was already at the bottom.

No, his mind reeled. *No, no, no—*

He tore his eyes away, reached up with his other hand to the railing, and hauled himself up, Erik's glove still in his hand.

Don't think, don't think right now, he told himself, pocketing the glove. He expected some emotion—anything—but his heart beat harder the closer he came to Di, who was still facedown in the grass. He quickly knelt down beside his friend and went to shake his shoulder, when his wound sparked and Robb winced back, shielding his face. He gritted his teeth and tried again.

"Di," he said, thinking that it was a good sign that his eyes were closed.

That meant he was alive, right? Or as alive as Metals could be.

People died with their eyes open.

"Di, I need you to get up," he added a little more urgently, as the telltale sound of boots in synchrony began to echo up the stairwell from the underbelly of the garden. He knew that sound like his own heartbeat by now. Messiers were terrifying, but they were not *subtle*. The Messiers would come and kill them—he was quite sure of it. Mellifare didn't seem very pleased that they had tricked her.

Robb cursed to himself and looped an arm under Di's shoulder, pulling him to his feet. His head lolled against his chest.

Robb dragged Di toward the edge of the garden—the same edge his brother had fallen from. He'd give his left arm for a comm-link to call Jax. Viera had fried his when she'd electrocuted him, and he felt the burn puckering the side of his neck. He wasn't sure how he had survived that, but he thought it might have had something to do with his mechanical arm—it had absorbed some of the shock.

At the edge of the garden, he heard the Messiers break out into the thicket of moonlilies and roses before he saw them. They crept through the bushes, surrounding him.

"We ask you—" began one.

"—to be orderly—"

"—and calm—"

"—while you wait."

"Wait for what?" Robb muttered.

"For Mellifare to get her heart," Di replied, lifting his head a little. The slice in his chest sparked, and he winced. "And then she will kill us all."

"Nice of you to join me. How're you feeling?"

"Not good," replied the Metal, and suppressed a painful groan. "I think it hit my memory core. You should have left me."

Something glinted far above them—a flash of a skysailer's

underbelly. Crimson wings. Diving down through the lines of traffic like a stone dropped from the sky.

Guess he didn't need a comm-link after all.

The skysailer swirled down beneath the garden on the other side, its wings as silent as a sigh. He heaved Di a little higher on his shoulder and said, "We're never leaving anyone behind. Never again."

Then he shoved himself and Di over the edge—for a split second he remembered his brother falling, falling, a crown of blood behind his head—before the skysailer appeared under them and they landed in a heap in the backseat.

JAX

Jax pushed up his goggles and glanced back at his new passengers as they struggled to untangle themselves from each other. "Welcome aboa— *Goddess*, Di, you have a hole in your chest."

"It is only a flesh wound," replied the Metal painfully, pulling himself up from the floorboard to the seat. "We need to get to the shrine."

"That doesn't look like just a flesh wound—are you sure you're okay?"

"The shrine, please. Mellifare went into my head. She knows her heart is there."

"*Ak'va*," Jax cursed, and tapped the comm-link on his lapel. "Ana, they're on their way to you."

There was only static in reply.

"Captain?" he tried again, but there was still no answer.

He exchanged a look with Robb. That wasn't good. The light under his skin whispered, telling him things he didn't want to hear. His face pinched. A horn blared, and he quickly jerked the skysailer out of oncoming traffic and down toward the cityscape. The Iron Shrine stood in the distance, surrounded by a large square, and then rows and rows of buildings, like petals of a blooming flower.

Suddenly, an emergency node blipped up on the holo-screen, and on every other skysailer's holo-screen around them.

CODE 49-1.

EFFECTIVE IMMEDIATELY.

He cursed and swiped the emergency node away. "Di, what code is that?"

"How am I supposed to know?" replied Di, almost irritably. "I have a hole in my chest."

Both Jax and Robb gave him a blank look. "Because you always knew this stuff before," Robb pointed out.

Di's eyebrows jerked up in surprise. "Oh. I did." It wasn't a question but a realization. He looked down to the wound in his chest and put his hand over it. "I would guess it has something to do with locking down the space station. Mellifare would not want anyone to leave. Not now. Not with her heart."

"So this is it, then," Robb murmured.

"Seems so," Jax agreed.

The Iron Shrine loomed in the distance, growing larger and larger with each passing moment. The rest of Nevaeh carried on like it was any other day in the kingdom, and the normalcy of it frightened him. The light under his skin crawled across the timelines, the near futures and past perfects, and he didn't know which were true and which were thwarted.

But it didn't matter—each of them ended in flames.

ANA

Ana slipped into the Iron Shrine.

While the fire had gutted most of the inside, the structure of it still stood like an indestructible mountain. Some of Nevaeh's citizens had already taken to repairing the structure. There was scaffolding on the outside, and the charred door had been replaced with fresh wood. She pushed against the towering ornate door, half expecting it to be locked, but it eased open.

Inside, at a passing glance, it looked as though the shrine hadn't burned at all. It oozed the warm, loving golden glow of a thousand candles set upon the rafters. They flickered in the draft from the open door and danced shadows across the walls, masking the blackened burn marks. The statue of the Goddess, alight with candles, towered at the head of the shrine, fifty feet high, just as Ana had remembered from her last visit. Dried candle wax pooled out of her cupped hands and dripped from her outstretched arms like pearlescent water.

There.

The heart must've been there.

Dozens of people knelt in the pews. They muttered softly to themselves, cadences of *The Cantos of Light* mixed with their own prayers. Four abbesses stood at the front of the shrine, holding lit censers, the smell of moonlilies fresh and strong.

"Oh no," she murmured. Everyone needed to leave. She cleared her throat and greeted one of the abbesses who came to meet them halfway down the aisle. "Madam, you're in danger here—"

"The Goddess will protect us," the abbess interrupted, her gaze lingering on her scars. "Please, come and worship."

Helplessly, Ana watched her walk back toward the front of the shrine, swinging her censer patiently.

Fine.

Setting her jaw, she took her Metroid from her holster and prayed that the Goddess would forgive her for this. She raised it into the air and fired a shot into the ceiling.

The people praying in the pews shrieked and ducked for cover.

"Everyone *leave!*" she commanded, her voice vibrating across the rafters. They turned to her, staring at her as if she was a phantom come home. They began to recognize the burn scars across the left side of her face, the thick slant of her brow, the bronze of her skin, the Armorov gold of her eyes. They recognized royalty in an orphan girl from the stars.

A ghost among marbled Goddess statues.

The Empress?

Ananke Armorov?

Empress Ananke?

Ana?

They stared at her in awe.

"I SAID LEAVE!" she roared, and her voice carried up into the rafters, quaking the candles.

The worshippers sprang out of the pews, leaving behind hymn books of the *Cantos* and their own personal effects. When the last person was gone, and the imposing doors swung closed with a *thud*, Ana sighed and holstered her pistol again.

"That worked a little too well," she commented to herself, and turned her eyes up toward the fifty-foot statue, and the Goddess's outstretched arms, hands cupped together. It looked a lot higher than she rememebred, she thought, shrugging out of the Valerio uniform to a dark undershirt, and tossed the jacket into the pews. Then she climbed up onto the pedestal where the Goddess's feet were planted.

The base of the statue was as thick as five tree trunks, but there were handholds to climb up the side of her, oddly enough. *Someone* had to light and change out the candles covering the Goddess's hands, arms, and shoulders, but she'd expected a ladder or something. Not footholds in the statue's dress.

She scaled the Goddess, careful to listen to her comm-link for any chatter. It had been increasingly quiet, and she didn't like that at all. She didn't look down, mostly because she knew what she'd find. The floor. Very far away. It wasn't that she was afraid of heights, but she *was* afraid of gravity at this height. Wax covered most of the statue, rubbery and soft. She found herself sinking her nails into it as she climbed up onto the arms and started to crawl across, trying not to knock the candles down as she went. The wax accumulated for centuries, because no one ever scraped it off, only ever adding a candle for each year since the Goddess's death. She knew that because of Di. The main character in his favorite book, *The Swords of Veten Ruel*, was raised to be a priest of the Iron Shrine, and so Ana learned that the candles were changed every three days, when the wicks burned low.

"It is interesting," he had once said. They were on a stakeout in the humid city of Ventura on Eros, hunkered down in a sky-sailer to wait for the leader of the Red Dawn to leave his cushy hideout. He owed Siege money. "There are magic spells and tactical battles and the very precise use of the trajectory of a turtle. It is quite thrilling. Are you interested yet?"

She quirked an eyebrow. "How exactly does it use a turtle?"

He began to answer, but then he must've thought better of it and said instead, "You will have to read it to find out."

"That's infuriating—read it to me, then."

"I do not have it with me."

"Then recite it," she had said, fanning herself with a piece of paper from the glove compartment. *Anything* to keep her mind off how miserable she was. It had been so hot, condensation began to collect on Di's metal body. "I know you know it by heart."

He had been quiet for a moment, but then he cocked his head and said, "In a time before our time, in the far weathered north of the Bavania Range . . ."

She had actually liked the story as he read it to her—well, *recited* it. Perhaps after this, he could read her some other books.

Of course she could read herself, but stories always sounded so much better when he read them. She was so lost in thought, she accidentally knocked off a candle, and it went skittering into the pews and went out.

Oh, oh, it was a *long* way down.

She quickly refocused on the arm and kept crawling.

There were thousand candles in the shrine. A thousand years. The prophecy had been right about that, at least. The Great Dark returned after a millennium.

She was surprised the wax hadn't melted off in the fire.

She crawled down into the Goddess's cupped palms. And there, underneath years of candle wax, was a dark shape that looked startlingly like a lockbox. She slid her dagger out of her boot and quietly began to dig for it. When the dagger struck the box, she quickly abandoned her tool and pried the wax away with her fingers, nails chipping as she dug the box free. She cleared the lock of wax, jammed the tip of her dagger into the lock, and twisted. The lock broke free.

She steeled her courage and opened the box.

A cool white light oozed from a small metal cube. A memory core. It looked so similar to the one she kept in her pocket now. She picked up the heart, and it vibrated—pulsing like a heartbeat.

This was the end of galaxies? This cube sucked the light out of people and feasted on their souls?

It was terrifying, how something so small could be so dangerous.

Gently, she took the heart in her hand, and she could hear it *whisper*—to her! She could see now why the Lady Valerio never wanted to destroy it. It was too important. There was so much more she could do *with* the heart than without it. It was childish to want to destroy something so perfect, something so—

The front doors to the shrine swung open, bringing with it a gust of wind that snuffed out half of the candles. The burst of cold snapped her to her senses, and she quickly closed the lockbox again. What—what had just happened? She remembered it whispering and then . . . .

Fear curled in her chest. The heart needed to be destroyed, but a terrible part of her wanted to open the box again, to keep it safe—

Mellifare stepped into the shrine, a feral scowl tearing across her face. She raked her red eyes across the shrine.

"I know you are here, Ananke," she said, her voice barely more than a whisper, but it carried all the way up into the rafters. The doors slammed closed behind her, trapping Ana inside.

JAX

Jax knew something was amiss the moment he saw the square in front of the Iron Shrine. Usually the square was teeming with people browsing the vendors set up around the square. There was always some sort of music, and the smell of freshly baked bread and meat skewers, but as he crested the last building and looked down—the square was empty. The stalls had been abandoned as if everyone had left in a hurry, baskets of fruits and vegetables overturned, mechanical parts strewn over the cobblestones glinting in the evening sunlight that came down from the harbor. He landed the skysailer on the far side of the square, beside the captain's. As he landed, he noticed bodies in the debris left behind, blood pooling beneath them. He couldn't sense their light at all, and he knew they were dead.

A single figure stood on the steps of the shrine, blocking anyone from entering.

Siege was leaning beside her skysailer, half using it for cover, her once-bright hair a simmer as she kept a hand on a bloody wound in her side, and Talle was on the ground beside her, wrapping up her own foot. Robb was already out of the sky-sailer before Jax could land it properly, rushing over to Siege, and once Jax parked he followed, helping Di out.

"Ana's in there," Siege said before any of them could ask how she was. The light underneath Jax's skin whispered the truth anyway, and it made him clench his fists. "We dropped her off and stood guard. I—I didn't see them coming. Mellifare tore through the square. Viera surprised us—stabbed me good. Everyone scattered."

"It's okay," Talle soothed.

"No, it's *not*. I have to get in there, starlight. I *have* to." Jax had never heard such pure desperation in his captain's voice before. It frightened him.

Across the square, the sentry on the steps did not move. Viera didn't waver as she stared at them, a lightsword un-sheathed in her hand. Her hair was no longer smoothed back but hung in her face, and beneath it her eyes burned a terrible, gut-wrenching red. Now that he concentrated, he sensed the HIVE—the thousands of souls—tied to her. If they came any closer, she would attack them.

"She was a Metal this whole time?" asked a voice behind him.

He quickly turned around to face Lenda. She looked as if she'd run a long way. The sanctuary was a few blocks north—he figured Siege had called for backup once Mellifare attacked. She stared out across the square to Viera on the other side.

"Yeah, she's a Metal," replied Robb. "Mellifare tricked us. Viera's been HIVE'd—Goddess knows for how long."

"And those people on the ground . . ."

"Viera was so quick, we couldn't stop her," said the captain, grinding her teeth. "I *should've* seen this coming. After all these times."

Jax didn't understand what that meant, but as he felt her light shift and flicker, he began to realize that he didn't know a lot about his captain.

"She's been standing there since Mellifare went inside after Ana," Talle said softly, and went to help Siege to her feet. Blood splattered Siege's shirt, quickly soaking through. "She hasn't attacked us yet. And all of the channels are down."

"Maybe Viera can fight the HIVE," said Robb, "like Di did."

"I don't think she knows she can," Talle replied. "And there's no way past her."

Lenda took her gun out of its holster. "All right then, I'll find out—"

Robb caught her by the arm. "That's suicide."

But the gunner shook her head. "Nah. She's family." Then Lenda set off across the abandoned square toward Viera, and in turn the ex–guard captain eased down to the steps to meet her.

As Siege rose to stand, she gave a painful wimper and leaned against her wife. "We need to get into that shrine."

"We can try," Jax promised her. "Di, can you—" He glanced back to the skysailer, but Di, it seemed, was gone.

ANA

Mellifare prowled deeper into the shrine, humming gently to herself. "Come now, you know you cannot hide from me forever."

Ana quietly shimmied across the arms. Her grip was sweaty, and the wax was slippery. The only sound she could hear was her hammering heart, and she hoped it wasn't as loud as she feared—

Her hand knocked over a candle.

It toppled before she could catch it and clattered on the ground.

The Great Dark turned her gaze up toward the statue—

When a bolt of lightning caught Mellifare on the side of the face, and she went stumbling into the pews.

Di dropped from one of the windows accessed by the outside scaffolding. He had a sword wound torn through his chest, too close to where his memory core should be, and it sparked even in the shadow of the shrine. He pulled himself up to his full height, even though it looked like it pained him. "Looking for someone?"

"You," Mellifare seethed, righting herself. She clutched the side of her face, where the skin had blackened and cracked. "Why do you stop me? You are on my side. You are with me."

"I am not with you, Mellifare. I was never with you willingly."

"Lies—I was in your head. I remember."

Di shifted uncomfortably.

"You promised me the heart, Dmitri."

"I am sorry mine was not enough," he replied—and winced. He must have heard the song.

Or realized how bad that pickup line was.

Ana curled her fingers into the soft wax underneath her. She had to keep going.

Don't stop, she coached herself, and began to creep forward again, her heart thundering like funeral drums in her ears. She had to go quietly, and quickly, while Di kept Mellifare occupied.

"And what did Viera promise when you turned her? Or was she dead before you made her a monster?"

"A monster? I gave you freedom."

"You took away who I *was*!" he snarled.

Mellifare laughed. "I made you better. Now where is my heart, brother?"

"I am not your brother."

Below her, Mellifare circled Di like a carrion bird did to a corpse. "You will tell me. You do not have a choice."

Then she flicked her hand. A bolt of light jumped out of her fingers and shot toward Di. He caught it in his hand and shot it back. It whirled over Mellifare's shoulder and slammed into the intricate stone molding above the door. A piece of marble cracked off and shattered on the ground. Mellifare launched herself at Di, arcs of lightning striking the pillars and scorched stone walls, leaving burned flower markings in their wake.

Goddess's spark, Ana cursed, and the hair on her arms stood on end. She doubled her pace to the shoulder of the Goddess and down the side of the statue. An arc of lightning shot up into the rafters, and Di went flying back into the benches, snapping them in half like a twig. She had to end this—fast. She jumped down the last few feet onto the pedestal.

"STOP!" Ana cried.

In the ruins of crushed benches, Di struggled to his feet, slipping on a piece of splintered wood. His moonlit eyes flickered, the wound in his chest sizzling. He was overheating again, and Mellifare looked barely winded as she jerked her gaze up to Ana, a smile curving across her lips.

Ana held up the box. "I—I have it. I'll give it to you. Just let us go."

The Great Dark clucked her tongue to the roof of her mouth and outstretched her hand to Di again. "Oh no," she purred as he tried to stumble away, and a blast pinned him up against the pillar. He cried out in pain. "You will hand it to me, and perhaps I will spare him."

"No," Di forced out. "Ana—*d-do not*." He pushed himself off the pillar, but it was clear he needed it to stand. His fingertips were blackened, burned up to his first knuckles. She resisted the urge to run to him, to make sure he was okay, to tell him to destroy the heart so Mellifare could never get it—

But Mellifare wasn't going to let her do that, so she had to improvise.

She walked up to the Great Dark, even though with every step her skin crawled at the nearness, and offered out the box. "I think this is yours."

The Great Dark looked down at the lockbox for a moment, as if not quite certain it was hers. Then the monster reached with trembling fingers and gently took the box. Ana retreated back to Di and quickly pulled his arm over her shoulder. The wound in his chest looked worse up close, a slice right through the center of it.

"Why did you do that?" he asked, his voice scratchy, like nails across metal. It reminded her of the voice he'd had in his old body. "Why did you give it to her?"

"Trust me, okay?" She subtly took his other hand and pressed it against her pocket. To the cube shape there. The heart. "Di— overload the memory core in the box."

"The what?"

"I swapped them—your old one is in the box." She led him, stumbling, toward the back exit, and he nodded and twisted his hand back toward the box. His fingers shook. Mellifare broke open the lockbox with her bare hands. At first there was delight as she stared into the box, but then it quickly dropped to rage—

She grabbed the memory core inside.

"What is this? Whose is—"

Di's fingertips sparked.

The memory core exploded in her grip, swirling outward in

a bloom. It rattled the rafters and filled the shrine with smoke. The shock wave swept up the walls, snuffed out all the candles, and plunged the Iron Shrine into darkness. She hauled Di to the side exit where they had escaped once before—in pursuit of Robb and the coordinates to the *Tsarina*—and pushed on the door.

ROBB

Viera attacked with a sweep of her lightsword.

Lenda deflected with the butt of her pistol and rolled away from her. Robb watched helplessly, his hand gravitating toward the lightsword at his hip. Lenda had terrible odds, but she was keeping Viera occupied. Somehow.

They needed to get inside and help Ana. The longer she was trapped in there with Mellifare, the less likely he'd see Ana again alive. He remembered facing Mellifare the last time in the shrine in the Iron Palace. It had been terrifying, and back then he hadn't known that she was the Great Dark. It was because of him Viera was dead in the first place. She had faced off against Mellifare in that shrine and given him time to flee after Ana.

And now Viera was dead, and Ana was fighting Mellifare alone.

He had to do *something*—

Jax stilled his hand reaching for the hilt of his sword and shook his head. Robb ground his teeth, feeling more helpless by the moment. "Maybe we can overpower Viera together, and then sneak in through the side entrance—"

"No can do, kiddo—that entrace was melted shut," a gruff voice said behind them. Everyone jumped in surprise and spun back to it. A tall and burly shadow towered over them, with curly peppery-gray hair and a handlebar mustache.

Robb recognized the man with a start.

"Mokuba! Finally!" he cried, pulling the burly man into a quick hug. Over Mokuba's shoulder, he noticed other people behind him—Red Dawn mercenaries and the people from the sanctuary on Nevaeh. "Did Xu and Elara—?"

"Take destiny into their own hands when the comms went down and rally the reinforcements? Why yes, Smolder, we *are* competent," interjected Elara as she melted out of the shadows, Xu beside her. "Though we kinda ran into some Messiers." She pointed her glowing boomerang behind her, and to his horror Messiers began to come into focus at the end of the street, patiently stalking toward them. "They're heading this way. There's a lot of them."

"They're coming from the other streets, too," Siege added grimly, nudging her chin across the square. A handful of Messiers in pressed blue uniforms came into the square. They advanced on the shrine—and on Viera and Lenda.

"Shit," Robb cursed. "Can't one thing be easy, just one?"

"*Ma'alor*, when has anything been easy?" Jax replied tiredly.

Xu assessed the situation. "I believe our best option is to try the front door. But they will attack if we make our move."

Siege forced herself to her feet. Her hair burned a deep, bloody red. She took out her Metroid and checked her bullets.

"Aye," she said, and the look on her face was grim. "And if we go over in our skysailers, we'll be shot out of the sky. Front door's the only way."

Talle gave a start. "You're hurt, Sunshine! We need to trust Ana."

"But I'm not dead yet."

"Even if we tried, there's twenty—maybe thirty Messiers already in the square," Jax added, but the captain wasn't taking their excuses.

"I'll get myself there, with or without your help."

Robb gave Jax a hesitant look, and then he glanced back at Elara and the rebels from the santuary, the last of the rogue Metals who had held out this long, and a few crewmembers from Siege's other fleetships. His family's militiamen were helping with the disaster of Astoria, evacuating all nearby buildings and making sure everyone in the gardens got out safely, while the Wysteria militia were trying to keep order in the docks above after Mellifare had cut off all incoming traffic. They weren't going to get any more reinforcements.

This was it.

The odds were getting slim. Robb really did hate his luck, especially now. He remembered back to the Wicked Luck game with that cheating bastard. Mellifare had a card up her sleeve, he had a feeling, but doing nothing was worse than waiting to see what trump card she'd play.

"Okay, Captain," he told Siege, voicing the consensus of the group, "we'll get you to the door. Just be ready to knock."

In reply, the captain pulled back the hammer of her Metroid. "They'll hear me."

DI

The exit door was melted shut.

A critical warning blinked in the back of his head, and his chest burned like someone had poured lava onto his ribs. The fight with Mellifare had made him expend so much of his energy. Another stunt like that—even as much as feeding energy into anything—would overload his hardware.

It would kill him.

Mellifare gave a feral cry, and he heard her prowling toward them in the darkness, pushing the pews out of the way as if they were made of paper. "I know you have the heart. I will find you!"

He and Ana ducked behind one of the pillars, and they pressed against each other in the dark. Without the candles, they could barely see anything—only the hint of smoke rising from the wicks, and the outline of the windows high above them, shedding light from the misty city outside. There were footsteps to their left, but were they just echoing from the right?

He could not tell.

"Ana," he said softly, "you need to get out of here."

"Not without you."

"I will distract her. What matters now is the heart."

She gave a start. "Are you sure?"

"I will be fine," he replied, but he could feel his eyes flicker again.

"No," Ana replied, and his face hardened. "I won't. I won't make you do that."

"I am *asking*—"

His chest sparked again, and he gave a groan, doubling over. Warning flared in his head. *CRITICAL MALFUNCTION*, it read. He pressed his hand against the wound, his eyesight glitching.

Distantly, he heard Ana calling his name, and then it was—

"Di, look! It's your name!" Nicholii laughed, flourishing his hand at the ancient stone wall. They were in the ruins near the Academy, waiting for Mercer to fix their skysailer. It had broken just outside the ruins, and no matter how many times he kicked at it, the damned thing just would not start. Nicholii had found a piece of charcoal in the glove compartment of the sailer and got to work alleviating his boredom.

Di was not amused. "Could you *stop* desecrating the ruins?" he asked, looking up from his holo-pad in annoynace. "You're the *prince*, for Goddess's sake."

Nicholii gave him a pointed look and, after *DI*, added *IS A SPOILSPORT* on the wall, and both Mercer and Selena Valerio fell back in peals of laughter. "Oh, whoops, now you're immortalized as a dick!"

Di rolled his eyes and glanced back at Mercer. "Honestly, can't you just call Cynthia and ask her to come get us?"

"And incur her wrath?" Mercer scoffed, wiping the oil from the skysailer's engines off his hands and onto his trousers. "The ruins have been off-limits since the Plague. Cynth and I might be betrothed, but she would *kill* me if she knew I went out here."

"No, she wouldn't."

"No, no, she would," Nicholii agreed. "She's terrifying."

"Don't let her hear you say that," Mercer chided. He came over beside Nicholii, took the piece of charcoal out of Nic's hand, and scratched out the *NICH* in Nicholii and put *DICK*. He gave his friend a shit-eating grin and handed him back the charcoal. "Why don't you call your father?"

"Pff! And have the royal guard scolding me for the rest of my life? I think not."

"Cynthia's our best option," Di added.

The memory was like a bright flare in his head—Nicholii tossing the piece of charcoal to him, and Mercer rolling up his sleeves with his greasy fingers, and Selena sunbathing on a thousand-year-fallen pillar, and—

"Where's Marigold?" Di asked, glancing around the ruins.

Selena pointed deeper into the shrine. "She went exploring— and Mercer, I think everyone's right. Cynthia's our best bet."

"I *refuse* to . . ." Mercer went on a rant about why Cynthia would be the worst person to call to come fetch them, but Di tuned him out as he went to go look for Marigold. He wandered deeper into the shrine, into a circular back room with a dry fountain in the middle. There were tiles on the walls, murals depicting the plight of the Goddess and her age-old battle with the Great Dark, faded and crumbling with time. It was a marvel that it was still here at all.

He found Marigold on the far side of the circular room, standing in front of an enormous iron door. The lock was so intricate, it curved in and out of itself up the flat surface of the door, and he imagined it would turn like a great machine work—cogs interlocking with each other and teeth turning. It looked a little like a map of the Iron Kingdom.

Marigold traced the circular lock where some sort of round and jagged key went. She did not hear him until he accidentally kicked a fallen tile, and she glanced over her shoulder. Her eyes focused.

"Oh—Di. I didn't hear you."

"Evidently." He came up beside her, studying the door. "What is this?"

Mari turned her gaze back to the circular shape where a key went and shook her head. "I don't know, but I feel . . . like I know this place." A laugh bubbled up from her throat. "Isn't that silly?"

"Perhaps in another life?" he asked.

She laughed in earnest this time. "Perhaps," she agreed, and turned her gaze back to the door. "I just feel . . . peaceful here. Like someday it'll bring me good things. And I'll be happy." She surprised herself by wiping a tear from her eye. "Goddess, I swear I'm not crying!"

In reply, Di dug a kerchief out of his pocket and handed it to her. "Your eyeliner didn't even smudge," he replied in good humor, and realized that Selena was calling them back to the front of the shrine.

"Hey, Di?" Mari asked, but her voice sounded different. It sounded like—*"Di!"*

Ana grabbed him by the arm and pulled him around the other side of the statue, as a bolt of lightning arced through the darkness. She grabbed him by the side of the face and made him look at her, the dim light falling softly along her scars. "Di— can you hear me?"

He nodded. "Yes."

"What happened?"

"Nothing," he lied, dazed, and pressed his hand harder against his chest. The blade *had* cut into his memory core. It was malfunctioning. He needed to keep himself together. Ana slid closer to him, and in the quiet he could hear her frightened breathing.

"I'm not going anywhere without you."

"We can't give her the heart, either," he replied.

Ana paused for a moment and then said, "Can you—could you free them? I mean—you can do everything else she can, right? Can't you—can't you go into *her* and disassemble the HIVE?"

The taste of the memory had unbalanced him, half of him still in that sun-drenched memory, and he shook his head. "I do not know."

"Do you think you could try?"

"I do not know." He tried to sound patient, but he was not patient anymore. He wanted to end this—to fix the mistakes he had begun. Perhaps if he had enough energy, he could force his way into her mind—but what if he tried and the HIVE consumed him again? What if it made him turn on her?

In the darkness, he felt Mellifare's anger roll off her in waves. She was getting closer.

"You know that captain of yours? She begged for her life, you know. Outside. Before I killed her."

He heard Ana suck in a breath, and he found her hand and curled his fingers through hers. He squeezed. *She is lying*, he wanted to tell her. *Siege does not die so easily.*

Out of the corner of his eye, he noticed as electricity surged around Mellifare's footfalls, like drops of water in a calm pond. The shadow lunged. Di grabbed Ana by the hand and pulled her out from behind the pillar and down the middle of the aisle. She stumbled on a censer that had been dropped in the abbesses' mad dash out of the shrine.

"She begged me to spare your life"—Mellifare's voice was so close, how was it so *close*?—"just before I killed her."

Ana let go of his hand before he could tell her to duck or dodge, felt for the censer on the ground, and swung it by the chain. It collided with Mellifare and knocked her sideways. Her footsteps stumbled like a pebble tripping across a pond.

"Siege would never *beg*," Ana snarled into the darkness. "She demands."

"Oh yes, darling, I demanded so much from you."

A shudder crept down his spine. It was Siege's voice, and not Mellifare's, the honeyed dip and swing of her accent. He felt Ana tremble beside him.

"It is not real," he told her, trying to convince himself.

"*I died*," the Great Dark went on in Siege's voice. "*You let me die, darling. You disappointed me.*"

"I . . . I didn't . . . ," Ana whispered.

He felt the HIVE shift then, pulsing, raging, and suddenly he shoved Ana out of the way. The next thing he knew, a hand grabbed his face—and red eyes sparked to life in the dark, illuminating Mellifare's twisted snarl. The electricity she had expended had cracked her skin, making chunks of it flake off. She did not look the least bit human anymore, the shadows clinging to her like an extravagant robe.

Lightning bolts leaped across his skin, leaving blossoms of black burn marks, sinking beneath his wires. His memory core in his chest flashed so hot he thought it would boil out of his skin—and there was a *pop*.

His eyes darkened.

Mellifare picked him up and launched him into the pews with enough force to snap them in half.

ANA

There was a loud crash. His name tore from her throat in a
wail—but he didn't respond. The light in his eyes flickered for
a moment—moonlit—and then was gone.

She gritted her teeth, anger pulsing in her stomach, and tore
the steel dagger out of her boot. All she could see were the red
pinpricks of Mellifare's eyes. Ana slashed her across the middle,
but Mellifare backstepped, and then again. Ana took the offen-
sive, remembering what Siege had taught her.

Don't let them stop, darling, don't let them think, she heard her
captain say.

Rage and regret pulsed through her in equal measure, and
she blindly jabbed into the darkness. She caught glimpses of
Mellifare only when she came too close, and then the darkness
swallowed her up again. Ana cursed, making herself stop, and
listened for footsteps, but her heart beat so loud she could barely
hear anything at all—

This was useless. *She* was useless in the dark.

"I'll barter with you!" Ana cried desperately, and with her

other hand she curled it around the heart in her pocket and brought it out. "Release the Metals in the HIVE, and I'll give you your heart."

Out of the corner of her eyes, she watched Mellifare's electric footfalls come to a stop a few feet away from her, eyes bright. "Liar."

"It's here and you can have it. Just release the Metals in the HIVE first."

"And give up my only power source for when you refuse to give me my heart?" Mellifare laughed. "Ana, I am not that gullible. I will just take it once I kill you."

Ana curled her shaking fingers around the heart.

She was afraid of dying—of ending like a sigh in the universe, inconsequential, a blink in time. She wanted to be more than a blink—she wanted eons with that boy of metal and moonlight. And she couldn't have it.

She just wanted more time.

With Di, with Robb, with Jax—with Siege. Her captain.

But time flowed in a river going one way, and she was on it for only a short while, while this monster had sailed the river for countless centuries, killing and taking and devouring worlds, and that she could not let happen anymore.

Because she did not want her friends—her home—to die.

But she didn't want the Metals in the HIVE to die either. She couldn't save both, but she couldn't choose one over the other. She wasn't a Metal, she had never been part of the HIVE, and yet she had the power to damn them all. She had a choice that wasn't a choice at all.

Destroy the heart . . .

Or let the Great Dark win. Let the Metals exist in the HIVE.

She now understood why it had won so many times over the course of its existence. Because it never had anything to lose, and Ana had everything. Di and Jax and Robb and Elara and Xu—*dying* so that she could succeed. And so she had to choose. There was no one else left to.

Her captain had not raised her to take the easy road.

"Fine," she said, her voice trembling, curling her fingers tightly around the heart as it pulsed against her palm. "Then you'll have to pry it from my corpse."

"That," Mellifare purred, "can be arranged."

She appeared in the darkness, sliding between the shafts of light that speared through from the broken windows above, and stalked toward Ana, electricity curling in her hands.

JAX

"Get to the door!" he cried, deflecting a lightsword as it came down on him and slamming his foot into the Messier's middle. It was infinitely harder to disable them without outright *killing* them. For every *one* Messier they took out, two more crawled out of the city to take its place. They were all converging, gathering, trying to fight their way into the shrine. Just as soon as Jax had decided to go for the door, what felt like every Messier in Nevaeh came to stop them. They poured out of the streets like ants, and in the middle of them danced Viera and Lenda.

He pressed his back against Robb's as four more Messiers advanced on them.

"Are they ever going to let up?" Robb asked, brushing his arm across his forehead. He was breathless. "Do you have any bright ideas?"

"I could kiss you again and maybe see if we get a break in the future?"

"Do you really think that'll help?"

"No," he said bitterly, hating he couldn't lie, "but it'd sure help me feel better."

One of the Messiers attacked. Robb shoved his foot against its knee, and it buckled inward, before he drove a lightsword through its skull and kicked the android back into its friends. If Jax wasn't so tired, he would have been incredibly turned on by how effortless Robb looked.

"Now!" Robb cried.

Siege, with an arm slung over Talle's shoulder, rushed past them toward the stairs to the shrine. A Messier gave a running start but was knocked off its feet by a boomerang. The weapon swirled back, and Elara jumped to catch it a few feet away.

Xu slammed their shoulder into the next Messier who came at them, blocking it from attacking as Siege and Talle hurried up the steps. Xu, one arm torn off, with a spear they had picked off an android's corpse, stabbed the Messier through the shoulder and pinned it to the ground.

The captain and Talle were almost to the door.

At least *one* thing was going right.

Robb wiped his forehead again with his sleeve. He glanced around the square and gave a start. "Lenda! Fend her off!"

The woman in question achingly got to her feet. There was a deep red wound on her forehead that bled down into her eyes, but she wiped the blood away. Viera had escaped her, making a beeline for the shrine to stop the captain, and she quickly raced after her, grabbed her by the hair, and swung Viera away from the stairs.

"Yes—they're almost to the door!" Xu reported.

"Don't jinx them," said Jax as he sliced through another Messier. He and Robb stuck close together, cutting down every Messier who came at them like they were an abundant weed patch encroaching upon the shrine.

A Messier with a halberd came swinging—

Mokuba blew a sizable chunk into its side with his antique Lancaster. The rebels and resistance swarmed around them, the noise so loud he could barely think. Robb grabbed the halberd out of the air, shoved it into the stomach of the next Messier, and launched himself in front and drove his lightsword down into a third body. Three more took its place.

This was hopeless—

For a second as he let his guard down, a Messier grabbed ahold of his ponytail and wrenched him backward.

"Ma'alor!" Robb cried, too far away to save him.

Another Messier raised its lightsword to slice him in half, but a bullet slammed into the side of the android's skull. Robb tossed him his lightsword. Jax caught it and, with a brief moment of sorrow, sliced it across his hair. The smell of burned hair filled his nose as he stumbled forward, away from the Messier.

Another bullet sliced through its shoulder, and it fell back.

At the top of the stairs, holding only a smoking Metroid, was Siege as she leaned on Talle for support. She cocked her pistol again and put five more bullets into the Messiers coming up on Robb and Jax. They dropped like trees in the wood, sparking and hissing from bullet holes in their necks.

She gave one last nod before she turned toward the large doors to the shrine with Talle and slipped inside, her tailcoats fluttering behind her like the last line of a story.

"*Ma'alor*, are you okay?" Robb asked.

"Yes," he replied roughly, surprising himself with the truth. A knot formed in his throat. "Yes, I will be."

ANA

Mellifare walked, slow and steady and patient, toward her.

It was the first time Ana remembered being this afraid. At least, since she was very little. When the fire broke out in the palace, she had been scared for her life—but this was different. This was the sinking, settling sort of fear. The kind that nailed itself to her heart and told her that it would stay.

Her captain told her it was okay to be afraid—that it just meant she had something she didn't want to lose.

But this was the kind of fear that told her that she would lose it, anyway.

She wasn't the Goddess. She didn't have celestial powers. She couldn't stop the Great Dark. She was just . . . she was . . .

She was Ana of the *Dossier*.

She was Siege's daughter.

That did *not* mean nothing. Her fingers gripped the terrible heart so tightly, her hand shook, and she pressed it against her stomach—against the scar she had survived. She had plenty of those now, each a story, each a part that made her stronger.

I'm Siege's daughter, she repeated to herself as she reached for the Metroid under her arm, the fit of the pistol so familiar it calmed her nerves, and unholstered it. She knew what she had to do, and Goddess damn her forever for doing it. She spun out her barrel to check her ammunition. Five. She had five shots.

Count your bullets, Siege had once said.

She aimed at Mellifare's left shoulder. "One."

She fired.

The bullet clipped the girl's right shoulder, but the impact made barely more than a punch.

"If you kill me," said Mellifare, "you kill all the Metals in the HIVE. All those innocent people dead—"

"Two—three," she counted.

She fired again, slamming another two bullets into the exact same shoulder. Sparks hissed from Mellifare's shoulder this time, and her arm fell limp, but her other fisted.

"You will not kill them," Mellifare hissed. "You are too *soft.*"

The pistol in her hand began to shake.

"Four," Ana whispered.

The bullet slammed into the left side of Mellifare's chest, and the monster's face crumpled into a feral snarl. "You missed."

She couldn't again. She had to steady her aim, even as the knowledge shook her to the bone. If she killed Mellifare, the thousands of Metals in the HIVE would cease to exist. But if she did not kill Mellifare, then the kingdom would fall to ruin.

"Why do you fight so much? Give up, Ana. Everyone you love—your captain, your lover, your friends and family—all of them," Mellifare said, so close now Ana could see the cracks in her skin and the metal underneath.

A shadow rose behind her, and Ana recognized the shape as surely as she did her own.

"Your loved ones are are dead—"

A bullet, straight and sure, pierced through her chest and came out the other side.

"Five" came the voice of her captain, standing in the open doorway.

Mellifare stumbled back, staring down at the hole in her chest. "You—you would kill me? You would kill *everyone*?"

"The people I love are never really gone," Ana said as the shadow's pale hand grabbed Mellifare by the shoulder and spun her around.

"And some come back," added Di, his eyes flickering, flickering, fading, and pressed his palm against her forehead. *"But not you."*

DI

The moment his fingers connected with her skin, he felt the energy inside her, crackling like lightning trapped in a bottle. It was the light from eons of souls she had absorbed, from countless worlds, and it was tainted; it was wrong.

The stolen energy came to his fingertips like light through a dark tunnel, pouring through his fingers and up his arm. Crackles of electricity screamed across his skin as his programs flickered back to life, his synapses rebooted, his senses sharpened. It was like taking a breath after a year underwater.

Do you have enough? Are you sated? he heard her whisper across his code.

No, not *nearly*.

Overflowing with her power, almost *drunk* with it, he sank into her code, burrowing inside like a worm, between the pointed talons and snapping red maw, into the gnarled root of her, this twisted and dark thing. He did not know if it was her soul or just her code—her malware—but it was corrupted all the same. And from her stemmed thousands upon thousands of threads in every direction, arcing across the kingdom, and with them he could see every Messier. Ones guarding airlocks on Nevaeh, others dragging rebels away on Iliad, and the ones newly changed and waiting in dreadnought holds.

It was the HIVE, singing the song he had been a part of, that had not been a song at all, but thousands of voices screeching in agony.

It reminded him of the white gurney in the hospital, the Plague eating up his hands, and a terrible and spiraling blackness that sucked in all hope and happiness and left him empty. When he was alive, he had been so afraid of death, Mellifare had looked like a goddess come to save him.

He wished he had been braver.

But if he had not become a Metal, he would never have met Ana, and a life with her—with Siege and Talle and Jax and the *Dossier*—was the best life he could have had.

And it was a life worth fighting for.

YOU ARE MINE OR YOU ARE NOTHING, the Great Dark screamed, but like it had torn through his code, he set upon it with a vengeance. And there was no firewall intricate enough to keep him out.

YOU ARE MINE OR YOU ARE—

One by one, he tore out the threads connected to the HIVE, severing them quicker and quicker, letting them go like balloons into the atmosphere, freeing them. D293. D849. D394. D091—so many numbers, once people, ones with names, and perhaps with a little help, they would be again.

YOU ARE MINE YOU ARE—

He tore out the Great Dark's memories of being Metal. Of the palace, of the kingdom, of all the people it had killed.

YOU ARE MINE—

Of the galaxies it had invaded. The Solani kingdom, among countless others. The eons of history it had devoured. The suffering, the bloodshed. He separated zeroes from ones, spreading through them as swiftly as ice across the windshield of the *Dossier.*

YOU ARE—

He tore the Great Dark asunder, until it was only—

YOU—

"They are free," Di said, and tried not to think about what he had just done—taken eons' worth of stolen light to free the Metals in the HIVE. The energy now hummed inside him, powering his wires, his core, his hardware, and he felt strange. Too full and empty all at once. It was a buzzing sort of feeling, his skin tingling with it.

"You promised," Mellifare whispered as she fell away from his touch, sinking down onto her knees. Her hair was burned at the ends. She held her broken chest and the memory core inside. "You . . . you promised me my . . ."

"He couldn't promise something that wasn't his to give," said Captain Siege as she came up to them, leaning heavily on Talle. Blood leaked from between her fingers as she held on to her wounded side.

Mellifare drew her gaze up to the captain. "*. . . Goddess?*"

"Siege," she corrected.

"It is so lonely in my head," said the Great Dark. "I do not want to be . . . a-alo . . ." Her eyes gave one last brief flicker, and her head bowed; and in a great sigh of time, and space, and stardust . . .

the Great Dark was gone.

ANA

"It's done," Ana heard her captain say, and her hair shifted to a yellowish white, like the heart of a candle. Her knees gave out, and she dropped to the ground. Her breath came out in short, sporadic gasps.

"Sunshine!" Talle gasped, falling to her knees beside her. "Di, hurry, there's a medical bag in the skysailer—"

"On it." He spun on his heels and broke into a run out of the shrine, tripping on an overturned pew as he went, out of the open shrine doorway and into the square filled with Metals, slowly blinking back to themselves, and people holding their wounds.

Ana's gaze drifted down to the wound on her captain's side, not quite understanding what she saw. Too much blood, too little time. It was everywhere, blending into her bloodred murder coat, painting up the side of her cream-colored blouse.

"Starlight," Siege sighed to her wife, "just let me . . ."

"Stay with me," Talle whispered. "I love you, sunshine." She curled her fingers tightly around her wife's shaking hands.

Siege looked pale—pale in the way Ana had seen corpses look pale, and her captain wasn't a corpse.

Her captain was . . . she was . . .

Ana sank to the ground beside her, hovering a hand over her bloody side. "You'll be okay. You'll be okay," she repeated.

Her captain smiled and, with her bloodied hand, cupped Ana's cheek. "I am so, so proud of you."

Sorrow welled up in her so quickly, she couldn't keep back the tears. "Don't say stuff like that. Why didn't you go get medical help when you could've?"

"You came first."

She gritted her teeth. "Di'll be back soon. You'll be fine—"

The captain rubbed Ana's tears away with her thumb. "We're all stories in the end, my darling," she sighed, and with every word she grew quieter, each strand of her firelight hair darkening like stars in a dawning sky. "You and Talle are the best parts of mine."

"Shush—save your breath," Talle scolded, her voice soft and trembling, but the captain only smiled sadly and took another painful breath.

No, Ana thought, glancing out of the open door to Di, rushing across the square to the skysailers, a sinking feeling settling in her stomach. *No, no, no, no—*

Her captain curled her bloody fingers into hers, and Ana looked back down to her, memorizing her face, the way her wild hair glowed and simmered like stoked coals, bathing her face in sunlight. She memorized her green eyes, her smirk, how her coat was ragged and patched yet had been cleaned and pressed with prestige. A hundred memories, a thousand moments she wished she had paid more attention to, a million seconds she had taken for granted.

She bent down, tears streaming down her face, and kissed her mother's forehead as the light faded softly from her hair.

ROBB

Black banners decorated the Iron Palace. If anyone didn't know they were coming to a funeral, he hoped they figured it out by the time they came into the ballroom. Most Ironblood funerals weren't held at the palace, families opting for quiet wakes at their private estates where the reading of the will came directly after the victuals. There was little pomp and circumstance, since most of the time it devolved into long-lost family members coming out of the woodwork to try to snag what few valuables they could get from the will.

But Robb was not only a Valerio—he was an Aragon too, since he took the captain's last name, so he had the power to buck a little tradition. Where the Valerios were notorious as sharp and merciless businesspeople, having investments in almost every type of company in the kingdom, the Aragons were magnanimous to the point where his mother had to spit out their name. He thought it rather fitting.

So tonight, for the first time in the history of the Iron Kingdom, there was a funeral at the palace. The lanterns in the hall bobbed with a new orange glow—as if they'd taken the light directly from Siege's hair. He wondered if that was Di's doing. He'd seen him messing with one of the lanterns in the hallway earlier today.

He hurried down the ballroom stairs and nodded to a few Ironbloods who looked vaguely familiar, adjusting his dark frock coat as he went. The Aragon symbol was pinned to his lapel, and he felt too many eyes lingering on it as he passed. A Valerio who became an Aragon, who had inherited both houses after his brother met his unfortunate end.

Goddess, he had so much wealth he didn't know what to do with it—and so much responsibility he got panicky just thinking about it.

"Thank you," he said to a passing waiter, snagging two glasses of rose champagne—Suvan'du, from the Aragon estate itself—and made his way toward a tall and slender boy. He stood out against the sea of black like a star in the night, the orange-yellow lanterns above making his skin sparkle like sunbursts.

"Hey, Smolder!" Elara yelled from the refreshments, and she waved with a beignet. Xu stood beside her, looking quite dashing in a golden tux. They were still missing an arm from the battle in the square, but a new one was supposed to arrive at the palace any day now.

After Di had freed the Metals from the HIVE, the Metals had returned to themselves as if waking up from a long dream. He saw it firsthand, as one moment Viera had lunged at Lenda, and the next she had fallen to her knees on the ground, the sword skittering away across the cobblestones.

Lenda had whirled back to her, dagger at the ready, but at the same moment the other Messiers had dropped their weapons, too. Viera looked around in confusion.

"Where—where am I?" she asked.

Lenda, hesitant at first, sheathed her dagger and walked up to the ex–guard captain."You're free," she replied, and stretched down her hand for Viera to take.

In the week following the death of the Great Dark, Ana returned to the Iron Palace with the crown, and she faced her people. She was met with so much love, she cried. She told the kingdom about Di, and how the HIVE had used him as a puppet Emperor. She wasted no time getting to work. Nevaeh was to be repaired, the Iron Shrine rebuilt, the garden of Astoria restored to its former glory. The dreadnoughts were quickly decommissioned. The special laws about "rogue" Metals were rescinded. She elected Xu as a liaison between Metals and the kingdom, and they had a chair on the Iron Council. So did a lot of other people who were not Ironblooded, and who did not come from prosperous bloodlines, but to Ana that didn't matter. If she was going to exist in a galaxy where an orphaned rebel could become the Empress of the Iron Kingdom, she didn't care about titles or bloodlines.

And quite frankly, Robb looked forward to the new dynamic in the Council.

Elara shouted with a mouthful of pastries, "You're looking hot tonight!"

"That's quite innaproriate to say at a funeral," he called back.

"Good!"

Robb waved her off and slipped up next to his partner, handing him one of the glasses. "Champagne to dull the boredom, *ma'alor?*"

Jax melted with relief. He looked as dashing as always, in a crisp lavender coat and pressed trousers. It was still a little startling to see Jax with short hair, falling just below his chin, but he was no less dashing. He wore starlike decorations on his head, too bright to be silver, that seemed to glow all on their own—the C'zar's crown. "About time you got here! I was worried I'd have to waste away over here alone," Jax said, and they kissed.

Robb couldn't help but smile. "I'll never get tired of doing that."

"We should do it as often as possible."

"Because you love to kiss me, right?" he asked.

"Because it makes the Elder Court so deliciously angry. An Ironblood and a C'zar? How *devious.*" He nodded over to a group of stodgy old men who were glaring daggers at them. "And also because I love to kiss you. That's a given."

"Thanks for the clarification—"

Jax kissed him again, longer this time, slower, running his tongue along his bottom lip, and when they parted, he lingered so close they shared a breath. "I clarify very well, thank you. Are they scowling yet?" he added, nudging his head toward the Elder Court.

Robb chanced a look. "Oh yes, scowls galore."

"Good."

He rolled his eyes and took another sip of champagne. "Is Di here?"

"Not yet."

"I heard he had a few, um, *appointments* with some engineers. Because of his—" He motioned to his chest. "What my brother did. It brushed his memory core."

"Yes, well, he's glitching—like he had been before this whole mess started. Except this time it's a little worse, I think."

"And Ana doesn't know, does she?"

"No, and speaking of whom, she's yet to grace the party. Fashionably late as usual." When Robb began to ask if he knew what was taking her so long, Jax nudged his head toward the other side of the ballroom to change the subject. Across the way, Lenda nervously clutched the arm of the newly reinstated captain of the royal guard. Lenda never did do well in crowds. They were talking with Mokuba and part of Captain Redbeard's crew, and Robb happily noted that at least *two* of them had gold teeth. "I never thought Viera and Lenda would become a *thing*. They seem to be having a good time."

Robb agreed. "I think Viera's smiling. Never thought I'd see that."

"At a *funeral*, too, *ma'alor*. Ghastly."

After a moment, Robb asked, "Ana *is* coming, isn't she?" in a low voice, so as not to alarm anyone.

The C'zar tilted his head one way and then the other. The light under his skin flickered playfully. "Why wouldn't she? She *is* Siege's daughter."

"That's why I'm worried."

ANA

She took the royal purple coat from where it was laid out on her bed and held it, trying to decide if she really wanted to wear something so . . . so *purple*. There really wasn't a better way to describe it. Purple and gold, the crown's colors—and so also *her* colors—although too bad she looked better in literally any other shade. The purple coat reminded her too much of her father's.

"You know, your father used to scowl like that too whenever he wore that color," commented Siege, who was lounging back in one of the cushy red chairs in the room. She had a flute of champagne in one hand, her hair peppery gray and wild, reaching toward the sky. She looked mismatched in Ana's room, in a worn black coat and trousers, and yet at the same time perfectly at home. She leaned her head on her hand. "Though you look so much like Nicholii I could cry."

"I do?" she asked, turning back to the mirror. "I don't *feel* like royalty."

"He never did either."

It was strange how you could be something but not know how. The coat didn't fit right, and she was afraid that the title *Empress* wouldn't fit either. It was more of a birthright, anyway. Something that she had just lucked into—there were other, better leaders out there in the kingdom, and she wanted to make sure they had a voice. She couldn't do it all on her own. She didn't know how.

There was a knock on the door and Talle peeked into the room. "Oh, here you are, sunshine. Are you ready to get going?"

"Are you sure you don't want to stay for the funeral?" Ana asked.

"Ah, I've had enough of those," said the captain, "and it's as good a time as any to disappear."

"And you can't tell me where you're going?"

Talle and Siege exchanged an unreadable look, and then the captain said, "I'm sorry, darling. We need to hide the heart, and the fewer people who know, the better. The Great Dark is gone—but we don't know if it's forever, or if we just destroyed a part of it, or if something else will come after the heart's power. We'll come back, though," she added when Ana started to look a little panicky. "We promise."

Ana nodded. She guessed that was as good as she was going to get from her captain. She played with the golden toggles on her coat as Siege stood, slowly, one hand on her side, and grabbed the golden-handled cane propped up on the side of the chair. As she turned to leave, Ana blurted, "Captain?"

Siege paused and glanced back over her shoulder. "Yeah, darling?"

Are you really the Goddess? Is the Great Dark really gone? Will you be back? She had so many questions to ask her, but none of them seemed as important as: "I love you."

Siege smiled, and the ends of her hair glowed faintly, reminding Ana of how once her hair had lit an entire room. She came up to Ana, and they were close to the same height now, but she thought she would always feel infinitely smaller against Siege—a shadow to rise up to. Her captain kissed her on the forehead and whispered, "To the ends of the galaxy, my darling."

Then her mothers were gone.

Pursing her lips, she blinked the wetness out of her eyes because she had cried too many times over the last week and slipped on the coat. The metal shoulders and the accolades on her lapel made the coat cumbersome, and it buttoned in this ridiculous way that must have been very fashionable a hundred year ago.

Was *this* going to be the rest of her life? Slipping into coats she didn't like, fretting about the state of the kingdom, and whether she ruled well, and what kind of world she would leave her own heir?

Her heir.

Oh, that meant love and marriage and—and other things. She barely knew what love was, and even so, she wasn't all that sure he loved her, too, and thinking about it got her nervous. Had the room just become stuffy? She began to unfasten the coat, one button at a time, almost tearing off the last one to get it undone, pulling at the collar of her blouse to get some air.

Stop thinking. You're okay. You'll be—

"That color really doesn't suit you," said a voice in the doorway.

Surprised, Ana glanced into the mirror, and behind her stood Di. He looked just as tragically handsome as ever, clad in an evening coat as black as coal, designs of golden suns across the collar and cuffs, a ruffly white ascot tight against his throat, his trousers as dark as his polished leather boots. His bloodred hair was half up in a bun, silver stitches sewing together the wound on his cheek. He had a box under his arm that was tied tight with a piece of string.

She spun around to him. "You always seem to find me in a state of undress," she noted.

She had barely seen him this last week, and standing there he looked both familiar and strange—someone she knew intimately and yet didn't know at all.

"Seems so," he replied. "You have a visitor who wants to see you. If you don't mind your state of decency, I won't say anything."

She was about to tell him to shush when a familiar whirring made her pause. Her eyes widened. It couldn't be. A moment later, a small square bot peeked over Di's shoulder, its lens widening at the sight of her.

"EOS!" she cried, flinging out her arms.

The bot gave a shrill beep and flew around Di to her, and she grabbed it and squeezed it tight to her chest.

"I thought you were fried!" She laughed. It wiggled out of her arms and nuzzled her cheek. She wanted to cry, she was so happy to see it. She asked, "How did you fix it?"

He rubbed his chest where Erik had punctured him with the sword. It was fixed now, she'd heard, the wires soldered, but rubbing it had become a habit, like with the scar on her belly. "Well," he began, "I broke the bot, didn't I? So I had to fix it. Besides, I thought you'd need your little companion back. It's much better use like this than you lobbing it at my head." EoS swirled away from her and bumped against the side of his head again. He glared at it. "Or not."

EoS blipped happily.

"Ah, you're right. Almost forgot. This is for you." He handed her the box from under his arm.

She took it, resisting the urge to shake it. "A present?"

"I surely hope so, or I grabbed the wrong box."

"Smart-ass."

"I'll take the gift back if you don't want it."

"No, I do!" She laughed, and then realized, "Wait, did you just use contractions?"

He touched his fingers to his lips in surprise. "Oh. I guess I did."

"If this is another glitch, you're keeping this one," she said with another laugh, and he gave a strained smile.

"Why don't you open your present?"

"Fine, fine." She busied herself setting the box on the bed. It was a simple beige box tied with string. She pulled it loose and quickly opened the box—and stared down at the mountains of supple red wool and brass buttons.

Di came up beside her, his hands patiently behind his back. "I seem to recall you were eyeing it in a storefront window a while ago. This one's a little different, but I think it suits you better."

EoS peered over her shoulder and gave a long, awed beep.

Inside the box was a coat as red as blood, its collar black to match its cuffs, brassy buttons gleaming. She ran her fingers along the intricate details of the lapel, suns and moons and stars in a tapestry that reminded her of Siege and Talle and the nights on the *Dossier* when she couldn't sleep, so she and Di watched the stars instead. It was built from the best parts of everything she loved. Its insides were a soft cotton she could sink into. The coat was so sharply fierce, she was afraid the threads themselves would cut.

Gingerly, she held it up. "Oh, I can't take *this*."

"It's a gift, so I insist." Then he outstretched his hand to the mirror.

Excitedly, she shrugged out of the purple coat and raced to the mirror to put it on. And *Goddess*, it was a perfect fit, brushing just above her knees. She spun around in it, grinning, as EoS swirled around her, obviously happy. It even had room for her pistols, and a flash grenade, and—

Except Empresses never wore pistols. They didn't carry flash grenades in their pockets.

And in the mirror, there was a bittersweet look on his face, one he tried to hide but couldn't. She could never read him before, but the more she studied the slant of his brow or the dip in the corner of his mouth, the easier he was to translate.

And no one gave gifts like this unless something was wrong.

Her smile began to drop from her lips.

Di asked, "Do you not like it?"

She turned to him, pulling at the cuffs. "Why does this feel like good-bye?"

"Ana . . . I . . ." He tried to find the right words, but he seemed not to be able to find any. He turned his moonlit eyes down and pursed his lips together tightly. "I can't—" He winced suddenly, his hand quickly going to the injury at his chest—and froze.

Like he had in the shrine—when they were hiding from Mellifare.

And now that she watched, she had seen this happen countless times before.

The terrible realization began to crawl up her spine like tiny spiders. She pressed a hand against his chest, where the wound had been. "Di?"

His eyes flickered.

"Di—Di, you're okay," she soothed, touching his cheek. Her fingers trembled. She'd never thought she would see this again. She never wanted to. She tried to be patient, to stroke his cheek, to wait—

Suddenly he jerked, the sound of a gasp escaping his lips, and he snagged her wrist, twisting it away from him. For a moment he looked at her as if he didn't recognize her—it was a look she had seen for six months while he was HIVE'd—but then remembered who she was and quickly let go.

He stepped away.

"I—I'm sorry. I can't . . . It's difficult to sometimes . . . I . . ." He pulled his hands through his hair, his face crumpling, because it was so apparent he wished she never had to see.

She took him again by the hand. "You're glitching, aren't you? Like you did before—"

"It's worse than before," he interrupted, unable to meet her gaze. "When I glitch, all I see are memories. I relive them—of when I was alive, and as a Metal, and HIVE'd, and I never know which it'll be."

"We can deal that. I can help you," she said, folding her fingers into his, but he tugged his hand away from her, and her heart sank.

He gave her a sad look. "What if I wake up from a glitch, all these screams in my head, and I can't remember you?" His face began to scrunch, wrinkles bunching his forehead, like someone trying desperately not to cry. "I wish I had never made that promise. The one in Rasovant's lab. I promised I would go away forever."

"Because I was in danger, and now I'm not," she realized.

"Yes." He balled his hands into fists. He was in pain standing there, as if waiting for her permission to leave. But if he left, he would go forever—she would never see him again. She would never talk with him, or laugh with him, or dance with him—

She looked down at her red coat. It was the color of a renegade, the cut of a rogue. It was not a coat for an Empress but for the captain of a ship.

Perhaps, in a different life.

"You should go with the captain and Talle," she said, and she didn't hear the words until after they were spoken. "Find a place to hide the heart. Go on a few more grand adventures."

Di hesitated.

"*Go*," she said, kissing his cheek. "I will always love you, Dmitri Rasovant, wherever in the universe you are."

Then she turned away from him because she could not watch him leave, like the captain left, like Talle left, and she exited the room with EoS at her side. She had kept the funeral waiting long enough.

She didn't look back.

ROBB

The room quieted as the steward announced in his nasal voice, "I present the Royal Empress of the Iron Kingdom, Ananke Armorov!"

The doors at the top of the ballroom steps opened, and a woman in a coat as red as blood stepped into the room. For a moment, Robb thought it was Siege—the way she held herself, how every eye in the room turned to look because she demanded it—but then he noticed Ana's short hair and the scars across her face, and his heart lurched.

However much of Armorov or Valerio flowed in her veins, she was the daughter of a starship captain and there was stardust in her blood.

She commanded the attention of everyone in the room without even saying a word, their gazes following her as she motioned to one of the servants at the bottom of the stairs, and they brought her a shot glass on a tray with a dark liquor.

"Thank you for coming to share this evening with us," she said loudly, and proceeded to the middle of the ballroom. Out of the corner of his eye, he saw the waitstaff bring out shots for everyone. Jax got two for them, and he sniffed his. Oh, that was some strong whiskey—the same kind he'd drunk on the *Dossier* when the captain had toasted to Barger and D09.

"Please, everyone take one," Ana urged, and waited for most everyone to before she began. "I will be the first to admit that I haven't attended many funerals. I'm lucky, I realize. When I was orphaned, I could have been found by a hundred different ships. By Captain Redbeard." She turned and toasted to him, and he returned the gesture. "Or the Red Dawn." Again, she acknowledged them. "Or Captain Cullen's crew, or a passing merchant ship. Or I could not have been found at all."

Robb scanned the crowd. "Where's Di?" he whispered to Jax. The Solani only shook his head.

He didn't come, he realized. Or—worse still—*he left.*

"But I *was* found," Ana went on, "and I was home."

"And so I want to make a toast to Erik Mercer Valerio. He might not have been the kindest individual, or the most magnanimous, and some of you might just be here for the food"—to that a few outlaws raised their glasses quietly—"but he was my cousin, and he was a Valerio—and above that . . ."

"Above that," added Robb, stepping up into the center of the ballroom and locking eyes with Ana. They raised their glasses together. His brother might never have gotten the chance to live in the palace, or sit on the throne, or command the kingdom, but at least he would have the kind of funeral provided for laying royals to rest. He wasn't sure if his brother deserved it, but he, and Ana, and Jax, and all the people who surrounded him, were better than his brother. And even so, in a small part of his heart, he would miss Erik, even if he didn't deserve to be missed. Love was strange that way, and complicated. He repeated, "Above that . . . he helped bring us all home. To those who set sail into the night—may the stars keep them steady," he toasted.

A hundred glasses rose up, and a hundred people said in unison, "And the iron keep them safe."

They downed the liquor and smashed the shot glasses against the floor, and the crowd followed suit. Glass scattered across the floor like glittering stars, reflecting the lantern lights above. Then Ana, without a moment's hesitance, turned and left the ballroom.

JAX

A twenty-piece orchestra struck up a tired tune in a minor key, and it made the air shiver with mourning. A strange feeling vibrated through him, the light under his skin shifting, whispering to him. Robb would turn to him, ask him to dance, and—

"Would you care to dance, *ma'alor?*"

And then, out in the garden—

"Please," he said under his breath, hopeful, and grabbed his partner by the arm and dragged him over to the ballroom's grand windows that stretched from the floor to the ceiling, overlooking the royal garden beneath. Moonlilies were just beginning to open, unfurling in bursts of white. The light inside him swayed and shimmered, and he was heady with the possibility.

Please.

A figure materialized out of the darkness of one of the arches. It was Ana, the brassy buttons on her red coat catching the moonlight like flares.

"Are we spying on her now?" Robb joked, glancing between him and Ana down in the garden. "Is that EoS?"

"We're just looking," he said, but when his partner raised an eyebrow he added, "And yes, that's EoS."

"You've seen this before."

"I hope so."

There was a shadow on the other side of the garden. It materialized out of an archway, a stranger in a billowing half cape. He crossed the garden in long strides. His hair was half pulled back into a bloodred knot, and the was unmistakable in the way you always knew the color of the sun, and following like a trail of suns were countless palace lanterns.

And although Jax couldn't hear him through the window and the noise of the funeral, he read Ana's name on his lips.

DI

A glitch festered at the back of his mind, and all he wanted to do was pluck his memory core from his body and finally *rest*. But as he stood in the cockpit of the *Dossier*, about to break away from the moonbay and leave the Iron Palace forever—he remembered how Wick used to kick his feet up on the communications console, and how Riggs's mechanical leg thunked up and down the hallway, the sound of Talle's laughter rebounding from the galley, so full of mirth it made his soul ache a little less, and the glow of Captain Siege's hair just before an adventure, and Ana's eyes glimmering yellow-gold of suns and new hope and excitement, so bright it blinded his memories—

And Siege turned around in the pilot's chair and gave him a knowing look. "You don't want to be here, metalhead."

·)●(·

Now he found himself standing in the middle of the palace's dark garden, as the most beautiful person in the universe stared at him as if he was a comet that had passed long ago and was never expected to return.

EoS bleeped, narrowing its lens to see if it really was him.

". . . Di?" she asked, his name barely more than a whisper. Her eyes were red as if she'd been crying, and she quickly wiped tears away with the sleeve of her new coat and sniffed.

An audience of lantern lights trailed out of the palace behind him, caught up in his magnetic pull like they had when he and Ana had waltzed what felt like centuries ago. He had been a different person then, and so had she.

Around them, the moonlilies began to bloom in the night, as they did every night.

"I am defective, but when I am with you I don't feel broken at all. I love you." He took a step toward her, and the lanterns followed, illuminating behind him like the dawning of a sun. "I am yours, Ana of the *Dossier*."

Goddess, those words sounded so bright in his head. He *loved* her. He loved her to the moon and back. He loved her to the stars. He loved her beyond that, and he would love her for a thousand turns around the sun.

For a long moment, she didn't move. Had he said the wrong thing? Had he not said enough? But there were no words left, even as he tried to find them to fill the silence of the garden. He was a jumble of someone who was and never would be, of mis-spent technology and second chances—and he was made from the parts of the universe that loved her.

"And I am yours, Di," she finally replied, and pulled him close to her. She kissed him on the lips, where their words still lingered, and the lanterns swirled around them, flickering like a thousand candles in a dark and empty shrine.

ACKNOWLEDGMENTS

Just so we're all clear: I'm writing these acknowledgments in Comic Sans, knowing that I'll convert it to Something Less Goofy by the time I get to finishing it. I find Comic Sans (or Courier, or Papyrus) relaxing when I'm writing something hard to put into words.

You've come with me this far, so I know you haven't set it down or forgotten it on a park bench somewhere, to which I say—thank you! If you want to skip all the random names of people you don't know, just jump to the end. That part's for you.

First, this book wouldn't be possible without my editor, Kelsey Murphy. You helped me push my craft and become a better writer, and that I will forever keep with me. Thank you for believing in me.

I also want to thank Jordan Brown. Thank you for letting me go with my gut—it means everything.

And honestly, this book would never have been possible without my agent, Holly Root, who is a freaking superhuman. You saw my potential in *Heart of Iron*, and the end of *Soul of Stars* feels like the closing of a well-rounded chapter. Here's to new stories, new characters, and midnight emails!

I also want to thank Renée Cafiero, the copyeditor and production editor for both *Heart of Iron* and *Soul of Stars*—thank you so much for your tireless work and for everything you have done for this novel. We've never met in person, but I want to thank you in the pages you helped bring to life. I can't express how much it means to me.

To Nicole Brinkley, you are the reason everything in this book is so sad. And to Kaitlyn Sage Patterson and Katherine Locke, you are the reason everything in this book is kinda happy. To Savannah Apperson, you are the reason I never stopped writing. To Ada Starino, Eric Smith, Rae Huffaker Chang, CB Lee, Paul Kreuger, Julie Daly, Sara Taylor Woods, and, honestly, probably a lot of people who I have missed, thank you for always believing in me when I didn't have the courage or the strength to believe in myself.

To my family, who finally stopped asking when I'm going to get a real job, thank god.

And lastly, I want to thank you, reader. I'm so happy that you went on this journey with me, about a girl raised in the stars, finding her home in the people around her. People who will never leave her—not really. I hope these characters will linger with you like they will me.

Sometimes the world sucks, and people suck, and life sucks, but with a few good friends, you are never truly alone. You will *never* be alone.

May the stars keep you steady, dear friend, and the iron keep you safe.

TURN THE PAGE TO READ THE
FIRST CHAPTER OF ASHLEY POSTON'S

IT IS SAID that the first king of Aloriya was born with fire in his blood. He was born in a time when the cursed wood that bordered Aloriya snarled and snapped at the edges of the kingdom, the same cursed wood that had been plaguing the people of Aloriya for as long as anyone could remember, but he was not afraid. He entered the wood, razed a path through the cursed wood to the magical city of Voryn, and struck a bargain with the Lady of the Wilds. What he asked for was simple—that Aloriya be protected from the monsters who lurked in the forest she commanded.

It is said the Lady took pity on the king, for he did brave her cursed wood, and gifted him a crown that would protect his people; but because she feared his magic, she made him promise that neither he nor any Aloriyan would ever return to her city. The forest on the edge of Aloriya would be forbidden to all its people. He agreed.

For three hundred years, Aloriya flourished. The crown was passed from father to son, from king to heir, and there were no monsters, no famines, no plagues, no wars.

And the city of Voryn, deep in the forbidden wood, fell to legend.

It is said that the Lady of the Wilds gifted King Sunder a glorious crown.

It is a lie.

~ 1 ~

THE VILLAGE-IN-THE-VALLEY

Cerys

THE WOOD CAME for us the day the king died.

At first it was only a few spots on an orchid, small black rotten dots that few would even notice. I didn't think anything of it. It hadn't looked like any disease I could remember; still, I simply bit my first finger until I could taste blood on my tongue, then pressed a droplet into the heart of the dying flower.

It bloomed once again, pale blue petals unfurling, growing to the size of my palm. I needed a bouquet to give Lady Ganara for that evening's coronation, after all. A little blood never hurt anything, and no one was ever the wiser, anyway. I slid the bloom back into the vase, beside baby's breath and a few sprigs of bluebells. Papa told me to only use my *talent*, for lack of a better word, sparingly. A gardener's daughter with blood that could raise entire forests? Only the royal family had magic in their blood. What would Aloriya think if they knew I had a touch of magic, too? Even if my power was small, I was quite sure I would be the talk of the town. And not in the good way.

"Morning, Sprout!" Papa greeted me, coming in through the front of the shop. He knocked the dirt off his boots at the door and hung up his coat. "It's a beautiful day for a coronation!"

"Don't jinx it," I replied, making a tag for the bouquet—*Lady Ganara*, I wrote in my tight, neat cursive.

Papa belted a laugh. "What could go wrong? The sky's bright, the sun's out, and there's spring in the air—I can taste it."

"Mm-hmm. Watch it start raining the moment Wen says her vows. 'Oh, I would be *delighted* to accept this crown . . . after the monsoon,'" I said in the princess—soon-to-be queen—of Aloriya's crisp accent, grabbing the crown of daisies I'd made yesterday from the counter and placing it on my head. I mocked the royal wave to the flowers in the shop. "Why, thank you for coming! I am *delighted* to ruin all your fine clothes this evening."

Papa laughed louder as he escaped into the kitchen just off from the shop. He clanked around in the cabinets to find a cup and poured himself some coffee. He smelled like soil and freshly clipped flowers already, in dirty brown overalls and hard work boots, chewing on a stem of mint. His sun-browned skin was spotted with age, but his gray eyes were bright—like mine. "I got a feeling I won't be comin' back into the village today. It's a riot up at the castle. The seneschal's about to lose her head, she's so stressed."

"Poor Weiss. I feel for her."

"I don't," Papa groused, coming back to lean on the kitchen doorframe, into the small flower shop at the front of the house. The shop itself was part of our house. Papa and I lived upstairs, but the kitchen was downstairs, and out the back door were the gardens where we grew most of our flowers. "The old crone yelled at me again this morning."

"Probably for trampling muddy boots all over the castle again."

"That was one time, and it was an emergency."

I snorted. What my father deemed an emergency was showing King Merrick four-leaf clovers, or roses I'd accidentally bled on that turned strange shades of purple. I highly doubted it was an actual *emergency*. The late king had been Papa's best friend—one of the reasons that Princess Anwen was mine. He had been in the room when the king took his final breath two nights ago, and we barely had time to mourn his passing, as the kingdom was to be inherited by his children—

Child, I corrected myself. Because there were no longer two.

Papa seemed to be reminiscing about the same thing. "It feels like it didn't happen. Like he's still here. I keep forgetting."

"I know," I replied softly.

He stood quiet for a moment longer and then blinked his wet eyes and cleared his throat. "Well! No use dawdling; we've got work to do." He hooked his thumbs into the loops of his overalls and came around the front of the counter. He took a look at the bouquets ready to be picked up and paused on Lady Ganara's. "Kingsteeth, those are some beautiful blue orchids." Papa bent in to smell them—and winced.

While magic couldn't be seen, it did have a distinct scent that lingered for a while where it had been worked. The smell was like that of the Wildwood—like a sunlit forest just after heavy rain. Orchids did not smell like that. He leveled a stern look at me. "Cerys . . ."

"I know. I doubt she'll notice, though. Last night the flowers were fine, but this morning they were speckled with these weird black spots."

"What kind of spots?"

"Rot, it looked like? It was strange—but I fixed them. I just used a drop. I don't see what the big deal is. It's just magic, like Wen and her family have."

Papa's lips thinned into a line, and he took my hands in his, turning them over to see the wound on my finger. "You need to be careful. Our town, our village, they love you so much. I'm not worried about how they'd react to you having magic. But there is magic . . . and then there are curses."

"And mine's a curse, I know."

He squeezed my hands tightly. "The Wilds touched you, but they didn't keep you."

I glanced away.

Papa let go of my hand. "Maybe add a few more sprigs of baby's breath to cover up the scent—and then close up shop at noon and bring the last half dozen rose bouquets with you to the castle when you come."

"Don't forget your garden keys," I reminded him as he turned toward the front door.

He snapped his fingers and retreated back to get them from the hook in the kitchen. As he passed by the counter again, he planted a kiss on my forehead. "What would I do without you, Sprout?"

"Forget your head."

He laughed. "I'll see you in a bloom."

"In a bloom," I agreed, and watched him as he left through the front door and started out of the village on foot. He would catch a ride with one of the guards at the bottom of the Sundermount, and they would take him the rest of the way up the mountain to the castle.

The castle of Aloriya was perched at the edge of the wood, among the peaks of the Lavender Mountains. The spires stretched like shafts of broken bone toward the stars. It was much prettier at night, when all the windows were golden and warm, driving away the coldness that clung to it in the daytime, lit up like a body that had finally found its soul.

After Papa was well on his way to the castle, I slipped out of my apron, poured myself the last bit of coffee from the press, and stepped out back into the garden. It was a quarter to eight in the morning; the shop didn't officially open until eight o'clock. My finger was still bleeding a little, so I ran it across the doorframe, and from it moss grew in a thick green patch, like a swipe of paint across the weathered wood.

I sat down on the stone bench outside the door and leaned back against the house.

The gardens were small, but what they lacked in space they made up for in colors—leaves of green and kaleidoscopes of flowers bloomed on stems and in the latticework creeping up the house, having taken decades to climb. Roses thrived in the side gardens, and strange star-shaped flowers clustered in the corners of the yard where my mother had planted some foreign Wildwood seeds. Papa and I didn't sell those—they might have just been flowers, or they could have been cursed, and while we didn't want to lose the memory of my mother, we also couldn't risk any part of the Wildwood spreading.

The village knew my mother came from outside Aloriya—something that didn't exactly help my dating prospects. There were only so many young people in the Village-in-the-Valley, and I'd gone to grade school with almost every single one of them; we all knew each other's stories—where we came from, what we wanted to be someday, who we wanted to marry—but no one was as whispered about as I was, the girl whose mother had been an outsider. Then, later, the girl whose mother got lost in the wood. The pickings were slim to begin with, and I honestly didn't have time for the ones who "could overlook my oddities."

It also didn't help that most of the village thought that my best friend was a stupid fox that wouldn't stay away from me, no matter how many times I tried to shoo him off. I had rescued him from a hunter's trap near the wood a few years ago, and since then, he apparently thought we were inseparable.

"Can you *stop* nosing through the baker's garbage?" I scolded the little jerk as he slunk out from underneath the bench, a hunk of some sort of pastry in his mouth. "One of these days Mrs. Cavenshire's going to catch you."

The fox didn't seem to care. He never cared. He just kept going through the baker's trash, then would hide in our garden, hoping that I'd keep away the hounds when they came sniffing around. Now the fox hopped up on the bench beside me and gave me an unreadable look.

"*Fine*," I muttered, and scratched him behind the ears. He began to purr—which was probably the most charming thing about him. "Today's the day, you know. Anwen's getting the crown. She'll be Queen Anwen Sunder."

The fox gave a lazy yawn.

A voice interrupted my morning solitude. "*Queen* sounds awfully pretentious."

I glanced up toward the pergola on the other side of the

garden as a gangly boy in threadbare trousers that barely came up down to his ankles, a wrinkled button-down shirt, and a brown vest came in. He had two fresh croissants in his hands from the bakery next door, and a wide smile on his face that made his cerulean eyes glimmer. A sliver of long golden hair escaped his newsboy hat, giving him away. As if his grace hadn't already.

"Shouldn't you be at the castle?" I asked the princess of Aloriya as she handed me a croissant.

"Shush and eat," Anwen replied, lifting the fox up from his spot and putting him on her lap as she sat down.

I twirled a lock of her golden hair around my finger. "Your disguise is coming undone."

"Again?" Wen made a disgruntled noise and took off her hat. Long golden hair spilled down her shoulders, reaching her lower back in soft curls. "It doesn't matter. You'd recognize me anyway whether I was a boy or, I don't know, a *goat*."

I laughed. "I should hope so; we've been friends since we were six—"

"Five," she corrected.

"Are you sure?"

"It was right after your father caught you cutting your own hair and you had bangs like—" And she angled her fingers slantwise across her forehead. "Do you think I'd forget something like that? My brother wouldn't stop making fun of you for weeks."

I shivered, remembering, and handed her the cup of coffee. "Well, *I* certainly forgot until this very moment. Your brother hated me."

"I don't think he did at all," she replied, and took a sip of coffee to wash down a bite of croissant. "I miss him."

"Me too."

We sat and ate our breakfast quietly.

There was still so much to do before the coronation. I had to finish up the rose decorations and tend to the arrangements already in the store, all before I loaded up the wagon and made my way to the castle to help Papa set up for the rest of the afternoon. I felt exhausted just thinking about it. And I kinda didn't want the coronation to come—ever. Because once Anwen was crowned, everything would change.

Anwen rubbed the fox behind his ears. "Cerys, do you think I'll be a good ruler? As good as my brother would've been?"

I gave a start. "Why wouldn't you be?"

She let the fox nibble on the rest of her croissant and gave a half-hearted shrug. "What if . . . what if the crown doesn't take to me? Father died so suddenly, and he never gave me the chance to wear it. It keeps the curse and the creatures of the forest at bay, but how?" She outstretched her hand, and as she brushed her thumb and forefinger together, a flame bloomed in the air. It took my breath away every time she called her magic, the same magic that ran in her ancient bloodline. The same magic that razed the cursewood three hundred years ago. The flame flickered on the tips of her fingers. "Do *I* do something? I don't know."

"You'll figure it out—you're a Sunder, after all. It's in your blood, in your magic," I replied, and put my hand over hers to smother the flame. "And whenever you need me, I'm here. I'll always be here for you."

"Promise?"

I was the royal gardener's daughter. There was nowhere else I was supposed to be. "I promise, Anwen Sunder."

A small smile graced her lips. "Thank you."

We shared the rest of the coffee as the cool morning mists that surrounded the Village-in-the-Valley slowly lifted. The sun was bright and golden, and the sky was blue, and spring grew warm and light in the air. Papa was right. It was going to be a beautiful day.

The fox shook his head, having gotten bored with us, and hopped off Wen's lap. He began to slink around the gardens.

"If you go for those strawberries . . . ," I warned him.

Wen snorted. "He's just a fox. He's not going to listen. Honestly, I don't see why you put up with him."

I cocked my head. "He'll make a great hat someday."

She gave a laugh, and then, unexpectedly, she turned to me. "Cerys, will you be part of my coronation tonight?"

It took me a moment to react. ". . . *What?*"

"You and your papa both—I want you with me up on the terrace, not hiding in the back by the garden wall. You're both family to me. I can't imagine starting my reign as queen without you. You . . . you're the only one who really understands." Her gaze turned hesitantly to the edge of the Wilds, the line of soft green trees that looked innocent, a mask for the curse within. "If I didn't have you in my life . . . I'd be alone."

But if I weren't in your life, your brother might still be alive, I thought before I could catch myself.

Wen smiled hesitantly. "Will you? Please?"

It was an honor, not to mention a breaking of tradition. Only those most important to the royal bloodline were allowed on the coronation steps with the anointed, and my papa and I were simple gardeners. We didn't command countries or save villages from disaster. We tended to flowers. We helped them bloom.

Anwen was asking me to be one of those most important people—and my heart swelled at the thought. I wanted to cry.

But when I looked back into her eyes, all I could see was the wood, as it surrounded us all those years ago. On the day she and I survived.

A thrilling sci-fi fantasy full of romance, royalty, and adventure

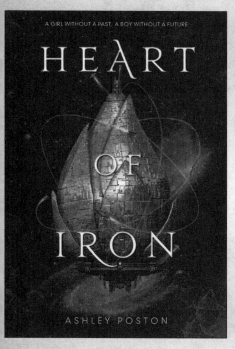

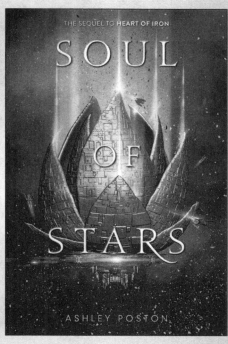

Read this action-packed duology filled with diverse characters

A DARK FOREST RIFE WITH SECRETS AND MONSTERS.

A captivating fantasy from **ASHLEY POSTON**.

JOIN THE

Epic Reads

COMMUNITY